Dead End

To Ambulance Crew

Best Wishes

Dead End

Kenn Gordon

To order additional copies of this book, contact:
Xlibris
800-056-3182
www.Xlibrispublishing.co.uk
Orders@Xlibrispublishing.co.uk
792261

I grew up in the Highlands of Scotland and I became a musician while still at School. Then I made my first musical instrument at the age of just 13 years, an Appalachian Dulcimer. I joined the Royal Air Force at the age of 18. I served for 9 years and worked at many of our secret establishments. Even during my military career, I continued to play in bands as well as to write music. When time would allow, I made guitars for myself, although most of these ended up in my friends hands. With the bands that I formed and played in, I have been fortunate enough to have recorded 32 albums. I later formed my own company making bespoke guitars (Gordon Guitars UK) The pressure of running so many ventures simultaneously eventually took its toll and a series of heart attacks followed. So I looked for a new and more sedate way to direct my creative juices and writing thrillers fitted that bill perfectly.

The first novel was entitled ALTERED PERCEPTIONS. It brought to life 'Team Seven' with Andy McPhee, Lachie Henderson, Abdalla Mohamed, Hans Gunnerson, Jane Miller and 'The Suit'. Andy and Lachie were childhood friends and both serving in the RAF when the UK's SIS (Secret Intelligence Service) coerced them into becoming a part of them. The reason was simple, Andy & Lachie came from the Highlands of Scotland. SIS needed boots on the ground that would fit in. Black Door operations were run by SIS and were totally unaccountable. They had one remit, Protect the UK from ANY and all threats, using deadly force. Team Seven would have to face treats from inside SIS as well as outside it. They would save the world in a dangerous game of cat and mouse. Biological, Chemical and Nuclear threat. Not to mention all the people from agencies outside SIS who had a kill order put on them by a corrupt Secretary of Defence.

Book Two THE RETURN OF SEVEN sees our heroes return to once again take on the threat of a Bio-Genetic weapon of mass destruction. Being hunted down by Neo-Nazis from around the globe. Then they will go to North Korea into the mouth of the dragon and Prison Colony number 22, they will continue to fight for their lives and for the innocents they have rescued. The will eventually bring down Governments and corrupt CIA and EU Financiers of hatred. Some will survive but some of the team will be lost along the way. Much of what goes on in this episode will be split between RAF Saxa Vord and on board of the replacement Catherine May, the original boat having been destroyed in 'Altered Perceptions'.

The third and final part to the Andy McPhee Trilogy is DEAD END. Having lost their homes in The Return Of Seven starts as they are sailing away from the Faeroe Islands and licking their wounds they have lost two of their members, but they have gained a new member Oran, a computer geek from Iceland who had previously done some work for Hans Gunnerson and the IDF. Oran will join the team on their third and final adventure but he is not alone for he brings with him, his protector CYBER, an Ovcharka or Caucasian Sheppard Dog. Probably the next best thing to a Grizzly Bear. This time Team Seven, first have to find somewhere to settle down. When they do they then have to tidy up a few loose ends from their previous escapade. Then just as they think their lives are back on track, Hans Gunnerson brings them some bad news, that will bring the team back into a service they had left behind. Politics and Corruption are never very far away. In this final chapter who will fall by the wayside and as they will question their loyalties not just with SIS but with each other. What will become of Andy and the rest of 'Team Seven'................. ....

CONTENTS

ACT 1

We barely made it out with our lives, well most of us did. Jane, the girl who I had planned to marry, was now dead. Her father, Dusty, had taken his own life, within minutes of learning that his daughter had died at the hands of a member, of the now defunct Neo-Nazi organisation, GRH or Gods Right Hand. The organisation had previously been getting its funding from the CIA and even from some within the EU. There had been those in the CIA, that had wanted to gain control, over the newly released Eastern Block Countries. They had tried to replace Communism with Nationalism. Team Seven had lost two of its fold but we had gained one new member.

Oran, he was a Computer Hacker and a certified genius from Iceland. I had just murdered his arch nemesis Jeon Chang. Chang was a Geneticist and computer whiz kid from North Korea. Except that he had been taken out of North Korea, by the CIA and then they in turn, had let the GRH have him. He had then managed to make an ex soviet bio-weapon, the like of which the world had not seen before, work. That is to say he managed to theoretically work, at least on paper. I could not let anyone have that weapon. We had destroyed the basis of it. We had destroyed the computers with the data on. Then I had destroyed the brain that designed it. I knew I had been his judge, jury and executioner.

Chang's family had been destroyed. His grand parents, parents, and even his aunts. We had not done this, it had been the fault of the CIA and the North Koreans. Two though, that the CIA and the North Koreans, did not know about, and that we had rescued, from inside a North Korean prison camp, had survived. They were both in the baby unit, at Raigmore Hospital in Inverness. Somehow or other, we would provide for them. My home had been destroyed as had Lachie's.

For now, Team Seven were sailing away from the Faeroe Islands on a highly modified trawler. There was still a price on our heads. Our crime if you can call it that was to serve our country, well SIS the UK's Secret Intelligence Service and to save the world for the second time in a year. We had funds, Hell we had more than we would ever need. This is more than could now be said, for the corrupt politicians around the world, along with anyone else who had any monetary involvement with GRH. Their funds which amounted in the trillions, had now been redistributed to good causes around the globe. Oran had hacked into all of their bank accounts and cleaned them out. Half of the money that we found, went to the World Health Organisation. The other half was divided into two. Part of it coming to Team Seven and the other part going to injured parties as compensation, for acts carried out by the GRH.

So here we were, sailing down from the North Atlantic Ocean, to the North Sea in winter. We had managed to survive one of the worst storms in recent years. We had lost our HIND-Mi24 attack helicopter. Not that it was really our own property, I guess it actually belonged to SIS. We had no plans at the moment, apart from to survive. Which for the greater part we were managing to do.

Team Seven permanent members were, Lachie Henderson, my lifelong friend, he was really more of a brother to me, than just a mere friend. Lachie was a Highlander and he looked the part, with his shock of ginger blonde hair and beard. Lachie stood an inch or so taller than me and was broader, none of it was fat though. Lachie like me had been serving the Royal Air Force. He had been in the RAF Regiment and would have gone on to transfer to the British Army's elite Special Air Service, had it not been for the interference of the SIS.

Abdalla Mohamed, probably one of the finest long range snipers in the world, as well as being a great gunsmith and firearms expert. Abdalla came from Northern Kenya and had been a senior officer in the Kenyan elite special forces. He was as black as the ace of spades and his face was covered with tribal scarification. He was a man's man and a great man to have standing beside you in a fight. Standing at six foot seven inches tall. Abdalla was our biggest member.

Hans Gunnerson was the Colonel in Chief of the Icelandic Defence Force and was now the only member still officially employed by the military. He was about the same size and build as Lachie only a classic V shaped torso with the build of a weight lifter. He was a soft spoken man and was a specialist is Arctic Warfare and Extreme Survival.

Then there was me, Andy McPhee. I had been a medic in the RAF and somehow ended up as Team Seven's appointed leader. There were other members as we were a family.

Sandy McKay who now owned a Pub in Keiss. Sandy was a retired fisherman and even looked a bit like a shaggy 'Captain Birdseye'. Sandy had been the owner of the original Catherine May fishing boat. He was the father of Rosemary and consequently the stepfather of Stu. There was not much about the sea that Sandy did not know. Then Stu McCormack, who was the owner of the boat we we currently on, the Catherine May II. The original Catherine May having been destroyed on the first mission 'Altered Perceptions', for SIS. That was about a year ago. Stu had originally been a deckhand on Sandy's boat, but was now the skipper of our new pseudo trawler. It may have originally been designed as a Stern Trawler, but now it was more like a luxury yacht. When Stu and his wife Rosemary, were not providing transport for us, they would legitimise their high life, by taking out the rich and famous who wanted to deep sea fish, with rod and reel. This they charged a hefty fee for, however the quality of the boat and accommodation on board, along with Rosemary's cooking skills, warranted this.

Rosemary McCormack, she was the wife of Stu and also chef and mother hen, to the rest of Team Seven. Rosemary had in her previous life, been one of the Chefs at The Queen Mother's residence, at Mey Castle in Caithness.

Mr Mark Henderson, father of my lifetime friend, Lachie. Mark had been a Shepard on the West coast of Scotland, before moving to the Highlands with Lachie.

Mr Craig McPhee who was of course my father. Dad had been in the military and then worked for a short while in the village of Keiss, before moving to Old Kinbrace. Both Lachie's and my home, had been destroyed by the Neo Nazis. That would bring us to our newest team member Oran.

Oran came from Iceland and had no middle or last name. Oran was a computer hacker and code cracker. He had worked, early on in his illicit career, for the hacking group 'Anonymous'. Then he had set up stealing money from the big conglomerates and hacking into every secure system he could find, including Homeland Security of the USA, the CIA, the FBI and several other secure servers. Then he was apprehended in a sting operation, headed by Hans Gunnerson. Hans had offered him protection, on the proviso that he would now work solely for the IDF and then he had sent him on to Team Seven, in order to hide him from the various security agencies, that wanted to lock him up in one super-max or another. Oran was now free from all obligations to Hans and the IDF. Oran was now just part of our extended family

There were the four legged members. of Team Seven. Kyla my Japanese Akita who was protective of me and to a certain degree all of Team Seven. My fathers dog Raven, a Jet black Great Dane. Finally as far as the dogs go, Oran's beast! Cyber. That would be a fair description. It was an Ovcharka. It was a dog, technically speaking, but I think it was more of a grizzly bear, and damn near as big. Oran was a small slight built computer geek, he probably weighed in at eight stone, when wringing wet. Cyber on the other hand weighed in at nearly twice that. Cyber was Oran's protector and when Oran commanded it, Team Sevens protector.

There was another part time member of our team and the was Sir Philip Reeves-Johnson, current head of the SIS. He was better known to us as 'The Suit' because, 90% of the time, he would be dressed in a Saville Row, Harris Tweed suit. We had Money, we had weapons and we had just made it out alive from something that should really have been handled by the governments of the west. Only they were to busy squabbling over jurisdiction. We only got involved because my father had been kidnapped, in a revenge play, due to the first mission, Altered Perceptions.

So, as I said, here we were sailing in the North Atlantic with nowhere to go. We were all gathered in the galley come lounge area of the Catherine May. We had drunk a toast to Jane and her father. Then we had drunk some more.

The Catherine May's onboard computer navigation system including its anti collision system, really was more like a planes auto pilot, but with the added bonus of what effectively was an auto park. This would allow the boat to actually dock itself. Except for the tying up part. Because of this Stu was down in the galley having a drink with us and toasting fallen comrades.

"So what happens now?" I asked to no one

"Once I sort things with the rest of the worlds security services, you can go back to your lives and SIS will of course pick up the cost of rebuilding your homes. You will be paid the same amount as you were previously. I assume that you would like to have the payments made in the form of cash?" Sir Philip Reeves-Johnson replied.

"Yes Sir Philip, you know how we feel about banks and traceable funds. We will arrange a time and a place for the transfer of funds. First though we will have to find somewhere to live at least on a temporary basis." I replied

"Mark and Craig can stay at mine if you like, at least until you have your homes rebuilt. There are plenty of empty rooms at the Pub, well its more like a small hotel really." Sandy said

"That's very kind of you Sandy"

"Hell its the least I can do after what you have all done for my Rosemary" Sandy replied

"I hate to be a pain in the ass, but I really do have to get back to my post, the PM and new Defence Secretary, will want a complete debrief. Also I will have to arrange, to have all the prisoners transferred from RAF Saxa Vord, to a more permanent and secure location. Then get the kill order on all of you, lifted as quick as I can. Flight Lieutenant Summers, will also require to get back to RAF Lossimouth. Stuart could you make for the Brent Bravo oil Rig? Then they can send a chopper from 202 Squadron, to pick us up."

"Sir Philip I had already figured that is what you would want, so Stu has already set course for there and I think we should be there in about 3 hours" I replied.

"In that case, if you will excuse me. I need to change back into civilian clothing." Sir Philip said as he plucked at his Nomex suit. Then he left the galley to get changed.

The Brent Bravo Oil Platform, used to be one of the biggest working oil platforms in the North Sea. In its prime it had over 100 men working on board her. Now she stood silent over the cruel and cold waves below. She stood alone like a windmill waiting for Sancho Panza, in the Don Miguel de Cervantes Saavedra novel 'Don Quixote' Yet she had given us refuge. Her gigantic legs were covered with seaweed and barnacles. The platform over, was made from concrete and steel. The paint what there was left of it, had mostly pealed away over the years of neglect.

Cosmetically on the outside she was a hulk, given its present state, the cost of making her capable, to be used for her original task and then the actual cost, of removing her from the concrete posts that bound her to the sea bed several fathoms below, was just to exuberant to justify moving her to a new location. So she remained where she was to slowly crumble into the sea, that had been her life.

I had already decided that I would not discuss the future of 'Team Seven' before 'The Suit' had left with the Sqn Ldr. I was tired, we had been in multiple time zones over the last few weeks. I would talk with Oran tomorrow, about ensuring that the innocents, who had been hurt over the course of the last operation, were cared for by the correct authorities.

As previously, we had hidden the new 170ft luxury Catherine May, under the gigantic legs of the now disused Brent Bravo, Oil Rig. I sat back and drank my whisky and absent mindedly, ruffled Kyla's fur. Kyla was my pure bred Japanese Akita, she was my companion. Kyla had saved my life and the lives of quite a few people over the last couple of missions. She was more like a team mascot, and one of our brave four legged protectors. I would go for a shower in a minute and then try and relax, after we would tie up at the Rig. I needed to have a long chat first with Stu and then with Rosemary, for what was floating around inside my mind. Then an even longer chat with Lachie.

I missed Jane. I missed her a lot. It had been a whirlwind romance that was for sure. We had shared so much over the last 9 months. She had even moved into my home, as my significant other. We had a reunion meeting, that had been scheduled to be held at Han's Icelandic Summer house. It would have been there, that I was going to propose to her. The ring was now, somewhere under the rubble of what had been my family home in the highlands.

I had not planned for a life with SIS. Like Lachie I had been in the Royal Air Force. SIS though, needed a team on location in and around our homes in the highlands. So SIS had arranged for a fake discharge and for Lachie and I, to be their agents on location. From there, everything took a distinct downturn. Even after the first mission and we thought we had our lives back. A son, who's father had been killed, by us saving the world. Decided he wanted payback and so we had been drawn into the seedy world of international crime, espionage and politics, to be with SIS once again. Hopefully we were now free of all that shit. It had been at a very high cost morally and emotionally. Not to mention financially, and yes, I knew we would be compensated for it. But this time, I would not rebuild my home where it had been.

I had grown up in the house located on the side of a hill, in the Strath Of Kildonan. I had learned to swim in the fresh and clear water stream that came out of the mountain side. Its water was ice cold, but still I learned to swim in a beautiful rock pool. This very same water was the water that fed our home. I learned to shoot in the Mountains and Strath's around that house. I fished in the rivers and I breathed the clean air. I hated the thought that we would never return to this house. That was the house that we had 'made safe' after the first time we were involved with SIS.

We had rebuilt and made a safe bunker under, without realising just how soon we would need it. I would have them bulldoze over the bunker and we would start again elsewhere. At the start of our relationship with SIS, I had said to 'The Suit' that "I wanted out" the suit had simply replied "There is no out for you." Well I figured they had their pound of flesh. I had no intention of giving them any more. Life previous to SIS had been so simple and a lot less fucking dangerous. Life at the moment, was not the life I had envisaged all those years ago, as a boy growing up in the Highlands of Scotland. Then again, the life I had chosen on the Royal Air Force, was not the life I was living just now either.

I lay back on my bunk bed in a small cabin that had originally been intended for the rich folks, that wanted to pay for the pleasure to fish, with a rod, in either the North Sea or the North Atlantic. Stu's boat was comfortable and the food that Rosemary cooked up, was fantastic. So I was not complaining about that, not even to myself. We were however cramped for space. Stu had done the best, he could given a bad situation. I never heard anyone ever complain about life aboard the Catherine May II, which was three times the size of the Original Catherine May and no one had ever complained about life on board the original boat. We were not the sort of folks that made demands for comfortable or high class surroundings. True we were all technically millionaires, but no one had let that go to our heads.

'The Suit' had contacted RAF Lossimouth and a helicopter was on its way to us, to collect those that were going to return to the mainland. Hans had also been called back as the Colonel in Chief of the Icelandic Defence Force. He had to go and give his report to the Chief of Staff at the UN. Apart from Jane and her Father, Team Seven had survived. Whether we would survive the aftermath of it, was a different matter altogether. Sandy called me to the bridge.

"Do you want the dogs to have a run on the deck of the Oil Platform?"

"Yes Sandy I think that would be a great idea."

The Brent Bravo Oil platform, was where we had hidden our boat. The rig stood almost seventy feet over the top of the Catherine May. The Oil Company stated it was too expensive to dismantle and they were in talks with the environment agency as to what should be done with it. When we first used it as a hiding place for the Catherine May, Sandy and myself had climbed up the rusty steel ladder on one of the gigantic legs. We had then checked out the rig. There was still a generator on board the rig, we had filled it with fuel and it powered up the lighting on the rig. It also powered a winch with a large cage attached. Previously, when the platform was still being used for its intended purpose, it had been used by the rig, when getting their re-supplies. The one time we had used it, to get the dogs up to the main platform in order to allow the dogs a proper chance to walk.

I could see the big yellow helicopter belonging to 202 Search and Rescue Squadron, from RAF Lossimouth. It was perched on the cantilever helipad on the top deck of the rig. 'The Suit' was already on the foredeck of the Catherine May with his kitbag. Hans had come to say goodbye to all of us and it was an emotional farewell. The Flt Lt was standing by 'The Suit'. We had said our goodbyes to them earlier. I respected and admired Sir Philip Reeves-Johnson, but hoped that this would be the last time I had anything to do with 'The Suit' and bloody SIS. Sandy went up and pressed the remote for the cage lift, it wound its way down from the platform above as the generator kicked into life. When it was a couple of feet off the deck, it stopped. Hans said his final farewells to us in the wheelhouse and went to join the other two on the foredeck, before entering the rusty steel cage and closing the gate. Sandy pressed another button on the remote and the cage went on its journey back up to the platform. They would then have to climb three sets of stairs before they reached the helicopter platform. Five minutes later we were all out on the top of the Catherine May, waving goodbye to the big Sea King chopper, as she was getting ever smaller, going on her journey and towards dry land.

ACT 2

"Oran, do you fancy going up to the platform with the dogs and me?"

"Sure Andy I could use the fresh air, not that I am complaining mind you. Just the hold where I do all my work, it has no windows so any chance at natural light is a bonus." he replied.

Sandy and Stu, had allowed Oran to use one, of the four stainless steel holds, on board the Catherine May. They had even allowed him to make modifications to it, such as welding brackets to the walls, in order to hold his massive computer screens. Stu had run power lines into it and allowed Oran to connect to the ships own onboard computer. Oran has able even to access satellites from what was euphemistically known as a grotto, because it was filled with his toys. These toys had at times saved our lives whilst at the same time, cost the lives of those that would do us harm. But it was still just a large metal box deep inside the hull of the Catherine May.

I whistled, and my fathers Great Dane, along with my Japanese Akita came running. This was the second Great Dane that my father had owned. The first had been with my father for over a decade, before it had been brutally slain by a mercenary, who was intent on making me into an ex-person.

Raven II, had been given to my father by Jane. He was still at that gangly all legs and a tail that would knock cups off coffee tables or whip an unsuspecting person on the back of the legs.

Oran whistled and his Ovcharka came and joined the two other dogs. My dogs were big but Oran's hound was bigger. Oran had called it a sheep dog when he first told us he had a dog, even if he had said he had a Caucasian Sheep dog, I would not have known what it was. What it was, was HUGE. The biggest damn dog I ever saw. Cyber was Oran's personal protector, but his dog like mine, had started to offer its services to all of our team. Like all the dogs they were part of this tight knit team. I went to the foredeck with Oran and the animals. I pressed the remote for the service cage. Lachie came out while I was waiting for it to arrive.

"Mind if I join you Andy?"

"Feel free Lachie"

The three of us and the three dogs went up in the lift, which stopped automatically on the first deck. We climbed the stairs up to the top deck and let the dogs have a run around on the helipad. When they had finished I sluiced it down and cleaned it off. Lachie stood looking out to sea.

"This is good mate"

"I don't follow Lachie?"

"Look Andy you can see 360 degrees."

"Yes so?"

"Well think about it, our homes were destroyed because we could not see what folks were doing or planning to do. There is no way anyone, could sneak up on us here."

"Are you suggesting that we should make our home on this rust bucket?" I asked Lachie

"You said it yourself before, it is just surface rust, and legs are sound, as is the platform. We have the resources, as in we have the money and we can bring in workers from another country to do the hard work on contract. Some of the rig, we would have to dismantle and other parts we could renovate. I am sure I read somewhere about a company from Malaysia, that restores these old rigs and make them into luxury hotels, or private mansions."

"Your serious, aren't you Lachie?"

"Yes I think so, the company that own this rig were looking to sell it as a marine conservation project. They wanted marine life to grow on the concrete legs, or something like that. I am sure Oran, could create some fake company, that fits that remit. You could make it real safe too. It could be self sufficient if we did things right."

That was how the whole thing started for our little commune. My father and I, had no home, Lachie and his dad, had no home, Oran had no home, Stu said he and Rosemary would continue to run their private luxury fishing boat, Sandy said he would take our parents to his pub, until we had things up and running. Oran said he would find the funds whenever we needed it and he would use a shell company to sort things out, in a way that nothing, would ever come back to us.

Three months later Oran set it up. We bought the rig from Brent. Technically we had purchased it, to convert into a Marine Bio Research Centre. The cost of the platform was just £250,000, this was what they estimated the scrap value, of the rig to be. The oil company were glad to see the back of it and could not sign over the papers fast enough. We used the Malaysian company that had experience in this type of renovation. A Further three months later and we had spent £3 million and were about half way through. Though most of the structural work had been undertaken and it was the decorative work now. We handed this over to a Saudi company and spent another two million and six more months of work before it was completed. Five and a half million pounds. It sounds a lot but for the size and the quality of what was effectively a stately home was not too bad.

The major changes were all inside. Whilst it still looked a bit tatty and rusty from a distance. It had actually been renovated to look like that, even the patches of rust that showed from the outside, were in fact painted on. Inside though was like a modern penthouse apartment block. We now had a properly enclosed lift that went down the inside of one of the platform's, three massive concrete legs. This allowed access to a new floating dock at the base. We had made the rig into a series of large self contained apartments. There was one each for Lachie, Oran, Abdalla and for myself. There were a further 10 suites, should Team Seven ever require them. Oran had a state of the art Computer Centre with ultra High speed satellite internet. Under another shell company, he had bought what was effectively, timeshare on a media satellite. We kept all the guns and ammunition that we had collected along the way over the past two missions and had set up our own armoury, which we had resupplied.

There were cameras all around our platform and they went to a bank of monitors in Oran's grotto, as with the one he still had aboard the Catherine May, this was filled with toys, which for the greater part could only be used by the magical touch, of our own electronic wizard. There were radar beams going all the way around the platform including the air space around us.

Part of the deck area we had made into a 'Fair Weather' area complete with Astro Turf and a Bar B Q area. There was a fenced off dog area where they could play safely and that was easy to clean. We had a heated indoor swimming pool and a gymnasium. We also had a small Cinema. In short we had every thing that you would expect to find in a 5 or 6 star hotel, except for the staff. New generators were backed up by under-water wave turbines, that worked on the swell of the sea. The windows were a type of glass which was a bit similar to one way glass, light could not go out, but light could enter. This meant that apart from the odd time when we would require deck lights to do work outside, we could not be seen. We had renovated everything that needed it.

Any time we wanted off 'The Rig' Stu would come and fetch us and take us to the mainland. Due to the size of the Catherine May, Stu would anchor off from Keiss harbour and we would take a RIB in, and then an old Ford Transit van, which we kept there, should we require it. Keiss was one of those picturesque small harbours, that are dotted around the rocky coastline of Caithness and Sutherland, in the North East of Scotland. People here tend to mind their own business, especially if your business benefits theirs. Sandy had bought the Pub come Hotel in Keiss, when he retired from the sea. Compared to hotels down South I guess you could call it more of a Bed and Breakfast establishment with a bar attached to it. This place suited our fathers requirements. They both loved to fish with road and reel, consequently unless the weather was really inclement, then our parents, when not sat on the solid granite harbour wall, they could be found sat on the grassy embankment that surrounded this little harbour. So Lachie and I saw our fathers often enough.

I had been going through my pockets one night when I found a piece of paper. It was the telephone number for Petrá. She lived on the one of the small Faeroe Islands. Petrá had helped me, when we were in trouble on the last mission. Around the same time that I found her number, Abdalla asked me what ever happened to the two North

Korean babies, that we had rescued with the Chang family. When the Chang Family had been murdered, the twin babies had been in Raigmore Hospital, in Inverness. I mentioned this to Oran and he said that he had tracked them to an orphanage just outside Inverness. I had asked him to get me some further details, as I felt a responsibility for them. He said that he could arrange all the adoption papers if I wished, then all I would have to do would be, to turn up at the orphanage with a woman, who I would have to introduce as my wife. I told him, that sort of life was not for me. Then, they had plagued my dreams and a few weeks later I had rediscovered the scrap of paper, and that plagued my mind for another week or so. Eventually I gave in and called Petrá.

"Hello"

"Petrá?"

"Yes. Who is this please?"

"Are you still looking excitement away from the Faeroe's?"

"Andy!!!! It has been some time, my Andy Andy Andy" she sang my name out in the same way as she had over a year ago.

"How are you? How are your Father and Brother" I asked. She had previously told me her father and her brother, worked on a fishing boat, while she looked after the family home and ran the Island's, small grocery shop. There was a long pause before she answered and when she did it was like being hit with a baseball bat.

"My Father and brother, they have died" she said

I wished the sea would just swallow me

"I am so sorry Petrá, I did not know. Please forgive me"

"How would you know Andy. It was about a month after you were here. Their boat was lost at sea. In the big storm."

I remembered the storm well. It had been one of the worst storms that the northern Isles had ever seen. Many of the fishermen had been caught out in it and several boats had been lost that week. I Had no Idea what to say to her next and like a bloody fool. I said the first thing that came into my mouth.

"Would it be alright If I came to visit you?"

"Yes Andy. That would be nice. When are you thinking of coming to the Faeroe's. Is your fishing boat near?"

When I had first met Petrá, I had lied to her, when we were battling the GRH, on the most North Easterly Faeroe Island of Fugloy. I had told her I was from a fishing boat and our radio was down.

"No Petrá, I no longer work on a fishing boat. I work on an Oil Rig. But I will tell you about it when I see you. I will call you soon."

"Andy do you promise you are coming to see me?"

"Of course Petrá."

"OK Andy Andy Andy see you soon." she sang and then hung up.

I went to the radio room and called the Catherine May

"Stu can you give me a lift to Svinoy?"

"In the Faeroe's?"

"One and the same."

"When?"

"When ever you can pick me up and take me there?"

"I am about four hours from you, if you want to go today?"

"Perfect see you then."

I went to the main lounge, this was our communal area, it was an open plan design, that backed onto our bar. Abdalla was busy beating Lachie at Cribbage. Oran was taking the mickey out of Lachie for loosing, at a game that Lachie had taught Abdalla.

"Hi Guys I am going to the Faeroe's for a day I will be back tomorrow. And will tell you what I have planned depending on how I get on tonight."

"Sounds underhand" said Oran

"Sounds Private" said Abdalla

"Sounds like a woman" said Lachie.

"Stu will be here in about four hours. Meanwhile I am going for a shower."

"Definitely a woman." said Lachie

I gave him the bird and went to my apartment. I stripped off and washed under the steaming shower for ten minutes and then I rinsed off under ice cold water for another five minutes. I shaved off three days worth of stubble and then dressed in clean Jeans and a fresh dress shirt. I splashed aftershave on and looked at myself in the mirror. Not too shabby.

I had a slight scar from a bullet crease to the left hand temple. To go with a larger one on my left arm. Both of these reminders I had received, in battle a year ago. Things could have been worse and their aim could have been better. I knew I would come in for some stick for dressing up. Out here in the North Sea there was not much reason for us to shave. Today was a good reason to shave, I was going to see a beautiful young woman.

Stu radioed to say he was five minutes out. I took the lift down to the floating dock and waited for Stu to come alongside in the 170ft pseudo trawler. It had been a replacement for the original Catherine May, which had been lost during the first mission. The original 50 foot fishing boat, had been traditional clinker built. The cost of having a new clinker built fishing boat was actually more than the cost of this new much bigger boat. SIS had paid for this boat, which had been a cancelled order, and as such Stu got a bargain. He had then set about spending almost a million pounds, on massively upgrading it into a luxury fishing boat. He would take rich customers out on week long fishing trips. The galley and the bunk rooms reflected the prices he was charging his customers. Stu though, had always said that his first priority was to Team Seven and their families. I clambered on board and joined Stu in the wheelhouse.

"Now then Andy, what is so important that you need a rush trip to Svinoy? Is it another SIS Mission and do I tell my family to go into hiding?"

"No Stu, nothing so exciting as saving the world. Just someone I have to go and see and ask a favour of."

"Would this someone be a woman?" He asked with a smirk

"Yes it would be, but not in the way you are intimating. I will let you know more, when I do. Do you have customers on board?"

"No Andy I was just out testing some new modifications to the boat. Rosemary is down below in the galley and she is dying to see you. I will be down in a few moments when I have us out to sea and the course set."

"OK Stu see you down below." I replied and went down to the beautifully equipped galley.

This is where Jane had died. A member of the GRH had been holding a pistol to her head. Jane had just sneezed and the gun had gone off accidentally and she had died instantly. The galley had been completely redecorated. Rosemary rushed to me and gave me a big hug and a kiss on the cheek.

"Coffee Andy?"

"Please Rosemary."

There was always a fresh pot of coffee percolating in the galley of the Catherine May. It had always been that way, from the time when all of us had been forced together. It did not matter if it was in one of our homes, or even in the field. We survived on coffee, more often than not with a good slug of Irish or Scotch whisky in it. I sat down at the polished Mahogany long galley table. Rosemary came over and put three mugs down on the table, just as Stu joined us. He sat down opposite me and Rosemary poured out three steaming mugs of black Arabic coffee. Then she put the pot back onto its holder over the stove.

"With or without?"

"That would be without, perhaps it will be a with on the way back. Will you be able to wait for a couple of hours for me?"

"This all sounds very clandestine Andy?" Rosemary replied

"No Rosemary nothing to worry about. This is a personal matter."

"Its a woman" Stu said with a wink

"Ohhh do tell Andy?"

"There is nothing to tell Rosemary, I just want to ask someone, to do something of a favour for me."

"Andy are you wearing After-Shave lotion?" Rosemary asked as she deliberately twitched her nose.

I must have gone bright red as I could feel the bottom of my ears burning.

"Yes Rosemary, I thought it would be better than working man's sweat."

The banter continued for the next three hours. We must have been travelling at close to 40 knots. However with the sea being relatively calm it did not feel it.

"Do you want me to tie up at their pier? I don't think you will get this boat into the harbour proper."

"That will be great if you can. Thanks Stu"

"OK lets go up and you can help put the buoys over the edge as we come alongside." Rosemary said

Rosemary and I followed Stu up to the deck and then Stu went into the wheelhouse. Skilfully he brought his large fishing boat alongside the end of the pier. Equally as skilfully Rosemary bounded over the edge of the boat taking the bow rope and winding it around a thick post. I threw down the stern rope and she tied that off to another stout post.

"Cheers Stu. I will see you in a couple of hours. If I am not back in three hours, come and get me I will be at the Svinoy grocery shop."

He gave me the thumbs up. I jumped down onto the wooden slatted pier. Rosemary came across and in her mother hen mode, that she so often had been, when all our lives had been in danger previously. She flicked my hair and dusted off the non-existent dust from my shoulder.

"Well I asked?"

"You'll do, I guess. You don't clean up too bad Mr Andy McPhee."

I waved to them and walked up the well trodden pathway to Svinoy village. I say village, it was more like a hamlet. There was a whitewashed, tin roofed church. A few houses and a singular shop come post office, which also had a house tacked onto the back of it. It was this house I was returning to. I walked up the narrow pathway to the shop. What had been a well maintained and beautiful garden, to the front of the house come shop, was now overgrown with tall grass. I opened the half glass door that led into the shop part of the building. A small bell rang, to announce the fact that I had entered. Like the garden it was different from the last time I had visited. The shop had previously been full of goods. Now there were only a few items left on the solid wood shelves. Petrá stood behind the counter. She was wearing a Norwegian style cardigan over a white blouse. She wore a pair of denim jeans, that hugged her bum nicely.

"Andy, Andy, Andy." she sang my name out with a distinct Faeroese accent, this was like a cross between a Shetland and a Danish accent.

"You do look a lot smarter, than when we last met. And you do scrub up nice, I have to say, young Andy. Come on through and tell me what it is that brings you to this far off desolate Island." She said, as she lifted the gated counter top up to allow me to pass into what effectively was the kitchen of the house behind the shop.

I followed her through to the hub of the house, it was unchanged since I had been there, a year or so ago. The large custard coloured, solid fuel Rayburn cooker, still standing against the gable wall. The very distinct smell of peat being burned. I guess that one of the other villagers had probably bartered peat for goods from the shop. Peat cutting would normally have been a big family concern, with everybody mucking in, to get the job done. However now her father and brother were dead, that would no longer happen.

Bartering still very much existed in the Highlands and also in these desolate and mostly agriculturally barren Islands, which were stuck in the middle of the North Atlantic. To my mind bartering, was a much fairer system than hard cash. I would guess that bartering, had been the original currency of the world, before the advent of coins around 2,700 years ago.

There was a scrubbed pine table and chairs. Then an old well worn and comfortable leather settee along with the matching chairs. At the other end was a long sideboard, which had a Ship to Shore UHF radio sat on top. It was took up space, next to a framed picture of a small fishing boat, that had a red painted Hull and a white top. Standing beside the boat, were two tall men. They both looked fit and well, they were obviously and without doubt, Father and Son. The Father had his arm, over the sons shoulders. They were smiling happily for the camera. I guessed this was Petrá's father and her brother. Being as how Petrá was not in the photo, I assumed that she had been the person behind the camera.

The oak rocking chair that I had sat in, over a year ago, to make my call to Sandy, in order that he might rescue us from the neighbouring Island of Fugloy, was still sat next to the radio. Petra interrupted my thoughts.

"Now then Andy, let me have a good look at you. Last time I saw you. You were wrapped up in Arctic Camouflage. I know fishermen Andy and I know you are not one of them. I heard tell, that there was a helicopter crashed on Fugloy. That would be around the same time, as you came over here and said you had lost the use of the radio in your boat. I also heard tales that the old whaling station was destroyed, in a series of explosions. Some of the men from the Islands around here, went and had a look a few days later. The Danish Navy, had it shut down tighter than a Synagogue's petty cash box."

"Really Petrá? Must just have been a coincidence"

"Well I do have to say, you present a whole lot better, than you did then."

"Petrá I am truly sorry to hear about your Father and your Brother."

"Thanks Andy, It was a difficult time. There were four men from our small Island, They had gone to fish for Cod around the northern fishery beds. Nobody really knows what happened. They never even got out an SOS. The other fishermen think it was a rogue wave, and it just rolled the boat. Now all but a couple of families, have gone from the Island and village. The shop, no longer makes any money. I will probably have to go to the mainland to get work. This has been our family home, for five generations. Anyway enough of my problems. Where are my manners. Would you care for a coffee?"

"That would be lovely Petrá."

"So what is it that brings my mysterious Andy, Andy, Andy to me?" she sang my name out again.

"Truth be told Petrá, I came to see you. I have a small problem that I could use some help with."

"Ohh?" she said as she brought the coffee over to me

"May I?" I said, indicating to settee.

"Of course you may, please sit."

I sat down and she sat down next to me. It actually made me feel slightly embarrassed and excited as her knees touched mine, when we turned to face each other. She was beautiful. But she was looking at the prospect of hard times, that much was obvious from the shop. Not only was the shop failing to make any money, but there were also a double income missing from the household. I had not said anything to anyone, in regards to what I was ready to ask Petrá and it felt awkward.

"So Andy what is it I can do for you?" she said and her brilliant emerald green eyes, glistened with devilment.

"Petrá if you were able to keep this house and have a job away from the Island, with a really good wage, would you consider it?"

"You don't mess around, when it comes to big questions do you Andy. Here was I thinking you had come to offer me a tropical holiday in the sun, or at least a night on the town."

"So?"

"What?

"What do you think?"

"About?"

"What I have just asked you?"

"Which part?" she said.

It was like having a conversation with Lachie when he wanted to be daft!

"All of it" I said and looked to her face for an indication of where here thoughts on it were.

"Well when you say a really good wage, what are we comparing it against, for it to be really good? As in, would that be a really good Island wage? Or a really good Mainland wage?"

"What would you say would be a good wage Petrá?"

"Andy, I would say for what you are asking, for me to leave my home and to keep it going while I am away working and live somewhere else. It would have to be at least 10,000 Faeroe Kroná each month."

"How many Kroná are there to a Euro?"

"I think 100 Faeroe Kroná is about 13.5 Euro or in your British Pounds it is £10."

"What if I could offer you £5,000 per month and pay for the upkeep of your house here?"

"Who do you wish me to kill Andy?"

"You would not have to kill anyone. I would also provide your own set of apartments with all the mod cons. And if there is something that you need, and it's not there, I will get it for you."

"Andy are you trying to buy my attentions?"

"Ohhhhh Hell No. No, It is nothing like that Petrá. I am looking for someone to be a nanny to two, one year old children. Their real parents are dead and I feel a duty of care for them."

"Why?"

"Why do I want you to care for them?"

"No Andy. Why is it you feel a duty of care for them? Did you kill their parents?" She asked.

I looked back into those emerald green eyes to see if she was playing with me again. It did not look like she was. I suppose in a way I had been partly responsible, for their parents death. We had rescued the family, from a North Korean death camp. Then we had managed to get them to the safety of the UK. At that point in time, the children who were premature and underweight, were dispatched to Raigmore Hospital in Inverness. The other 12 North Koreans that we had rescued, were murdered, by folks working for the CIA or the North Korean government. The family would no doubt have died a cruel death in the Prison camp. But they did not deserve the death they got either. Now the two children, which were just over a year old were in an orphanage just outside Inverness.

"No Petrá. I never killed the parents, I knew the family and they have no other living relatives. I am in a position to help. But I have never had children, so would not know where to begin."

"Andy I have never had children either, what makes you think I would be any better?"

"Because Petrá, you have a gentle nature and you looked after your father and brother and there is nothing closer to children than full grown men."

"OK, on that point you are correct Andy. All men are just big kids at heart. I will think about it while we drink our coffee. Would you like a Whisky to go with the coffee?" She said and sprang up from the couch and bounced on her toes across the room.

She came back with a bottle of Shetland Reel and two tumblers. After poring two very large measures, she handed one to me. I now had a coffee in one hand and a large Whisky in the other. Petrá sat down next to me again and sat with one leg tucked in under her bum. She sat facing me with her Whisky in her left hand, her right hand was across her lap.

"Well Andy, I do not even know your last name."

"Its McPhee, my name is Andy McPhee."

"Mr Andy McPhee. It has a nice ring to it. Well Mr Andy McPhee it is a pleasure to make your formal acquaintance. My name is Petrá Johansen. Skál! Andy McPhee." she said as she raised he glass to mine.

"Skál" I said in return, hoping it was the correct thing to do.

"If I do chose to accept this post, where will I be living?"

"You would live with the children of course."

"Andy, I am not a stupid woman. Even in the Faeroe's, we have televisions. So where is the house?"

I knew at some point that question would come. I had not even managed to adopt the children at this point, yet here I was out here trying to engage Petrá, as a live in nanny to the twins.

"Petrá. I need you to trust me. I will not harm you, or allow harm to come to you. I would like for you to come with me on my friends boat, to where my home is. My friend Stu McCormack and his wife Rosemary are down at the pier in their fishing boat the Catherine May. When I say fishing boat. It is probably not like any fishing boat, you have ever been on. It is more like a luxury yacht. At least walk with me, down to the pier and meet with them. Then I will ask you again, if you wish to see where you would be working. It is only 3 to 4 hours away."

"Your boat is three hours away" she said and I almost bit, until I saw that flash in her bright green eyes. She threw her head back and the bright flame red, hair fell in cascades over her shoulders. She laughed and I laughed. Then we drank our Whisky.

"Yes Andy McPhee. I say yes. I will come and meet with Stuart and Rosemary on their boat. But I will think about the job, a little more."

She clinked her glass against mine and we drank our coffee and whisky. Then she pulled on a shawl and we walked back down the path to the Catherine May. I helped her aboard and we went down into the galley where Stu and Rosemary sat at the table. I made the introductions and we sat down.

"Your boat Stuart, it is very shiny and very fancy for a fishing boat. What is it that you fish for? To be able to afford such a boat? I am sorry that was rude of me. Please forgive my rudeness. It is none of my business."

"Don't worry Petrá, Stu and I, we take stupid rich people out to fish, in the deep waters with rod and line. They have more money than sense. So we have a boat that makes things comfortable for them. Also for Andy and our friends, we use the boat for pleasure" Rosemary said

"You could say, we have a little club, that we all belong to. Some of us have been friends since school other are more recent. We are all lucky people, we have some wealth, but we also enjoy our privacy. If you would still like to see our home? Stu can take us there now. he will of course bring you right back to your home when you have seen it. What do you say?"

"I say this is a strange boat that has such a small crew, for such a large vessel."

"It is completely computer controlled, except when I don't want it to be." Stu said

"No catch and you have my word that this is all above board. Come see the place and have a meal with us." I said

"OK." Petrá replied

"OK What?" I asked

"OK I accept your word"

"You'll come?"

"Yes Mr Andy McPhee, I will come on your friends fancy fishing boat and look at your home."

"Do you not wish to close up your home and shop?"

"If they wish anything, they will leave money for it. There are only two families left in the village. So lets go and see the mystery house."

"OK Stu, I will cast off I am sure Rosemary can look after our guest." I said and got up and walked out of the Galley. Stu followed me on to the deck.

"Wow Andy, she is a cracker!"

"Its not like that Stu, I have been thinking we are going to need some hired help on the rig, its a big old place. Truthfully its as big as a stately home."

"It is that Andy and damn near as nice inside too. I shall not press you though. You know we owe you and Lachie, real big time."

"No you don't mate. We are a family no one owes anyone. We have been through hell and back with each other and seen our share of losses. Perhaps now, if I live off the grid, I can have a quiet and safe life. I just wish our parents would join us on the rig, now its completed. But they are stuck in their ways, not to mention being stuck in your father in law's pub." I said as I cast off.

Then I went back down below to the galley. Rosemary and Petrá were in deep conversation. I grabbed a couple of cups of coffee and joined Stu on the bridge. Stu pushed the throttles all the way forward and this highly modified boat rose up on her hydrofoil and shot through the water at more than 40 knots.

"I have modified the engines and also added a pneumatic hydrofoil blade, that coupled with the extra deep screws, now make this the fastest trawler around. The bigger twin rudders also give me the handling of a much smaller boat. Its always fun to see the faces of the folks I take out when I open up the throttles. They love it." Stu said

"I have to be honest with you when, you told me before you could make this run like one of those torpedo boats. I thought you might be talking metaphorically. You made it happen for real, I am impressed." I replied as I sipped my coffee and looked out on a still and dark ocean ahead of us.

This time, with a fair sea and equally fair winds, it took just a tad over 3 hours, before Stu pulled back on the throttles and navigated to the floating dock, under the previously disused oil platform formally known as Brent Bravo. This was now our new home. I went down to the galley as Stu tied off.

"OK Girls time to view the palace. If you will take my hand and trust me, when I put a blindfold on you. Honest it is just so that the surprise you see, is just that. A surprise."

"OK, Mr Andy McPhee but I should warn you I am a Black Belt at Origami. One false move and I can fold you into twelve.!" Petrá joked.

I carefully wound one of Rosemary's shawls, into a blindfold and gently tied it over Petrá's bright green and playful eyes. Then I led her up the steps. I helped her to step over and on to the floating dock. I held on to her slim waist as he came down onto the floating platform, I held on longer than I had intended to, and in embarrassment I let go of her waist. I carefully took her by the arm and led her into the lift, along with Stu and Rosemary. The doors closed and the lift went up to the main indoor area. This was our communal relaxation area, with bar, and recreational area. The doors opened and I removed the blindfold. Lachie and Abdalla were sat with Oran and the three dogs.

Each of the men had a beer and there was some kind of heavy metal music playing. I was going to ask Oran to turn it off when Petrá said

"Skálmóld my favourite band, how did you know I like them Andy?" she said still with the fun in her voice

"I did not. Petrá, please meet Oran. He is the smallest man and probably the smartest man among us. He has no other names, just plain Oran. Then the big man over there, with the long blonde hair and beard, is my lifelong friend Lachlan Henderson or Lachie to his friends. As you can see he thinks he is an extra for the movie Braveheart. Sat next to him the really, really, big man is another of my true friends. He is Abdalla Mohamed. Abdalla comes to us from the Northern reaches of Kenya. For all of his size, he is one of the most gentle people, I have had the pleasure to make the acquaintance of. The other two people you already know. Where are my manners. What can I get you to drink Petrá?"

"I don't suppose you have some Icelandic Vodka in that well stocked bar of yours, do you?" She said while looking around the large space and pointing over to our drinks bar.

Abdalla got up and walked to the bar.

"Miss Petrá, I believe that our friend Mr Hans, has a couple of bottles behind the bar. I shall have look."

With that Abdalla ducked down behind that bar that we had modelled on the bar at the Kvosin Hotel, in Reykjavik. It was where we had stayed for a short time on the last mission. It had been a nice, until the GRH, had decided that they had wanted to make us into ex-people. They had come off second best, but the hotel had suffered a fair amount of damage in the process. Hans, who was at the time and still was, the Colonel In Chief of the Icelandic Defence Force. Had managed to make any problems there, go away under the auspices of it being an act of terrorism. With all the terrorists having been killed in a failed attempt, at a copy of a Mumbai style attack. Abdalla popped up from below the polished mahogany bar top with one bottle in each hand.

"Miss Petrá it would seem you are in luck. There is a choice. You can have Reyka or you can have Mountain Vodka."

"Can I please have the Icelandic Mountain Vodka on ice. Reyka is a bit rough." Petrá said as she sat down on a chair next to the others.

Abdalla poured a good measure into a glass with two large ice cubes in, He added a slice of lemon and passed the drink over.

"Miss Rosemary what would you like?" Abdalla asked

"I will just have a beer the same as you boys."

When we all had our drinks and filled the time with small talk until Rosemary said she could prepare something for all of us to eat, while I showed Petrá around the rig. We had set the apartments around second and third decks. A total of eight apartments on second level set. There were a further two much larger apartments on the next level. The first level was set to all the recreational areas, where we had the Kitchen, Bar, Cinema, Gym and open plan garden area. We also had a small indoor swimming pool attached to the side of the gym. I showed her to one of the large apartments, which were fully self contained. Although we tended to eat most of our meals in the main kitchen, which was located through the swinging saloon doors behind the bar. Each apartment had three bedrooms and fully fitted bathroom along with a fully fitted kitchen. There was a large lounge with doors leading out on to a balcony. All the apartments had a small balcony accessed through a set of sliding glass doors. Although at this point I did not show her the balcony. They were fully triple glazed exterior windows and centrally heated. All the flooring was high end solid hardwood parquet or covered in plush, deep pile carpets, complimented by underfloor heating. Next I showed her the indoor pool and gym, along with garden area that was surrounded by our offices and guest accommodation.

"Its beautiful Andy, so much space and so many rooms. And you have your own private harbour?"

"Would you like to see the outside?"

"Please" she said like a child with a chance to go on a fairground ride.

I led her up to the top floor which opened on to yet another garden area with Bar B Q set off to the side. Behind that we had our generators, I walked with her to the edge where there was a strong six foot high chain link fence that went all the way around this level and a gateway leading onto the Helipad.

"I don't understand Andy? It sounds like there is water all around? Are we in the middle of the sea on a boat?"

"No Petrá this is my home and it is an old Oil rig that we have put new life in to. This is where you would live. We also work from here. You will want for nothing and when the children are old enough, if you wish help in teaching then I will get help as required. Now I am sure you have a million questions, but we should eat first. Rosemary is an excellent chef."

I walked her back over to the lift and we went down to the first level. We joined all the others in the kitchen, at a huge rustic dining table, which was made from a massive slab of polished Indian Teak. Rosemary had designed the kitchen herself, so it had the best of the best and none of it would look out of place in the kitchen of a Michelin Star restaurant. We ate a fine meal and then went back to the bar area for another drink.

"Petrá, Stu will take you home and I will give you my telephone number. If you wish to join our family. Let me know. But please do so soon, as I need to sort things out."

"Yes"

"Yes? Yes what?"

"My answer is Yes!"

"You will join us?"

"Yes Mr Andy McPhee. I will join you and your strange family."

"OK that's great, in that case, Stu will take you home. to allow you to sort your life out, on Svinoy."

"No I am staying, I needed a new life and this will be it. All I need are some new clothes." Petrá said

"This is so cool, I can take you shopping tomorrow." Rosemary said excitedly and continued.

"It will be so good to have another girl around again." Then she looked embarrassed. I had lost Jane just over a year ago. She would have been my wife, if all things in life had been equal. It was taking time, but it was not so much getting over her loss, but learning to live without her. I also had the realisation, that life goes on. Jane and Rosemary had been close to each other and would often be sat, just talking about normal things in life. Rather than plotting the deaths, of fellow human beings as SIS would have us do.

I had not told Petrá what sort of life I had led. Hell I did not even have her charges, the twin Korean kids. I would need the help of 'The

Suit' as well as that of Oran in order to have them officially adopted by me. That was a joke at the moment!! I was a hired killer for SIS, at least I had been up until a year ago. And a Year before that I had been in the Royal Air Force as a Medic. What would I put down as my trade? Medic? Assassin? Murder?

"OK that is fantastic, I assume that you and Stu are stopping over tonight?"

"Absolutely Andy! Petrá and I have to plan which shops, we are going to visit. You are going to have to give Petrá some spending money. We cant have your newest member of the team, looking like she works for McDonald's or KFC. She is part of Team Seven now." Rosemary said.

"Lets drink to that" said Abdalla.

"Lets get drunk to that." said Lachie.

"Looks like its going to be a late night." said Stu.

"I'll get the drinks in then." I said.

We sat around drinking as old friends, talking about life before Team Seven. I told her about my growing up in the Strath of Kildonnan and my lifetime friendship with Lachie. Lachie talked about that and then his life in the RAF regiment. Stu and Rosemary talked about their life and love since childhood and the life at sea. Rosemary recounted about helping her mother, cook at Mey Castle and cooking for the Queen Mother. Abdalla spoke of his childhood of growing up in a small village in the North of Kenya. How he won a scholarship to Oxford University. Then how he joined the Kenyan Army as an officer before becoming a firearms expert and his promotion to a senior officer. Then of his chance meeting with Lachie and me and then the rest of Team Seven. None of us told, of the things that we had done with Team Seven. Team Seven exploits were never mentioned in any conversation at that time.

We were just like minded and wealthy friends. There would be a time for explanations. Perhaps I would tell her tomorrow. The least I could do for now, was to pay for a new wardrobe before I did tell her. We drank the night away and danced in our private bar. In the morning after, I had showered, then went to the kitchen and Rosemary had already cooked breakfast for everyone. Petrá had nearly finished hers.

"Good morning sleepyhead"

Every time she spoke, it almost sounded like she was singing. I grabbed a coffee and went to my office next to Oran's grotto. I had a large safe there, I opened it and drew out £2,000, in advance wages for Petrá. Then I changed my mind and made it £5,000. I was unsure just how much women's clothes were. I knew that when Jane went shopping for clothes, she would always come back with arms loaded up with bags. I walked back to the kitchen.

"This is for expenses. You should be able to buy what you need with this, if not, ask Rosemary for some more and I will square it up with her" I said as I passed over the wad of used banknotes.

"No Andy this is way too much" Petrá said and tried to give it back.

"No it looks about right" said Rosemary and pulled Petrá's hand back

"Looks like you have just been tucked up" Said Lachie who had just come in the kitchen.

I looked at Stu, for some kind of assistance.

"Don't get me involved, its bad enough that I will have to take them clothes shopping and act as the donkey. But it is a dangerous thing to tell a woman what to buy and what looks good and even worse what does not look good on them. So I am staying out of this one."

After breakfast, Petrá left on the Catherine May with Stu and Rosemary saying they would be back tonight or tomorrow morning. Stu said he would call if they were going to lay over. I waved them off from the floating dock. Then went to see Oran.

Oran was our certified computer genius. He had been used by the IDF, in return for them keeping him out of jail and out of the clutches of the FBI, who wanted him for hacking into various systems. These included Homeland Security, the CIA along with the IDF's own servers. For his involvement in the last mission, he had been granted immunity and was no longer working for any government body. He had decided to join Lachie, Abdalla and myself in living Off-Grid. Oran had created new identities for all of us and placed us theoretically around the four corners of the world.

"Hi Oran, I need a really big favour."

"Is there any other kind these days? So what really big favour can I do for you today Andy?"

"I want you to adopt the two Korean kids."

"No way Andy I am not parent material."

"OK I could have phrased that better. I want for you, to arrange for me. To adopt the two Korean children."

"So what do you need me for?"

"I need a fake identity and a fake address and fake references, well pretty much fake everything. Then I want it to go like clockwork, and have all the boxes ticked."

"You mean you want to just go and get the kids and bring them here, and have folks looking for them elsewhere."

"That would be yes and no, Yes I want to bring them here and NO! I most certainly don't want, any fucker, EVER! looking for them ever again. As soon as we have them, I want them to get brand new identities. Those kids, have had enough bad things happen to them, in just one year. WE are in a position to help them. I feel a responsibility for them. We rescued them and then let their parents get killed under our watch. Can you do it?"

"I thought you wanted something big, like bring down an international terrorist organisation or a corrupt section of the CIA. Man this is a simple job. Want to sit and wait while I do it? Or wanna get me OJ?"

"I will get a OJ for you back in a minute"

By the time I had returned with the OJ, Oran had a fake ID for me as Patrick Amadam and for Petrá as Haley Amadam. All the paperwork for the adoption was arranged for Mr & Mrs Amadam to collect the twins from the Orphanage. The New names and Birth Certificates were also being sorted. Along with trust funds. The children were now to be called Finnbar and Ainá Amadam. Their birth dates had also been changed to one month later than their real births. That was the way things worked out and they did work our extremely well.

ACT 3

Five years later, the kids had grown up and they called me dad and Petrá they called mum. Now that Petrá and I were married, we were more than just an item. Petrá had completed her Open University degree in Teaching. She was now qualified, to teach children up to the age of 12. Lachie was married now, to a girl he had dated when he was a teenager, Morag McKenzie. Like me they chose to stay on our home on the rig.

Abdalla was engaged to a girl that he knew from his childhood and as with all of us, we all had fake identities. We were all going to Kenya for the wedding in few weeks time.

The only one of us, living out here in the middle of the North Atlantic, not in a steady relationship, was Oran. He still spent most of his life in the ethos of the internet.

Hans Gunnerson, who had been one of the original and official members of Team Seven was still the head of the Icelandic Defence Force and now worked at NATO.

We still had our reunions with the singular difference, rather then us taking turns in hosting our get-together's, They all came to our place here on the Ocean. We would see Stu and Rosemary at least once a week, and they would re-supply the rig. Lachie's father and my own father, had moved out from the pub in Keiss and had moved to the Island of Svinoy. They chosen run Petrá's old place. They never needed the money from the shop. It just gave them something to do, to while away the hours in their retirement.

Rosemary's father, Sandy, had died last year from a heart attack. We had honoured his last request and had him buried at sea. The

North Sea, had been his life and in many ways his mistress. So it was right and proper that he go to her on his death. Oran had made sure that the pub Sandy had owned, was purchased by one of the shell companies he had set up. Then he had rented it out and all the money from it went to Rosemary and Stu.

We had not heard a single thing from 'The Suit' or SIS in almost six years We had everything we required on our luxury home built inside the old Brent Bravo Oil Rig Platform. Because of the way that we had designed it, unless you were directly overhead and stationary you would not even know that the use had changed, or for that matter that anyone lived here. We were a hamlet, that was far out in the middle of the sea and we were happy with our existence.

We watched the kids growing up. When they were older, we would have to look at a better level of education and probably boarding school. We would cross that bridge when we came to it. Petrá had already helped the children speak English and Faeroese. Abdalla had taught them Bantu Swahili, Lachie had taught them Scots Gaelic. I had helped with basic Latin and Irish Gaelic. So even at the age of six, they were multi lingual.

We taught them other skills to go alongside their basic education. These were the skills that Team Seven possessed. They were skills that we hoped, that they would never require. Unarmed Combat and Shooting. This was part of their daily education. Oran helped them with computer skills. We were no longer a Team we were an extended family.

Then one day, that all stopped. Our radar had picked up a chopper heading directly for us, on an unscheduled approach. They circled our home from a distance, then the radio burst into life. But not before we had a lock on them with a SAM.

"Team Seven this is Carl Gunnerson and I request permission to Land." I recognised the voice and looked at Lachie and Abdalla.

"Permission Granted" I said and disengaged our defence system. Carl Gunnerson was the nephew of Hans and was also a pilot in the IDF. He had at first unwillingly joined us on the last operation. Then he had stood back to back with us and even on occasions saved our lives. He was a man we could trust. The small Jet Ranger came in and dropped Hans off then the helicopter took off again. We all rushed up to the helipad to greet Hans.

"Hans what brings you all the way out here, last I heard you had a desk job at NATO Headquarters in Brussels."

"Hello my friends. Yes I am still there."

"What brings you here today, I mean apart from the Carl and the helicopter?" Lachie asked

"Lets go down inside its a bit windy up here today for a reunion" I said as I grabbed Hans's backpack and followed Abdalla and Lachie back down to the communal lounge. When we were all seated and the kids had said hello to 'Uncle Hans' Petrá took the children back to their studies. Morag went back to the kitchen, she said she had to keep an eye on things in there.

"Not that it is not nice to see you again, but what massive problem, brings you out here unannounced Hans?" I asked

"I always said you would have made a great policeman Andy. So I will cut straight to the chase and there is no easy way to say it. Sir Philip Reeves-Johnson, has been kidnapped!"

We all knew Sir Philip better as 'The Suit' and that he was the top man in the UK's Intelligence and Secret Services. But we knew him better as our friend and part time member of SIS's Black Door ops 'Team Seven'.

"Who took him?" I asked

"We don't really know yet" Hans replied as he sat down.

"Where was he take from and when?"

"He was taken from his Buckinghamshire home, last night."

"So why are you here? You could have talked to us on the secure sat phone, or on the dark web chat room."

"Because apart from Carl and myself. He is the only other man in the real world, outside the team, who knows your real identities and your location. Whoever took him, they brutally murdered his wife and his son. His son had just arrived home for the school holidays."

"What are SIS doing about it?" I asked

"They say they are following up and chasing clues. Which is really security speak for 'We don't have a clue'."

"Mr Hans. In your position, you tend to have a grip on what is going on around the world, in and out of the security services. What is your take on things?" Abdalla asked

"So far I have no idea. All I know is Sir Philip once told me, that is he was ever in trouble, then 'Team Seven' was his best way out."

"How do you know about it so quickly Hans?" Lachie asked.

"When the head of a security service inside NATO goes missing, then all the NATO Security Services become involved. The only clues are the weapons that were used. According to the first reports from SIS, His security detail was taken out by a 50cal rifle. SIS seem to think that a BOYS ATR was used. There are security cameras around his home. Before the cameras were all taken out, a couple of them caught flashes of gunfire but without sound. There is only one way that could have happened." Hans said

"Mr Hans, you are saying they used a Suppressed 50cal sniper rifle? But my understanding is that you can't suppress a BOYS because of the size and type of explosive cartridge that it uses."

"Abdalla you do not know about this version, because they are still in secret trials. It is a modified BOYS 50ATR or BOYS 50cal Anti Tank Rifle. Some of the specialist forces inside NATO have been testing a version of this rifle, that has been modified for Sniper use. It had a full barrel suppressor of the same type as you would find on the VAL Silent Sniper, that the Russians invented. Only it is really not as silent. Its not a new weapon. Just this version that is a lot better than its predecessors. This rifle has been around since WWII. Previously back then, it only had a limited range of between 300 and 500 yards. With the larger charge and more efficient barrel. Plus the fact that it is made from a combination of ceramics and titanium, it is lighter and much more transportable. This is a version that has been updated for use with modern depleted uranium armour piercing shells. Because of its increased barrel barrel length from 33.5 to 52 inches. Some boffin thought that it would also make a hell of a sniper rifle. They managed to take the kick out of it, by using a floating barrel system, which allowed it to become an accurate weapon. The range of it now, with modern digital scopes like the New BAE advanced, has increased it to an effective killing range of almost 3000 yards. No one so far has been able to make it quiet enough for sniper use, until now, or so it would appear. There were rumours that the KOFC had cracked the problem and also managed to make a fully automatic version of the BOYS ANTI Tank 50cal Rifle. We have to assume that KOFC, really have managed to sort the problem of the suppressor. Because the shots that killed Sir Philips security detail were only from 200 to 300 yards and his protection squad, would have heard something as big as a 50, even with suppressor. Yet it would appear none of Sir Philips detail reacted to it being fired."

"OK Who or what are the KOFC." I asked

"Mr Hans are you saying my Country is behind this?" Abdalla asked before Hans could answer my question. Then Hans answered both the questions together.

"No Abdalla, what I am saying is, the State owned Kenya Ordinance Factories Corporation have perfected a weapon that NATO have been testing. We can account for every test rifle. Going on the lists that we got from the manufacturers. So either someone else is producing these or someone has managed to get one from source."

We tossed ideas back and forth and it was decided that under the command of Hans, we would act as special agents for NATO. We would move our parents temporarily back onto the rig and that would include Stu and Rosemary. As soon as that was done Hans would have his Private helicopter come and collect us and we would try and find 'The Suit'.

I went to see Petrá and told her quietly so that the kids did not hear.

"Petrá I have to go away for a while as do Abdalla and Lachie. All the families are coming here while we are away, They will take care of you"

"Be safe Andy and come back soon."

I had told Petrá enough, so that she would not ask any questions. Oran would act as our link while we were away. The children were still to young to understand so I just told them I had to go to the mainland for a time and I would bring presents when I returned. I knew that Stu would look out for all our families and he could handle any of the weapons that we had in our armoury or for that matter the armoury he had on board the Catherine May.

"We left the next morning with Captain Gunnerson behind the controls. The man flying it, was an old friend. Carl Gunnerson, Hans's nephew. This time the helicopter was a plain white Sea King, without any markings or tail numbers. It never ceased to amaze me how Hans could just lay his hands on transport like this.

Hans went and sat beside his nephew and we sat down on the webbing seats. I knew this had to belong to the military even though it was painted white. If it had been a civilian chopper then at least we would have proper seats. Abdalla was sat beside me and Lachie was sat opposite, within minutes into the flight though, Lachie was asleep.

We still had no Idea of where we were going, only that it was in the UK and that somehow Hans was in charge of the investigation. I looked out the window and watched my home in the North Atlantic recede as we headed for the mainland. I looked as the countryside below us changed all the time. It amazed my how many different types there were, in just one small Island. From Heather and woodland covered to barren shale, and from chalk to rolling greens. As we came into land, I thought I recognised the place but was not entirely sure. It was a military base that much I knew. However when we landed, I knew exactly where I was. This was Royal Air Force Halton. It was here, I did my trade training as a Medic, almost two and a half decades ago. I looked around. We were at the south side of the camp, on its small airfield which was located behind the Technical Training blocks. This was where the boy entrants and apprentices were trained. Up beyond them was Station Headquarters. To the left of that would be the Number One School for Dental Training, Then incredulously beyond that, a main road. The B4009 ran right through the middle of this base. Across the road was the Guard room and then up to the RAF Hospital and the accommodation sites. I doubt if there was ever much secrecy about this place. Lachie and Abdalla joined me and then Hans came out and joined us. Carl stayed with the helicopter.

A black Range Rover 4.6 HSE pulled up and the RAF driver got out and gave me the keys. Then he walked away. Hans walked over and took the Keys and walked to the back of the SUV, then he unlocked it and lifted up the tailgate. He reached in, then passed out three tactical vests, which from the weight of them I guessed they were armoured. They each bore the NATO Logo on both the front and the back. Each also had a small patch that said GDR Investigator.

"What's this mean Hans?" I asked pointing to the patch

"Service General du Renseignement. It used to be for War Crimes Investigation Branch, but now it is more of a Secret Police within NATO"

"And we, are now in them?"

"You are, if I say you are. You know my new posting was direct to NATO Headquarters. What I did not tell you, was that it was to command this branch."

"Don't you think that Lachie's long hair and Braveheart look might not be entirely military?"

"Andy in the Norwegian military, the men can grow their hair as long as they like and the same applies to facial hair. There are other military units that encourage their members to look more civilian such as Delta Force and even your own Countries, SAS. So he will fit right in. Now please put your vests on and then help yourself from here." He said, as he lifted the lid on a large lock-box in the boot of the Range Rover.

"They are Heckler and Koch VP9, they come with a 13 round magazine and you will find a leg and shoulder holsters for each of them. They also have a further two magazines with them."

"Mr Hans. Why would we need to carry these firearms openly here in the United Kingdom?"

"The GDR are always armed and always have permission in any NATO Country, which is why you will also need these" he said as he passed us our NATO Identity Cards. I looked at mine 'A. Castle' and then looked at Lachie's which said his name was, 'A. Knight', Abdalla's read 'A. Bishop'.

"I am betting Hans's, says 'A. King'?" said Lachie

"No Lachie, mine says Colonel in Chief H. Gunnerson."

"It could be worse I suppose he could have seen Reservoir Dogs I could just see Lachie as Mr Pink" I said

That got me the bird from Lachie. We put Our vests and guns on and then attached our I.D. with their Velcro backing the front of our vests. Then I climbed in the front beside Hans with Lachie and Abdalla in the rear seats. Hans drove away from the small airstrip and down towards the village of Halton then down to the T-junction. Then he turned right, for the village of Tring. After about a mile we turned left past a civilian police car, that was parked at the entrance to a private road. The road went on for a further 500 yards, through an arboretum of Elm and Oak trees. Then as we came upon a circular driveway. We were stopped by a man armed with an automatic machine pistol. Hans showed his ID and we were allowed to pass. There were more people with guns and a lot more suits. Hans pulled up at the main doors of the large farmhouse. It was a substantial building and was probably over one hundred years old. I suppose you could describe it either as a large farmhouse or a small stately home. I would say that it reflected the character of 'The Suit'. His tweed suit fitted this house like a glove to a hand.

We exited the car and stood there, while Hans went off to find out who was in charge. I looked at where the cameras were, at least before they had been smashed. There was one on each end of the house pointing down towards the driveway and another two that were about six foot off the ground pointing, so that any person coming to the front door would always be caught on camera. I noticed two others high up in the trees on either side of the road. I had seen two, at the front gate where we slowed for the police car.

They had not removed the bodies of the security detail, from outside the home. I could see two just outside the front door and another to the far right of the house. I was sure there would be others. I think it would be normal, for a man in 'The Suits' position. He would probably have a detail of between six and eight allowing for shifts. Plus he would no doubt have a couple of drivers. I had no idea of what we would find, once we entered the house. Apart from, I knew his wife and son had also been killed. I was running through the possibilities. Of who could have accessed the house, to get a lie of the land, prior to the attack.

'The Suit' would have to entertain, the head people in various security agencies. This would mean that he would also have a domestic staff, who may or may not live on the premises.

Hans came back with another man. The man was about 35 years old and wore a dark blue business suit. Along with a crisp white dress shirt and some regimental tie. His shoes were polished to a high shine. He was lean and stood just over six foot. Even though he was not particularly old his hair was thinning and going silver.

"This is Sir Philips number two, John Stephens. John this is my team." I noticed that Hans did not bother giving our names, was it because he thought that John could read our chests or that he might slip up and use our real names. I did not know, or really care. I was unsure, what we could do to help here, that the experts they already seemed to have on hand, were not already doing.

"Nice to meet you all, terrible thing, really terrible. I just hope you lads can sort this mess out. Right I will leave you to get on Colonel." He said and walked off and got in the back of a black Jaguar, which then drove off.

"Lets go see what is what, and see if we can figure out how this went down" Hans said as he led the way.

"Mr Hans, 'The Suits' protection detail, were they all killed?"

"Yes Abdalla, whoever they were, they left no witnesses behind. All the domestic staff and all of Sir Philips family along with all his protection squad and drivers." Hans said as he showed his ID Card to a young police officer, standing guard over one of the bodies.

"Shit Hans, that is a lot of carnage for just a kidnapping. And no one saw or heard anything?"

"Lachie, it is a bit like where you, used to live. His nearest neighbour is over a mile a way. No one would really have heard much, apart from perhaps the odd shot from the 50cal. Even then, they may have mistook it for one of those bird scaring devices, that the farmers around here have to protect their crops."

"Which branch of the services were his detail from?"

"That is actually a good question Andy, no one seems willing to answer that at the moment. But if I had to guess I would say probably SAS or the Political Protection Squad of the Metropolitan Police force. They also do Royal Protection duty, actually they both do. The metropolitan tend to source the RPS or Royal Protection Squad from the SAS anyway. Being a betting man, my money would be on them."

"Do we know how many shooters yet, or even how many came to attack this place. It looks like it would be the sort of place that would be easy to defend. I notice no broken windows, so I am guessing bullet proof glass?"

"I don't know about the glass but I suspect you are right. Given the amount of dead bodies and the calibre of some of the weapons used.

The outside detail were shot with 50cal the internal shooting seem to be a mix of 9mm and 7.62mm." Hans replied

"OK Lets see the mess" I said as I walked first to the right hand side of the house, where one of Sir Philips detail lay dead. A sheet had been laid over the body. I lifted it and there was a fist sized hole right through the centre mass of his chest. His Sig Sauer 9mm lay on the ground next to him. I begged a pair of neoprene gloves from one of the many specialists who seemed to be everywhere. After putting them on, I lifted up the gun and I sniffed the barrel and checked the magazine. The gun has not been fired recently and the magazine was full. He never had a chance to get off a shot. So either the shooter, already knew where the security detail would come from, or had deliberately lured him to that spot. I lifted the outside of the dead man's jacket, he had been wearing a bullet proof vest under, for all the good it had done against an anti tank rifle. The actual bullet was probably somewhere in the woods, behind the house. I laid the sheet back down and walked to the other side of the house. As before Hans, Abdalla and Lachie came with me.

The man on this side of the house had been shot in the same way. Except his firearm was still in its holster under his jacket, again he had not fired a single shot.

I walked to the front door of the house. The security guard was headless and like the man before him, had not even taken his firearm out of its holster. The blood splatter said it all really. Massive lump of lead, hits a relatively soft mass of bone and grey matter. Lump of lead wins. Its a bit like a juggernaut hitting an egg, SPLAT! The blood and brain matter, had fanned out from where the man had originally been standing, to way past where he had fallen. The man had then slid backwards, so he had ended up against the bottom step of the large ornate staircase.

To the right of where he had fallen, was a woman. She had been shot with a small calibre pistol. From the looks of things it was either point blank or very very close to it. The skin around the entrance wound was burned and blackened and there was a lot of starring around it where particles of explosive powder had been forced under the skin. The exit wound was small, which meant that it was a full metal jacket. There had been no flattening on impact with the bone on either side of her head. The bullet had caused massive damage to the skull which was swollen grotesquely. I looked around to see if I could find a bullet hole in the wall. This would have given me a good idea of where she had been standing and facing when she was shot. I could not find the bullet. The blood splatter tended to the conclusion that she had been coming down the hallways toward the front door, possibly to answer it. I assumed this was 'The Suits' wife.

So far that gave us a minimum of three shooters At least two outside the front of the house using 50 cal anti tank rifles and one inside using a small calibre hand gun.

I followed the Hallway down to the Kitchen. The cook was dead, again shot with a small calibre hand gun.

The Maid at the back of the kitchen told the same story, small bore firearm, yet no bullet or casings left behind. It looked like this was a professional hit and they had cleaned their brass. Outside the back door there was another member of the protection detail he had been killed with a 50 cal to the chest. His pistol was in its holster.

I walked around the back of the house to the side entrance and to Car, a Jaguar. just like the one that 'The Number Two' left in. The driver was sat in the drivers seat. A 50cal had gone through the rear window, then exited the front window. During its flight it had destroyed everything in its path. This included the drivers headrest and then his head. Given the angle that the bullet had exited at and driven itself through the front end of the bonnet. That would mean that the shooter had been high up in one of the trees behind the house.

We walked the downstairs of the house. There were no more bodies. There had been signs of a struggle in the Library.

We walked upstairs and found the boy in his bedroom. It was a typical teenagers room with bright posters of cars and bikini clad babes on the wall. He was sat at his computer with a small hole to the back of his head and on inspection the bullet had exited through his nose. From where he was sat, the bullet should have then punched a hole through the computer monitor. Due to the amount of damage on the exit wound, it must have been a soft nosed bullet, or even a dumdum. There was very little left of the boys face. He had like most of the victims, not seen anything before they died. So now that gave us a minimum of four shooters three of which used 50cal super rifles and one possibly two inside the house. And then there was 'The Suit' so a vehicle capable of take six persons or the use of two vehicles. I walked back down the ornate staircase to the front hallway, where I met back up with the others.

"All the staff accounted for?" I asked Hans

"According to John Stephens, yes."

"What about Gate Guards? Where the Police Car was." Lachie asked.

"Apparently Sir Philip asked for them to be removed a couple of weeks ago, or there would have been two more dead men. That's for sure." Hans replied.

"I have seen all I need to see, anyone else want to see more? Hans?" I asked. He shook his head and as we had all decided we had seen enough. We walked back to where 'The Suits' car was, to see if I could find the bullet there, but strangely like the man at the foot of the stairs no bullet.

"Hans do you suppose that once the bodies have been removed, you can have the SIS folks, look for any of the bullets. The one that went through the security guard, who had his pistol out. The bullet will be somewhere in the woods behind the house. There is a fair chance it is embedded in one of the trees about three or four feet off the ground. Also there should be more all over the place. Get them to use metal detectors and sweep the whole bloody estate if necessary."

"OK Andy I will ask them to do it?"

"Mr Hans, is there somewhere we can go to discuss this and to use a base of operations?"

"We are going to London just now, to see SIS. I will ask them to sort this out for us." he replied

We piled back into the Range Rover. Within minutes Lachie had balled his jacket into a pillow and put it between his head and the window. It did not take him long to be gently snoring away. Abdalla put in a set of earbuds and listened to his music from his MP3 player. Hans turned the news on and took us down to the A41 and then into London proper. I was not looking at the street names. We pulled off the road and before we could enter the garage at the base of a tall building, Hans pressed a button on an intercom with camera over it.

"Can I help you?" a voice with a metallic sound enquired

"GDR Investigation Branch" Hans replied and held up his ID to the camera lens on the intercom. Two sets of vicious looking spikes, retracted into the roadway that led towards the building and into its underground parking garage below. It was one of the newer buildings in the street. Presumable its predecessor had been knocked down to make room for a new high tech, high rise home, for the UK's spy industry. Once we were in, the spikes came back up. Hans got out and I noticed he kept his firearm on so we all followed his lead. I also noticed that there were a lot of cameras around the garage. The underground garage was partially filled with high end cars, Jaguars and Range Rovers mostly. I did however notice a Bentley sat in a far off corner, presumably the head honcho's private car. We walked to a set of brushed stainless steel doors and entered the elevator. Again there were cameras inside the lift. Hans showed his ID to the camera and indicated that we should do the same. After the rest of us did, a panel slid back to reveal a series of buttons and Hans pressed 2. I had expected the lift to go up but it went down. When the lift stopped and the doors opened The first signs of real Security showed. A Pair of heavily armed men in Black Nomex complete with Nomex Balaclavas and mirrored glasses.

"Your firearms please?" The first man asked

"GDR we keep them" Hans said and showed his ID again. That elicited a smart salute from both the guards who went back to their posts. We walked over to a reception desk, where a young lady was sat. Again there was a camera over it.

"John Stephens please" Hans said and slid his ID card over. The young lady took it and slid it over a scanner, then passed it back to Hans. Each of us had to do the same before reattaching them to out Tactical Vests. A middle aged woman in a grey stripe suit and black court shoes, came out from behind a set of frosted glass doors and asked us to follow her. Her heels, made a loud clicking sound on the highly polished floor. We followed her, back through the way she had come. Once again there were cameras over the door, in fact I noticed that each doorway had cameras over them. She knocked twice on the door and then opened it, she motioned for us to stay while she went in alone. then returned a few moments later.

"Please go in"

We did. The office was large and well lit. It had quality furniture and looked like some top class designer, had furnished and decorated it. Fake windows lined one wall they must have been made from gigantic TV screens as there was a view of the outside, showing a vista of trees with clouds moving behind them. It gave the room a feel of being on the bottom floor of a plush house and grounds.

John Stephens was sat behind a large Oak desk, which had a green leather top. There were two traditional phones on the top, one cream and the other red. Some form of desk ornament that held two smart looking pens. I noticed there were no IN or OUT trays. Presumably that was in his secretaries office. He had a single folder in front of him, which he closed as we entered. His office looked efficient and spacious. He stood up and offered his hand to Hans. Hans shook it and John indicated that we all should sit. The seating area was a pair of green leather Chesterfield sofas, which faced each other, over an Oak coffee table, that matched the desk, which John Stevens had previously been sat behind. There was a single matching Winged Chesterfield chair, sat at one end of the coffee table.

"Have you had a chance to walk the scene?" John asked as we all sat down.

"Yes we have. Thank you"

"And?"

"It is really too early for us to make any conclusions. Has there been a ransom demand?"

"No Colonel, nothing at all."

"We were told that Sir Philip, asked for his security to be relaxed at the main gate to his property?"

"Yes that's right, it was about two weeks ago." Stephens replied.

"Why did he do that?" I asked him

"I am afraid I cant say."

"We will want to look at his house again, at some point. Do you have the video footage from his home?" Hans said

"Yes we do but unfortunately they don't really show very much apart from a couple of flashes before they all go dead."

"Can we have access to the footage from his home"

"Yes of course Colonel" He pressed a button on his desk and the woman in the grey skirt suit, came in with a pad and pencil in her hand.

"Yes Mr Stephens?"

"Can you please make sure that these gentlemen have access to all the footage, from around Sir Philips home."

She made some notes.

"Will there be anything else?" Stephens asked Hans

"Can you arrange for us to have some offices to work from and staff as we require them. Also we will require secure accommodation."

John simply nodded to his secretary and she made more notes.

"Any thing else you require" he asked in a tone that indicated he was already bored with us and our questions.

"I know its strange but I would like to chose my staff from outside of SIS and we will vet them first. If that is all right by you John?" Hans said

John actually looked very uncomfortable at that last request, but nodded once again and the lady with the grey suit, made more notes.

"I am sorry Colonel that I cant spare more time with you this morning but I have another meeting scheduled at number 10, and the P.M. does not like to be kept waiting." He said as he stood up and offered his hand to Hans once again.

"My secretary will sort all your requests out, so if you will excuse me." He said. Then he indicated with a sweep of his hand that we should leave the confines of his office. We walked out single file and I gave his office a once over before leaving.

"OK First we require secure office space, without cameras or any listening devices." Hans said the secretary

"I am sorry all of our offices have cameras outside and inside for security. I have arranged a suit of offices, at the end of this corridor, if you gentlemen will just follow me."

We followed her down to the corridors end and into a large office space with other offices inside. There were cameras outside the door and two more inside the door. Lachie took his HK out and used its butt to smash the two cameras inside the room. The woman looked shocked.

"You cant do that." She said

"Well I just did. We want our office to be private." Lachie replied. Hans looked a little angry at Lachie's actions, but said nothing. Lachie just shrugged his shoulders. I actually thought it was a good move. The woman left us to get settled into our office space. Hans picked up the phone. And obviously there must have been someone on the end of it and then Hans put the phone down.

"We should get Oran down here" I said

"I will arrange the helicopter to collect him" Hans replied to me

"Mr Andy. You know he goes nowhere without Cyber." Abdalla said

"So much the better Abdalla." I replied

Hans put his briefcase on one of the desks and opened it up. And took out what looked like a small transistor radio. He pulled the Ariel up and started to sweep the room. When the light flashed red he stopped and then removed a listening device from where his hand held gadget had located it. He went round our offices and found two in each room. He put them all in a metal waste bin and put them outside the main door to our offices. Hans lifted the telephone again and said

"Can you come in here please"

The same woman in grey came through the door with a notebook in her hand.

"How is it I may be of service to you Colonel?"

"Contact whoever it is that is in charge of your internal security and have them come up, or down here now please, whichever way it is for them. I am sorry I did not catch your name Miss?"

"Susan, just plain Susan."

"OK just plain Susan. Can you have them come down here?"

"When would you like them Colonel"

"I thought I made it perfectly clear, I want them here now please, and have you arranged our accommodation?"

"Yes Colonel I have booked four adjoining rooms at the Guards Club Hotel."

"OK Susan that will be all for now."

"Talk about prunes, that woman's face when you requested their security people" I noted

"I would say definitely more towards the lemon side of things" Lachie added to my observation.

Hans plugged a small box into a computer port on a desk and then he plugged his laptop into that. I must have raised an eyebrow or something. Because Hans looked up and said.

"Hardware 128bit modulating encryption. The same as the one Oran uses. The only way anyone can see or access information between our two computers is to have one of these paired devices. So any messages between us and Oran using this, really stays, just between us and Oran. It can not be cracked by coding, because its is a hardware computer scrambler. It continually changes its code every couple of seconds. So even if you could crack the software that runs it, any additional hardware would show up as an intruder at which point the system would close and have to be reconnected using just the original paired devices."

"See, I knew that" Lachie said with one of his wry smiles.

Our office space was as big as John Stevens but without the fancy monitors for windows or the nice designer furniture. We had even removed half the furniture by putting the waste bin outside the door with their eavesdropping devices in it. I waited while Hans's computer, powered up and when had finished typing then he closed the computer down again.

"I have messaged Oran and he is waiting for Carl." he said and then continued.

"So what is it that we know?"

I went over to a large white board and picked up the black marker that was in the pen rest. I started by drawing a plan of 'The Suits' House and grounds.

"So, there were no men, posted at the main gateway and we are told that 'The Suit' requested that they were removed two weeks ago. Then we know that with the exception of one man, all the other security guards were shot without even having drawn their firearms. The other household staff did not appear to have put up a fight, same applies to the family. The duty driver was sat in the car and was also not expecting to be shot at. 'The Suit' apart from the signs of a struggle in his library was taken, there was no blood in there. There is absolutely no sign of how or where he was taken."

"Go on Andy" Hans said as he walked around the desk he had been sat at.

"I looks like there were two shooters at the front of the property somewhere in either side of the driveway. There was also a shooter at the rear of the property. They must have been on the left hand side of the house, as you look from the front, because he would not have wanted to be in the line of fire from the right hand side of the shooter to the front of the home. Inside there looks to have been one possibly two shooters and they took out all the domestic staff, plus the family as well as taking 'The Suit'.

The thing is I have seen the suit fight and he is seriously good at unarmed combat. He once took Lachie down without throwing a single punch. I think he knew the person, that took him and they got the drop on him somehow. I think that is why the security detail also went down so easy they either knew the attackers or were distracted by someone they actually knew."

"I agree with Andy on this" Hans said

"Mr Hans what I do not understand is why have they used what is effectively a secret version of an Anti Tank weapon when they could just as easily used any silenced sniper rifle, there are plenty of them to chose from. This is overkill to the extreme. They did not have to kill the family or for that matter the domestic staff."

"Again as Andy said, perhaps they knew the people that took Sir Philip. You are right also Abdalla, this is almost like an all out assault." Hans Said

"Mar Hans, This has military precision written all over it. No witnesses. Meaning they all knew who it was. This was carried out by someone who was not just known to Sir Philip, but was also known to the security details and to the domestic staff. That should limit severely, who we should be looking for." Abdalla said.

When he spoke, which was not that often we tended to listen, because Abdalla always chose his words carefully. At first I thought it was because he was used to talking in another language, but over the years I found he chose his words to be accurate.

"We need to see the video from when it happened we also need to see the video from two weeks before, right up until last night." Lachie said

"Why last night Lachie?" Hans asked

"Because if I were the person that took the suit, I would want to know if there was anyone on my tail. I would also take a look at the video from his office from two weeks ago until today. And see who's face pops up."

We were interrupted by a knock at the door.

"Come in." Hans said

A tall thin man came into the office. He wore a dark blue suit, white shirt and a royal blue tie. His shoes were neatly polished.

I had a habit of always looking at peoples shoes. My father had once told me you can tell a lot about a man, from what he wears on his feet. A dedicated person will always have clean shoes. A person of quality will always wear quality on their feet even if they are not a dedicated sort of individual. A slob will always be just that, dirty cheap shoes. Me, I also looked at their wrists. People who are efficient tend to be good at time keeping. They wear a good quality watch. Conscientious people were a real timepiece and not a quartz watch, because apart from time, its shows dedication and that they also want their image to be taken seriously. It does not have to be a Rolex or a Cartier on their wrists, nor does it have to be gold or diamond encrusted. In fact they are more likely to wear a stainless steel timepiece that is waterproof. So they will wear an automatic or wind up watch. Something like a Seiko or similar. A cheap plastic quartz is just that. A good timepiece though, is quality, and will always be quality.

"My name Mathew Warms. I am the head of internal security. How can I help you?" He said. He wore a Seiko with a leather strap

"Simple this office is NOT and I repeat this, IS NOT to be listened in on, nor is there to be any video of the inside of this office."

"I am sorry Sir, All our offices have this for security."

"Mathew, Do you know who the GDR are? And I do not mean the German Democratic Republic."

"No sir I do not."

"Well let me enlighten you, It is a secret Investigation branch that oversees, internal investigation within NATO. Being as how SIS falls into that catchment. Then that means we are above you. I am the most senior officer for the GDR and you can see from our badges that these men are my investigators. So what we say goes. Is that Understood?"

"Yes sir but I will have to check with Mr Stephens first and he is out of the office at the moment."

"I thought you said you understood?" Lachie said

"I do"

"So?"

"What?

"What is it you understand?"

"That you are the investigation branch for NATO."

"And? Do you want to be running security for a shopping centre tomorrow?"

The man was becoming increasingly more flustered. Hans pressed the button on his desk and 'just plain Susan' entered with he pen and paper.

"Susan have you told this man that John Stephens has given us complete autonomy and authority?"

"Yes Sir."

"Then please tell him again."

"They are correct. You are to do everything as requested by this team."

"Thank you Susan that will be all for now" Hans said as she left.

Lachie got back into the driving seat. He did have a way of making people flustered.

"So?"

"I don't understand."

"You just told me you did understand."

"Sorry Yes."

"Yes?"

"What?"

"I do understand Sir"

"So?" Lachie was on a roll but time to save this security officers brain from a major malfunction.

"Mathew. No cameras and No listening devices. EVER. Got it?"

"Sir. Yes Sir."

"Right lets get on, I want the tapes of Sir Philips offices from three weeks ago until now. I also want all the security tapes for his house for the same period. I want to interview anyone who has been on his security detail for the last month. If you can get me a list of their names please. I want a list of people that Sir Philip has had appointments with for the last month. Thank Mathew." Hans said and Mathew the security guy, left.

"Hans, you will need to add another room for Oran and make sure that the Guards Club, know that he has a dog as well. You will also have to arrange for Oran to be on team with ID and all the other bits."

"You are right Andy, I will arrange that just now." Hans said as he typed away on his computer.

"Mr Hans you said that the rifles that they use, are experimental and that they are currently undergoing trials. That must mean that there are only a few out there. We should be able to ask the Factory. Who they have sent them out too? You should let me talk to the factory. Because these guns come from my country, the are more likely to open up to me. Especially if I can do it in a face to face basis."

Abdalla always put the term Mr, Mrs, Miss or Master, in front of peoples names when talking to them. He did it as a mark of respect to the person he was having a conversation with. We had tried to get him to just call us by our given first names, but to no avail.

"Very well Abdalla I will let you get on with that. Lachie I would like you to interview the security staff. I will work with NATO. Andy I want you to work with Oran when he gets here and see if we can police the scene ourselves. You can choose which laboratory you wish to do the forensic work for you. I will get the paperwork drawn up. So we know what we have to do. It is all to one end game and that is to get Sir Philip back. We will have to figure out the who, why and wherefores out along the way. This does not look like a kidnap for cash, more like a leverage or information sort of thing. That means if they get the info they want, then Sir Philip is dead."

I wiped the white board, I knew that someone inside the SIS would want to watch whatever we did. I did not wish to make things easy for them. I would wait until I had Oran with us, before I dug too much deeper. That would be later today, possibly tonight. We left the underground park and headed for the hotel. We put our weapons in a lock-box and checked in. Once in our rooms we washed and changed. After going to the lock box to retrieve my firearm, I put my HK on a belt clip at the back of my jeans and put my T-shirt with my tweed jacket over and I went down and joined the others in the bar. It was a swanky joint. An old fashioned type bar, with waiter service. We sat at an empty table and a waiter appeared.

"Are you Gentlemen ready to order?"

Hans ordered for us, three large single malt whiskeys and a large dark rum on ice for Abdalla. We waited for the drinks to arrive and then looked around. There were several other tables with people sitting at, but it was the one by the doorway, that interested me the most. The drinks arrived and whilst I sipped mine I looked over the top edge of the glass. There was just something wrong about the two men sat there. We chatted amicably and I kept watch. We had a second drink. And I noticed that the two men had not yet ordered a drink. Now I was sure, that they were here for us, either to watch over us or to harm us. I was not sure which.

If they were there just to watch then OK. If on the other hand they wished to harm us, then they were seriously under estimated us. 2 of them against the 4 of us. Good odds for us, Hospital time for them.

"What's up Andy you seem distracted?"

"Without turning around take a look at those two guys by the door sat at the first table. You should be able to see them by looking in the bar mirror, over my shoulders."

Lachie lifted his glass and like me, made like he was drinking. Then without taking the glass from his mouth said

"I see them Andy, what makes you think they are iffy?"

"Well we all have had two drinks and the waiter works the room real hard. So why do they not have a drink yet?"

Lachie put his glass down as did Hans

"You have a good point there Andy. What do you think we should do about them?"

"For now nothing. Oran and Cyber have just arrived with Carl"

Now the odds had gone up so it was 2 of them against 6 of us plus a grizzly bear. Serious hospital time and possible missing limbs if Cyber got involved. I motioned the waiter over and ordered a J20 for Oran and a Double Vodka for Carl. Then as an after thought a large bowl of water for the dog. The waiter stalled and then changed his mind when he saw Cyber up close and personal. All the time I kept an eye on the two men at the doorway. We greeted Oran and Cyber and most of the folks in the bar moved further away. This suited me fine as

I did not really want any one, listening in on our conversation. Lachie was just about to order another round of drinks. When I noticed that one of men at the table by the doorway, appeared to be talking into his wrist. None to smart a way to make a radio call! This meant that the odds were lower than 2 to 6 but I still doubted that they would manage to take us down, while Cyber was here, at least not without a running gun battle on the streets of London. Given that we had a license to carry firearms and the power of SIS, I still did not fancy their chances.

"OK Now I am 100% sure Hans, I think we should leave this hotel and take a walk somewhere and find out who these guys are." I said.

Hans signed for the drinks giving his room number and we walked out into the chill of the night. We exited, the RAFA Club was next door to our hotel and the ROCK SHOP on the other side. Over the road there was a park of some kind. If I had to guess I would say that this was the park, that backed onto Buckingham Palace. We crossed over the road and entered the park following the footpaths around. We went past the Bomber Command Memorial.

"Oran can you make Cyber play fetch?" I asked him.

"Why?

"For one, it is the sort of thing that people do with their dogs, when they walk in a park with them and for two, you can then tell me if the two men from the bar are behind us."

we walked on without talking and Oran came back to us with Cyber

"Yes Andy they are behind you about 40 yards."

"Abdalla would You and Hans go straight on and Lachie and me we will go to the left. Oran take Cyber and go right and circle back to this point. Can you do that Oran?" He nodded.

Oran was the only non military trained person, on our team, he was learning from us but we still had to look out for him. As such we tended to give him the safest jobs to do. Besides we really counted on his abilities, as our personal go to geek. God help the person that attacked Oran because they would probably be eaten by Cyber before they could either complete their task or run from it.

Hans and Abdalla shook hands with Lachie and me, like we were saying goodbye and we waved Oran and Cyber off. Then we went left and started to circle back to where we were were now. As soon as we were out of sight of the two men we raced around behind them and hid behind some bushes. Hans and Abdalla had done the same and were on the opposite side, equally well hidden. Oran had turned around and was now walking towards the two men. He stopped abut 5 yards from them, One of the men shouted at him

"Where did your friends go?"

Oran said nothing, Cyber growled. He asked Oran again this time he pulled out a gun. By which time Abdalla was now standing behind both the men and Lachie had joined him. All this was unbeknown by either man. They had concentrated on Oran. Abdalla reached over and as fast as I saw any man move, he literally bashed their heads together and they fell limp onto the path. Equally as quick Lachie relieved them of their guns and put them in his pockets.

"Now what?" Lachie asked

"Lets take our friends here and have a quick chat with them. See that bandstand over there."

Lachie and I had one guy between us and Hans and Abdalla had the other. We followed the path down towards the bandstand. With each man held between two of us. We were almost there when I saw a Policeman walking towards us.

"Start singing lads"

"I belong to Glasgow dear old Glasgow toon
There nothing the matter with Glasgow toon
For its going round and round." I sang in a drunken voice and Lachie did the same.

"Evening Osshifer" I said in my best inebriated voice

"Looks like you lads have had a little too much to drink now. Be on your way and keep the noise down." the Constable said

"Yes Shir, Mr Polishman" Lachie said back to him and waved at the police officer.

The policeman walked on following the pathway. We walked on in the other direction and in the dark of night to the empty bandstand. We sat them down next to each other and slapped them awake.

"Well Hello there, now who do we have here.?"

I reached in the jacket belonging to the taller of the two. I pulled out his wallet. Drivers License says John Smith! As do the bank cards. Then I did the same for the other man. Strangely his were the same, only his picture on the drivers license differed from the first guy.

"Lachie what do you reckon the chances are of us bumping into two men named John Smith on a walk in the park."

Both men were starting to come around. One made to get up, ready to launch himself at Lachie, he should have stayed still as a blow to the back of his head, from the fist of Abdalla, put him right back to sleep. His friend seeing this decided to stay sat down. Oran had now arrived with Cyber and the small bandstand became almost full.

"Your real name please?" Hans asked

No answer.

"Who are you working for?"

No answer.

"Why are you following us?"

No answer.

"Andy can you go and fetch some suitable transport?"

"Sure thing." I replied and went off to find something.

We would need something big enough to carry seven men and a bear, well that was the closest thing in size I could think of, that came close to Cyber. I needed some transport fast. There was a Mini Bus outside a bar. It was all dressed up with balloons and streamers. No doubt for a Stag or Hen party, but it was perfect. It only took a minute to pull the ignition wires and find the correct two. I touched them together and the engine came to life. I drove away slowly and then around to the closest entrance to the park. I parked up and left the Hazard Lights flashing. Then I went to the bandstand. The tall guy was just coming around. We walked them around at gun point to the bus and then drove away.

"Where to boss?" I asked Hans

"The only place we will not be in trouble"

"The HQ?"

Hans nodded and then gave me instructions to the SIS underground garage. When we got to the building there was a guard at the entrance. Hans showed his ID and the guard pressed a button and the spikes in the ground shrunk away. As soon as the bus was inside they came back up again. In the lift Hans showed his ID to the camera and the panel slid across allowing Hans to press button 2. The lift went down and we marched them down to our offices within SIS. Once inside our underground offices Hans closed the doors and put the lights on

"Call your friends."

"What?"

"Lift your arm up and call your friends"

"I don't now what you mean" The tall one replied

"I watched you in the bar, You were passing information to someone via a mike on your wrist. Don't make us strip you to prove a point" I said

He sat still and said nothing.

Abdalla pulled the man's jacket off, it revealed a wire that travelled from the cuff to a small radio pack on the man's belt. On inspection there was a tiny receiver in the man's ear canal.

"This is the part where we beat the shit out of you and in the end you tell us who you are, who you work for and anything else we want to know. Or we feed you to the dog. So what is it to be?" Lachie asked him

"Those were our buddies that were murdered while guarding Sir Philip."

"You guys are SAS?" I said

"What's it to you?"

"So why are you following us?"

"You should know you are the bastards behind all this. You and the rest of SIS. Do what you got to do, but can you just get on with it."

Lachie pulled of the shirt sleeve first, off one man and then of the other. Both had the commando dagger with wings, through a scroll that said 'Who Dares Wins' the motto of the SAS.'

"From what I know about you guys, you have a code of honour. We are here to investigate the deaths of all the people at Sir Philips. We are independent from SIS" I said as I showed my GDR ID card.

"So you guys are NATO police or something like that?"

"Something like that" I replied and continued

"So who is on the other end of the radio?"

He did not say a word to begin with, then he seemed to make a choice, and that choice was, that we were actually on the same side.

"There are two more of us, they will be in an old blue ford transit outside this building. The are probably working out a way to take this place. Your best bet is to let one of us go and get them to stand down. Or the likelihood is that the next time you boys exit the garage you will meet with a nasty accident."

I looked at Lachie and Abdalla and then over to Hans. They all gave tiny nods indicating that we should let one of them go and bring in the rest of the SAS team. I gave him back his jacket.

"I'll do it, I will walk him out" I said

"Be careful Andy!" Lachie said

"Always" I replied and walked back to the lift and then up to the garage with the SAS Guy. I let him walk in front of me when we exited the lift. We walked towards the exit ramp. I kept myself tight behind him as we walked up.

"Over there" he said

He pointed to an old style and somewhat beat up Ford Transit. I followed him up the ramp and we were just about to exit, when a hand grabbed me by the forehead and pulled my head backwards. I could feel the cold steel against my throat. The blade was with its flat side pressed hard against my Adams apple. I was left with no doubt that in a second it could be the working edge of the blade.

"Where's our other man?" he hissed in my ear.

"He is safe and well, ask your buddy over there."

"He is telling the truth. I think these are actually the good guys. They are GDR NATO Internal Police. Sort of like CID. For the Secret Services."

The pressure of the blade against my throat eased off a bit and I found I could now swallow even though my throat was actually dry.

"Guys I am unarmed, I left my firearm and knife inside, you want justice for your buddies? Then help us."

The man with the knife to my throat looked towards someone I could not see. Then that person stepped out from behind the edge of the building.

"Who are you, apart from the GDR, you don't look military to me."

"We are independent civilian contractors. It was our old boss that was taken and his family that were murdered. So you see, like you, we have the same axe to grind."

"OK, Say I believe you what happens now?"

"Now you come in and meet the rest of the team. Then we decide, how best to use your skill set in catching and punishing the bastards, that did this. Sound fair?"

The man who had been in the shadows gave another nod and the knife left my throat. I instinctively put my hand up and rubbed the part where the knife had lain moments before.

"OK If you guys will follow me" I said and walked back to the elevator. The three of them followed but they kept themselves spread out. It was a smart play if there were a trap. Only when I was in the lift did they join me. I held my ID up to the camera and the doors closed and the panel slid across. I pressed button 2.

When the lift stopped and the doors opened they made sure I was standing at the front. These were not amateurs they knew what they were doing. So whoever had killed their buddies must have been skilled. I walked down the corridor and knocked on the door before opening it. I knew our team would be taking no chances either. I felt rather than saw guns come up behind my back. Abdalla opened the door. I motioned with my hands for our team to lower their guns. Abdalla did and let his HK hang by his right leg. Hans put his in its holster under his jacket. Lachie waited a little longer, his gun had been pointed directly over my left shoulder at the man who was behind me. I nodded and Lachie lowered his gun. I walked into the room with the other three surviving members of the SAS, who were on Sir Philips detail. I introduced our team. They were less inclined to give out their full names.

There was Micky who was a Warrant Officer, John who was a Sergeant, John 'O, the guy that had gone out with me. He was a Corporal and finally there was Staff Sergeant Paul. All of them carried ID that said they were John Smith.

"We all need to talk, but away from here. As you may know my name is Hans, or to be more precise, I am Colonel in Chief Hans Gunnerson of the IDF, or if you prefer, The Icelandic Defence Force. My current posting is to NATO in charge of the GDR. This as you

know is the investigation branch for NATO. If you men will trust
me, I can arrange accommodation for you. In return, I will need to
ask you some questions. I will need honest answers. Unofficially I am
quite happy for you to be the instrument of punishment, on the men
that killed your friends. If this is acceptable to you then we can move
forward if not then you go on your merry way, but be sure to stay out
of our way and our investigation."

I looked around the room which was filled with hitherto
unprecedented levels of testosterone. We all wanted the same thing
at the end of the day. However no one wants to be the little dog in
the pen. I knew that technically we were the big dog, even without
Oran who was sat quietly in the corner of our office suite. Cyber was
standing, silent but attentive. It was the Warrant Officer who broke
the silence.

"OK, if we work with you, what is your end game?"

Hans looked around the room and then said.

"Our end game would be to ensure the safe return of Sir Philip
and to find the who and the why, behind the murder of all those
people, at Sir Philips home. How does that sit with you?"

"I think I can speak for my men in this, We are happy with that,
so long as we get the men that killed our buddies."

"Thank you Micky. So lets get you some accommodation. How
do you feel about the Guards Club, where we are staying. NATO will
pick up the tab. But no side games, we all work together."

We left in the Mini Bus and the Ford Transit. When we arrived
back at the park, I parked the Mini Bus close to where I had stolen
it from. After wiping down the steering wheel and door handles we
walked to the entrance of the Guards Club. The SAS team were
waiting for us. Each of them held a large kit-bag. Hans led the way
into the hotel and arranged for the four men, to join us on the same
floor, as we were staying on. After getting booked in, Hans told them
and us to come to his room. He told Oran to stay in his own room
with Cyber for now. There were not nearly enough chairs in Hans's
room, so most of us sat on the floor with our backs pressed against the
walls.

"When was the gate detail, removed from Sir Philips home and who authorised it. It seems to me that you four were probably the main gate guard?" Hans said

"We were told by SIS that Sir Philip felt that there was no need for men on the gate of his home." Mickey replied

"When you say that SIS told you, who and when?" I asked

"We received all our instructions the same way as normal, which was via our CO in Hereford. We got a physical memo."

"Micky be specific on this. Who gave you the order to stand down from the gate?"

"It was a memo on our units note paper, it was passed to us by our L.T. He received the memo from HQ and physically gave it to me. So we stood down, but stayed ready."

"Do you still have the memo?" Hans asked.

"Sure, I have it in my kit bag, I can get it for you if you like."

Hans nodded and the WO left to get the memo.

"What unit are you with?" Abdalla asked the Staff Sergeant.

"We are part of a joint services unit that makes up the RPD."

"Which is?"

"Royal Protection Detail. There are about 100 of us, but we get sent out as small units, for Royals and Political figures, as well as for the heads of the Security Services. We were a team of eight. The drivers came from the Police ATU. Anti Terrorist Unit. The cars come from the RPD and are completely bullet proof, at least they were until this happened. It is a matter of honour for us now. The SAS have never lost any of their charges until this. We also have brothers to avenge. We have lost guys before, but have never lost any on home turf. Apart from accidents that is. We are happy to help you, so long as you let us finish it."

I knew they were talking about executing those that had carried out the attack. There would be no trial, not by NATO and not by the Crown. There would be no plea bargains, nor would they have lawyers. Hans seemed happy enough for things to go down this way. I was not so sure. Yet who was I to compare my moral balance or compass with theirs. Had I not done the same thing just over five years ago.

I had taken a civilian who was unarmed and shot him in the back of the head. He had committed small crimes, but he had the propensity to commit a crime so heinous, that I and I alone, had been his judge jury and executioner. Those were my corrupt morals. These men had simpler morals. Simple you kill one of us then you will pay with your life, no matter how long it takes.

The WO returned and passed over the memo to Hans. Hans looked at it and passed it over to me. The memo was on MOD Form 4A and purported to be from SAS HQ Hereford. It was addressed to

OIC Unit 5 RPD.

'With immediate effect.
There is no longer a requirement for this unit to cover
The front gate of the property.
This is at the formal request of OIC SIS
The Squad, this memo concerns, are to return to base
ASAP and await further instructions.
Signed
M.T.Sutterton. B.Gen
Special Air Service
Headquarters
Credenhill
Hereford

The form looked legit I passed it to Lachie and he gave it to Abdalla after reading it.

"So Micky why did you not return to base?"

"We did, but as soon as we heard about the attack. We then asked for permission, to help with the investigation. Our OIC granted that permission on a face to face. You will find no orders for it. Technically we are on extended leave. I know what you guys are thinking. Is it real and is it normal to get orders this way? Yes its real and yes sometimes we do get our orders in the field this way. For the greater part we get written orders, it stops mix ups and gives the crown its accountability and the transparency, that the politicians seek. So yes these days, it is relatively normal to get orders this way. The top dogs thought that radio, was too easy to crack so personnel voice, face to face or orders handed over in written format, as we have here."

"Hans let us assume, that the orders that are written here did in fact come from SAS HQ. Being as we are all ex-military to one degree or another. We know apart from shit which flows downhill, that the orders do the same. The CO at Credenhill, he got his orders from somewhere. Who commands him?" I asked.

"Well above him you would have, The SAS General, then the Field Marshall, then the Secretary of Defence and then the PM." Micky replied.

"So the SIS folks, they could not change the orders without the involvement of the Army?"

"I don't so. You think its an inside job?"

"To tell you the truth Micky, I don't have a clue at this point, I am just looking at the options. According to SIS, Sir Philip requested they be withdrawn. That seems to tie in with the memo, that you got from your OIC. If it were fake, Sir Philip would have immediately noticed, the lack of his forward gate guard though?" Hans said

"No not necessary Colonel. Sir Philip spent most of his time away from this home. From what I can gather he had only just returned that night. A lot of the time he would spend at his club, especially of he had a meeting in the morning, or if he was due to fly out somewhere the next day."

"Who knew Sir Philip's routine?"

"We would only get details 12 hours in front. They would come direct from SIS. Through our OIC"

"Who in SIS?"

"I am sorry, I don't have the answer to that, but I would presume that it came from Sir Philips own office."

"OK. There are a few things here that we need to understand, before we can actually move forward.

One, we need to check that the memo, did actually come from the SAS, OIC.

Two, what is the point in using a weapon that is actually secret and only on a test list? This would limit it to the people that have access to it. We were looking at a unit, that has access to three of them as well.

Three. Why such a level of violence?

Four. Who it is, that have actually taken Sir Philip?

Finally five. Why?

Once we have at least some of those answers, we will have something of a starting point. Lets go back to the house tomorrow and see if we can work the crime scene again. I will arrange for you guys to get better transport. OK that's it for tonight guys, see you all at breakfast." Hans said

The SAS guys left us in Hans's room. There were a lot of questions and so far bugger all, in the way of answers. I got up from my place on the floor. And started to pace up and down. I don't know why I did that. It is just I seem to think better, when I am on the go.

"What bothers you Mr Andy?" Abdalla said

"Just about everything. But if I take it in the order, that Hans has set out the problems. First The SAS Team said they got the Memo from their LT. So, I would say that there is a good chance that the memo is real. Even if it was written, with flawed information. We have been told that the BOYS 50ATR was used by some of the attackers. We have not had ballistics on any 50cal bullets yet, so how the hell do they know its a BOYS? It could just as easily be a AS50. Who is it? that first stated that a BOYS Rifle was actually used? There is no doubt that some of the SAS guys were killed with a high calibre weapon, it does look like a 50cal, but other than that I personally can see no evidence that it was a BOYS ATR. The violence was unnecessary, sure kill the protection detail as they would shoot at you, but why murder the domestic staff and the family? It is almost psychotic. From the looks of the library 'The Suit' put up a fight. We have seen 'The Suit' in action, so I would guess there was more than one person, in there with him. Finally there was no brass. These were professionals that did this, at least from our first run over the place. The four of us are sniper trained. We should take a look at the scene as if we were the shooters. Perhaps we will be able to see something we have missed. Hans you are the policeman, you should look at the house and see if you can find anything. We will have to use an independent laboratory for any forensics. That way, no one else will be able to manipulate the findings."

"Andy you think that the information from SIS is flawed?"

"To tell the truth Hans I don't know, I would just like to err on the side of caution, the sooner we get accurate answers the sooner we can find 'The Suit'."

"Lachie you have not said much, what are your thoughts so far."

"Hans, I am thinking that is a lot of firepower, to snatch one man from his home, when surely it would have been easier, to snatch him away from his home. He would have had a maximum of two in the detail and one driver. But more likely a driver in one car and a pair following in another car. Taking this house would have been like taking a fort. A road snatch is just so much simpler and a lot less collateral damage involved."

"Mr Hans I agree with both Mr Andy and Mr Lachie. I also think it was a much bigger team that would have been required to take the home. I think that the protection detail probably knew at least, some of the team that attacked them."

Rather than eating in the Guards Club. I decided to go for a walk, Oran and Cyber came with me. We found a Kebab shop, called Chez Radwan. We bought a couple of large Doner kebabs. While the man behind the counter was cutting the meat from one of the large Doner Meats on skewers, he chatted amicably to us. I had thought at first he was Turkish but he explained that he was Syrian and had moved to Britain for a better life. He had originally intended to train as a Doctor, but that in order to pay for his life he had started making Kebabs and selling them. He claimed that Doner Kebab was a Syrian recipe and that the Turkish kebabs were inferior and cheap imitation of the real thing. I apologised for thinking he was Turkish. He said that's the thing about life you can never be sure of anything until you try it. True to his word his Kebab was probably the best I have ever eaten. I thanked him and paid for our food then we left the shop. We ate as we walked and talked.

"Oran can you find out, who here in the UK, have the 'BOYS ATR' for testing?"

"I can do that Andy just as soon as we get back"

We walked around the corner and back into the park. It was now about 11.30pm and people were starting to make their way home from pubs and early closing clubs and theatres. It was a Monday night and most folks would be getting up for work in eight hours or less. So the park was becoming empty. The police had moved the homeless folks on, from the public areas. These homeless and unfortunate folks, would now move to the far less glitzy areas of central London. Most of them would end up in the doorways of smaller shops in the side streets. It was this, that made them a lot easier to spot. These were not SAS, nor were they police, but they were not homeless bums either. If they had been, they would have been out looking for somewhere sheltered to sleep the night. They would not be in the park pretending to be drunk or scavenging in the many, now empty litter bins. Knowing you are being followed is not as scary, as not knowing 'if' you are being followed. It was a whole lot less frightening with Cyber walking beside us.

Oran had been given Cyber as a puppy, at that age Cyber had been a ball of fluff, that ball of fluff had grown into this Caucasian Shepard Dog or Ovcharka. It is a dog, but in size and bulk it was closer to being a grizzly bear. It had grown to become a protector for Oran. Cyber's head came up to Oran's armpit and probably weighed in at almost twice that of his master. Oran had been the sort of person that the thugs on a beach would kick sand in their face. Oran was somewhere between five foot six inches tall and five foot eight inches. He probably weighed in at eight stone when wringing wet. Perfect meat for the bullies. That was before Cyber came into his life, now when people saw Oran walking towards then, they would give them both a wide berth. The men were following at a distance from both sides of the park. I instinctively felt for my HK. I did not tell Oran, about the three guys. I watched out the peripheral edge of my eyesight, without turning my head. They kept a respectable distance and did not threaten in any way. I decided to let them follow. They sure as hell would not get any info from us, as at the moment we were blank canvases. They followed us all the way around the park and then sat down on a bench opposite our hotel, as Oran, cyber and I entered.

I went up and to my room. I would tell the others about our shadows in the morning, as I did not see any kind of hostile threat from them at the moment. The following morning after I had showered and dressed, I went down to the dining room for breakfast. I sat at a table alone in the dining room with my back against the wall, so I had a good view of the road outside. There were two of the guys from last night, camped out on a bench, on the other side if the road from the hotel. I saw Lachie and Abdalla enter the dining room, as the waiter was at my table, I ordered a large pot of Arabic coffee and two full English breakfasts, also a breakfast that had beef sausage, with lambs liver and kidney. This was instead of the bacon and pork sausage, that made up a full English. This breakfast was for Abdalla in deference to his Islamic faith. I waited for them to sit before I told them about the guys outside.

"We have some shadows, and they are not SAS. If I had to make a wild guess I would say that we are being watched by the very folks that have asked for our help."

"Mr Andy why would SIS, want to watch us? When we have offices in their building and we are staying in a hotel they have arranged for us."

"To make sure we stay within the constraints of the B.S. we have been fed." Lachie said.

The coffee arrived and our conversation died until the waiter had gone back into the kitchen. By which time Hans had now joined us and ordered his breakfast of buttered kippers and toast. "Morning Hans, we need new digs, we seem to be the subject of school project."

Hans gave me an enquiring look

"What Mr Andy means, is that we have pick up some fleas."

Hans gave Abdalla the same look

"What they both mean, is that we have the wagging part of Cyber." Lachie said

"Have you three been to the bar this morning? I am afraid I don't understand school projects, fleas and dogs."

In unison we all tried to explain at the same time. And without turning around. He said and then continued

"Do you mean the two tramps opposite and the street cleaners at each end of this hotel?"

"OK so you saw them, I have to admit I missed the street cleaners as I was not looking for them. I saw the bums last night. The point is I don't think we should stay here, I don't think we should go back to SIS, at least until we have all the answers. Perhaps we should use our own premises and then send SIS the bill when we are done. But we will have to have leave our Range Rover here and then reach out to the SAS. We should do all this when we get back here tonight after we have been to 'The Suits'.What do you think?"

"That sounds like a good plan, but what about the Laboratory? There are only a few specialist ones to chose from."

"Mr Hans, why do you have to use a laboratory in the UK? Surely you could use an independent from anywhere in the world."

"That is a valid point Abdalla, and I agree with you on it. Hans can we bring our own specialists onto our platform and provide whatever equipment they require? Doing it that way there is no way anyone can interfere with the results. We could set them up under the watch of Oran, if he is agreeable. I am sure, he could set us up with an encrypted laptop and cell phone. A bit like the one you have Hans.

You and your nephew are the only people, outside those who are actually living there, who know where we are based. Once we have collected the actual evidence and have the answers from it, we can hopefully hunt down 'The Suit". It will also mean that we do not have to rent anywhere. Add to that, it would be physically impossible to sit outside and spy on us without being seen. Unless anyone can think of a better idea. We have all our families safe there. We have the use of the Catherine May and I am sure we could fabricate some kind of cover to go over a helicopter."

As with all the missions that 'Team Seven' have undertaken it was fluid and self forming. Plans were continually changing and re-evolving. Nobody objected. There was only one other wrinkle to be ironed out. How to contact the SAS, after we left? As I really did not want to leave them out of the loop. I would let Hans sort that part out. After we had breakfasted, we met up with the SAS boys and drove to 'The Suits' home. There was still a single police car at the end of the long drive. Hans showed his ID Card and we drove down and parked outside the front door. The SAS Boys pulled up behind us. Hans walked away from the house and like true conspirators the other seven of us followed him. When we were about 100 yards back down the driveway, Hans stopped and turned to face us.

"We seem to have other people following us." He said for the benefit of the SAS. Then continued.

"They were outside the hotel last night and even followed Andy and Oran into the park. So we are going to move base. Can we use you lads as our local folks? We don't like the attention that we are getting. Our plan is to set up our own forensics Lab in a private location. But we will want to sort, some form of communication. We want to get Sir Philip back. He was our boss, on a couple big missions. We also want to see justice done, for the teammates that you have lost. First let's work this site. See if we can find any of the sniper lairs and work our angles. Who knows, we may actually find one of the rounds that were used. At least that would give us a definitive calibre, that the snipers used. Right lets go and see if we can find out where the snipers were. We should split up one of us with one of your men and meet back here in one hour."

We set off looking for signs that someone had laid down in the small woods to the front and the rear of the property. Each of the four teams, worked diligently and we met back at the front of the house an hour or so later.

"Any one find anything? Because Micky and I could find nothing, to the right hand side of the house. Which kind of blows my theory about two shooters at the front."

"Mr Andy we found nothing at the rear"

"Same here" Lachie said

"Likewise, which makes no sense. If there were three shooters outside, we might possibly miss seeing one shooters nest, or position. We were at the back of the home directly across from you and Andy. Even if we had not found the nest we should have found the round that took out the Protection Detail at the right hand side of the house. Not only could we not find the bullet, we could not find any marking to the trees. There is no way that the bullet, could have travelled through the woods behind the house and into the farmland beyond, without it striking at least a couple of trees. Even if these snipers were good enough not to leave marks from where they were set up, and if they cleaned their brass. There would still have been some damage to the trees behind from the bullet."

"OK Lets try the inside of the home." I replied

I looked at where the security guard had been standing and where the bloody mess was behind, where he would have been standing. I put myself in his position and looked out, then I walked back to where he had come to rest. Again there was no bullet or even bullet hole behind him. There was lots of blood where the folks had been killed but no bullets or even a sign of one. We went out to where the car was, The driver had been removed. There was damage to the car and to the bonnet. I followed the line that the bullet would have travelled from the hole, in the 'not so' bullet proof rear window, through the back of the headrest and then through the windscreen. Finally through the bonnet then the radiator and front grill. That would have made the bullet's resting place about twelve feet in front of the car. We searched on our hands and knees. All we got for it was sore knees, from crawling around on the flint chippings of 'The Suits' gravel driveway. I went back to the house and went upstairs to the boys room. I looked but no bullet hole in the computer or in the plaster wall behind.

"Right just how the fuck can so many people be killed here with a variety of weapons and there be no bullet holes. How can there be no evidence!!! SIS said they had no fingerprints, No hairs nothing. Yet they tell us that the SAS guys were all taken out with a BOYS 50cal. I don't doubt that they were shot with a large calibre rifle and that even after the first shot, they were still caught with their pants down, or it was that silenced that they never heard it being fired. I. That said, I like the rest of us, have fired 50cal rifles and even with a suppressor on it still makes enough noise for it to be heard when fired from 25 yards. The SAS Guys would know what a suppressed shot sounds like. From the direction all the men were facing, which is away from the house and towards the main road. I would suspect that they would have at least seen the flash as they were fired. This would have given one or perhaps two experienced men, like the SAS are, a chance to dive for cover. I just don't get it."

"Andy come and have a look at this." Hans said indicating I should go with him over to where the car was sat. and then he continued, while standing at the front of the car.

"What do you see Andy?"

"A car with a fucking big bullet hole, well technically it has an entry, a hole through the back of the car, at the top of the rear window then through the headrest, and then finally an exit hole through the bottom of the windscreen and bonnet. What am I looking for?"

"Take a look Andy." Hans said

I stood at the front of the car and then I went around the back of the car. I even looked through the windscreen at the rear of the car I could see the line the bullet had taken. I knew that no one had been able to find the shooters lair.

"Sorry Hans I am lost."

He took a laser pen out from his pocket put it in the hole of the front windscreen then lined it up with the one in the headrest and finally the one in the entry point of the rear window. Then I saw what Hans was talking about. The red dot was on a wall behind the car. The dot was almost a foot under the top edge of the wall. There was no way that the shot was fired here.

"What the fuck?" Lachie said

"This car and the man in it, were not shot here."

"OK we need to photograph everything and then we need to get hold of the original Scenes Of Crime Pictures. Hans who were the first folks on the scene?"

"The local police, got an anonymous call. The caller stated they thought they heard gunfire and screams."

"OK first, there is no way anyone could have heard screams from 'The Suits' house, unless they were right here. So we need to get the reports and photos that they took. Before SIS claimed the scene."

"We, can get all that for you. We are technically part of the Metropolitan Police in the Royal Protection Squad. Where do you want the info sent?" Micky said

"We will give you an email address. Andy will work that out with you. But for now Micky, we are going to sort our new lab and office space. We need one more favour from you. We need to collect our kit and Oran from the hotel and then we have to go to RAF Halton. We could use you guys, running some form of interference for us, just in case someone decides to follow us again, from the Hotel. Can you ensure that? We will need to change our transport. So If you want to swap our Range Rover, for your Transit that would be good."

"We can do that" Micky said with a big smile.

That is what we did, we changed transport and we did not contact SIS. We did however contact Carl Gunnerson and arranged for him to meet us at RAF Halton and then he flew us back to the Rig.

ACT 4

As soon as we landed back on our platform, Hans and Lachie, along with Karl set about creating a temporary box frame around the helicopter and then covered the outside in tarpaulins. So now it looked like there was a green box structure rather than a helipad. I went down and said a really quick hello to all the families, that had now come to the rig, in order to be under our watchful eyes. Then I went with Oran, to one of the unused apartments.

"If we empty this, of all furniture. Do you think we could set up a basic forensics lab in here?"

"Depends on what you want to check on Andy?"

"Some basic forensics, ballistics and possibly some blood-work. Also we will be conducting our own postmortem. Perhaps a bit of computer forensics. Along with a basic mock up of 'The Suits' home and surrounding land. Just tell me what equipment we need for it and if there is enough space?"

"Space is not a problem but you are going to need a spectrometer, Post mortem table and Electron Microscope. Along with the usual things that would be required for a post mortem. A clean room we can build inside one of the bedrooms. The computer stuff is not a problem, I already have everything you will need. I say you, though I suspect that it is going to be me?"

"Yes Oran it will be you. I am going to put you in total charge of the laboratory. Order what you need and arrange for it to go to the dock at Keiss and Stu can collect it from there. Make sure it is addressed to the Catherine May. If you go and see Hans, he has all the digital images from 'The Suit's' home. OK lets go to the bar and sort everybody out." I said.

I went down to the main deck area, where we had made a general communal lounge, come bar. There were a lot more people here than when I left. My father along with his gangly companion Raven II. My fathers friend and Lachie's father, Mark Henderson, was here. Stu McCormack and his wife Rosemary were here. The twins Hals and Finn along with Petrá. Then of course there was Carl Gunnerson and his uncle Hans. Added into this Lachie, Abdalla, Oran and myself, while not forgetting my Japanese Akita, Kyla and the gigantic Caucasian Sheppard Dog, Cyber. So fourteen humans and three dogs. It would sound like a lot of people, had it been a house.

However this had once been an Oil Platform with over 100 men, living and working on it. We had turned all the work and accommodation space into living and a different kind of workspace. So we had a lot of area to play with. We had luxurious space.

We had never really worked in a military structured, sort of way. Sure we had previously had ranks, but in a most unmilitary fashion, I had been elected leader. Now however we seemed to be working under Hans, which was fine by me, as if I were honest, I prefered to follow than to lead. We were not really working for SIS either. We were working for NATO. No one had discussed wages, but at some point, I would want to send out some form of bill to someone. That, or Oran would just steal it, from one source or other, no doubt linked to either SIS or NATO.

I knew we needed to unravel lots of puzzles, in order to find 'The Suit'. I was also sure, that SIS knew a lot more, than they were telling. I knew that the SIS had the ability to back track satellite imagery, yet they had apparently, not done this simple task. We were brought in almost 24 hours after the incident happened.

The local police had the scene for less than an hour before SIS claimed it. I wanted to see the local police officers notes. I wanted to know, where the original emergency call came from. When every one was seated and the kids were in the play room. I raised these points.

Oran said he would get the satellite images. Hans said he would see if he could get the SAS guys, to get all the information from the attending police officer.

Abdalla said he would look into the BOYS ATR Link. Which left me and Lachie at a bit of a loose end. There was one question that no one had really asked. What if 'The Suit' was dead? We ate and slept on the rig for two days waiting on equipment and for information to arrive.

It was the equipment that arrived first. Oran and I had already cleared out one of the spare apartments and set up a clean room in what was one of the bedrooms. We had set up a command centre and office in the lounge area. SIS, apparently were not happy, that we had moved from the Guards Club. They had asked the SAS to locate us, they in turn had said they were looking.

Oran had been in contact via a laptop, he had given, to what was left of Sir Philips detail. Hans had told SIS, that his team, which would be us, were chasing down evidence. So we were still able to have a two way communications with them. Micky had been able to locate the Police officer, who had been the first on the scene. The officer had been wearing a body camera, and they had sent the video footage to us. However since the night of Sir Philips abduction, the attending police officer had been involved in a serious head on collision, with an articulated truck. He was currently in a coma, in Stoke Mandeville Hospital. That in itself meant that he had either suffered a broken back or that he had a brain injury.

I had my doubts about this being an accident, given all that was going on. Micky had also sent the officers notes, and the names of those who had attended the scene afterwards. With the help of Abdalla and the fact that Abdalla, had been one of the most senior officers in the Kenyan Army before joining Team Seven. Oran had been in contact with the KOFC or Kenyan Ordnance Factories Corporation. And had been able to get a complete list of all the units that had been issued with the Beta or trial version of the MKVI BOYS 50ATR. Abdalla had since found out that they were also sending out information to countries around the world, that the KOFC had a new and improved 'Silent Version'. Although There did not seem to be more information on where and who, were testing this version. KOFC had stated in their advertising blurb that this rifle and others in the same series would be game changers in the field of covert firearms. The specs they had on it were impressive though. So much so that I asked Abdalla was there any chance, that we could have one for 'Testing' His reply was that the KOFC would only deal with governments direct. Both the East and the West bought firearms from this company. The blurb from the KOFC that I looked at, gave projected prices per unit. The base price of a non-silenced 50cal MKVI BOYS was $75,000 US. That sounded a lot but not so, when it was stated that they had done a deal with BAE, who would be providing a new version of the digital scope. This new and improved version, was smaller and lighter than the BAE digital scope, than the one we were actually using on our own sniper rifles. Our scopes, which we had managed to acquire, when they were in the test stage. Had originally been valued at £500,000 each. So now this scope had been miniaturised and now fitted to a 50cal with an effective kill range of 3,000 meters plus. I had made shots at 2,000 meters and that was at the absolute limit of the rifle and of the scope, not to mention my own ability. So a rifle that could take a man or light armoured vehicle out, at a distance of 3 kilometres, was indeed a game changer. You would never see where the shot came from and by the time you heard the shot, assuming the wind was blowing in your direction. You would already be eights seconds into the hereafter. Now $75k sounded not just fair, but positively cheap. BOYS had also said, that their Silenced models were available with interchangeable barrels. To cover all standard munitions from 9mm to 7.62, or even from 45 to 50. Each interchangeable barrel also came with its own integral chamber. Meaning that the Barrel, Silencer and chamber were a single unit that clipped in and out of place with the stock and firing pin. I also looked at the shares for KOFC and they were soaring. It would appear that the arms market were ready for this sort of weapon. I looked up who in the UK, had been given this weapon for testing. There were only two units in the UK, that had been issued with them. They were the SAS and the RMC-SBS. These two units were the crème de la crème of the UK's covert fighting forces. I would have expected them, to have trials with this weapon. We had contacts in the SAS, so it would seem the simple thing to have Hans contact them and then get Abdalla to go down and see one of these beasts first hand. The claim on their website, was that is you were more than twelve yards away, you would not hear this fire. I for one found this a big pill to swallow.

Even the VAL Silent Sniper they said twenty five yards. The VAL was only a 9mm. Having used the VAL personally, I would have probably gone for a bit more than that and said forty to fifty yards, before it was totally silent. Like most things these were subjective and you had to take into consideration is you were using High or low velocity rounds. There is a country mile between the sound of a sub-sonic round and super-sonic round. The environment likewise plays a huge part. The concrete jungle amplifies the sound of a firearm, no matter if it is suppressed or not. Fire the same weapon from inside a close wooded area or in thick and deep grasslands and the result it a lot quieter. Somebody though, I feared was yanking our chain.

It was beginning to look like the whole murder kidnap thing was staged. That is to say, the Scene had been staged either for the SAS or SIS or more specifically, it was set for us.

"Hans can you get us a couple of really good, forensic crime technicians, I mean from the Icelandic police force. Can we have them on loan for as long as required?"

"I will arrange that. Do you wish them brought directly here or something a little more covert?"

"I Like the covert thing. How long do you suppose it would take to get them say about an hour away by sea. We could have Stu meet one of your cutters an hour or so away from here."

"OK I will let you know where and when to send Stu out." Hans replied.

"I will have Oran help me make a cardboard mock up, of 'The Suits' house. We should be able to make an approximate scale replica, working from the photographs we have. Hans you say the unit you head up is the Police for NATO?"

"Yes Andy? Why do you ask"

"So can you give Oran permission to hack a computer at SIS?"

"Who's computer?"

"John Stephens and see if we can use the SAS boys to watch him, covertly of course."

"Technically we are the police for all of NATO, even so no sovereign nation likes to be spied on by their own allies"

"Then we best not get caught. You told me before that Oran was the best hacker in the West. And we killed the best hacker in the East. So that makes Oran the best in the world. Right?"

Oran piped up,

"Trust me Andy, when I am in their servers, they will not even know I have been there."

"OK Oran, can you start work on the reverse satellite imagery, and see if we can see, what actually went down at 'The Suits'? So far no one had shot at us, or even tried to blow us up. That in itself was quite refreshing."

The way things had started for us on the two previous missions, was for people to blow us up, and then try to turn us into ex-people, by trying to shoot or stab us. I had my doubts, as to just how long benign nature, of our involvement would last. The more I thought about this, the more I was sure this had less to do with 'The Suit' and more to do with the something that the SIS, were either involved in, or that they had known about. I had no idea, who was actually the puppeteer this time around.

I left Oran and Hans, working out which techs, they would be best suited to what we were looking into. Abdalla was in contact with a friend of his in the Kenyan Government. That once again, this left Lachie and myself twiddling our metaphorical thumbs, for now. I was not sure which would arrive first, the Boffins or the Boffins Hardware, that we had ordered.

"Lachie I could use your thoughts mate, and please don't give me that self denigration of I'm just a Rock Ape."

"OK Andy I am just a Rock Ape.............But. What if this was simply about money."

"Go on Lachie"

"What if 'The Suit' was somehow tied up in the contracts for arms, and they are holding him in order to ensure that the UK, buy a contract for these new canons?"

"I suppose it is possible. We know that the next person above 'The Suit', is the Secretary Of Defence. Perhaps we should look at a way of watching the SOD. Just in case someone tries to manipulate him."

Petrá walked in and was making a coffee for herself and had overheard the conversation.

"Andy can I say something? I know, I am not a military person, like the rest of you. But I can think of a simple reason behind this."

"Petrá you are as much a part of Team Seven as anyone. If you have something to say, you don't have to ask permission. We are always open to anything, that could shine a light on things."

"What if it is about the guns?"

"How do you mean?"

"What if it is about forcing the price of the guns up as well as creating a demand for them. If the makers claim that the guns are so silent, that even a Crack SAS unit could be taken out, without any of them knowing a shot had been fired. And the claim was, that all the shots were fired from a range of approximately 150 yards or less. Then a lot of countries would want this. Yes?"

"I follow where you are going with this. But we have not been able to say how all the people were shot. At least not with any certainty."

"What if that did not really matter?"

"Sorry Petrá now you have me lost."

"What if all they needed to do was create an illusion, a misconception, that all these people were killed in a raid on the home. What if they were not killed there, at all. What if they were just placed there."

"OK Petrá, Lets say, that we work with that theory. Why then not just kill Sir Philip as well as the rest of his family."

"I do not know Andy, It was just a thought I had."

"Thanks Petrá. It is something for us to consider. Even if it just creates more questions than it gives us answers."

After we had all eaten dinner and all of us had spent time playing with the twins. Technically I was the adopted father and Petrá the adopted mother, The reality though was much different. We were all, their parents. The children belonged to us all. Belonged was not the right term, we were just a family all of us. No child could have had more love given to them, than the twins we had adopted. They gave that love back in spades. They were smart too and we home schooled them here on the rig. They would have more languages than most children, they would have skill sets that would protect them in later life. They would have no problems gaining employment. In the years they had lived with us, they had grown up so fast. They were competitive, yet loving of each other. I hugged them both and gave them a goodnight kiss. This routine would normally have taken a few minutes, but today it was a full house so to speak, it took almost 30 minutes, before they were packed off to bed and their night time story read by Petrá.

I had lived with Petrá longer than I ever had with Jane. I loved Petrá. She was perfect and beautiful, smart and funny. About a year after she started to look after the twins. I had told her the truth, about why we lived out here, literally in the middle of nowhere. I told her about the dangers that we had faced in the past. I even told her about Jane. I just needed to be honest with her. Most of what we did, had involved lies, in the past I had been forced to be dishonest with my father, just because SIS did not want anyone to know that we were their hired guns. I would not have been surprised, if Petrá had left and gone to live back on the Faeroe Islands. What Petrá had said about illusions and about the ability to force the price of the guns up, made sense except that KOFC, sold guns to lots of countries and any scandal, could effectively force the cancellation of of Billions of Dollars of weapons. I went and saw Abdalla to find out how he was getting on with obtaining a Mk VI BOYS ATR. I wanted to know if the ones the SAS and SBS were the exact same spec as those that were now being produced by the KOFC. Abdalla was helping Oran set up his computer workstation in what was now going to be our Forensics Laboratory.

"Hello Mr Andy. How is it I can be of service to you?" he said

Abdalla, had since the very start of joining Team Seven, added the prefix of Miss or Mister to all of our names as well as the deference of Master for young Finn. We had tried just to get him to use only or first names or call us Mate or Buddy. He had though stuck with the prefixes. He had grown up in the North Eastern edge of Kenya. He had tribal scarification to his Face and to his back and shoulders. Women liked him for many reasons, not least of all was his voice, which came out as a gentle rumble, the sort of sound that made Barry White, sound like a boy soprano. He had received another scar to his face on our last foray into the murky world of international espionage and terrorism. This scar almost detracted from the tribal scarification, which was symmetrical. He was a Muslim who believed that Allah was his God. He believed we were wrong in our faith, in the same way as most faiths, believe they are the only ones who have it right. This though. did not mean he hated and non Muslims. He was a liberal and tolerant man. Abdalla was supposed to be getting married to Basoos. She was a woman from his home village. We had all spoken, but so far we had only done so, using our dark web chat room. She was a beautiful woman. Her name meant 'She was the daughter'. I wondered if any of us would be able to get away to go to his wedding, hell I wondered if he would be able to make it on time.

"Abdalla have you managed to locate one of these big guns for us?"

"Yes Mr Andy KOFC are going to fly one out to us. We need someone to go to collect it though. They are flying it in to Lossimouth tomorrow. They say however, all the 'Silent Models' are out on trials and that perhaps we should talk with the SAS and see if they will let us go to their live fire range in the Brecon Beacons"

"The only people that I can think of that would be able to collect this without raising suspicion, would be someone from the SAS team. I will have Hans get hold of them. Then Carl will have to take the chopper to collect the gun from him. Stu is pretty busy tomorrow he has to collect the equipment for the Lab and then go and meet up with the IDF Cutter and collect the boffins. Then bring them back here."

As it turned out they arrived together. Gunter and Johan along with all the techie stuff, that Oran had ordered which was crated up. It took several hours to get the Two boffins and all the equipment set up, in what was now the forensic laboratory. Introductions were made and they were allocated one of the apartments to share. We had just enough space, around our gigantic slab of teak, in the kitchen diner. The main members of Team Seven would talk about the kidnap of 'The Suit'. All this would take place after the children had gone to their beds. We had kept the apartment, know known as 'The Lab' locked as we did not want the children frightened by the photographs which were plastered across one wall, an almost floor to ceiling wallpaper made up of the gory pictures of dead and destroyed bodies. Some of the still frames that we had isolated from the video sequences taken from the police officers body camera along with our own pictures taken both with and without the bodies. When the kids had gone off to bed. Abdalla, Lachie, Hans, Oran and myself joined the two new boffins in the lab.

"First off gentlemen, thank you for coming here to help us with this investigation. I am sure that Hans has told you everything you do here is secret and not to be spoken or written about, anywhere outside of this unit. Your contracts will also state the penalties that breach of this would incur. So now I have said that. I would like you both to take a look at the photographs and at the scale model over there. When you have done that, we would like your first impressions." I said

We left the two boffins chatting and making notes. We went to the kitchen area where Rosemary had set up a large coffee machine, along with sugar, cream and cups. We kept the talk between ourselves completely off the topic, in case we accidentally led them down a wrong path. After an hour we went over to the two scientists.

"Well gentlemen. What can you tell us so far?" Hans asked

"Is this a joke?" Johan replied

"No. Why would you ask us that?"

"Because this is not any kind of murder scene."

"What makes you say that?"

"Because if you look at the man, who was shot at the front of the stairs." Gunter said pointing at one of the 8×10 photos and then continued

"The blood splatter pattern, is all wrong. The same with the woman in the hallway and the teenager at the computer. From where the bodies are, they do not match with where the blood and other matter is."

"Anything else?"

"Not unless you can shine a light on exactly what went on here. We look at the evidence, but even we need to know what it is we are supposed to be seeing. So we need a story behind it, that we can either prove or disprove. Do you have any evidence apart from the photos?" Gunter asked and then he continued, without giving us a chance to answer.

"On the evidence so far, that we have to go on, and only on the small amount of evidence. The entire murder scene is nothing more than a poor quality movie mock-up. Made to look like there was either a massive attack force, that surprised everyone. Or that the people providing security are rubbish. We both think the people were killed elsewhere and then put in place. Then a lot of blood and other material was thrown about to simulate massive trauma spray and misting as well as arterial spray. We would both bet, that the blood types would match the victims but that under closer inspection the DNA's would not be a match. It is easy enough to buy bags of human blood in all blood groups. Then just spray it around."

"Thank you gentlemen you have given us a lot to go on with. We will be in the main lounge area if you need us"

We left Oran and the boffins and went to the bar. After we all had a drink we sat down to discuss how to proceed next now we had some confirmation of what we already suspected. That the shooting had been staged.

"Your guys are good Hans. They got it right away. So if this was staged and I think all of us, actually thought this fairly quickly. All the people at 'The Suit's home, were killed elsewhere. From the way I see it, the Driver was actually shot while seated in the car, only the car was not where the shooting happened. Whilst we know, sort of what happened, we don't know where it happened and that is still a fucking mystery." I said

"What if they were not killed on the night they were supposed to have been killed?" Lachie asked

"Surely SIS would have known if 'The Suit' and or his detail had not reported in" I said

"Mr Andy, if 'The Suit' were away from home he would only have a small detail with him and they would just check in by phone, I think."

"That is a valid point Abdalla, I will contact the SAS boys and ask them what the procedure was for Sir Philip, when he was away from home."

I was just about to get another drink for everyone, when the two boffins now dressed in matching white coats came walking across the room towards us.

"We need to go to the scene" Gunter said

"You guys drink?" I asked

"Brennivin" they both said in unison

"Hans?" I asked

"Very well, but this is my own private stock." He replied in mock anger Then went behind the bar, put two tumblers on the counter, reached down and came up with a bottle of green spirit."

"Ice" he asked them

They looked at one and other and then is what would appear to have been a much practised answer, again they said in unison

"No!"

Hans poured out two generous measures and brought them over to the seating area where we were and gave them to the scientists.

"We have to see the crime scene, first hand"

"I am sorry gentlemen, that will not be possible for security reasons, and for your own personal safety"

Again they spoke almost in unison like they were linked by some form of data cable

"Could we have a live video feed where we could control the camera?"

"I will see what can do, in the meantime please make yourself at home and use any of the facilities that we have here. Do not worry there will soon be lots of forensic work for you to do" Hans replied

The slightly shorter of the two then asked an incredulous question.

"Can we have one of the bodies, one of the ones that were hit with the high calibre weapon?"

Then before I could answer the taller of the two said

"Because we will be able to tell a lot more about the weapon used by seeing the damage. You see there will be traces on the bones of the man and possibly even some rifling marks, on his bones or on the protection vest he was wearing. Even microscopic traces of gun oil used in cleaning the rifle can lead us to which outlet or unit the gun came from."

"That makes sense to me, but I am not even sure we will be able to get access to the bodies, let alone become latter day Burke and Hare? What do you think Hans?" I asked

"I will see what I can do. Although I don't know how yet." he replied.

"I can arrange it." Oran said

"Wait! A minute Oran. I am not sure I want a dead body on the rig, and where the hell are we going to keep it. Before you do anything Oran, let us sleep on it. Then perhaps we will sort it, OK?"

They all nodded. I finished my drink and went to join Petrá in our apartment. Petrá was curled up in front of the TV watching a DVD of some chick flick.

"I might have to go off to the mainland for a few days"

"Andy you have always told me what I needed to know. So I am asking you, is it going to be dangerous?"

"I don't know Petrá, but we will be going as a team. All the families on the rig are capable of looking out for each other. They will look out for you and the kids as well. If you need anything while I am gone, just ask Stu, or Rosemary."

"Promise you will be careful Andy."

"Always and I have Abdalla, Lachie and Hans looking after me as well. I doubt it will be as dangerous as the mission that led me to you babe."

"I know you do what you have to do. Just remember the children and I need you back in one piece." Petrá said

We went to bed and made love gently and lovingly. Then she curled herself into the fetal position and we went to sleep spooned like that, with her back against my belly. There were no curtains or blinds on our windows, there was no need for them. Our apartment was on the south side so we saw the sun rise and set from our bed. This was one of the most amazing things to wake up to. The triple glazing kept us warm in winter, and in the summer we would sleep with the patio door open. Often I would stand on our small balcony and just look out to the sea. In summer there were no flies or mosquitoes to worry about. Unlike those on the mainland. We would get the occasional sea bird that would have strayed way too far our to sea and needed a rest. I woke this morning and there was no sunshine just low cloud or sea fog. I carefully slid out of bed and went to the bathroom. Shaved and showered and then I dressed. Then went down to the central kitchen behind the bar. Rosemary was already there and had the coffee burbling away. Its fresh scent wafting into the air. I exchanged pleasantries with Rosemary and waited for the others to show up for our breakfast meeting.

"Andy I know that I am technically the senior officer in this investigation but I just feel that things would run smoother, if you actually were to take point on things. If someone says no to you, then I can step in as the Polar Bear in the closet, so to speak." Hans said as he filled his coffee cup up.

I looked around the room to try and gauge the reaction of the others there. Lachie, Abdalla, Carl and even Oran nodded. The two scientists took no interest in things. I looked over to where Petrá had joined with Rosemary and Stu, they all gave a thumbs up.

"How will that work with the authorities?" I asked him

"Simple Andy. I am going to make you temporary Officer in charge of the UK Branch of the GDR."

"But Hans, we do not have a branch of the GDR in the UK, do we?"

"We do now." He said with a smile and a wink.

On previous missions I had been made the leader of team seven, because of our locality and because I was not really a foot soldier. So I could overlook operations and the others, could do all that soldiering stuff. I was not sure how the new temporary head of SIS, would take to working with me. but it had always been alright with 'The Suit'. In fact he was the one, who actively encouraged me to lead Team Seven. I could still sense them all looking at me, to see if I would issue some edict or order. That was something that I never did. I would always ask. Sure to those outside of Team Seven, I could be a bit harsh towards, primarily because I did not tolerate fools, nor did I suffer bureaucracy well.

"OK if you are sure that is the way you want things done Hans. So to my scientific friends, first welcome again and thank you for the work you have done so far. You also confirmed our suspicions about the slaughter at 'The Suits' home. That is to say we agree that they were not actually killed there. This leaves us with another problem. If they were not killed there. where were they killed? Also where was 'The Suit' taken from? We need his appointment diary and I know that the SAS guys, are going to send up all the video from the security cameras around 'The Suits' home. I would like you two to work with Oran on enhancing any images we get from them." I said indicating to Gunter and Johan.

"Oran can you also backtrack on any satellite that may have been over 'The Suits' home for the three days. That is to say the day before, the day of, and the day after this incident. It might not tell us exactly what happened but it might tell us what did not happen."

"Are you saying you disbelieve SIS?" Hans asked me

"I would say that the jury is out on that Hans. What is the first thing you look into in a murder Hans?"

"That is simple. Who has the most to gain from the death. Are you saying you think Sir Philip is dead?"

"No I don't think he is dead, but like murder, we need to see who gains the most here."

As with all the missions we had survived. We did so because we always worked on the fly. Continually changing our methods, to match the problems that would unfold.

"So what is the plan of action?" Lachie asked

"No plan apart from, lets find out first, who did NOT commit the murders, in order that we can rule them out and hopefully point us in the correct direction. Let's start with John Stevens. See if we can find out what he was doing, covering the same three days. So, we are going to have to go to the mainland and hopefully, our SAS brothers can find us somewhere to stay off the grid. Lachie you can arrange that with Micky. Abdalla we need to know everything there is to know about that fucking Anti Tank Rifle. The KOFC must have records for every single one they have made and where it has been sent. Lets face it, there are not that many of them out there yet! Rather I should say, there should not be many of them out there. We only have other peoples words, that they are in limited supply. Carl you will have to take us down to somewhere in or near London? In order for us to be able to get to SIS, as well as to hook up with Micky. Going on everything that has ever happened with us and SIS, I would recommend that we wear body armour and carry firearms openly, as we have done up until now. Only this time, we chose what firearms we carry. I prefer my Sig to the HK. The only way we can walk around London like that, is to be dressed as Metropolitan Police officers. So first I ask John, and if he cant do it, then I am sure that Hans will be able to arrange that for us."

Hans gave a little nod of his head.

"We will all keep in touch using either secure sat phones, secure laptops, or if close enough scrambled Motorola radios. OK Lets load up and get moving. Hopefully we will be back here in just a few days."

I went over to Petrá and kissed her then whispered I love you in her ear. We wandered off to our apartment. I needed to change into Nomex and body armour, which I would wear under my police uniform. I chose my Sig Sauer rather than the HK just because I felt more comfortable with it. The children were awake so I kissed them both and told them, daddy had to go away for a couple of days work. And that I would bring back presents when I returned. I always did, even though for the greater part, they were only small things. It was just the act of giving that felt good to me. We could all afford big expensive things, but I did not want the kids growing up without realising the worth of bigger or more valuable items.

ACT 5

We landed at a small but derelict farm on the outskirts of the M25. Micky was there with a couple of his lads. They had managed to somehow or other acquire a couple of Police Range Rovers, or at least that is what they looked like. They were probably our old Range Rovers with a new paint job. He handed out some police uniforms and baseball caps to us. We now looked like Anti Terrorist police. We still had our GDR passes so our first port of call would be SIS. I asked Mickey to make sure that any of the evidence he had managed to get, was automatically sent up to Oran. It really meant that it was sent to the post office in Keiss and then collected by Stu.

It is actually quite amazing, how even the most stubborn of driver, will move out of the way when he sees a police car, in his or her rear view mirror. The result being our drive into central London, even during rush hour, was actually quite simple. After going through all the security and parking up in the underground garage and then going through the usual hoops we finally made it to John Stephens secretary.

"I would like to see Mr Stephens please."

"I am sorry you will have to make an appointment and he has no spaces free for about 2 weeks."

"Excuse me Miss?...."

"Susan."

It would appear that as with the SAS all being called John Smith, all secretaries at SIS were called just Susan.

"OK Susan. You do realise that we represent NATO?"

"I do, but I am afraid he is a busy man."

Having been to his office previously I knew the way there. So we walked past Susan and down the corridor. Stopping at his door. Susan followed us and tried block the doorway to his office by putting her body literally, between Abdalla and the door.

"You cant go in there he is in an important meeting." she protested.

"Excuse me Miss Susan" Abdalla said and simply picked her up off the floor and then placed her gently on the other side of the hallway. I knocked once and waited. No answer. So I knocked a second time a little louder.

"Come." A single word command from inside the room.

So we did. We filed in and as Susan was about to enter, Abdalla closed the door and stood with his back too it

"What is the meaning of this? You cant just barge into my office any damn time you like." John Stephens, protested.

"And I object to being given the run around by you and your office. You have not been very truthful with us. Even without the forensic evidence. I could see that the people at Sir Philips house, were not killed there. I would have expected any sniper worth his salt, to have taken his brass, but for the bullets to disappear. Was too much. The question I keep asking myself is just what the fuck has a Kenyan version, of an old Anti Tank Rifle, got to do with all this. Who gains by killing a SAS protection squad? And why would Sir Philip be involved in something that is effectively under control of the Army purchasers. They would be the Generals and the Politicians. Not under a bunch of spy's? So John, if I may call you that," I did not give him a chance to answer.

"Can you tell me why the head man in the UK's alphabet soup of the spy world, would somehow be involved in such a way, that his family would be killed and he would be taken?" I stopped to let him answer.

He looked up from behind his desk and put the telephone receiver, that he had held absent mindedly in his right hand since we had entered the room, back down on its base unit.

"There are some things I can not tell you as they would be above your pay grade."

I put my hand up to stop him

"There is NOTHING, that would be above my pay grade since we first started working for the GDR. In fact I would say that there have been things that happened, that we have been involved in, which would be above your pay grade. So lets start with the conversation again. Only this this time lets see if you can do it without the secret society bullshit. So no baring of the left breast, no rolling up of the trouser legs and definitely no fancy hand shakes. Just the truth."

"I really don't know what you want me to say?"

"How about we all sit down, and you start at the beginning." I said as I motioned to the twin sofas and the wing chair, around the coffee table. This time though, I sat in the wing chair forcing Mr John Stevens. to sit next to Abdalla. After he sat down I indicated that he should continue by rotating my index finger.

"What is it you wish to know?" he said

"I want to know, what went on at the farmhouse?"

"I don't know."

"Where is Sir Philip?"

"Again I don't know"

"Why were his wife and son murdered?"

"I don't know I can only speculate, that the kidnappers wanted to leave no witnesses."

"Did your office have anything to do with the accident that befell the attending police officer?"

"Most definitely not. SIS do not do that sort of thing."

I remembered back to our first mission, when SIS Black Door operations had tried to kill us all, albeit under the instructions of then then corrupt Secretary of Defence. So I knew that SIS would quite happily order, the murder of innocents as collateral, in order to achieve a desired conclusion. Short of waterboarding John Stevens, I doubted we would get much in the way of truth out of him today. He was not a field operative. He was a political monkey, who some day would no doubt end up as Foreign Secretary or Defence Minister. So I thought I would try a different tack.

"How well do you know the Reeves-Johnsons?"

"Very well, actually I went to school with his wife. I say school it was at university, Caroline and I attended Cambridge University together."

"Who called the shooting in?"

"I'm sorry, I don't understand you?"

"Who was it the called the police?"

"It was an anonymous telephone call, then the police contacted my office."

"OK we need to see Sir Philips files, for anything he was involved with over the last 3 months or so."

"I am sorry you can't."

"You know we have the authority."

"Yes I do, and it is not that I am unwilling to help. Sir Philip used a physical encryption on his computer and also the only way to access his safe is triple biometric data."

"When you say Physical Encryption what do you mean by that?"

"Like the computers that your own and Colonel in Chief Gunnerson uses. It is a matched 128 bit encryption dongle that is attached to his computer, then a password and finally his finger prints are scanned."

"And the biometric safe?"

"It has a similar system only more complex. Insomuch as it requires a tiny sample of his blood. There is a pin prick that takes his blood and scans it for his DNA as well as checking that the blood is oxygenated. It is a method he invented."

"You say he invented it?"

"Well invented is perhaps a stretch. He said that by using all the systems together along with the blood test would stop someone from just removing an eyeball or a thumb. A retinal scan, can be replicated by simply going to his optician and stealing their retinal photographs that the optician will have. Oxygenated blood, complete with the DNA has to come from a live person. So you cant just cut off a thumb and use it to enter the safe, even if you had all the other information. So you see I cant help you on that even if I wanted to."

"You don't want to help us?" Lachie interjected

"I never said that. I said that even if I wanted, to help. I could not, because of the systems he has set into place."

"Do you use the same system" I asked him

"Yes"

"Can we look at your files?"

"Yes but you will not find anything in there, that will be helpful in finding Sir Philip? As we worked on different levels and cases. My remit is to check on political security. Sir Philip was more the espionage side of things. As I am sure you know he is very much a hands on sort of man."

"You said he IS a hands on man, So you know he is alive?"

"No."

"No?" Lachie asked

"What?"

"You said No? But I am not sure what you mean?"

Now was not the time for one of Lachie's brain melts so I cut him off.

"Do you know if Sir Philip is alive or not?"

"No I don't. When I said he is a hands on sort of man, it was a figure of speech."

"OK thank you Mr Stevens. That will be all for now."

I stood up just as Susan entered the room with two of SIS own, Nomex clad and suitably armed, security guards. Both held their automatic guns at the ready.

"You guys don't want to do that." Lachie said

"On the floor now" Shouted the shorter of the two

"Its OK, you men can stand down" John said and then continued

"These gentlemen were just leaving anyway."

ACT 6

We left and met up with Micky at a disused Brick Works on the edge of the M25 London Ring Road.

"So what's new?" Micky asked, as he lit a cigarette with a brass Zippo lighter.

"We need to steal one of the bodies, most specifically your man that took the round to the chest." I said

"Are you fucking mad?"

"No Micky. You know that old adage, that dead men tell no tales? Well we have a boffin who thinks, he can tell us which Unit the 50 cal came from."

"So why cant you take your boffin, to the morgue and do his work there."

"Because I think the powers that be, don't want us to find out what is actually going on. I also think they know a lot more than they are telling. Besides we have a totally independent lab, that no one but ourselves can have access to. OK independent might be a bit of a stretch. But it means that no one can interfere in the results. I promise you that your man will be treated with as much dignity as if he were one of our own."

"OK where and when?"

"Can you get him out of the Aylesbury Mortuary tonight and get him down to RAF Halton airfield."

"You don't want much Andy, do you?"

"We all know that the scene was staged at Sir Philip's, as such we can assume that the footage caught on the security cameras is also bullshit."

"Yeah I think we are all in agreement with that Andy. So where does that leave us?"

"Well Micky, there is something."

"What's that?"

"The attending police officer as you know is in Stoke Mandeville Hospital. I am sure that you believe in coincidences as much as I believe in Fairies. I think he may have seen something, or they, whoever they are, think he saw something. I am going to have our lab take a look at his body cam footage. I know the guy has some pretty serious injuries but I want to move him and get private medical care. He is a single bloke so at least we will not have to move a family. If this guy comes too, he may have some info. I will arrange to have him taken from the hospital and transferred by helicopter to our base. I want to ensure he gets the best of care. I am completely sure that the emergency call, to the police was staged. So there is no mileage to be had from that. We cant get access to Sir Philips files, because he installed a very good biometric system. That said I will have Oran take a look and see if there is some kind of back door in. There is something about this John Stevens that just does not feel right, I am going to have Oran, look into his background and do a bit of rooting about. The BOYS rifle figures in this somehow, it all just a little too overkill. No pun intended. As you know Abdalla just happens to be Kenyan, but he does not know any more about this rifles success, or lack of it, as of yet. He is going to take a trip back home to Kenya, to follow up on things there."

"I am, Mr Andy?" asked Abdalla's

"Yes Abdalla. You can use the cover of going to see that beautiful young fiancé of yours and use your standing in the Kenyan Elite Special Forces. Wine and dine some of the top people from the factory and see what you can glean. I will get Hans to arrange a military flight tonight for you."

"I doubt if the police officer will be of much use to you. My understanding is the accident pretty much killed the guy. He is in a coma and from what I hear, he will be pretty much a cabbage if and when he wakes up. So what else do you need from us?" Micky said.

"I want you to follow John Stevens wherever he goes. He is at the moment, the temporary number one at SIS, that will mean that he will have a protection detail, probably from your mob. Hopefully there will be some of the guys you will know, and that might make things easier for you. I want to know where he is 24/7. He should be an easy man to follow because he is nothing like Sir Philip. He is a politician, Sir Philip was an old school spook from the days of the cold war. I doubt if this John Stevens, has ever done a Dead Drop in his career, let alone learned spy-craft."

"You don't trust him?"

"I will make no bones about it Micky, I don't like him he is a weasel. But what is worse, is he is dangerously ambitious. He will sacrifice any one, so long as it means he gets promoted, or gains something else on the back of others. It is not just Sir Philip's job he wants. I think he wants to be the SOD, or even the PM's position."

With that we agreed to meet at the Airfield around 10pm. I contacted Hans and made the arrangements for Abdalla to go down to London. It was decided, it would be better if he went on a civilian airline. We got him on an overnight with British Airways, first class. So he could get some sleep before arriving. After a quick stop at some clothing shops, Abdalla was dressed like a moderately wealthy business man. He would look the part in Kenya and probably even, get a Royal tour of the Arms Factory. Hans arranged for Carl to bring the Sea King in and collect us, along with the body of the dead soldier and hopefully along with the injured policeman. That was providing all our other plans worked.

The SAS boys left in the Transit, taking Abdalla with them and gave us back our Range Rover. Lachie drove while I tried to sort things in my mind. We all knew that SIS were a bunch of slippery bastards, but this John Stevens was even more so.

"What's up Andy?"

"Apart from the obvious. Like we don't have a clue, as to what is happening you mean?"

"Aye."

"I don't know how yet, but I am sure that John Stevens, is mixed up in this somehow."

"I kind of gathered that when you had the SAS guys arrange to follow him."

"I don't know which part of this is a red herring."

"What makes you thing there is a red herring?"

"Because whenever SIS are involved, there is."

"Fair Point mate." Lachie said and mashed the accelerator to the floor."

"What you doing Lachie?" I asked as the speed of the Range Rover went from a steady 70 miles an hour to 110 and kept climbing.

"Its not every day you get to drive a Police Range Rover." He chuckled and flicked a switch on the dashboard and the flashing blue lights came on. After that the M25 ring road that had previously been clogged with traffic, seemed to open up in front of us, as the other cars moved over to let us pass.

We arrived back at RAF Halton and drove to the side of the Airfield. Lachie switched the engine off and then put his jacket over the steering wheel and promptly went to sleep. I listened to BBC Radio two play some golden oldies, as I waited to see who would appear first, either Carl or the SAS guys with the corpse. The Sea King was first. Lachie never even raised his head. I waited until the rotors had spun down and walked over to greet Carl.

"Hans tells me we have some cargo take back to your Rig?" Carl said as he shook my hand.

"Yes there is one and possibly two if I can swing things."

Lachie finally woke up and joined us by the chopper. He shook hands with Carl, then looked at his watch. We still had two hours before the SAS Guys were due to meet up with us and I was sure they would be spot on time. I had though formulated a plan in my head to get the young police officer released into our custody.

"Glad you are awake Lachie, we need to borrow an Ambulance"

"When you say borrow do you mean you want me to steal an ambulance from the Motor Pool?"

"No Lachie, the ones they have there, are the green Land Rover, military style ones. I need one of the white ones from the Hospital."

"Care to tell me why we are stealing an ambulance?"

"We are not stealing it we are borrowing it and they will get it back in one piece. I want to get the injured policeman, out of Stoke Mandeville. Carl will come with me in the Ambulance and you take the police Range Rover. Carl and I will wear some white coats, which we can borrow with the ambulance. If you then put on all that police tactical stuff including the chequered baseball cap. We can say, that he has to be moved to a place of safety as there is a credible threat to his life, which is not far off the truth anyway. Then we bring him back here and take him with us and the dead soldier back to the Rig. Hans has arranged for medical people from the IDF to stay with us as long as required. We can set up one of the apartments as a mini Hospital ward. There should be a portable oxygen tank and resuscitation kit in the ambulance that we can borrow just in case. I will try and take what we require from Stoke Mandeville under some bullshit story or other. Enough innocent people have died already. So unlike normal, lets keep it that way."

"Le me get this right, you want to kidnap the injured police officer from Stoke Mandeville. You think we will get away with it?"

"Sure we will Lachie you make a great policeman and if anyone asks about all that hair, you just say that you are in the Anti Terrorist Squad."

Lachie and I walked up to the hospital which was on the other side of the camp. I was still wearing my police outfit. No one bothered to stop us. At the side of the Hospital there were six ambulances, lined up neatly in the parking bay. They were pretty much the same as their civilian equivalents.

"Lets take the one furthest from the main doors. They will always run for the first ambulance so I doubt if they will go for this one on the end. at all tonight."

I tried the Ambulance door and was surprised to find it unlocked and even the keys were ready in the ignition. I looked in the back and it was fully kitted out for any eventuality. Except there were no white coats. Going into a working hospital would be too risky. As I did not want to alert anyone to what we were doing. Now all we had to do was to get some whites to wear. I started it up and we headed back down to the other side of the camp. The Number 1 School of Dental Training was closed for the night, they would have white lab coats in there. I parked at the side and peered through the window of a dental lab. I could see several white coats, hanging on the back of a door. I stuck some surgical tape across the small window, in the way Hans had taught us and then gave it a sharp crack with the butt of my Sig Sauer. It made a lot less noise, than just breaking the window without tape on it. After pulling the loose glass off with the surgical tape. I then quickly opened the larger window, next to it. I climbed in and snagged two coats off the back of the door. As soon as I was in back in the ambulance, I donned my white coat. We drove the short distance to the Air Strip where the chopper was waiting. Lachie got behind the wheel of the Police Range Rover, Carl put on his white lab coat, and got in the front of the Ambulance, next to me. I knew that Stoke Mandeville was only 5 miles away. Lachie put the Hospital address, into his vehicles Sat Nav system. As we left the RAF Base, Lachie turned on the blue lights and I followed suit. We raced through the narrow lanes, with Lachie leading the way, to the Specialist Spinal Hospital.

On arrival Lachie led us into the main hospital reception area. Wearing his tactical vest and police baseball cap, he went to the reception desk. Carl and I followed. Even though we had white coats on underneath we still were wearing our Nomex. I just hoped that the staff would notice the whites rather than our tactical trousers.

"Good evening Miss. Who is the senior person on duty here tonight?" Lachie enquired

"That would be, our consultant Orthopaedic Surgeon, Mr Hamerston." The young lady replied

"Can you page him please, and tell him it is a matter of great urgency."

"May I ask what it is about?"

"You can ask, but unfortunately as it is a matter of National Security. If I told you, I would have to kill you."

The woman went ashen white.

"I am only kidding. But unfortunately I still can not tell you"

She smiled and picked up the telephone on her desk, and spoke quietly into it. Then she replaced the receiver.

"He is on his way down."

"Thank you" Lachie replied.

As we waited on the consultant, I looked out the front door of the hospital. The flashing blue lights of both our vehicles, cast eerie shadows across the hallway we were waiting in. The door of the lift behind us opened and a tall thin man of about 50, came out, wearing green hospital scrubs.

"Hello I am Doctor Hamerston. How can I help you officer?" He enquired.

The Doctor seemed to take it on face value that Lachie was some form of policeman.

"Good evening Doctor. I am Sergeant Knight, with the Anti Terrorist Squad. We have just received information, that there is a credible threat against one of your patients. So we are taking him into protective custody. He is one of our own. Police Constable William Green. We have an Ambulance waiting outside to take him to the spinal unit at RAF Hospital Halton. Where we are better set up to protect him. I am sure that you can understand this. Because of the immediate and credible nature of the threat, which is only against our man. We can not leave this until tomorrow. We shall of course be setting up a road block, on the road into this Hospital. So you and your other patients will be protected." Then he continued and said to us.

"Can you two men get the Gurney from the Ambulance please"

Carl and I went to the ambulance and came back with the patient trolley. Then all of us entered the lift, which stopped at the first floor.

"This way please" The doctor said

We followed him down a short corridor and then into a side room. The young police constable was lying there, His condition must have stabilised, because he was breathing on his own.

"I will get some nurses to help you with the transfer, if you will just wait here." The Doctor left the side room and went towards a nurses station.

"Lachie go with him and make sure that he only calls the nurses." I whispered

Lachie walked down the corridor behind the doctor, who had just lifted an internal telephone.

"Janet can you call the Met........"

That was as far as he got before Lachie put his finger on the disconnect button on the phone.

"I told you before Doctor that I am with the Anti Terrorist Unit and there is an immediate and credible threat to our man. Now lets just get him on to the trolley and get him to safety"

"Very well Sergeant, but I need to see your ID Card first."

The doctor had grown suspicious. As Lachie brought him back into the room. The Doctor was still protesting. Lachie drew his pistol and pointed it at the Doctor, who immediately stopped talking.

"We really are the good guys." I said.

I had hoped that we could just go in and take the patient without any problems. However the Doctor had obviously taken note of what we were wearing under our white coats.

"Who are you really?" he asked quietly

"Like I said we are the good guys. There really is threat against this man. There are some people who would rather he did not wake up to tell tales. Truthfully we are taking him to a place of safety. So can you please help us get him on this trolley."

"This is my patient and he is far to sick to be moved. I must ask you to leave."

"Sorry Doctor. We cant do that, at least not without our man there" Lachie replied, and then continued

"You can either help us get him on the trolley or you can watch." I said as made the scoop board ready

"Stop! I will help you" He said in a defeated manner.

"There is a canvas transfer sheet under him, you need to put the scoop board between the bed sheet and the transfer sheet. We need to have three people around one side of the bed to carefully roll him toward them. Then we put one half of the board under and gently roll him the other way then put the other half of the back board under him and fix it together. Then we can use the transfer sheet to get him on the gurney. OK?"

We transferred him to our stretcher and then Lachie put a sleeper hold on the doctor and then carefully laid him on the now empty bed. The Nurse we locked in one of the offices, after taking her mobile phone and ripping out the telephone line in that room. She would be able to escape in a few minutes

"That should buy us 10 to 15 minutes. So lets get out of here as fast as we can." Lachie said

That is just what we did, we returned too the Airfield at RAF Halton and pulled in, just as the SAS Boys arrived with the Ford Transit. All Four of them piled out of the van and you could almost feel the deference, to their fallen collogue. There was a sombre feel even before we had exited from the Ambulance and Range Rover. I went over and shook Micky's hand.

"Was it an easy extract?" I enquired

"Yes Andy there was no security at all unless you count the low end burglar alarm on the front door and John 'O bypassed that quick enough."

"Good, I hate to put a rush on things but we have the Police officer in the Ambulance. We borrowed the ambulance from the hospital here. Also Lachie had to put a sleeper hold on one of the Doctors at Stoke Mandeville. Pretty soon the real police are going to be looking for him and the ambulance. So we need to load up and get gone from here as quick as we can."

"You actually managed to get the injured police officer? I thought they said he was as good as dead, at least mentally? Then You stole this ambulance?" Micky said

"We have a medical team waiting to look after him as I am sure you are aware I doubt his accident was an accident, If and when he wakes up then he may be able to tell us something about what he saw at Sir Phillips home." I said

"The ambulance is not really stolen until this miss it" Lachie interjected.

"You know we could take the injured policeman to the Credenhill Barracks, we have a great medical centre there. Plus we could protect him from any outside threat. I mean who would be stupid enough to attack the barracks of 22 SAS?"

"Kind of you to offer but I think it would be best if we kept him hidden for now, lets face it whoever took Sir Phillip was not afraid of the guys from your unit who were there. Would you like any help getting your comrade into the chopper?" I asked

"I understand mate and thanks, but we will load him up ourselves if that is OK by you?"

"No probs" I replied.

They all went around to the back door of the Transit and opened the doors. There was a black Rubber body bag laid on the floor. Each of the four SAS men took hold of a grab handle and gently lifted the fallen member of their team out. The carried it with reverence across to the open door of the Sea King, and laid the body gently inside on the floor of the helicopter. Then they all stood back and in unison offered up a salute. Even though none of us were in official uniforms, we also saluted the body of a fallen soldier. Then Micky came over to the ambulance and he and his men helped us to gently carry the stretchered policeman on the scoop board on to the helicopter and carefully secure him into place for the journey to the Rig.

"You can have the Range Rover back now and I will be in touch as soon as we have some information. Your teammate will be treated with the utmost respect. You have my word on that Micky."

"Thanks Andy, we appreciate that. What do you want to do with the Ambulance?"

"Can you use it?"

"Yes mate if we use the Transit along with the Range Rover and Ambulance. It will give us a variety of vehicles to tail that snobby git in London. So if you don't mind we will take them all. We can collect you when you come back."

We said Our goodbyes as Carl got the rotors turning and we loaded up and closed the door. I went and sat in the Co-pilots seat next to Carl. Lachie lay down on the webbing seats and got ready to sleep again. He had told me lots of times you take food and sleep when you get the chance, because in the field you never know when you will next get a chance. He was certainly living by that mantra.

Carl took off from the airfield and I watched as the three vehicles moved off down the road on their way back to London. As soon as the chopper had enough height, Carl brought the nose down and headed for home. I looked out the window and I could see the lights of towns and villages pass away before us. The transponder fitted to this Chopper must have been given the all clear for any and all of British air space, as we were not challenged on the radio, even though I knew, we must at some point be flying over restricted space.

Carl took us across the country towards East Anglia and The Wash, then headed north towards our home. We talked a little, partly because of deference to the body, as we sped over the sea just above the small waves. Partly because I was trying to figure out what was going on. It was in the small hours of the morning when we arrived, at what Lachie now called the 'Brent Plaza'. Carl brought us into land on the helipad. Lachie as easily as he had gone to sleep was now wide awake,

I on the other hand was knackered as I was sure Carl was. Stu was standing at the side of the helipad waiting to help us.

The rotors spun down and we all helped to first carry the injured policeman, down to the next deck. There was an IDF Doctor and Nurse, waiting in one of our guest apartments. The apartment had been converted into a mini hospital ward. We left them with their patient and went back up to the helicopter, then carried the body-bag down to the laboratory. The two forensic scientists were waiting to take custody of the fallen soldier. I wondered if one day, this would be my fate? I was surprised to see the two boffins up at this hour.

"Please treat him with as much respect as you can gentlemen" I said as I help to lay the body-bag down on the stainless steel table.

The two white coated scientists seemed to act in unison and when they spoke it was as one voice. At the same time they carefully touched the rubber bag.

"We will, you have our word on that."

"What do you wish us to do with the body when we have concluded our examination?" Johan asked. I had not even thought about what we should do, or even how we would store it.

"You will have to refrigerate it" Gunter said

"I will sort something out before morning, if that is OK?"

"Yes we will start work right away" Johan said

"Are you not tired" I asked looking down at my Omega Seamaster, which showed the time to be almost 2am.

"No, we knew that you would be here at this approximate time, so we rested earlier in the night" Gunter added

"How long do you think it will take you until you are finished with the body?" I asked them

"They looked at each other and whispered in Icelandic with a lot of shaking and nodding of their heads. Then once again in unison they turned to me a said

"About three hours."

"Then about another three to six hours to run tests on the results of the Post mortem." Johan added.

"Thank you" I said and we left them to do their thing.

I let Carl and Lachie go ahead of Stu and myself then I whispered to Stu

"While your tied up here, can we use the chill room on your boat for the body of the SAS soldier that the boffins are working on, or do you have a better Idea?"

"I would prefer we did not use the chill room, but I can reduce the temperature of one of the forward holds on the Catherine May to just above freezing, if that will do? Its just I would not like Rosemary to suddenly go into the Chill room for some food and find him, just laying there."

"Thanks Stu, I fully understand and I appreciate that. I just never thought about it, when we decided to set up a lab here. I never really expected to be keeping a body here either. But enough about that. Is everybody OK here?"

"Of course they are mate. You know how Rosemary is, she organises everyone and everything. Its even worse for me, now that she has Petrá to help her. They can be like the mothers from hell"

"Hell, I am sorry Stu, I will ask Petrá to back off a bit."

"No Andy, don't do that. They are great together, I meant it in a jovial way. They are good together, It's actually is good to see them working together so well. By the way, they are in the Kitchen waiting for you, as is Morag. The Kids tried to stay awake because they knew you were flying back in, but they crashed out at about 9pm."

"I am real sorry to put on you Stu, but I have a feeling that things are beginning to go pear shaped again. I will pay you for any lost business. But I want to keep you and the Catherine May handy."

"No sorry I cant Andy."

"You cant?"

"Nope...........I cant take any money from you. Hell we are as much of Team Seven, as anyone else. So I am sorry. NO CHARGE."

I laughed and patted him on the back as we headed on down to the kitchen. I could smell the coffee and I could also smell bacon cooking. Rosemary, along with Petrá and Morag were busy cooking up a storm. Petrá saw me and ran to me with the spatula still in her hands.

"Hello my love, are you hungry."

I had not really given it much thought, but it had been a while since I last ate. I also missed my secret pleasure of a nice cup of Arabic Coffee.

"I guess we are all a little hungry and I am sure that the Boffins upstairs could use something to eat and drink as they are going to work through the night."

"We have already thought of that and will give them a call as soon as it is ready, while you were away Oran installed a new internal telephone system so I can just dial their apartment number and hay-ho, Alexander Graham Bell, eat your heart out." Petrá said as she planted a big wet kiss on me.

"Love you"

"I love you too" she said and hugged me.

Lachie came in with Carl and Oran. They sat down at the table and Rosemary started to serve up our early breakfast, Petrá brought over a large pot of fresh coffee, while Morag placed a large plate of freshly made toast in the middle of the table. Then she picked up a cordless telephone from its bracket on the wall and pressed two numbers on the dial pad. After a few seconds it was obviously answered

"Breakfast is ready in the kitchen if you wish some.......OK See you in a minute"

She put the telephone back on the clip and set the silverware on the table before filling two more mugs off fresh coffee and setting them down on one side of our long teak slab of a table. So it was breakfast for 10 hungry mouths.

For many people, that would be a challenge but for our mother hen Rosemary it was no sweat, especially now she had the help of Petrá and Morag.

"Thank you Rosemary and also you other girls, for this fine meal. Rosemary, it is possible that the two medical people will need feeding at some point later tonight."

"I have already fed them before you got here, what about the patient." she replied

"I think it will be a while before he is eating solids, but if you check with the Doctor after, I am sure he will let you know what the patients nutritional requirements are. At the moment, the man is in a drug induced coma. He is very ill, we have brought him here for his own protection."

"Who is he in danger from?" asked Morag

"The same people that probably killed 'The Suits' family" Lachie said

"Are we in any danger here?" she asked

"No we are all quite safe here. That is why we brought all the families in. This is the safest place on the planet. The only person that is not here from Team Seven, and discounting our parents, who really knows us, and where our home is, is 'The Suit', and he will not tell even if he was asked and I am sure the folks that have taken him don't care about us. Anyway I am bloody hungry, lets eat." Lachie replied. The two scientists arrived just as Rosemary was serving up the last plate of steaming hot food.

As was his way, Oran then covered his breakfast in tomato ketchup, much to Rosemary's disapproving look. Rosemary was a great chef and her food was delicious. I along with everyone else had asked Oran, to at least taste his food, before covering it in red goo made by Heinz. I suppose to Rosemary, it was a bit of a slap in the face metaphorically speaking. So I understood her glare at Oran. Oran was a genius, but for a man of 30 something, not that any of us really knew his exact age, he tended to be like a petulant teenager in his habits. If he was not working on solving problems for us, he would spend his downtime on playing computer games against other faceless and like minded computer geeks. We had beautiful gardens on two levels which were totally enclosed to their sides, consequentially we had a great suntrap for anyone who wanted to sunbathe, when the weather was warm enough to do so. In all the years we had lived her in our little commune on the waves, I had never seen Oran sunbathe. He had used the swimming pool and occasionally when the weather was hot, he would come out into the sunshine but never without a T-Shirt on and three quarter length shorts on. He was from Iceland, so would have been naturally pale but because he spent most of his life in a darkened room on his computer, he was paler than most Icelanders. He had not, had a hair cut in six years. It was long when he arrived to us, now his hair was pulled back into a ponytail, that was down around his waistband. The same also applied to his wispy beard, it have never been trimmed. It was like a students beard short and wispy, and nothing like the monster ginger beard that Lachie wore. He too had his thick curly hair tied back in a ponytail although Lachie, did allow Rosemary to trim his hair and beard, nonetheless he still looked like an extra from Braveheart.

When breakfast was finished I offered to help clear up but when Rosemary was on the Rig, then this was her kitchen. So we went through to the Bar come Lounge and sat down to discus things. It was not that we excluded the girls from anything, just that there was nothing that would really require their involvement at this time.

I sat down with Lachie, and Stu We chatted about the way things were going for us, which at the moment was exactly nowhere. What did we know? We knew 'The Suit' had been taken, his family killed and the scene at his home staged. We knew that SIS were telling lies to us, but that really was situation normal. Somehow the big anti tank rifle was involved in what was happening. It was more like the things we did not know, that bothered me. That was pretty much everything. We had zip, to go on. Hans had once said, I would have made a great policeman. I think that might have been a bit of a stretch now. We had no clue as to who had taken 'The Suit' or why, or even where. We had no ballistics yet. We might have a witness from just after the incident at the farm, assuming he could remember anything after he came out from the Coma, that the doctors at Stoke Mandeville, had put him in. The SAS guys were chomping at the bit, it seemed they wanted revenge, pure and simple. They would get it providing we could solve the case. I think we still had trust, between them and us. However the longer this thing went one, I was sure the quicker that would wane. We would have to start getting some sort of results. The day went on as a fairly normal sort of day, that anyone in our position could have. Hopefully the two boffins upstairs would have some answers for us later today. I was chatting things over when Petrá came into the bar with Morag. It was not just us men that had formed a bond, the girls had too. They all knew what we had done in the past, they knew roughly what we were involved in now. Petrá had asked me if we were in any danger, especially as I had called everyone in. I had told her and the others at the time that it was just a precaution, now I was not entirely sure. The one and only witness to whatever went on at the suits home, was laid in a coma upstairs. It had been declared to be a terrible road accident. I never liked coincidences, especially where SIS were involved. The past had taught us to be wary. So were we all safe? I doubted it. I just did not want to tell them how I felt at this time. In the early evening, Carl returned to the rig but with no more information than we already had. He had left Oran and Cyber down in London trying to hack into "The Suits" computer. I finished my drink and went in search of the Doctor.

ACT 7

He was in the medical suite that we had set up. I knocked and waited. It was the nurse who came to the door.

"Hello would it be possible to have a quick word with the Doctor?" I asked her.

The Nurse was pure Scandinavian, tall, slim, blonde hair, blue eyes and pale freckled skin. She opened the door completely to allow me to pass. The Doctor was checking the drips, that led to the veins of the young police officer. The face of the constable was bruised and battered. There were several large wounds that had been stitched up. The entire right hand side of his scalp, had been shaved. This had the beginnings of stubble growing, but it did nothing to hide the long semicircular incision which was the result of some recent medical procedure. I guessed that he had suffered a fractured skull during his 'accident'. The medical team at Stoke Mandeville had presumably opened him up to first relieve the pressure on his brain and then to set the broken pieces of bone, or to replace them with a metal plate of some form.

"Hello Doctor, my name is Andy" I said as I stuck my hand out to greet him. Then continued.

"This is my home. I hope you find your accommodation suitable. If there is anything you require then please just let any of our team know."

"Hello Andy, It is a pleasure to meet with you. I am Doctor Jon Einersson and this is my Nurse is Sárrá Ísleifsdóttir." He said with a sweep of his hand towards the woman, whilst shaking my hand with his other arm.

"Hello Sárrá" I said to her and got a slight nod in response.

I looked around the room that had been turned into a medical ward. I assumed that Oran had arranged for all the necessary equipment to be delivered. I wondered if he had actually bought it with our money, or if he had used someone else's account. Not that it really mattered who was paying for it, so long as when the Police Officer woke up. If and when that happened, we would be able to talk with him and hopefully. Then perhaps we would be more enlightened, as to what the hell was going on. Having been a medic I knew the policeman was getting good care.

"How is the patient doing?" I asked the Doctor

"He has a compression fracture to C3 in his neck and it was pinching the spinal cord. He has a swelling to the brain from the blow he sustained to the head. That was probably the blow that fractured the vertebrae, in a moment of whiplash. He has several broken ribs to his left hand side. There was a compound fracture to both his left and right femur, along with shattered patella's, probably caused by both his knees striking the underside of the dashboard when the engine in his car was forced backwards in the collision. He is out of danger, as far as life and death are concerned. The hospital he was in, stabilised the neck fracture by fusing C 1, 2 and 3 together. His ribs will heal. Walking though, even if it were not for the neck fractures, will always be difficult. When all the swelling has gone down, I will remove the damaged patellas and replace them with new nylon ones. And then apply casts to his broken legs which as you can see are still encased in metal framework. Whilst he is in a medically induced coma, the head injury is actually relatively minor. He has a slight bleed, but all the swelling had gone down. The injuries to his face are all superficial and will heal nicely. I have reduced the medication that he is receiving in his drip, so that he should regain consciousness tomorrow. I have been told by Colonel in Chief Gunnerson, that it is important for you to talk to this man as soon as possible. As such I will inform you as soon as he wakes up."

"Thank you Doctor, I think you have answered all the questions I was going to ask you. If you require any other equipment please just ask any of us. You are welcome to enjoy any of our facilities during your time with us." I said as I shook hands and left the Doctor and

Nurse to their duties. I went to my own apartments, Petrá was already waiting in bed for me.

"Sorry darling I had to check on the policeman." I said

I stripped off my clothing and walked naked to the bathroom. Then stepped into the shower cubicle and turned it on. I let the hot and steaming water pound the tension out of my back muscles. After washing thoroughly, I rinsed off and turned the tap to cold. I stood under the freezing water for as long as I could stand it, which felt like 10 minutes but was probably closer to 2 minutes. Then I turned it off and dried myself and wrapped the towel around my waist. I wiped the steam from the mirror. I looked at my reflection as the water beads ran down the silvered glass. It was now a little over six years since I had been seconded into SIS. It had aged me. I had scars that most normal folks don't get. I had been shot and wounded. I was still fit and I kept my body in tone. The one thing I could not control were the ravages of age. It took longer to recover from injuries, my once black hair was now tinged with grey and I was actually going prematurely white, around the temples. My face looked haggard especially as there was grey and black straggly beard on my chin. I decided to shave off my beard. Not as easy a task, as just shaving. First cutting with scissors and then shaving twice until my face showed clean. It took a few years off the way I looked, not that I really gave a shit about that. I just preferred the clean look. Petrá has seen me both with a beard and without I wondered which she preferred, I was sure I would find out in a minute. I switched off the Bathroom light and hung the towel up. I walked naked into the bedroom and slid under the sheets and lay next to Petrá. She moved over and wrapped an arm over my chest. Like me Petrá liked to sleep naked, our bed faced out towards the window and the sea beyond. We had a south facing room so the sun rose on the left and sank on the right, while all the time being in total view from our bed. We did not have drapes or blinds across the window as as we had one way glass and there was no one to see us anyway, when we were alone in our apartment. She snuggled closer and we fell to sleep in each others arms.

I awoke to the sunrise on another beautiful day, with not a cloud in the sky. It was looking like it could be a day to sit in the garden area. I say garden we had tubs of flowers and raised boarders but we had Astro Turf instead of real grass. That actually worked well for me as I never had green fingers. Originally, we never even had raised flower beds or potted plants, that was before the girls moved on to the Rig. We had our own mini desalination plant, but we never wasted any of the fresh drinking water or for that matter any of the rainwater that was stored in several large tanks. This water we used for the plants. As well as distilling it before it was sent to an even larger Fresh-Water tank.

I grabbed a mug of coffee from the communal kitchen and joined Petrá and the kids, who were playing French Cricket along with Rosemary and Morag. They were on the bottom garden area when Lachie called to me, from the lounge come bar area. This was separated from the garden by a wall of folding glass doors. When the weather was clement, as it had been for the last couple of days. We just folded the doors back so that the garden and Bar B Q area became one with the bar and lounge. It also made things much easier for access to our kitchen. I had been thinking about firing up the charcoal Bar B Q, before Lachie had called to me. I walked over to the lounge and sat down on one of the many chairs that randomly covered the floor.

"What's up mate?" I asked

"Oran has just messaged. he has some information for us, but only wants to give it to us in person."

"That's strange because if there is any secure way of sending info via computers or satellites, then Oran would be the man to make it happen"

"Did he give you any idea as to what he has discovered?"

"No not specifically, just that what he has found, is gonna blow your mind."

"He used those words, specifically?"

"Yes Andy, it is pretty much verbatim of his message"

"OK we better send Carl to collect him also see if you can get Hans on the Dark Web chat room."

Lachie said he would and then went to what was our control room but was really Oran's suite. He had set up a large screen monitor that almost filled one wall. It was where we all tended to hold our Dark Web conferencing. I went back to see Petrá and explained that I would have to do some work and that I would be in Oran's grotto. Abdalla was still in Kenya, Hans was back in Brussels, Carl was somewhere down near Halton, Oran was presumably at SIS Headquarters. The SAS Team were located in and around Mayfair. That just left two full time members of Team Seven on the Rig, Lachie and myself. I knew we also had Stu, Rosemary, Morag, Petrá along with the Doctor and Nurse, not forgetting the two boffins. I did not include the kids in the numbers. If things went tits-up as they had a habit of doing so, when SIS were involved. I needed to know, we could defend ourself if required.

I was worried about Oran, he was on his own inside the lions den, so to speak that is. I was sure that the SAS team, would protect him outside the SIS Building and it would be a brave man who would actually tackle Oran head on, when Cyber was with him. The message that Lachie had received led me to believe that not only had Oran discovered something important but he also suspected that SIS, were on to his discovery. Lachie joined me in Oran's apartment, and he clicked a few keys on the computer Keyboard. Hans's face filled the screen. He was in full dress uniform.

"Good morning to you Hans. We have sent Carl to pick up Oran"

"Good morning Andy, Lachie. Where do you want him collected from?"

"We think he is in danger, so I would like the SAS Boys to get ready to snatch him and take them to wherever Carl can pick him up from"

"What makes you think he is in danger?"

"Just that his message was a little weird and I have one of those feeling that I cant shift. Oran is basically on his own. He is not military as you know. He said he has some info that would will 'Blow Our Minds'. If that is the case, then SIS will want to know it as well. I don't trust them, well that is to say, I don't trust their number two, who is currently running things. Abdalla has not contacted us so far, and we have had no new info from the SAS guys. The patient that we have, should be coming out of his medically induced coma today. Hopefully he will have some answers for us. The boffins will also be giving their results to us sometime soon."

"OK Andy I will get Carl to pick up Oran just as soon as I can set things up with Micky. Do you have any idea at all, what it is he has discovered."

"No, like I have said, he said it is game changer and that it will 'blow my mind'."

We said our farewells and then Lachie and I went to the lounge area next to the garden. I sat down opposite him and looked over his shoulders to where the girls were playing with the children. It would have been an idealistic lifestyle that we had here on the Brent Bravo platform, were it not for the fact, that I was sure that we would be in the face of danger once more. Whatever happened, we had to ensure, that SIS and for that matter, anyone outside our circle, never discover our home. I would do anything to ensure the safety of not just the children, but the other innocents who were on the fringes of Team Seven. We had been told that we were no longer an active team, that was over a five years ago. I wondered, if we should not have become involved in the search and investigation for Sir Philip. However when I thought about it, I knew that 'The Suit' would shift hell and high water in order to protect any of Team Seven. I was 100% sure that even under interrogation he would not give up our identities, or location. I watched Finn strike the ball with the bat and the ball sailed high over Petrá's hands and then hit the fine netting that ran all the way around our leisure areas. Previously before the children had joined us on the Rig. We had just installed waist high fencing. In the interests of safety and because we kept losing balls to the north sea, we had installed full height netting that went from the floor of the first level to the floor of the second level, the same was done between the second and third levels. The top level was just a six foot high chain link fence. The cantilever helicopter platform that rose of the third deck and over the sea almost 170 feet below. The Helicopter platform had a fence that folded down to allow for safe landings.

"Andy" Lachie said and stole me from my thoughts. Then he continued.

"Behind you." He said pointing over my shoulder.

I turned my head to see the two boffins, they were walking toward us, their white lab coats flapping in a combination of the light breeze coming of the sea and the their own rapid walk toward us. Normally I was quite good with names but for some reason I could not remember theirs.

"Mr McPhee, we have conducted our investigation into both the crime scene and into the dead security guard." The taller of the two said as he looked down at his clipboard.

"We were right in our first conclusion, just on the visual information given to us at the time." the shorter man said. He too looked at his clipboard as he spoke to us.

"In short it was a put up job." the taller said and then passed over his clipboard. I looked down and it was written in a language that I did not recognise but assumed to be Icelandic.

"And this says what?" I asked him.

"That we were right" He replied.

"OK Lets have some specifics please, because even I, could see that it was a staged scene. What we require are facts and not suppositions." I said to no one in particular.

"We know that the blood spray, did not belong to the man who's body we have in your boats hold. The blood, was human blood, but as we suspected it did not belong to the man. It was not even the right blood group. It would appear that the majority of the blood that was sprayed around was O Positive. The man who's body, we examined. His blood group is A Negative." he said

Then his partner took up the conversation. It was like a practised thing that they did. One would start a conversation and the other would end it.

"But the really good information, we have, came from the bullet wound that the soldier received. We told you before that perhaps there would be traces of gun oil residue that would be left on the man's wound, or even on his protective vest. Again we were right there was some gun oil residue. In order to understand our findings you have to first understand how we reached our conclusion. We take scraping from the area around the entry and exit points then we introduce this into our electronic-spectrometer. Next we tell it all the results of previous spectro analysis results which we have on file, in this case it was to test for various oils. We actually have a complete spectro analysis of just about everything in our digital library. We would be happy to share this with you."

I made a rotation movement with my finger intending for him to continue. It was however his partner that took up the results with us.

"We did find gun oil, and it is the standard kind, used by the British military. However we can then break that down into batches, which actually differ ever so slightly. The gun oil used in this instance belonged to your Military Intelligence investigation branch number 6."

"MI6?" Lachie asked

"Yes I believe that is what you call them" The tall one interjected and then he continued.

"We can tell you also that they were not killed with the BOYS ATR."

I was going to interrupt when the shorter man looked at his clipboard and took up where his partner had left off.

"You see the BOYS uses a much bigger charge than any other Fifty calibre rifle. Once again when we look through the spectrograph we can see this as clear as day. Had they used any of the other rifle barrels that we are told would fit this particular weapon then things could have been difficult for us to categorically prove one way or another. Because the charge on a Boys is so much larger than any other, what we can say this was not a BOYS." He stopped for breath and the other man took up where he had stopped.

"We can actually tell you, which model of rifle he was shot with. You see we also looked at the markings on his protective vest as well as the markings that were left on the edges of the bones around the entry and exit areas of the wound. We removed a piece of bone and also a piece of his protective vest and looked at them under the Electron Microscope. This is where we found the most damming evidence."

As if on cue the other boffin took over.

"When we look at a bullet under a microscope you know that we can match this to the gun fired. This is the normal way that a lot of murders are solved by looking at the striation on the actual bullet and then matching that to a the rifling of a rifle or other firearm type. We though did not have a bullet. So we first had to find the bullets markings that were left on the bone and metal of his vest. It was a back to front sort of puzzle. I am sure you know that when a bullet is fired down a rifle then it spins and it picks up all sorts of markings from the chamber to the end of the barrel. We call this rifling or as I have said, Striation. It is like a fingerprint of a weapon. By looking at a bible of weapons we were able to match up the rifling to a make and model. We can not though, without the bullet match it to a specific firearm."

I was going to ask a question when he had stopped to take a breath, however once again the other boffin took up the reigns of the conversation.

"The firearm in question or should I say without any questions is the AS50 Sniper Rifle. In the UK there are only a few units to have this rifle. They are the SAS, SBS and the Intelligence services. This should limit your search. Sor either the Bullet and, or the Gun Oil came from MI6 and the weapon came from SIS, SAS or SBS. But we have some even better news for you."

"Better News?" I enquired.

I thought to myself, so far none of this is better news because it means that almost everything we had thought, was now nothing more than bullshit. And that Abdalla had been sent on a fools errand. Once again his twin took up the results of their tests.

"We did a blood test and guess what we found?" he asked.

His question hung in the air like that for several moments until I realised it was not a rhetorical question, but one that Lachie or I were supposed to answer. I took the bait.

"So what was the big mysterious result then?" I asked of them.

They both stood there and looked at each other and then in unison they said

"It was nothing mysterious, just a strange thing we found."

Once again I rotated my finger and the taller one continued where the other had left of. It was like being at a children's show, with tweedle de and tweedle dumb.

"He was dead when he was shot. That is not the best part" He said excitedly. And continued.

"We can not find a cause of death"

"What do you mean you cant find a cause of death? If it was not the bullet then it had to be something else, these were fit young men in their prime so they did not die from a heart attack." Lachie said.

"Well it is because we can not find a cause of death that makes it so interesting. Normally we can say that they had a heart attack or they had a stroke or they were shot or suffocated or even poisoned. All the ways you can kill a man they have results that show in toxicology or in tissue samples. Yet we can find nothing. There is no such thing as the perfect murder. Yet we are stumped."

"OK Gentlemen could you please write your reports and would it be possible to have a copy in English please? Thank you for your hard work so far. I would like you to stay with us a bit longer in case we need your services again. You will of course be fully recompensed for your time here. For now however you should relax and enjoy our amenities."

I stood up and shook their hands and they went back to their laboratory in their allotted accommodation.

"What do you make of that Lachie?"

"Well it just goes to prove you cant trust a thing that SIS Say. This is not just about kidnapping. We know now it has fuck all to do with that big gun. Yet why would the lanky bloke down at SIS want us to follow that route?"

"I have not got a clue at the moment Lachie, perhaps they wanted us to follow the BOYS clue, in order that we did not start looking at other reasons, behind 'The Suits' kidnapping. First thing for now though, is to get Oran and Abdalla, back here as soon as we can. We will have just about enough room to squeeze everyone in. Lets go back to Oran's den and give Abdalla a call and then, see what Hans has to say about it all."

That is what we did, well that is what we tried to do. The first thing we did was to place a satellite call to Abdalla, without result. It could just be that he was sleeping but that did not stop me from worrying. So we called Hans again. He said that he would catch the first military bird out of Brussels to the UK then he would have Carl pick him up. I went down stairs and joined Stu on the deck of the Catherine May.

"Stu I need you to go and collect Lachie's dad and mine."

"Is there something happening that we need to be worried about?"

"No I don't think Stu, so I am just erring on the side of caution."

"OK Andy I will give them a call on the ship to shore and then go out to collect them. What do you want to do about the body of the dead soldier in my hold."

"I will let you know in five minutes if you can hold off?"

"No problems Andy you know the Catherine May will always be at your service."

I climbed back on to the floating dock and took the lift up to the first deck. The I sought out Lachie.

"We are going to have to do something about the body in Stu's boat, I think it is starting to worry him. We need to talk to Micky and see if he will agree to a burial at sea. I grabbed a satellite phone and headed up to the Helicopter deck. I dialled the number he had given me. After several minutes the number was answered.

"Credenhill how may I direct your call?" A woman's voice

"I need to have contact with Unit number 5 of the RPS"

"Who shall I say is calling?" she asked

"Just tell them it is NATO GDR."

There was an awkward silence then a man's voice came on the phone.

"Adjutants office how can I help you" he said politely

"I need to talk to Micky from team 5 of the RPS"

"I am sorry I think you may have been put through to the wrong person. We do not have a team 5 in our RPS."

"Wait" I said before he could hang up on me. I found that the military and the UK's secret service had a really annoying habit of just hanging up on a conversation, when you were trying to get your call, directed to the right person

"Yes?" he said in a disinterested way

"You are the adjutants office right?"

"Yes"

"And you would be the adjutant for Brigadier General Sutterton?"

"Yes?"

"Well in that case he will be seriously hacked off at whoever blocks this call to him. I know there was a Team 5 and I know they were attacked and I know they lost men. So please can you put me through to him. Tell him Micky from Team 5 gave me this number."

The line went silent and I thought I had been cut off, I was about to start swearing at the phone.

"Hello this is Brigadier General Sutterton. First who is it calling me, second why are you calling me and third how the hell did you get this number?"

The voice was calm yet authoritative. This was a man who not only demanded respect but earned it. He did not bother to play on his rank. He was a hands on man who probably hated being stuck behind a desk.

"Hello Sir, my name is Andy Knight, I am part of the GDR team, set up by Colonel In Chief Hans Gunnerson. We are working on trying to recover Sir Philip. We understand that your RPS team 5, were his protection detail. I know that you lost a good number of your men the night Sir Philip was taken and his family murdered. I need to get in touch with Micky, to see what he wants us to do with the body of one of the security detail. We have conducted our own postmortem and will happily share the outcome of that with you. I will do whatever Micky wants us to do with the body."

"When you say you conducted your own postmortem, I assume that you are the people responsible for the theft of his body from the Aylesbury Mortuary?"

"Yes Sir, and it would be kind of foolish of me to attempt to deny it. Though we would prefer to see it as us conducting and truly independent enquirey."

"Tell me are your results any different from the initial report that they were shot?"

"The tests that were conducted under the strictest of conditions, state that this man did not die from a gunshot wound to the chest. In fact our laboratory report, states that he was dead before being shot. How he died we do not know yet, but our team are working on that at the moment. As soon as we know, you will also know."

"So you are claiming that the cause of death as given to us, by our own head of intelligence has somehow got it wrong?"

"Yes Sir and further to it the wounds inflicted upon your men were not caused by the BOYS ATR Silent Sniper rifle."

"And you have proof of this Mr Knight"

"Yes Sir we do. It looks like someone, deliberately wants us to follow a red herring, rather than find out what really happened and how your men died. If I can be quite candid with you, I do not entirely trust the current head of SIS. I have spoken with your men and even had them help us, I trust them and I trust their judgement."

"Can you call me back in about 10 minutes Mr Knight. It will give me time to talk to my team on the ground."

We said our goodbyes and I hung up. I was sure that he would not only be checking out our version of the events but he would be in direct contact with Micky. I was also sure he would be working on a way to track my call to him. That was something I could not allow. I needed Oran here, He had told me before that I could use the internet to make a telephone call. I knew that our internet was as secure as they come. Our IP Address was bounced all over the world and it actually changed every 2 seconds. There was no structured way either, it was totally random and no way to trace. So rather than using the Sat Phone this time I would make the call via Oran's computer. When the 10 minutes were up, I dialled the number using the telephone program on Oran's Computer. I was put through to the Brigadier Generals office, without any fuss this time.

"OK Mr Knight, your story seems to check out with our team on the ground. Can we send a chopper to collect our man from your location?."

"I would prefer that we bring him to you."

"Can I ask why."

"Lets Just say we have trust issues, not necessarily with you personally just a sort of in general type of thing. We like our privacy. So where would you like him sent to?"

"Mr Knight please show a bit of respect. He is not a parcel or a letter for royal mail delivery"

"I am sorry Sir, it was not meant in any disrespectful way." I knew he was actually trying to spin the conversation out in order to track my position.

"Can you bring him down to our team?"

"Yes Sir"

There was a slight delay in him answering, so I filled the gap myself.

"We will take him to the same location, where Mickey sent him from. By now you will also have found out that your man there with you, has been unable to track this call. So in the interest of trust why don't you tell him to go and get a coffee."

"Mr Knight are you always this distrusting of people?"

"Yes Sir, I have found I stay alive longer that way."

"Very well I will tell Micky to meet you at the point he left you at. It would appear that your suspicion has rubbed off on my own men as Micky was reluctant to tell me where he left you. You stated earlier that you have some proof that my men were already dead, before their bodies were used for target practice. You also said that you don't yet know how they died. What would be the point in killing a man twice?"

"The point would be, if the first time was an accident that someone did not want us to know about. Or it could be just to throw red herrings into the mix. At this juncture, I don't have an accurate answer. I do have suspicions as to who is behind it, however the why at this point eludes me. One thing I am sure of is that Sir Philip is still alive."

"How do you come by that conclusion?"

"Because I have seen people try to kill him and they have all failed. I think if they had been going to kill him, they would have done so with everyone else at his home. I think they killed his family in order to force him to do something."

"Like what?"

"Who knows with SIS. We all know what a slippery bunch they are. And yes I know that technically, we work for NATO and should trust them. Anyway I have to go and get your man ready for transit. I will be in touch soon. Thank you for your time." I hung up.

Now I would have to contact Hans and Carl. We would have to collect Oran and then return the body to Micky. They would then take the body back to Credenhill and no doubt sort things out for a quiet yet sympathetic military funeral. He had died on duty that was for sure. After getting hold of Hans, who was just about to board a flight the UK. Carl was already flying the body, to to a farm on the M25 ring-road. Micky and his boys would ensure Oran and Cyber got there without any interference from anyone else. I went and joined Lachie in the main Kitchen behind our bar.

Without offering or being asked he poured a coffee for me and then he put a slug of Jameson's Irish Whisky into it.

"The Boffins have just been down they want to see you again, as soon as possible."

"Any idea what its about?"

"I think they have found out what killed everyone at 'The Suit's' farm."

"Well lets go see them" I said and walked with my coffee to the lift, rather than taking the stairs.

I was not being lazy I just wanted to drink my coffee as we went. I knocked and waited for the door to be opened. As with everything they did, it was done in unison. With one of them opening the door and the other beckoning us to enter. I went in first and Lachie came in behind me.

"Lachie tells me you have some news for me"

"Yes we have" Gunter said excitedly

"We should have seen it first, but we were not looking for this kind of thing" Johan added

"We had to look again at the tissue samples we had taken." Gunter said and continued.

"But the trouble is that some things in the blood do not show after a time-frame of several hours"

"Yes you see the human red blood cell, carries oxygen to the brain and to other parts of the body. But the body can be fooled into believing that other substances are oxygen" Johan said

I put my hand up to stop them.

"Do you mean like Carbon monoxide poisoning?"

"Well yes and no" Johan said and Gunter continued for him

"When someone suffers from carbon monoxide poisoning. The oxygen molecule that would normally attach itself to the red blood cell after being inhaled into the lungs in the form of being mixed in the air. The lungs then extract the oxygen and pass it into the bloodstream to be used by the body. Now if Carbon Monoxide replaces the oxygen then the body can not operate. Because CO is odourless and has no colour you don't know its there. However I am sure that the SAS Soldiers could not be overcome quickly enough for them not to realise something would be wrong. Also most other toxic gasses have some form of smell. So it had to be something that would be ultra fast acting. We do still think, that they were killed by some form of carbon monoxide poisoning" Gunter stopped for breath and Johan took up the explanation of what they felt had happened

"So because Carbon Monoxide is quite slow acting, we started to look for things that would be quite fast acting. I remembered a situation in Russia where they used an experimental form of Fentanyl this is a synthetic form of this opioid. Fentanyl as I am sure you are aware has been used as a palliative pain relief drug. However this synthesised version of the drug is called Carfentanil is one hundred times stronger than Fentanyl, five thousand times as strong as Heroin and a horrendous ten thousand times as strong as Morphine. As you know, Gunter and myself work for the IDF. We have heard, that the Russians have been working on manufacturing an aerosol version, of this drug which could be released into the air in a cloud format. They did make a version of this drug as far back as the mid 1970's. It is the tiny quantities, that made it almost impossible for us to detect." Johan said and Gunter picked up the reigns again.

"We think that a cloud of this highly modified form of Carfentanil was somehow enveloped the team at the home of Sir Philip. Then at some point later they were exposed to a fatal dose of Carbon Monoxide. The Carbon Monoxide poisoning hid the fact that a synthetic form of Fentanyl had previously been used on the SAS man. When they were dead, they were shot, in the case of the man we have examined, he was shot with a 50cal high powered rifle. The idea being to make us think that it had been an armed attack on the home. How a cloud of Carfentanil gas was dropped in or around the farm we do not know. I can tell you they probably did not suffer, they would all have simply gone to sleep and never woken up."

"Thank you Gunter and Johan for your hard work. I have arranged for the Soldiers body to be repatriated to his unit. We would still request, that you stay here until we have everything sorted. This is partly for your own safety and partly to protect us. Can you please write up a full report in English. As I have said before please feel free to use all the facilities that we have here. I will try and make your stay with us as short and as pleasant as is possible. As you work for the IDF I am sure that you will understand the operational restrictions that I have to place upon you."

We shook hands and then left to discuss the results of the Boffins findings.

Lachie and I went and snagged a beer from the bar before sitting down in our garden area.

"Not wanting it to sound like a pun, but don't you think that all of this is just a bit heavy on the overkill. First taken out with some kind of opioid gas then, exposed to deadly levels of Carbon Monoxide, before being shot at dawn, with a 50 cal rifle. Any one of these things could have been the one that killed them." Lachie said

"What if the point of the overkill, was to hide the real reason for their deaths?" I replied and took a deep swig of my cold beer.

"It still makes no sense, even if it were to cover up the true reason for the deaths. We still have no clue as to what that was."

"I know Lachie, lets hope that Oran has found something, that we can work with. He should be here in a couple of hours."

I tried to think of any reason why 'The Suit' would have been kidnapped and his entire protection detail, domestic staff and family were wiped out, in the manner that they had been. We finished our beers and went to play ball with the kids, then all to sudden I heard the sound of the helicopter coming over the still waves of the ocean below. He came in at wave height and then brought the chopper up and landed gently onto the helicopter pad, two stories above us.

Oran went straight to his grotto and told us he had to check a few things out, before he would talk to us. Cyber was excited to see everyone and ran around the children who were also running around in circles with Kyla. At that precise point it was almost a normal life in a normal home, albeit way out here all alone. The children squealing and shouting and the dogs barking happily. Petrá and Morag were smiling and chatting to each other as they watched the children play with the dogs. Even the two boffins were down at the side of the garden enjoying a beer. I knew that as soon as we had our dinner, things would revert back to the 'normal' Team Seven life. That was the life where we had to bring all our families into the safety of our secret hideaway. We would go back to running to and from danger. I knew that we would soon be wearing our firearms. As soon as we had our parents here, we would go into our automatic mode. That was where every official member and every unofficial member would know their primary tasks and we would work as a single unit. Primarily for the protection of all of us.

Morag called us all to dinner and even though things were a little snug we all sat down to eat at the slab of teak in the kitchen. Rosemary was in her primary role, in her mother hen mode, fussing over everyone, ensuring that we all had enough to eat. When dinner was finished, Petrá would take the children to our schoolroom. Stu had gone with Rosemary to collect our parents from the Faeroe Islands. Then he would swing by Keiss and fill up on fuel and Rosemary would restock our larder from the small supermarket in Keiss village. Lachie and I would go and speak with Oran and see what was what. I had sent a message to Abdalla telling him some of the details and I suggested that he return as soon as possible. Hans was already en-route to us. In the meantime Lachie and I went to see Oran in his grotto.

ACT 8

"Welcome back Oran and thank you for doing this for us. So what is it that you have discovered from SIS?" I asked

"A lot of things did not add up to begin with, but I hacked into 'The Suits' laptop. I bypassed at that biometric shit he had installed. I did the same to the number 2's, without John Stevens, knowing. The first thing I discovered is that 'The Suit' did not send any email to Credenhill, to request that the gate guards be removed. There are some other emails on Stevens laptop, that are heavily encrypted and one of them that I was able to see part of, seemed to involve an investigation into something to do with Stevens and Guantánamo Bay. I have not managed to get much in the way of the detail of it. There is also an email in 'The Suit's draft folder. That email that was actually in this folder had no addressee on it, so perhaps he still had to complete it."

I held my hand up to stop him.

"Not necessarily, one of the old school tricks as far as people like 'The Suit' go, is to use the trade-craft that they have learned. He may have written a message and put it in his draft folder for someone else to access, and then delete or to even leave a reply. That way the email could not be tracked as it was never actually sent. The fact that it is still in the draft folder, would lead mean to believe that the person the message was for never actually got it." I said and nodded my head for Oran to continue.

On 'The Suits' Computer I found some reference to someone called 'Simon' who had a meeting with 'The Suit' a few days before, Sir Philips home, home was attacked. There was a mention of something about Cambridge University. I also went through his photographs that were stored on his hard drive, mostly they were personal ones of the family holidays and birthdays. That is when something looked wrong for me."

"How do you mean something looked wrong?" Lachie interrupted

"Well I don't think the woman and the boy at 'The Suits' house are actually the Wife and Son. They are similar and with them both having been shot in the head they may well have looked at first glance, even to someone who knew them, to be the wife and son. So I compared a picture of the family taken at Christmas to the pictures from the farmhouse."

"And?" Lachie said impatiently

"Well unless Mrs Reeves-Johnson, has had her ears pierced since Christmas, then the woman at the farmhouse was not her."

"Surely John Stevens would have recognised the bodies, even with the facial damage."

"What about the boy, was he a plant as well?"

"Yes Andy, it would look like it. His eye colour even accounting for 'red eye' correction is wrong. He also has a small almost unnoticeable freckle or mole on the left side of his jaw. The body in the morgue does not have that. The staff and the security detail though they are who they are supposed to be."

"Andy do you think that 'The Suit' knew he was going to be targeted and got his real family out in time?"

"It is possible but no I don't think so Lachie. 'The Suit' is not the sort of man to save his own family and then let his own protection detail be murdered in cold blood. So I don't think he installed a clone family. I think someone else did but without his knowledge."

"You think that John Stevens is behind this don't you Andy?" Oran said

"I don't know for sure, but I am 100% certain that he knows the woman and the boy are not 'The Suits' family. He would have been at many social functions at 'The Suits' home. Also he knew the wife, from his university days. Why he has not shared that information with us is the real question now. We need to start with a fresh look at all this. So it is probably best that we wait for Hans to get here and then take the lead from him. I know he handed the reigns over to me, but I think that in light of the small amount of facts that we do have. It would seem pertinent that he take over as lead investigator in this once again. Meanwhile Oran if you can keep on at whatever files, you have been able to lift from the computers at SIS. I would say that the Video evidence from the security cameras around the farmhouse, have only got the little bits on that we were supposed to see. I am more interested in what the Policeman saw. His body-cam video has been deliberately corrupted. Again If I let you work on that, just in case you can get anything from it. We only share what we need to, with or SAS Friends, I don't want them going in hell for leather and killing for revenge, without us first conducting our own investigation. So now lets go see the Doctor and see when the policeman can be interviewed." I said and wound our short meeting down.

We never recorded anything or wrote things down. Written evidence had a nasty habit of coming back and biting you on the ass. Lachie and I went to the pseudo medical bay that was set up in one of our guest apartments. I knocked and waited. The nurse opened the door and invited us in. The Doctor was sat at a desk making notes on the patient, These I would have to destroy at some point. He stood up and offered his hand I shook it and got straight to the point of my visit.

"When will we be able to talk to him?"

"He should be conscious any time now, but there is no guarantee that you will be able to have a conversation with him. He may not remember anything. It is quite common for patients who suffer a head injury in accident, to find they cant remember anything, for some time before the collision occurred. He may have suffered some brain damage. If you wish me to call you as soon as he awakes, I can do that for you, or you can sit at his bedside and wait."

"If you could give us a call when the patient wakes, please Doctor"

Lachie and I left the Hospital room and went to see our respective partners. I sat with Petrá and the kids was they bathed in the afternoons sunshine. It would be tonight before the Catherine May returned. Then depending upon flight times, Hans should be with us. Abdalla would be last, as we would have to arrange for either Carl to fly him in, or for Stu to pick him up from one of the many small harbours dotted around the North East coast of Scotland, which we tended to use. When we were inside Oran's place, he had all his computers switched on. There were three large screens each with something different going on. We stood by Oran and watched him work all three screens at the same time. Without looking up from what he was doing on the keyboard in front of him, he spoke to us.

"The screen on the left shows how much of the encrypted hard drive of 'The Suits' computer I have managed to decrypt. Its not a lot at the moment and mostly it is going to be plain text documents. It will enter all the keystrokes, and that will just show as on continuous string of letters and numbers, that is what your are seeing at the moment on the centre screen. I will then put that text file into another program and that will intuitively break the string up into separate words. It is not going to be perfect and it may put wrong words from the string of letters, but we should be able to get the meaning of the text. The Photographs however and any maps or drawings will be much harder to recover, not impossible, just harder and will take longer. It will be several hours before I can give you the essence of any complete document."

"Thanks Oran, do you want me to take Cyber up on to the top deck for a run?"

"Sure Andy, also I have run out of J20 in my fridge do you think you could grab me some from the bar?"

I agreed and we left with Cyber and I collected Kyla and with Lachie we all went up to the top deck. This suited me because I wanted to toss some ideas around with Lachie. Not that I was trying to keep anything from the others just a basic brainstorming session. We took the stairs rather than using the lift. When we got to the top deck we went up to the Helipad. The sun was high in the sky and there was a gentle breeze coming from the west of us blowing off the mainland of Scotland. The six foot high fence that went around the top deck was in the up position, so was safe for the dogs. The two dogs ran around and Lachie and I started to toss our ideas out.

"If 'The Suit' knew this was coming, he would have moved all his staff out of harms way, so it is fair to assume he was not prepared for whatever happened there. Yet his number two had the gate guard removed, so he had to know something was going on. He knew Mrs Reeves-Johnson, so he knew, that was not her lying dead, on the floor of the home. The same would apply to the boy. Yet he positively identified them, as being the wife and son. There are only two reasons why he would do that. One he knew before any attack and had managed to get the wife and son out, and to a place of safety. Or two, he was in some way complicit in what went on there. We now know, that they were not shot at the home. So it stands to reason that they were all somehow tricked into either going somewhere else, where they were exposed to this Carfentanil stuff. Some time after this they were deliberately or accidentally, I say accidentally because we do not have proof one way or another at the moment, exposed to lethal levels of Carbon Monoxide. Then at some time after that, their bodies were then used, for target practice with a variety of weapons including an AS50. After which the bodies were taken back to the farmhouse and placed in position, the blood and other bodily stuff was thrown around to simulate that they had been murdered there. The big question here is how the hell do you get the family, the domestic staff and the full security detail to come away from the relative safety of the farmhouse, and into a situation whereby they could be drugged into unconsciousness, before being killed. The security detail was from the RPS these are not amateurs, they are skilled soldiers. If any unidentified aircraft had so much as come within striking distance, then the SAS boys would have gone into defensive mode. Personally I cant see how a vapour cloud could have been dropped on them without anyone knowing. So without a shadow of a doubt it had to be someone they trusted. Also the real wife and son, must have gone with them, at the same time everyone else went. What reason could there be, and one that would sit well with the security detail, in order for them all, to leave the farmhouse together?"

"In my honest opinion Andy they would only all leave together, if there was a credible threat received and if that information came directly from a credible source, such as 'The Suit', the OIC the RPS or from MI5 or even MI6. If the number one of SIS was unavailable, then from the number two as in John Stevens."

"I have to say I agree with that part Lachie. So who out of that alphabet soup were involved. We cant prove any of it yet, nor do we even have any kind of reason as to why. Lets suppose that the number two at SIS is involved in something that he should not be, and that the number one found out about it, that would give a reason, but again we have no evidence just suspicions. Why lead us down the path of the BOYS 50ATR? Why save part of the SAS unit and yet sacrifice the rest of them? Are they somehow involved? Why would SIS have anything to do with Guantánamo Bay, to the best of my knowledge that was purely an American concern. We had been played by SIS before, are we being played again? We still have no clue as to who it is, that has 'The Suit' or for that matter, where they are holding not just 'The Suit' but the wife and son".

We went back down and I joined Petrá in saying goodnight to the children. Then we all went to the lounge area to await the arrival of Hans and Abdalla. While we waited, Sárrá the nurse came down to us and told us that the policeman was awake. Lachie and myself followed her back up to the mini hospital ward. When we went in the officer was having a sip of some fluid that was in a glass which the Doctor held. He was sipping through a straw. The doctor moved back and he and the nurse left the room allowing us to have complete privacy with the young constable.

"Hello William. My name is Andy McPhee and this long haired yeti is Lachlan Henderson. We are with a specialist unit from SIS, which is part of our countries secret service. You have been taken to a secure location, for your own safety. I will get right to the point. You responded to an emergency call, at a Farmhouse near Tring. Then the following day you were involved in a road traffic accident. Do you remember any of that?"

"I remember it all and I can tell you first, it was not an accident, I was involved in. The truck drove straight for me and then he drove off and left me for dead."

"OK do you want us to call you William, Will or Bill?"

"Bill is fine"

"I need to ask you some questions first, about what you saw when you got to the farm. You see someone has deliberately wiped your body cam and your notes, have all gone missing as well. Take your time and tell me, what you can remember, can you do that for me? If it gets too much for you, we can stop until you are up to it."

"No its fine ask away"

"OK Bill, from the lead up, to when you arrived at the farmhouse. What is the first thing you saw?"

"I got the call, when I was just leaving a domestic incident, in Tring village. As such, I was just a couple of minutes away. So I responded that I would investigate and headed out there. I almost did not make it to the farmhouse either, as a bus and a couple of Range Rovers, nearly took me out at the T-Junction. These farmer types they race around the country lanes, like it is their own private race track. Anyway, I was told by dispatch, that the address was one of the ones with a Royal Protection Squad. So I did actually expect to see armed response officers on the gate. When I got to the address there was no one on the gate. I followed the road down to the house, and it was like a war zone. There were bodies all over the place, along with blood and guts splattered everywhere. I called it in. While I awaited CID I went and checked all the bodies just in case there was someone alive. They were all dead. About ten minutes later the Murder Squad arrived. Then within minutes some guys from SIS, your lot I think, arrived in a chopper and said they had jurisdiction and that we, the local police that is, were to stand down. I went back to the station and completed my notes and handed my body cam over, to the chain of evidence officer. I had never seen anything like it before. It was like a scene out of a Quentin Tarantino movie. Then I completed my shift and went home. The next day I was on my way into work, when a mad man, in a big truck, drove right at me without even slowing down. Next thing I know is I wake up here, by the way, where is here?"

"Thank you Bill, you say that on your way to the incident, you were almost taken out by a bus and a pair of Range Rovers?"

"That's right at the T-junction near the farmhouse"

"Can you remember anything at all about either the bus or the two Range Rovers?"

"Not really apart from they were dark and they were exceeding the speed limit."

"Which way were they heading?"

"I am sorry I don't follow?"

"Would you say they were heading towards London or away from it?"

"Out in the sticks with all the small side roads, it could have been either, but if I had to guess I would say towards London"

"One more question Bill, What order were they in, as were the Range Rovers in Front or behind?"

"One in front of the bus and one behind it. You think they had something to do with what happened at the farm?"

"I think that fact that you saw this bus is the reason that someone tried to kill you with a truck."

"Jesus!"

"OK Bill. You are in a secure and safe location. We moved you here in order to protect you. It is my belief that had you come out of your coma in the hospital you were in, then you may have met with a fatal accident. The people that put you in there in the first place would not want you talking to anyone about that night. We have a specialist Trauma Doctor and Nurse here, just to look after you. If you wish anything please just ask for it. Apart from taking you home at the moment, as we feel it would not be conducive to your continued recovery and recouperation. I don't know if the Doctor has told you about your injuries?"

"No not really."

"OK Bill, there is no sugar coating here. You suffered a fractured neck which Stoke Mandeville hospital fused three bones in your neck, so that you are not paralysed. You can see you have two broken legs, your knees are shattered and you have several broken ribs. You suffered a fractured skull and a slight bleed on the brain. Oh and they shaved just half of your head. That is the bad news. The good is that when the swelling on your knees goes down, the good doctor will replace your shattered knee caps, with new nylon ones. Then he will apply full casts to both your legs. They will be on for 8 to 12 weeks. I see you are wiggling your toes so that is good news on the spinal front. The ribs there is not a lot to be done, just give them time to heal naturally. Your memory seems to be OK too, so all things considered, for a man who had a fight with a speeding truck you are doing quite well."

"Ya think?" he said with a twisted smile.

"Talk Soon, get some rest Bill"

We left and the Doctor and nurse, who had been waiting on the other side of the rig, they returned to their room and patient.

ACT 9

"So what do you think Andy?"

"To be quite honest Lachie, it is just like everything that SIS is involved in, more smoke and mirrors than clarity. I would say that its safe to assume, that the bodies were brought back in the bus that Bill saw. The Range Rovers I doubt belonged to the Young Farmers Association. They were probably owned by some organisation who have an of alphabet soup for a name. God knows who they represent at this time, I don't have a clue. Lets look at the things we know rather than the things that we don't. First we know that 'The Suit' is missing. The woman and the boy, who's bodies were discovered at the farmhouse were not 'The Suits' wife and son. We think that the BOYS ATR is a red herring. We know that John Stevens ordered the removal of the gate security. We know the murders took place somewhere other than the farmhouse. We know that it has to be someone, who had access in some way, to this Synthetic Fentanyl based stuff. We still don't know any of the whys. So lets follow up on the bits that we have to go on for now. Then take things from there. Lets get Oran, to use his Satellite access and see if he can backtrack the two Range Rovers and the bus. Also check all the traffic cameras between the suits house and a 50 mile radius. We know what time Bill saw them at the Tring Crossroads. So it should be a simple matter, for Oran to find out where they came from. Then once again we see where things take us from there."

That is just what we would do. I went and sat with Petrá and watched the sun go down over an almost perfectly calm sea, as we waited the arrival of Hans and Abdalla. It was Abdalla who arrived first on the Catherine May. Along with our parents. Then about an hour later we heard the whoop of the Sea King coming over the waves. After securing the helicopter and bringing up the canvas walls, we all went down to the bar. I asked the two scientists to go to their quarters and that we would call them if required. Then we told Hans and Abdalla of our findings. We formulated the basis of a plan on the information that Oran was updating us with. We sat together as a family and as a team. I had deliberately kept the IDF doctor and Boffins out of the meeting, firstly because of security and secondly because they really did not need to be involved in the side of things, I knew what Team Seven would be doing in the near future. Oran had managed to find the Bus and Range Rovers by simply entering the time and the location give from the young police officers statement. Oran had a full map that showed their route to a disused military base, at RAF Daws Hill. He had then set up satellite surveillance, under the auspicious of our GDR NATO Investigation. This operation was limited to GDR Eyes Only, as such even if John Stevens wanted to access the information, he would be unable to, without requesting it directly from GDR. We decided to wait a day or two, before we took any form of real action and left it up to Oran to follow activity at Daws Hill. Hans was helping Oran, with the recovery of text documents, recovered from 'The Suits' hard drive. If for some reason the SAS security detail, had been fooled by John Stevens, into thinking that there was a credible threat, to not just 'The Suit' but also to his family. Then they had them taken to RAF Daws Hill underground bunker. Even Sir Philip, may have been fooled into believing that he needed make his family safe. So a bus would be required to take the family, staff and security detail along with an armed escort, to the front and rear, making it a military style convoy. It would then be an easy matter, in the bunker, to expose them to this knock out gas that would only take seconds to work. After which, put all the unconscious people that you wanted to kill, back into the bus. Then run a pipe from the exhaust back into the bus for an hour. After this, set the bodies up and shoot them. Finally take the bodies back to 'The Suits' home and lay them out. Next, splash the blood and guts around and job done. At first glance it would look like there had been a massive assault on 'The Suits' home.

Add some finesse to it, like one of the detail with a gun out and stick another one in 'The Suits' car. That would intimate, that they had been suddenly and brutally overwhelmed. Which was the initial assessment. Introduce the bullshit, about a secret version of the BOYS, which was actually under trials. Again this was another distraction that worked. This had originally left everybody chasing their own tails. So we were now looking at this from a completely different point of view.

We had to now believe, that not only was 'The Suit' still alive somewhere, but so were his family. After two days of watching Daws Hill. It was obvious that there was still some activity there. We contacted Micky and told them to meet us at RAF Halton Air Strip and to bring all the transport they had. The active members of Team Seven along with Carl would be going and we would once again be armed for bear.

I selected my Val Sniper along with a pair of Sig Sauer automatic pistols. Abdalla and Hans were both hostage rescue trained, so they would take the lead and I would act as backup with Carl. Lachie would act as oversight and watch our backs. The SAS would fill the gaps should there be any. I went to my apartment with Petrá who like all of our spouses, had been at the meeting. She knew where I was going and roughly what we were planing to do. This was to be first and primarily, a Hostage Rescue mission where we hoped that we could recover, alive and unharmed Sir Philip and his family.

It would be a live fire mission and we expected a reasonable amount of resistance. I took a shower and Petrá helped me into my Nomex suit which fitted to my body like a glove. I put on full Kevlar body armour. My Sig's were in double shoulder holsters and I had a pair of Bussé combat knives into their sheaths, attached to the webbing belt they sat nicely within reach in the small of my back. Petrá said nothing as she helped me put on the tools of my new trade. These were the tools, that unlike my first trade of saving lives, these now dealt out death. I knew Lachie would be doing the same and that Morag would be helping him into his own equipment. We did not, really need the help of our spouses. It was more of letting them be involved and to show them, that we were well armed and more than able to look after ourselves.

I had lost track of the number of live firefights that we had been in, since our induction into SIS some six and a half years ago. How many times, had I thought, it was going to be my turn to die. Worse was how many lives I had taken from others. I had shot, stabbed and beaten men to death. It was not something I was proud of, in fact I was mortally ashamed of it. I had known, it had to be that way, it would be them or me. That is with the singular exception, of Chang. That had been murder pure and simple. I could have arrested him, but the knowledge that he possessed in his twisted brain, was too dangerous for any country to own, even ours. I had been his Judge Jury and Executioner all rolled into one. I hoped, I would never have to do that again. The only people that knew of that act, were the active members of Team Seven, along with God.

"Be careful Andy, I need you and the children need you. Remember you are a father now, you are not that single man, running around like James Bond, that you used to be."

"Don't worry Petrá, Lachie will always have my back and he will be watching over us. So I will be safe."

She pulled me close to her until I could feel her firm breasts pushing into my chest. Then she slipped her hand down to my crotch, and a twinge of excitement rose in me.

"Careful darling, the boys will think I am carrying an extra weapon down there"

"Then you better look after him, because I don't just want you for your mind Andy McPhee, I want you for your body too." She said, as she stood up on her tip toes and kissed me passionately on the lips. It always seemed to me that she sang my Name. The children came running into the room and Petrá removed her hand from my crutch."

"Daddy has to go and do some work with Uncle Lachie and Uncle Abdalla. Uncle Hans is going with them to help as well. So say good bye children" Petrá said

I swept both the children up in my arms and kissed them both on their foreheads.

"Don't forget to bring back presents daddy" said Ainá

"Come back safe Daddy" said Finn.

Of the two children, he was one who was growing up fastest, in terms of maturity. He already knew that sometimes Daddy had to go a stop 'Bad Men'. Without even being told, he had worked it out, that this would involve some risk, and that men sometimes got hurt. In a way this was good because I was sure that these children, would never have a normal life. They would always be the children of Team Seven. Being a member of Team Seven came with it good and bad points. Good we were rich and lived, for the greater part an idealistic lifestyle. Bad because in the real world, there would always be people that wanted revenge, or people that wanted to ensure the secret information that we possessed, stayed secret, on a permanent basis. When three men know a secret, the only way it can remain a secret is for two of them to die. I did not think that we were in any immanent form of danger, but I realised that it came with the job.

Abdalla had taken his usual arsenal of weapons. Which really meant he had a Sig Sauer, an AS50 and a lot of explosives in the form of fragmentation grenades, attached to his webbing belts. I knew in his backpack there would be more along with plenty of full magazines and Claymore Mines.

Lachie like me had opted for a pair of Sig Sauer's although he had one on a thigh holster and the other under his left arm. He also carried his AS50 which was fitted with a suppressor making it even longer than the designers had intended. The rail on top held the new BAE Advanced digital scope and the Bifold legs were folded away under the barrel.

Hans had a silenced HK MP5 along with his beloved Desert Eagle Magnum 50, there was no point in even trying to silence this weapon. But what it did have was the stopping power of an AS50, just in close combat mode. Abdalla handed out the new NATO improved gas masks, just in case someone decided that they wanted a rerun of the Carfentanil. Each of us wore a secure encrypted Storno Radios, fitted with throat mikes and earbud receivers. Hans was able to get hold of some of the plans for the underground bunker of the Ex Cold War era, Daws Hill RAF Station. He had, with the help of Oran, installed a 3D map onto the PDA's that were now strapped to our forearms. We knew, that underground we would have limited range on the Storno Radios, so it was essential that we go over the incursion plans and make sure we knew where everyone, was supposed to be.

We would hand out some Storno's, to the SAS boys, when we met up with at Halton. I was sure they would have their own collection of weapons. We would only kill if we had to. If 'The Suit' and his family, were not still being held there, we needed to know, where they were. This meant, that we would require to interrogate someone, in order to find out where that was. This on the flip side meant we definitely needed a live tango.

Stu would be in charge of the rig, while we were gone, and would protect it if necessary. I knew all the people there on our home, would be in safe hands.

After taking down the Tarpaulin that surrounded the Sea King Helicopter, we loaded up and Carl started the engines. True to form Lachie lay back in his webbing seat and within minutes of our take off, he was snoring quietly. I tried to do the same, but sleep would not come to me. It had been just over five years, since we had seen any real action. I knew we continually trained for this sort of eventuality. I wondered if we were just a little too old, to be taking on terrorists and others. Now that we were approaching our 40's, I doubted we were as fast as we used to be, but on the flip side of this, I also thought that we had the experience and had been battle hardened, in true hand to hand combat. We would have the advantage of surprise. We would be landing almost 30 miles away for the target, then we would drive the rest of the way, until we were within walking distance of the RAF Daws underground bunker.

In the 1970's and 1980's there had been a peace camp on the outside of the wire fence. They had been an offshoot of the Greenham Common Women. They had been protesting against the USA, storing their Cruise Missile system here at Daws. This was a base that the Americans had been using since the end of the second World War. They had always been secretive about what went on in there. Some said it was part of the American Nuclear Missile system and as such put the UK at further risk from the Soviets. No doubt during the cold was there were many secrets to be had within its Razor Wire fencing. Now however, officially it had been closed down and technically it was up for sale. Although no one seemed to be in a hurry to sell it. It was located on some of the most expensive building land, within the UK.

I was sure would be snapped up by some shrewd investor, given a real chance. So why had it not be properly marketed???

I suspected that It may have been decommissioned as an active Airfield and normal working Military base, but that some arm of the security services, still walked its quiet and echo filled corridors. Possibly it was a black ops site for interrogations, could it even be an SIS holding site.

I did not even notice the sea and then the land, pass away beneath us. It was only the change in the engines pitch that took me from my conscious and subconscious thoughts. Lachie's head, rose from where his chin had been resting on his chest. His hands automatically carried out an equipment check. I followed suit though in a less automatic way. The chopper landed softly, on the small airfield at the back of the training hangers at RAF Halton. When I pulled the side door open I could see four vehicles with their lights pointing towards our chopper. We decamped and after making sure we had not left any of our equipment on the Sea King, Carl took off. He would find somewhere more private to set it down until we needed him.

Micky came over and shook my hand. Like us they were kitted out in camouflage and each soldier carried firearms and knives. Hans handed out Storno radios to them and we did a radio check, to ensure that we were all on the same channel. Then we split up and each of us teamed up with a SAS man, in their cars and vans. They were different from the ones they had when we were last here. These were less showy forms of transport. The car I shared with Micky was an old Ford Escort, it probably had more rust than paint, Lachie was in a Ford Transit van. with John'O. It claimed to be a Green Grocers, delivery van. Abdalla was in a Small VW Polo, which probably meant, that his knees were tucked somewhere under his chin. Hans was taking up the rear and he was paired up with his SAS man in a small Escort van. At least we would not not look from the outside, at night, anything other than just some random cars.

We went towards RAF Daws in a loose convoy. Its strange I did not feel excited nor did I feel worry. I would be happy when it was over, that much was for sure. I had trust and faith in my fellow team members. I also trusted the members from the SAS, they were without doubt the best covert fighting force in the world. Most of the operations they carried out, they did so in complete secrecy. The one of the few public displays of courage that people still talked about, were hostage rescues, such as the Iranian Embassy siege. This had taken place in London, in May of 1980. A group of six armed men stormed the Iranian Embassy. They took 26 people hostage, including a British Police officer. That officer had been on Embassy Duty. The terrorists had demanded the release of Arab prisoners in Khuzestan and that they then be given safe passage. The then, Prime Minister of the UK, Margaret Thatcher, would not acquiess to their demands. On the sixth day the gunmen, murdered one of the hostages and threw the body out of the Embassy. As a direct result of this happening, Margaret Thatcher, ordered that the SAS go in and gain the release of the other hostages. They were authorised to use deadly force, even though technically they were not on British Soil. The SAS called the mission 'Operation Nimrod' They abseiled down from the roof and forced their entry through the first and second floor windows. In just a little over a quarter of an hour they managed to rescue all but one of the hostages. They shot dead five out of the six gunmen, that had taken the embassy. Some of the gunmen it was claimed, were summarily executed after being wounded. This claim came from the surviving gunman, who was later charged with murder and other terrorist offences. He was sentenced to 27 years in British jails.

There were far more raids that have not been under the public eye. It was said that Margaret Thatcher used the SAS, as her own personal Army with a shoot to kill policy. So they were good guys to have on your side in a fight and bad guys to be on the wrong side of. The chances are that if you saw their face in battle it would be the last face you saw.

ACT 10

We were about 200 yards from the wire fence that still surrounded this cold war secret military base. From where we were in a hollow I could see no security guards, but I have always found that its a good idea to assume that they did have lookouts posted. I looked around to see if there was a good spot for Lachie to overlook us as we made our incursion into the base. There was only flat ground around the front edge but there was an old Trailer with advertising for some pub or other.

"Lachie do you think you could get on top of the trailer without being seen and still be able to cover us?"

"No Problem Andy" he replied and set off at a low crawl until he reached the field, where the trailer was parked. I watched him as he silently made his way on to the roof. The trailer was several years old, but fortunately the rot had not set in to it yet.

"Andy let Abdalla and me take the point, when we make it as far as the main doors to the bunker then if you follow in on our line. Micky If you could split your force and cover our flanks that would be much appreciated. We need to do this as silently as possible. We don't even know if there are any tangos in there, or even how many men they have. We should assume, they have at least a six man team that would be one driver for each vehicle and one riding shotgun. There may of course be more men. They are going to be professional, remember they took out a full SAS team, apparently without any losses of their own. They don't mind killing innocents, we can see that because of the domestic staff along with the woman and the boy. If you can take prisoners, then do so. If not take them out quietly."

The SAS guys nodded and Micky went to the right with one of his men and John 'O went the other way with his partner. Now we had flanking cover, and from our rear we had cover in the form of Lachie, with his sniper rifle.

"You are clear to go Hans. I see the bus. I have absolutely nothing on thermal so they must be behind that big bloody door. Watch out for booby traps."

I followed in behind Hans and Abdalla about 20 yards behind. When Hans reached the fence he connected a wire with crocodile clips on each end, these he set 4 feet apart on the fence then he proceeded to cut through the fence, until he had made a large enough hole for a man to easily walk through without touching the wire on either side of him. Hans signalled me over and I belly crawled to the fence where he and Abdalla were waiting. I assumed that the SAS guys were doing the same thing at their area of the wire fence.

"What gives with the wire?" I asked pointing to where he had placed the crocodile clips.

"Even through this may no longer be electrified they may have a small charge running through it, and I don't want to set off any alarms."

I messaged the others.

"Wait here until Abdalla and Hans reach the piece of flat ground by the edge of the road that goes into the bunker."

As soon as they were in place I followed through the hole in the fence and took up position. I watched them go, looking through the BAE sights on my VAL. I set it to night vision and they appeared in a ghostly green but perfect quality. I swept my scope around the area and could see the two SAS guys to my right but not the ones to my left, they must have been in a hollow.

I turned my sights back towards Abdalla and Hans.

I thought I saw movement to their left. It might have been the other SAS Team but I was not sure. In our first mission we had worked out a click code when we thought that our radios had been compromised.

"Lachie" and then I clicked once and dropped my radio channel down 3. Lachie must have remembered as well

"What's up Andy?"

"Can you see the SAS guys on the left of Hans and Abdalla?" I said and then waited for him to get back to me.

"Negative they must be in a hollow or behind something but nothing showing here"

"OK Lachie just nerves I guess" Click I went back up to the main channel. Just as I was sure, that I had been seeing things I saw in my peripheral vision, something move. I rolled onto my back just as the shape lunged for me. Instinctively I reached behind my back and pulled one of my razor sharp Bussé knives. The shape landed on top of me and I saw an arm raised with a dagger ready to stab me. The blow never came though as the knife I had brought around to my front, more out of muscle memory than anything else, it had slid to the hilt into the chest of the man who fell heavily upon me. I rolled over taking the man with me. Once again out of pure muscle memory and training, I clamped my left hand firmly over his mouth, just in case he would scream out. I need not have bothered, my knife was buried in the heart of my attacker and he had died the moment he fell upon me. I ripped of the black balaclava he was wearing. I almost shouted out. John'O. I clicked my radio once

"Andy?"

"Lachie I have just been attacked by John'O. He is dead."

"Say again?"

"I said I have just killed John'O, he attacked me. Something here is way fucking wrong." I clicked my mike once

"Hans" I clicked once again. I hoped that he would remember the code we had come up with during the fire fight at Altnabreac.

"Hello?" Hans's voice came over the radio

"Watch your back I have just been attacked by John'O" I replied

"Andy are you OK?" Lachie's voice

I could feel, rather than see Lachie swing the AS50 to cover my position.

"Yes mate John'O is down and out. Hans I think I know why the four gate guards were removed. But I will tell you in a bit, for now we have to assume that we have been led into a trap. Hans and Abdalla you need to be back to back, and keep in the hollow. Lachie can you cover my six as I make my way out."

"Roger Andy I am switching from Night to Thermal so I can cover you better." his reply came. I knew Lachie would give his life in order to save any one of us. Now we were in a game of hide and seek, in the dark against 3 members of the most elite fighting force in the world. We would have to rely on our close friendship and even closer working relationship that we had built up over the last six and a bit, years. Lachie's and my friendship, went back to childhood. Abdalla had taught hostage rescue and sniper training to the SAS and SBS. When we first met Hans he was teaching the SAS survival techniques. I was sure of one advantage that we had over Unit 5 of the SAS's RPS. That advantage was that, we were all trained snipers, and we were good at it. All of us had kill shots of over 2,000 metres. So long as we could put distance between us and this rogue SAS unit. Then we could turn a disadvantage, into a big advantage. I was in the process of making my way back to the wire fence when Lachie's voice came over the radio.

"Stay down and hug the ground, you have a weasel coming up on your left. He is about 10 yards out. Don't move"

I knew I had the VAL silent Sniper rifle with me but if I switched the scope on its glow would be seen from 10 yards or even more. So I did as Lachie had told me to. Once again I caught something in my peripheral vision. This time it was a flash from the barrel of the AS50. It was a suppressed shot and a subsonic round. But I still heard it, perhaps because I was listening for it. I know it was my imagination, as I visualised the flight path of the heavy 50cal round. I knew without looking that it will have struck home. Either a head or a chest shot. It would have been catastrophic, John'O's, partner's body, would have been thrown backwards by the kinetic energy. If it had struck the man's head, then it would have removed it from his shoulders. If the round had hit in the chest and even if he had been wearing body armour. The round would have torn through the Kevlar and then through the skin and bone that lay beneath it. It would have shattered like matchsticks, the ribs. Then even if it missed the heart, it would have pulled it from the Veins and Arteries that held it in place. The blood around it would be boiled by the time the bullet exited and ripped the spine and any surrounding connective tissue. Around 2 pints of blood would have instantly been turned to a red mist and a pink froth. The body dead, seconds before it finished tumbling to the ground. Nothing can prepare the human body for this massive shock. Which would have killed the man first? Pain? Blood Loss? Heart Failure? Shock? Perhaps all of them together. Violent death is never a pretty thing.

Even before Lachie had radioed to tell me the tango was down, I heard 3 massive booms which could only have come from the hand canon that Hans carried. He had loaned it to me on the last mission. I had used it to fire at fleeing target. I had actually shot at the RIB Craft that a man was escaping in. I had fired it, just as the small boat hit a wave, the shot had removed the man's head completely. The recoil was so massive that my wrist was sore for days. I was confident that I would suffer from tinnitus later in life just from that one shot. So I recognised its sound.

"Hans, what the situation?"

"Micky and his mate are down and out of the game. We are both safe." He replied referring to Abdalla and himself.

"Hans can you and Abdalla move back to Andy's position."

"Roger Lachie, we are moving now"

"I can cover from my position, Lachie can you over-watch?" I said
"Roger."

When we were all back a safe distance from the main door to the bunker at Daws Hill, we regrouped where we had left the cars.

"I think that those four are in it with Stevens"

"If that's the case Andy, then why all the roll play? Why not just take us out. They have had plenty of chances" Lachie said

"Perhaps they wanted to know how much we knew about what was going on?" Abdalla said

"Hans we have just killed four members of the SAS, when that gets back to Credenhill we are going to have every current member of the SAS and all the previous members, out for our blood. I think it is safe to assume that, the people that took 'The Suits' detail out, are either serving members of the SAS or private mercenaries, who are ex-SAS. Hans do you wish to take control of the mission? After all you are the only real serving member of the military amongst us."

"No Andy, I think that Sir Philip would say this is still a British problem and he would have chosen you anyway."

The others gave their thumbs up. So here I was again. Not really a place where I wanted to be.

"OK we only have the one AS50 here at the moment and the VAL, so we have one long range and one short range sniper rifle. Here is what I think we should do. We should set up two sniper nests with the ability to catch them in cross fire. Lachie, I will spot for you. Abdalla can have the VAL and Hans can spot for him. If that is OK by everyone?" Again I got the thumbs up from the others. So I continued

"Right lets hide the transport and set our nests about 400 yards out from the main entrance to the bunker."

"OK by me Hans said. Lets do it."

I set off to where Lachie had originally set up his sniper position. We looked to see if we could find somewhere that offered more cover as well as a good line of sight. It took us about 20 minutes of scrabbling around in the ditches and undergrowth until we found somewhere suitable. I wanted us set up before the light of dawn came. I pulled up tufts if long grass and weeds along with small branches and twigs and made a halfway descent hide that gave us an elevated position overlooking the main blast doors and road into the camp. I had not realised it at the time, due to the adrenalin dumped into my bloodstream, but I was covered in John'O's blood he must have bled out while he lay on top of me. What I thought was moisture from the damp ground was approximately a pint and a half of blood spread liberally down my front. I was thankful for two reasons though, first that it was not my blood and secondly that Petrá could not see me like this.

"Lachie any ideas as to what is going on here? And please don't give me 'I am just a lowly Rock Ape' rhetoric."

"OK even though I am still just a Rock Ape, I have not got a fucking clue mate. What I do know though, even if I cant as of yet prove it is. Mr John fancy pants Stevens is mixed up in all this. Somehow he has managed to get the SAS to wipe out their own folks and a bunch of innocent civilians. Why he has done this, totally eludes me at the moment. Do you suppose the Brigadier General is involved?"

"I cant see any way for these SAS foot soldiers, attacking us, without the involvement of their Commanding Officer. The fact that he sacrificed his whole team, can only mean that he is involved to a high degree. We really do have to stop killing people Lachie, we need to get a live one to talk to us."

"I agree."

"What with?"

"You have to stop killing people?"

"Me?"

"Yes?"

"Why?"

"Well it was you who killed John'O, and caused the shit to hit the fan."

"He was about to kill me."

"OK fair point. But how do we catch a live one?"

"With bait is usually a good way."

"I am just a lowly Rock Ape."

"Not you Lachie, well it could be you."

"WHAT?"

"Don't worry I need you behind the sight of that big gun."

"So tell me what have you got in mind?"

"I am about the same build and hair colour as John'O. All I have to do is black my face up like his. I can do a Glasgow accent like his. I can slip through the wire and stagger around a bit and fall down in a gully moaning. Lets face it I am covered in his blood anyway."

"Then what Andy, they come out and rescue you? Then they find out you are not John'O and they kill you!"

"That's not quite the plan."

I told Lachie what I had in mind and I asked Hans and Abdalla provide cover if I needed to make a run for it. I would never ask one of the guys to do anything that I was not willing to do myself. This was something I had actually learned from 'The Suit'. He had never asked us to do anything he was not prepared to do. He had stood beside us on the battlefield. Now it was my turn. I was about to step up to the mark.

I crawled through the morning dew and was actually happy to see that where John'O had fallen was still in the same hollow as I had killed him in. I could see it from where I was, but there was no way that those in the bunker could see it from their vantage point. I knew that John'O would have been wearing his radio when I stabbed him. I hoped that it was still on the same channel that he would have been talking to his comrades rather than the channel that we had asked them to be on. So far so good. I moved closer to the fence. The hole was still there, either they had not noticed it, which I doubted, or they thought that we had made a run for it. I was suddenly very grateful that I had not let the SAS boys know our home location.

"Lachie can you see me?"

"Roger Andy."

"Abdalla?"

"Yes Mr Andy, we have you in a perfect crossfire."

I think that was supposed to make me feel safe, but all of a sudden it made me feel very fragile. I slipped easily through the gap in the fence. I slithered forward until I reached the body of John'O. I checked his Storno, it was set to the same channel as we had asked them to use. I knew that we still had our radios set to another frequency. I keyed my throat mike.

"He has his radio to our old frequency."

"Fuck it Andy, Abort and come back" Lachie said

I was just about to when I noticed a small in-ear transmitter. I knew these existed, Just we never bothered with them, because they have a very limited range.

"Hold on lads He is wearing some kind of in-ear bud trans device."

I carefully grabbed hold of the 'pull out tab' and removed it, then I checked his body and found a wireless box about the size of a cigarette packet which had a TX button on it. The box was attached to John'O's webbing. I unclipped it and put it in my pocket. Then I put the bud in the opposite ear from my own Storno Earbud.

"Game on lads keep me covered"

I put John'O's Balaclava on and removed my twin shoulder holsters but put the Sig Sauer's in my belt beside my twin Bussé knives at my back. It was a tight and uncomfortable fit, but better the discomfort, than being unarmed I thought. I crawled to the front edge of the hollow, and started to wave one of my hands over the front. Then I pressed the transmit button on his radio box.

"Arrrrgggghhh" I moaned and did it a second time while pressing the TX button on John'O's transmitter.

"Come on tae fuck lads, I'm wounded and yeas fuckers hae left me oot here aww the night." I carefully moaned in my best Glasgow accent, hopefully sounding the same as John'O

"John'O? Is that you?" the voice in my ear came.

I knew the voice just could not place it. I was betting though, that John'O would have instantly recognised it. Play safe I thought don't over play it,

"Awww come on away lads. I am fucking bleeding to death oot here. The fucker knocked me oot and then stabbed me." I made up my mind I had to show myself.

I got Up to my feet and then staggered back down into the hollow."

"Awww gimme a break lads don't leave me here to die. That not the way we dae things. We dinnae leave a man behind."

"John'O, can you make it to the door."

"For fucks sake can yeas no see, I cannae even fucking stand man. You might as weel pit a bullet in ma heed man, but dinnae leave me here to die slow. Arrghh"

"OK John'O, well get to you. Hold on for a little longer."

"They have opened one of the doors and there are two of them coming with a stretcher. They are coming at a Zig Zag run." Lachie said in my other ear.

"Don't shoot them unless you have no choice" I said

I crawled forward to the edge of the hollow, they were about 100 yards out. I knew all they could see of me was my blood covered hand over the edge of where I was laid. I pulled my Sig out from behind my back and released the safety. Like we had been taught by Abdalla, all those years ago, at the firearms training centre. Always keep your weapon cocked and always have one up the spout. I would have to kill one of the two men, but not until they were on my position. I needed to incapacitate one but keep him alive. The problem with being a stretcher bearer, is that it is impossible to make an accurate shot, while running with a stretcher in your arms. They were doing it stupidly in my opinion. I would have had one man, run with the stretcher and the other man keeping watch and at the ready with his firearm. It looked like today their mistake, would be my saving grace. I moaned some more, a little more desperately.

"Hang on John'O almost there."

I rolled back down into the hollow so my back was on the ground. I had my Sig in my right hand, partially hidden by my right leg. They came over the top of the ridge and went to put the stretcher down. I brought my arm up quickly and shot the guy at the back, twice in the head. It exploded like a watermelon and he fell backwards. That had taken about three quarters of a second to snap off the two rounds. The soldier at the front suddenly realised his mistake, He had laid his SA80 Automatic, on the ground next to the stretcher. He reached for it and I shot him in his right shoulder. My bullet spun the man around, so that he faced the way he had come from. But even before his involuntary spin the 9mm round had torn through the cloth of his camouflage battle dress and the webbing strap over it. That was both good and bad. Good for me and bad for him. Because the webbing strap had flattened the bullet a little, it had also slowed it down some, not enough though to stop it doing some serious and painful damage. The bullet punched its way through the skin and muscle, then it sought out the bony parts. First the Caracoid Process of Scapula, which it shattered into thirty pieces, then due to that impact the bullets direction changed a little, helped in some way by the soldier starting to spin. Next it tore the Coracoacromial Ligament completely free from the bones, to which it had previously been attached. The bullet smashed into the head of the humerus ripping it out of its socket and totally destroying the ball joint at the top of the arm. The bullet was slowing fast now, but it was also starting to roll end over end now. The lump of metal that previously had a perfect torpedo shape, now resembled an almost cuboid blob of metal. Still moving end over end it ripped through the muscles and tendons at the back of the shoulder before punching out through his skin and tearing a good sized hole in the back of his uniform. A red mist filled with bone particles and fibres from his clothing, shot out from the gaping wound that was now on his back. The soldier continued his spin and then one of his knees gave way and he twisted to the ground. Pain is the bodies protector. First it tells you that the body has been damaged in some serious way, and then when it gets to a point where the body itself can not operate, it temporarily shuts things down and the individual looses consciousness.

Time resumed its normal pace and the wounded soldier now lay at my feet. I looked to where his partner had fallen the entire top of his head above his nose was now a bloody pulp. One eyeball, lay forlornly on his bloodied cheek. The other eyeball no longer existed, only a big hole. He had died without knowing the pain that his comrade had felt and would probably revisit in the near future. That was of course assuming, we could get him out from here alive. Not to mention getting myself out alive in the process. All this had taken a little over a second and a half. I lay back and looked at the carnage.

Again, I remembered something that Abdalla, had told me shortly after I have killed my first man. I was worried about being visited at night, while I slept, by the faces of those I had killed. He told me that might happen, but the worst thing was to be visited by the faces of your fallen comrades and knowing that perhaps you could have done something to save them. Or worse that you did nothing. I had killed more men than I cared to count. Most I had killed, to save others, that would never know. I had also killed men, to save my friends and to protect myself. I knew that these rogue SAS men, would have killed me the moment they found out I was not John'O.

"Andy?"

"Roger Lachie, I am OK."

"There are three more men coming out of the door and they look to have machine guns in their hands. Stay low Andy while we neutralise the threat." Abdalla said

I moved up to the front of the hollow and kept myself hidden behind the dead soldier. I saw one man fall before I realised that Abdalla must have used Han's Desert Eagle. The boom of his hand canon was unmistakeable. Another man fell to a silenced round from the AS50. The third man decided that discretion would be the better part of valour. He would have made it back to the door were it not for Lachie who fired a second round off within a second and he shot the man in the centre of his back. Three shots three men down. The door to the Bunker closed. I started to move backwards, dragging the wounded SAS man with me by holding onto his webbing straps.

It is remarkably hard thing to do, to pull a dead weight along the ground. It would have been easier for me to throw the man over my shoulder, and run with him, than it was proving to drag his sorry ass dead weight. That said, were I to pick him up and throw him over my shoulder, there would be a really good chance of me catching a round in the back, from those ensconced in the bunker. It was slow going but eventually I got to the fence line. I dragged him down into a ditch at the side of a field next to the edge of RAF Daws Hill. I removed the borrowed in ear transmitter and put it in my pocket.

"Lachie can you go snag one of the Vans that the SAS guys had, and bring it somewhere near my position?"

"Roger will do" Lachie replied in my one remaining earpiece

"Abdalla, stay where you are unless you want to move to the wooded area to your left?"

"OK Andy, moving back to the treeline now."

I waited in the ditch with my injured and unconscious prisoner. I checked his pulse. It was good if a little weak. But that would pick up when I got a saline and dextrose drip into him. He would live for now. I took a blast dressing from my pouch and a small tube of clotting gel. This was an anti haemorrhagic compound that effectively stopped massive blood loss, until a patient could be cared for in hospital. I squeezed some gel in the front and rolled him over and repeated the same process on the exit wound, then strapped on a blast bandage and tied it under his limp and useless arm. He started to come around. I took out one of my Sig's from where I had replaced them, in my shoulder holsters. His mind was still fogged with the pain and the massive dump of adrenalin. He groaned and swore. I could relate to that getting shot really fucking hurts. And the wound that I had inflicted upon him was the worst sort, well apart from being killed I suppose. A bullet wound that involves a bone injury hurts, but the ones that involves major bone joints, they tell me make you just want to die.

"Who the fuck are you?" he asked through gritted teeth

"Now that is the wrong question. Well being asked the wrong way around. The question is, who the fuck are you? Apart from being a member of the SAS. But no matter we will get to all that later. First we have to get you patched up, you are of no use to me dead." I could hear something coming over the field. I kept my Sig Sauer pointed at my new best friend. Who, I would be keeping alive at all costs. He was the key to unlocking whatever was going on. There was a Ford Transit

Van bouncing its way across the ruts of the farmers field. It swerved to a stop next to me. Lachie jumped out and down into the ditch with me. Between the two of us we lifted the soldier out of the ditch and threw him bodily, into the back of the van, I got in behind him and Lachie slammed the door closed. Then he got in the front and put it into a low gear and bounced us all the way to the other side of the field and back on to the tarmacadam road. Our prisoner was now once more out cold, no doubt from the pain of being thrown around.

Lachie drove down towards the wooded area to the opposite side of the entrance to Daws Hill. He slowed to a stop and the back door was opened. Hans and Abdalla both jumped in and we set off down the road. We would have to get under cover and then we would have to get Carl to come and collect us. For now I needed to catch my breath as my own adrenal gland dump was telling me.

I knew that technically I was no longer a medic, I was a hired gun for SIS, even if this time I had not been asked directly by SIS. We were doing this to rescue 'The Suit' because he was a Team Member and like the SAS, we never leave one of our own behind, dead or alive.

ACT 11

Lachie found a disused barn, down a side track and pulled the van into it and out of sight. I treated the wound on the man's shoulder as best I could but I would need somewhere a bit more sterile if I were to be successful, not that I really cared that much about him. He would have killed me, given half a chance. More fool him for falling for my little ploy. I really wanted some answers, but it would have to wait until after we got out the hell out of here.

"Hans we need to get Carl, but we are going to have to use a different location than Halton. Then we are going to have to make a switch somewhere along the line. Oran can backtrack satellites but I don't know if he can take control of their satellite and manage to make us disappear."

"Andy you would be surprised by what Oran can do. given access to them. I will make a quick call to my boss in NATO."

"See Andy even Hans has a boss!" Lachie said

Hans left the van and was talking on his satellite phone. Initially he seemed to be angry then he seemed resigned. He disconnected his call and then made another call, before returning to the van.

"Well?" I asked

"My boss, has said categorically no, to us having permission to access any of the UK satellites."

"Fuck, that will make things difficult for us getting out of here then."

"Oran though has told me that he can access it and actually make it look like it was accessed by SAS Command, He will switch it off and delete any video of us either arriving at or leaving Daws Hill. They will not be able to back track to here from Daws Hill. I have arranged for the loan of a helicopter from the Danish Air Force who are on exercise here in the UK at the moment. They are far more loyal to the Icelandic Defence force, than they are to the UK or for that matter to NATO. They are also going to send one of their buses, to collect us. They will be here in about 20 minutes. Carl is on his way to them at the moment."

"That sounds perfect Hans, but where are we going when the bus gets here?"

"RAF Strike Command at RAF High Wycombe."

"Talk about hiding in plain sight. How do we explain this fella here?" Lachie said pointing over his shoulder with his thumb. "Simple its a Danish training exercise, just the same as the British Military TACEVAL or Tactical Evaluation." Hans replied

"So where are we going to debrief this fella?" I asked

"Somewhere far away from here, and from High Wycombe for that matter" Hans said.

I filled a syringe of Morphine and injected it into the wounded SAS Man. I wanted him quiet for now. He could make as much noise as he wanted later. We sat around making small talk for about another 15 minutes. A plain grey coach pulled up at the end of the lane. Hans ran up and quickly directed the bus down to the barn. We loaded our equipment and our prisoner into the bus. Then set off for High Wycombe. The journey went without incident. At the gate to RAF Strike Command. The Gate Guard looked at the temporary pass that the driver of the Bus showed and then waved him through without checking the floor of the bus where we were all laid down. We were taken around the back of the Station Headquarters and then to the far side of a waiting helicopter. The doors to the chopper were open and Carl was standing there waiting. We were loaded up in under two minutes. Hans said something to the Danish serviceman, who nodded and then fired a smart salute, they then left in the bus. The rotors were turning as I pulled the side door closed. I sat back and let the tension ease away from me. Lachie had zip tied the prisoners legs to a metal buckle on the side of his webbing seat. The Plan was to first get to a secure location and then for Carl to return the Danish helicopter. After that he would go and collect our chopper. Even I did not know where the secure location, that Hans had chosen for us, not even when we landed. What I did know though, was, that it was bloody cold. Summer was waning and wherever we were, we were close to the sea. I could smell the sea air, I could hear the waves, I could even hear the call of the seagulls. We decamped from the chopper with all of our stuff and a backpack of stuff that Carl had brought for us. He shook hands with his uncle and closed the door to the chopper, to presumably return the way he had come.

"OK I give in Hans, where are we?"

"Why you are in Scotland of course." Hans replied

"I think he wants you to be a little more specific Hans." Lachie said as he re-zip tied the prisoners feet after he had cut them loose when we left the chopper. The man was starting to come around.

"We are are on a small and temporarily uninhabited Island on the West Coast of Scotland, in the South Hebrides."

"Right, well, I am so happy that we have narrowed it down to two or three rocks on the edge of the Atlantic Ocean"

"OK Andy because it is night time I will tell you where we are. We are on the Island of Mingulay. I had heard of this Island but had never been here. I was told that the fishing was particularity good here. I knew from my Scottish geography that it was part of the Bishop's Isles, in the Outer Hebrides of Scotland. It was also one of those places that you don't want to walk the cliffs at night, as they were amongst the highest cliffs in Scotland. Hans pulled a map from his backpack. Then a penlight torch. He laid the map on the ground, holding the penlight torch in one hand and the map down with the other. We are here, he said pointing to an area near the Eastern coast of the Island.

"We need to be down there" he said pointing to the coast then continued

"Its not far, about two or three hundred yards is all, then you will know why I chose this Island." He folded the map up and then we split the guns and backpacks between Lachie and myself. Abdalla and Hans half dragged half carried the prisoner down to the area, Hans had indicated. I knew we were next to the sea, by the sound of the waves, the sound had reduced to just a gentle lapping. I soon found out why as we stepped down onto a beach of soft sand.

"The Island is off limits to the public at the moment, due to foot and mouth, at least that is what it will say on the news tomorrow, This will stop the people that wish to come and view the Islands wildlife. The Island is ours for two or three days. So can you make this man fit to talk to us Andy?"

"I think it will be better to put a drip up first and get some fluids into him and then tomorrow he will understand his situation a bit better I think."

"OK Andy you know best. Fix him up. We will all take turns at guarding him, not that there is anywhere for him to run to. Just don't want him cutting our throats in the night while we sleep."

After I had set our patient up with his fluids and pain meds, I went for a walk around the immediate area. We were in a horseshoe shaped bay, that was filled with a beautiful soft sand. Had we not known, that we were in Scotland, you would have thought we were on a tropical island, apart from the fact it was cold that is. Even by the moonlight I could see that the sand extended out quite a way under the crystal clear water. I also knew that the water would be cold and nothing like the waters in the Caribbean. I almost took off my Goretex boots to paddle in the water. I thought better of it and headed back up from the beach to the grassy mounds that formed a border around the cove. I could see shapes that were definitely man made in origin. Like many of the smaller Islands around the coast of Scotland they had long since become uninhabited, and nature at reclaimed what man had built. There would once have been a thriving village community on this Island. The would have made a living from fishing and basic food crops like potatoes and perhaps a few green vegetable. There would have been sheep and possibly a milk cow or two, if not a cow they would have milked the ewes and made cheese. The cliffs around the coast of this island would have been filled with nesting birds and Sea Gulls eggs would have been gathered as a luxury. By today's standards a poor existence but by the standards of two hundred years ago, it would have been a good, but work filled living. Nothing would have been wasted. Rocks would have been gathered to build basic 'But-n-bens' a two room house that a whole family would have lived in. One room would be a Kitchen, scullery come living area and the other part, which may or may not have been separated by a wall, but more often than not it would have been a blanket of some kind. hung from string or wool. Sometimes when the weather was particularly rough they may even have shared the home with their animals. The roofs would be made from turf cut from the land. Peat would be cut for the fire. Any driftwood that came upon the shore would be far too valuable a thing to be burned, it would be used in construction of roofs, or formed into tools, or even into fencing.

Now all that remained, were the foundations stones. There were no walls high enough to hold a roof, from what I could see there was very little around here, that could be classed as a shelter, should the weather suddenly change. I walked back to where the others were. Abdalla had set up a small firepit and was heating up some field rations.

"Coffee?" Lachie offered me a tin cup of steamy black caffeine infused liquid. He followed that up by tossing me an energy bar which I caught in my left hand while holding the tin cup in my right.

"Mr Andy you should play cricket."

"Never could abide that game Abdalla, I was always more of a rugby type of person, all that tea and sandwiches never did it for me."

"What he means Abdalla, is he was more a cold beer and a meat pie sort of person."

"When do you suppose we will be able to talk to him?" Hans asked pointing to the man who was now wrapped up in a thermal blanket and our Jackets over the top of him.

"Well assuming that he has not yet developed a major infection, he should be able to answer questions by daylight. But a lot depends also on how far you want to question him."

Not a lot more was said and we took turns at sleeping and then Abdalla made breakfast of Coffee and Energy bars. I suppose it would be the same for lunch and dinner. Still it made us appreciate Rosemary, so much more.

The man was awake and watching us all closely. He had said nothing even when Abdalla had given him a coffee. I noticed he never gave him an energy bar to go with it. I knew that soon, things would not be friendly. I also knew that I would not interfere in anything, that would take place. He was part of the team, that had something to do with the death, of all the people at the farmhouse. He was part of the team that had kidnapped our friend. One way or another, he would tell us at least some, of what was going on. He might even tell us the extent of what he knew. I knew he would not survive the day. It was not like we could let him go, but at this point, he did not know that. As soon as he did know, he would tell us nothing more. I hated torture, I hated to hear a man beg and scream and offer anything just to make the pain stop. I also knew how to make the pain last and how to switch off the parts of the brain, that would cause the body to go into shutdown mode. I had used those methods before. I had injected Adrenalin into a man we had previously interrogated on the last mission. What would I be willing to do, in order to protect any member of Team Seven? I would do the same as they would do for me, anything!

The sun had risen, on the far side of the island and it was just starting to meet the edge of the hill behind us. Time for questions. I hoped that we could get the information we required without having to be overly barbaric.

Hundreds of years previous to our landing on this tiny Island, it had been invaded by the Irish, along with the Vikings. They had combined forces in order to steal more of everything, be it land, goods or even the women. Strangely they had a moral code amongst themselves. Even though they were guilty of the act of theft from peoples of other lands, they would never steal from each other. That was considered to be the lowest crime of all, for in order to steal you first had to deceive. That sat along with the dishonesty of a lie. You could kill a man and then admit to it, in order to accept your punishment, in an honourable way, But to lie about it, then you would be cast out. An outcast was then fair game, for anyone to kill with impunity, for it was not considered to be murder, if you were to do away with an outcast. You were merely cleansing the land. So the question now, would this man, who was now our prisoner, admit to his wrong doings and tell us why and where 'The Suit' and his family were?

"Its time." I said to the man, and also loud enough for the others to hear.

"What for?" The man said

"Answers" Lachie replied

"To what?" The man said as his eyes were darting to and from, each of us.

"Why questions of course" Hans Said

"I only have to give my name, rank and serial number. I am Mark Colish, I am a Sergeant in the Special Air Service service number is 5762213."

"Wow that's nice, what do you think Andy?" Lachie asked

"Not a lot, what about you Abdalla? Do you think that will suffice?"

"Mr Andy, no I do not think it will suffice. Am I correct in thinking that you would prefer me to conduct the interrogation? Or would you prefer to do this yourself?"

"No Abdalla, I think that because this concerns a member of our own team and a friends to all of us. I think this should be a joint venture." I replied

The SAS man's eyes continued darting from one of us to another, backwards and forwards as the conversation was going on. He was pretending to be nonchalant but I knew it was just bravado. I had seen men like him over the past few years, in the missions that we were involved in.

I remembered a man who was ex Israeli Shayetet 13. They were supposed to be able to die without passing any secret. I had seen one of their guys, beg for his life after we keelhauled him. So I knew that the man, we had here, he would give up the secrets that he held. The question was, how long would it take? And how much pain could he stand?

"Abdalla, I should like to start and if it is OK by the rest of you guys we can take turns?"

This was partly to let the others know that I would not expect them to do all the work and partly to install a sense of fear and foreboding into our prisoner.

"So now we have done the easy part Mark. Now lets get some more information. If you are SAS? Why did you turn on your brothers and murder them? I was under the impression, that the SAS, had a code of honour. You never leave a man behind and will die trying to protect that honour?" I said

No answer was forthcoming just a blank stare.

"Lachie can you please zip tie his hands behind his back. And then hog tie him to his ankles." I said. I knew that just tying his hands together behind his back would cause him immense pain and discomfort to his wounded shoulder.

Lachie stood up and started to move towards the man, who suddenly found his voice.

"So are you so chicken shit that you cant take me one on one, even with this bullet wound in my shoulder?"

"No, I know I could take you, with that bullet wound in your shoulder, after all I was the one that did it to you. I am sure you would try to put me down if I gave you a chance. The thing is though, you see this is not what you could call a fair fight for you. There will be no Queensbury rules here for you, it will be a very unfair and one sided affair. Now I know you SAS guys do all that anti-intergeneration shit and can hold out to sleep deprivation and the lights in the eye stuff. But we are not going to be that nice. In fact, first there will be pain, then there will be questions. Now I am going to inject you with some Adrenaline. Initially it will make your heart race, but what I am really going to use it for, is to stop you passing out, when the pain becomes to much for the body to bear. Then I am going to inflict some serious damage to your body and then I will ask you some questions. Are you following me so far?"

"Fuck You!!"

"Mr Andy it always amazes me. The English language is one of the most effective and descriptive languages in the modern world and it has gone from 'Yes, I understand the ramifications, of me telling you lies and the punishments, that you have set out for me, should I not comply' to 'Fuck You' in a single statement."

"Indeed Abdalla, I will let you educate him, when it is your turn to ask him questions. I am sure by then, he will have learned some manners and be a bit more polite. Now back to you Mark. Are you ready?" I said and shifted my gaze back to him.

I was still unsure, what I was going to do to him, but I knew it had to be really painful. In order for the questions that would come after, to have an effect. The man was looking just a tad less confident, as Lachie had him trussed up like a Christmas turkey. Due to being hog tied he was now forced to lie on his uninjured side. I could see even though I had put coagulant, into the shoulder wound, it was now seeping blood through the bandage. I walked over to where my medical bag was and took out a syringe and made a big deal of loading it up with the Adrenaline. I removed the dextrose drip and put the syringe into the cannula on the back of the man's hand. I injected him and watched his pupils. as they first became small and then massively enlarged, before retuning to a relative normal. Then I waited for the tell tale sweat on his forehead.

"Ready?" I asked. He said nothing.

I bent down and none to gently, removed the bandage from his shoulder. Then scooped out some of the Xstat until I could see deep into the wound from the front, then I repeated the process from the back.

"You know when I shot you, apart from the obvious things like mangled flesh, muscle and bone but it also mashed up a lot of nerve endings and it is those that will really cause you some severe discomfort." I removed my Bussé knife from the back of my belt. I made sure that he saw it. I pushed it into the wound from the front looking for the brachial nerves that run just under where the ball joint used to be located. I watched his face for that electric shock moment, that would tell me, I had found the nerve endings that were already broken and inflamed. The damage was such, that were he to live, he would never have totally recovered from the wound. The sudden jerking, told me that the tip of my knife had found the thin line I had been seeking. He tried but he could not stifle a scream. I did not have to move the knife much, just tiny movements were enough to elicit shrieks of pain now. I kept this up for about five minutes. Was I evil? No more so than they had been, when they had murdered their team mates and innocent women and children. I would not go to heaven that much was for sure. He puked up and I had to make sure he did not choke to death, at least before he gave up some answers. I removed the knife and wiped it on his trouser leg before putting it into its sheath at my back.

"Now that was fun wasn't it?"

"You Fucking Bastard!"

"Who me? No mate I know my father and he is safe. Although I am sure, if it were up to you and your buddies, that would be different.

So now you have had a taste of the pain, you will know that we are not hear for laughs, nor will we hold back, in any way, to get at the truth. So lets start again. Why did you kill the rest of the SAS protection squad along with the civilians."

He looked up at me, with eyes that showed hatred and defiance but made no reply."

"OK Mark, are you sure you want to go down this road?" I asked

Still no reply. I rolled him over so that the exit wound of the bullet I had fired at him had made. The one thing I always carried with me in a small pouch was table salt. I had found it improved the taste of field rations. I took the small vial and opened it, then poured the contents into the wound at his back. He let out a guttural howl. The salt would continue to work its way through the wound for some time, before the pain would subdue. I took no pleasure in what I was doing to a fellow human, but I would do anything to save a team member and if that meant I would be as barbaric as the other side, had been and perhaps even worse, then that is what I would be.

I walked back over to a rock and sat down while the soldier cried. There was no way I could make the pain stop immediately. So I left him continue to writhe in pain, He banged his head up and down on the ground below. He would have kicked and bucked had his legs been free to do so. They just pulled uselessly against the binding of his wrists, which were beginning to show signs of distress to the skin, which was being torn by the plastic bindings. I looked away and over the ocean towards mainland Scotland. The man's screams would not carry that far. He called upon the Sweet Mother of God and Jesus, he called me a Bastard, a Cunt, a Fucker and other things that I could not quite grasp due to his sobs of pain. I threw the remains of my coffee on the ground.

"Why?" I asked him

No reply.

"Well in that case I guess I cant help you. Lachie your up."

I went and sat down on a grass covered rock, that could once have been part of a house or stock pen. Lachie walked up to the where the man lay and planted his foot heavily on the soldiers shoulder. This elicited a loud scream. Lachie rolled him on to his back so that the man's hands were behind his back and he feet together on the ground with his knees in the air. Lachie looked around and then went a picked up a grapefruit sized rock. He hefted it in his hands as he walked back towards the prisoner. Tossing the rock from hand to hand. Then suddenly lifted it high in the air and without any warning brought is crashing down onto the left kneecap of the soldier. Once more he screamed and then he puked up a little bile. It looked like he was going to faint so I went over and administered a little more adrenaline as well as breaking an ammonia capsule under his nose forcing him back to his pain.

"What about now" I asked

"What do you mean?" he replied

"Why did you kill your team members?"

Lachie walked back over to the man and squeezed the shattered knee cap, causing the man to cry out.

"Stop please stop."

"Then answer the fucking question" Lachie said

"It was an order. I was just following orders." he said

"Who's Orders?" I asked

"I don't know it was just orders?"

"You must have known, who gave you the orders?"

"The team leader."

"Who is that?"

"Mickey"

"Who gave him the order?"

"I don't know, honest I don't."

"How did you get them, to go to their deaths?"

"We told them it was an emergency and that they, the family that is, were in danger from a hit squad."

"Carry on"

"Well that is pretty much it, they all got on the bus and we got in our cars and made it a convoy. Two of us in a car in front and the same behind. The family and all the domestic staff were in the bus. We took them to Daws Hill and then there was a gas released into the bus that knocked them all out. Sir Philip and his family were removed from the bus and handed over to our the team at Daws Hill. Then we attached a hose, to the bus's exhaust and fed that into the bus. And that is how they died in their sleep. Honest they felt no pain at all. They just went to sleep with the original gas and then the exhaust fumes killed them."

"And that makes it OK?" I asked

"It was orders I was just following orders, that's what soldiers do."

"What happened to Sir Philip and his family?"

"I don't know, we just handed them over to the crew at Daws Hill and then we were told to stand down, but later we were called back. We were ordered to make it look like an attack on the home and shoot up the bodies. Then the next day we were told that there was a team from NATO, going to come and investigate."

"What about the woman and the boy?"

"They were targets selected by Mickey from Ireland and from Wales. They were kidnapped and then given the same treatment as the others. They were fairly close to the looks of Sir Philips, wife and son."

"What happened next?"

"We took them to the home and made it look like a murder scene. Then we contacted the police anonymously using a burner phone that would show we were near Sir Philips home, and said we heard screams and shooting. Then we destroyed the sim card and phone. Only after we had done that, we could not get the bus started. By the time we got it started, we only just made it out from Sir Philips home. A police car responding almost ran into us as we were leaving. SIS took over the investigation and it was then, they ordered us to follow you and your team. We were also ordered by Mickey to make sure the Police Officer could not give any kind of evidence. So we crashed a truck into him. I guess he is dead by now."

That last comment got him a swift and almighty kick in his side from the size 11 boot, that belonged to the powerful right leg of Lachie. It was some time before he could continue speaking.

"Keep talking if you know what's good for you?"

"Well that is pretty much it. You know where the rest of the team is."

"Do you believe him?" I asked jointly of Lachie, Hans and Abdalla.

The only answer came from the deep bass voice of Abdalla.

"Mr Andy, I do not think he has told us every thing that he knows about what is happening. He was inside the bunker at RAF Daws Hill.

Therefore he must know more than we do. Would you like me to ask him some questions?"

"Abdalla you know, that we know and trust each others judgement and I trust yours, as I have done, many times before. Your judgement has saved our lives on numerous occasions before. So please continue."

Abdalla walked over to where the bloodied and bruised man lay on the ground, in the fetal position. With a single hand Abdalla picked the man up off the ground and replaced him on a rock. So that he was almost in the sitting position. Then he drew his knife and cut the binding that held the cable ties on his ankles and wrists. It was like watching an elastic band taking shape after being released. He fell off the rock but at least this time his legs were out in front of him rather than tucked up behind him. If the prisoner thought that this was a matter of hospitality, then he was sadly mistaken. I had seen Abdalla use his skills as an interrogator a number of times previously. He was precise and methodical in this, as he was in everything else in his life. Deftly he ran the blade of his knife up the front of the soldiers jacket and shirt. Then he pealed it back like the skin of a banana. It revealed a well tanned and fit body, well with the exception of the big hole in his shoulder. There was a large tattoo of some Celtic design. Next he sliced up each trouser leg and removed the underwear the trousers completely from the man. He sliced the shirt off the man who now apart from his boots was completely naked on the ground.

"Mr Andy, Mr Hans and Mr Lachie. Would you be so kind to help me with this man to the shore. I fear that he might injure himself If I were to do this alone."

Between the four of us we now grabbed the naked man and carried him down the beach and laid him down next to the waters edge. I was sure there must have been a reason for Abdalla asking for our help, other than the fear of the man being injured. So we waited to see what was going to happen. Abdalla removed his own shirt to reveal his tribal markings that matched those on his face and upper arms. All, bar one of them, looked masculine and authentic African tribal marks. One though was the result of an explosion and that had left a long scar down the right hand side of his face. In a way this detracted only slightly from his natural masculinity. His powerful and muscular body now loomed over the man below him. Abdalla stood astride the now naked man and pointed his knife towards the soldier.

"Today you get the chance to go from childhood to becoming a real man who can walk with the tribal elders." The man lay there and said nothing. His lips were closed tightly together in defiance. Abdalla leaned forward over the man, he put the tip of the blade just under the right eye. The man stayed perfectly still. Abdalla increased the pressure ever so slightly and a single drop of blood formed at the tip of the blade, and then that drop rose up and lost its balance to run down the cheek of the soldiers face. Abdalla pulled the knife down so that it had created a one inch cut the ran perpendicular on the face. Then he moved to the left eye and repeated the same process. Still the man did not move. When Abdalla had made a dozen or so cuts to the face he stood upright and looked back down at the bloodied face below him. Abdalla looked a little disappointed and yet a little impressed, by the man who had not even cried out, as the cuts were being made. Although that said, they were made with a razor sharp edge that would not have inflicted a great deal of pain. Probably not much more than a Bee sting. Torture is only useful if you get information in return. The threat of more cuts had not brought forth any more information, that left just one recourse, although the man's fate had already been sealed the moment he had pulled the metaphorical trigger on his teammates.

The one thing that gave us the edge over him was we knew the outcome. Hans came down to the beach and took over from Abdalla. The thing about waterboarding is you might know that your torturers will not kill you, but your body is always in denial of that fact. I knew it was going to be the next move, especially when Hans went up and came back down to the waters edge carrying what was left of the soldiers shirt.

"You are a brave soldier, and you are to be commended for holding out for so long. You can save yourself a lot of anguish just by answering our questions." Hans said as he tied the sleeves of the shirt around the man's neck and then took the back of the shirt and pulled it down over the face of the man and tucked it into the sleeves around the mans neck. Then he took a couple of handfuls of sea water and dribbled it over the cloth of the shirt back. The result was almost instantaneous.

The soldier kept turning his head from side to side to avoid the flow of water that was dripping down from above.

"Last chance"

Nothing. Hans grabbed the man by his boots and dragged him just far enough into the water so that the occasional wave would roll over his face.

"Names?" Hans shouted at him

Still nothing. Hans dragged him deeper into the sea so that his head spent the majority of time under water. There were garbled sounds. Hans dragged him so that he was totally submerged with his hands still bound behind his back and his ankles tied together. Hans let go of the man's feet. Not a lot happened to begin with then the bound man with the shirt over his face started to panic. Once that kind of panic sets in, there is nothing short of removing the danger, that will stop it.

People talk about being in a blind panic. The vast majority of whom, have not got a clue as to what real blind panic is. The sheer terror it brings to its victim. There is no precise definition for the term Blind Panic. However it is widely presumed by psychologists that it is a protection mode, set in place by the brain, when it does not wish to face up to, some evil that it sees as a threat to its continued existence. For the first time, the soldier feared that he would not be walking away from this. Being shot had not frightened him, it had hurt him physically but his mind had stayed focused. Now he could not focus, the real fear was blocking all the sensible things like, 'they wont kill me they have to follow rules........ They are part of NATO.'

His mind was saying ...... 'they are going to let you die this time?'...... 'can I save myself?'..... 'Will they believe what I tell them?'...... 'Can I get away with a lie and buy myself some time?'...... 'No they wont believe me!'..... 'Will they believe the truth?'...... 'I don't know'....... 'Quick hurry'..... 'I cant breathe'...... 'I can feel the water in my lungs.'

"HELP ME!!!!"

He had not realised that he had said the last two words out loud. Hans let him lie in the waves for a bit longer and then he reached down and lifted his head out of the water.

"NAMES." Hans shouted at him.

Then without letting the man answer he dropped him back down under the waves. This time he put his boot on the man's chest. With the shirt over his eyes the man could see nothing all he could feel was that every time he tried to breathe his lungs were filling with salt water. His mind was screaming to him 'GIVE IN'....... 'its your only chance'........ 'PLEASE DON'T LET ME DIE'...... 'I don't want to die this way'....... 'Why am I afraid?'...... 'I don't know but I am really fucking scared'......

"I GIVE IN"

Again he was not aware he had screamed through the waves. Hans lifted his head out of the water again.

"NAMES?"

This time Hans let him cough up the salt water and puke all over the inside of the shirt that still covered his face. After about three minutes Hans asked again.

"Names?"

"John Stevens" the man coughed out.

"Who else?"

"I don't know."

Hans looked each one of us in turn and got a single nod from all. Then he dropped the man back down into the ocean and let the outgoing tide do its work. We regrouped back up on the grassy area to the top of the beach.

ACT 12

"What now?" Hans asked

"I say we go into Daws Hill and clean it up and then we go look for John Stevens." I replied.

I knew Carl would be along at some point to collect us. We made use of the time by heating up some field rations and then catching forty winks. Lachie had already made himself comfortable against a small hummock. The air was beginning to chill a bit and I could see big white-caps way out to sea. The sea around the Island was calm enough at the moment but from experience, I knew that the seas around the Scottish coastal Islands, can change almost as rapidly as they can go to calm. From the North the sky was also darkening rapidly. It might just be a small squall or just as easily it could be a serious storm. In and around the Highlands and Islands of Scotland there is no hard demarcation between the seasons. Winter can be October to April or just December. Summer can go from March to October or not really exist at all. Most folks living in the UK, forget they are actually on just a rock, stuck out in the North Sea, so our climate is more changeable than say North America or even the biggest island, Australia. These large chunks of land, have a more set climate, rather than the almost daily changeable, weather patterns that the UK sees. I made myself a coffee and took another, over and gave it to Abdalla, as I sat down next to him.

"Mr Andy, do you have a plan, for when we get back to RAF Daws Hill?"

"As always Abdalla, I will just wing it. I don't have the luxury of a plan yet. But I guess we will have to find a way in and take care of things there. Hopefully there will be some clue as to where 'The Suit' and his family are."

"Mr Andy, you were worried about the death of that man just now? You know they would have killed all of us and probably tortured us to find our base and then they would go and wipe out every one on the Rig, that even knew about Sir Philip. I am sure that SIS have been trying to find us. Which is why we have to act first and we have to be definitive in our actions."

"You told me a long time ago that I would see all the faces of the people that we were involved in the death of, and I do see them all in my dreams."

"Mr Andy, I believe I also told you that the ones that would haunt you the most, would be those of your fallen comrades and that they would never leave you. So we have to make sure that we strike first and always strike hard. Until now, we never chose the battles that we have faced. This time we have to either save a comrade or avenge the death of him. This is just our destiny. I know its is not the destiny you chose, but nonetheless it remains yours. I know you struggle with the way, we sometimes have to do things. It is one of your greatest attributes. You become the conscience for the rest of us. Think of our team as a big tool chest. You are the Micrometre device. All of the rest of us are the big functional tools like hammers and wrenches. Each of us are part of a full tool kit."

I was not sure I agreed with Abdalla's liking us to just tools in a box, but I got where he was going with it. I thanked Abdalla and lay back on the cool ground and awaited the arrival of Karl. I had rested I guess until my body had recharged itself. I sat up and looked around. Lachie was still snoring, Abdalla was laid back on the grass with his eyes closed. I knew from the past though, whilst he might look asleep, there was a pretty good chance of you getting hurt if you tried to sneak up on him on the assumption that he was oblivious of your presence. Hans had made a small fire inside a stone firepit he had constructed with some rocks from the now broken buildings. He was boiling up a mess-tin of black coffee. It did not really matter if we were in the field or back on the Catherine May or even the Rig, we pretty much survived on black coffee, sometimes with a splash of Irish Whisky poured in for good measure, this though, was not one of those times.

We had not taken much in the way of rations as this was a short stop that we had planned, so it was just coffee and energy bars. I stood up and stretched my muscles. The sky was now completely different that it had been a few hours ago. There was no doubt about it now, we were in for a beast of a storm. There was a sea-foam, forming on the beach below. The sky had turned an ugly dark grey. The wind was starting to rise. It was not so much as a cold wind but it was becoming powerful enough, that when we moved up from the hollow, we were camped in. You would have to stoop into the face of the wind. I guessed the wind was starting to gust at about thirty miles to forty miles an hour. Knowing the highlands and islands as I did, I knew that we would have to get of this Island soon, as the weather was closing in fast. I squatted down next to Hans and took the mug of coffee that he offered me.

"What time do you think Karl will get here?"

"A lot depends on that" Hans said, pointing with his cup towards the impending weather front.

"Yeah I saw that, I think it will be here in about two hours. I really would like to be gone from this rock before it gets here."

"Karl will have to have flown a criss cross flight, so as not to be followed, he will have switched aircraft a few times, as well in an effort to confuse anyone, who did manage to track any part of his journey."

"Hans see if you can get him on the Storno."

I stood up and walked towards the shore where only hours before I had witnessed the death of a SAS Soldier. He had known he was following illegal commands. Yet he had continued to follow them. I did not know if it was for extra money, or out of a sense of loyalty to another. Either way his game was run. I don't know if I was looking out at the sea, searching for his body or looking to see if I could see Karl coming for us. Neither were anywhere in sight. I looked towards the mainland of Scotland which had just visible this morning, but now was nowhere to be seen. The rain from the dark great clouds were moving towards us and I heard the first roll, of a distant thunder storm. The sea had changed from bright blue to almost black in colour. The sky at this time of day should have been light, was now more like the dead of night. The waves I could hear crashing to the rocks on either side of the beach that we were camped next to. The rollers that had been far out in the deep waters of the sea, were now pounding onto the shore of the Western Isles.

This storm was coming down from the North. It was, what the old sea farer's would have called 'A Rammage, Blashie and a Blufferet.' These were descriptive words of the old west coast folks, that made a living by the sea. These old words sounded right, I could see the tall grasses being bent level at the edge of the sandy shore the top layer of sand was now being driven with a forceful wind and where it met the rise of the beach as it met with the edge of the grass it was whipped up into the air to be forced back inland in painful blasts. The sea foam followed it up and was now clinging to anything that would give it shelter from the wind. I walked back down to the relative shelter of the hollow where we were camped. Camped was probably an overly poetic word, we had no shelter nor did we have the accoutrements that you would associate with camping.

"Any joy?"

"Nothing and I don't think he will be able to fly in this weather. I suppose he could, if we still had the HIND-Mi24 but we only have a couple of small birds and the big Sea King. Even it is limited in its ability to fly in high winds. I will try the Satellite phone and see if I can contact Oran. Perhaps he can get hold of Karl, without giving out his position."

"Well Hans, if anyone can, then I am sure Oran can do it." I said as I finished my now cold coffee.

Abdalla was stirring, so I poured him a coffee and passed it to him.

"Mr Andy, I do not think, I like your weather. One day sunny and warm the next day cold and wet." He said as he wiped the driven rain and sea spray from his face.

Lachie had merely rolled over and turned his back towards the impending weather front. A bright flash of light followed some seven seconds later by a huge roll of thunder, told me the storm was fast moving. I did not know the lay of the land on this rock, so it was probably best if we stay in the semi shelter, of our dip, in this forlorn landscape. I had seen fast moving storms before, though they were mainly in the Caribbean, these could be furious and deadly hurricanes with winds of 200 miles and hour. Hurricanes do hit the UK from time to time, but we do not have a season for them. It was not hours before the force of the storm intensified. It was more like forty minutes.

Even Lachie had given up on any attempt at sleep. The four of us were huddled around Han's small firepit, which was threatening to go out at any moment. I shouted over to Hans.

"Did you get Oran?"

"Yes and no"

"I don't understand Hans?"

"I did get through to him Andy, but the weather is making it difficult, for a two way conversation. From what I heard, he said Karl is grounded, apparently this is just the front of a massive storm. Heading down from the Arctic. It seems to be mainly down the west but is also causing problems on the east of Scotland. He said we are to stay where we are and not to move. Oran has located us from our Sat Phone. So for now we are stuck here."

"Thanks Hans." I shouted back at him over the howling wind and constant rolls of thunder.

Even the sound of the waves smashing against the cliffs of this little Island threatened to deafen us. Over the next hour the weather grew continually worse, the wind was howling like a banshee. We had given up on small talk because it was so difficult to actually hear what was being said. It was not below freezing, but we were soaked to the skin and the wind-chill was in danger of making us hypothermic. The fire had died almost thirty minutes ago, so there was not even any warmth, to be had from that. The height of the waves threatened to breach the crest of the grass mound, that surrounded the beach. Small stones were now being thrown in the wind, chunks of driftwood that would normally, have lain on the shore. Were now natures munitions, for her wind canon. We huddled together sharing our body warmth such as it was. The thunder storm was overhead now, and there was no delay between the flashes of lightning and the ear splitting booms of thunder, that shook the very ground that we sat on. This was natures battlefield and we were on the losing side.

Mixed in with the sheets of rain and sea spray there were now hailstones some the size of golf balls. Even with our body armour on, we were battered and bruised by these icy bullets. Sometimes the ground would be white with the hailstones, and then the rain would wash them away, until they were replaced by another hail shower and further Thunder and Lightning. The tempestuous storm had been raging for about six hours and did not seem to be showing any signs of letting up. The first symptoms of hypothermia had started to show with Abdalla's chattering teeth. The satellite phone buzzed in Hans's back pack, and we almost missed it. It was just by pure luck, he was reaching in to get an energy bar for Abdalla. Hans pulled the phone close to his ear and cupped his other hand around the mouthpiece. After a few moments he closed the phone and this time he put it in the pocket of his Nomex suit. Then he picked up his backpack and shouldered it.

"We have to go."

"Where to Hans?" I asked

"There" he said pointing down to the beach, which was so covered in sea foam, it did not look like a beach at all. Only when the brown foam, was lifted off the sand, by a gusts of wind, could you identify it as something that resembled a sand covered cove.

"Are you mad Hans? They only place around here with any shelter from the wind at all is this hollow." Lachie shouted about the banshees wailing wind.

"Trust me Lachie, we all need to move down to the middle of the beach, unless you have any plans to stay here, for the next two days. While the storm runs its course." Hans replied.

"OK Hans whatever you say, I trust you." I said and put my own backpack on, then helped Abdalla on with his. The four of us gathered up anything, apart from the fire that had shown we had been on the island and headed out of our dip and into the harsh face of the wind. We held onto each others webbing to make sure we were not thrown back by the wind. The sand picked up by the wind burned our faces as if we were being sandblasted to remove rust or paint. By the time we had finished walking onto the beach, the water was swimming around our boots. Hans took out a laser pen and swept it across the rain filled seascape in front of him.

I looked to where he had pointed the laser and saw nothing but rain and sea. Hans took out his Sat Phone and started to speak then he closed it and put it away again. Then once again he went back to shining his laser, over the waves. I thought I was seeing things to begin with, I saw a bright white light sweeping the sea, before it too was obscured by the rain and waves. Then I saw it again and knew it was not just in my mind. Hans turned his laser pen towards the light and secured a triple flash followed by another and then another.

When it was about 400 yards from the shore I could see it was a bright orange vessel and the light kept flashing is groups of three. It was definitely coming in our direction. When it was about 200 yards out, it looked like some strange shaped tube. Then at 100 yards I knew exactly what it was.

This was one of the two, self righting totally enclosed lifeboats that Stu had bought, to add to his boat the Catherine May. He had then got his friend Gordon, who was a mechanic from Kinbrace, to come down and beef up the engines. He had made them more comfortable by installing better seating with full cross harnesses. Stu had told me shortly after he had bought them. That they were designed to be dropped, from as high as 200 feet, into the water below oil rigs. They were totally enclosed and self righting. They were to be our refuge from the storm.

Looking out to sea just now, I then noticed that the other of the two, he had bought. It was about 50 yards behind. The first of the two boats powered its way onto the beach and came to a sudden stop as there was now insufficient water below it to allow it to move and it was effectively beached. Moments later Stu's head, followed by his body, showed at the back of the beached craft, waving madly for us to go to him. We were waist deep in the swirling water and some of the waves, crashed over us as we finally got to the bright orange rescue vessel. One by one Stu helped us on board and gladly we entered the boat and out of the storm that still raged outside. When Stu had closed the door. I asked him how he was going to get his beached craft off the shore. He just smiled and told us to get strapped in and then he too strapped himself into the coxswains seat.

"OK Rosemary are you ready I have mine set for reverse?" He said into the headset

"Full power now!" he said.

I could feel something tug, at the back of our boat and the power of the engine below me, made our orange tube shake.

"Try again, watch for the waves coming in and time it for the big one" He said, into his headset microphone.

Then he waited for the tug on the back of our boat, as soon as it came, he pushed the throttles all the way to their stops. Our tube shook and then jumped backwards. I felt the back of the boat bite down into the water below. Then we were rolling in the sea.

"Andy can you slip the line that is outside the door"

I got out of my seat opened the door and was greeted by a face-full of north sea. I saw a rope looped over a lug at the rear of the boat and I slipped it off it fell into the boiling sea behind us. Then I got myself back inside and locked the watertight door, then buckled myself into my seat, making sure the straps were tight. I knew this would be a rough ride in this small torpedo shaped lifeboat. Skilfully Stu reversed the boat and turned it back into the waves, with steady use of both the throttle and the small steering wheel in front of him.

"You can haul in now Rosemary. We're clear and heading back now" He shouted into his headset microphone, above the noise of his engine.

We bounced over and under waves for the next forty five minutes. Most of us were good sailors, with the exception of Abdalla, although now, no longer in danger from hypothermia. He was however in danger of reviewing his last meal. Stu powered the engine back, then set them to reverse and then lined us up. Powered us backwards before switching off the engines. I felt our boat move backwards and upwards at a steep angle, then we were gently brought to a level stop. I unstrapped as did the others and the door was opened from the outside by my father. As we climbed out the second of the lifeboats had made its way into the rear hold that had been customised for these two lifeboats. My father, had now gone to open the door on that one. Rosemary came out and smiled at us.

"Who is driving the Catherine May?" I asked Stu

"That would be Petrá."

"Seriously? In this weather?"

"Andy, even Finnbar could skipper the Catherine May. You know its all computer controlled. Anyway enough of that for now. You guys look like you could use a hot shower and a good meal. Get yourself down below and get warmed up."

The next few hours were spent in a continual roller coaster ride. The Catherine May was large for most Scottish Fishing boats, but even she struggled in the maelstrom of the weather outside. Some of the waves threatened to swamp us. Stu said that the computer did all the hard work, but I knew that in a storm of this magnitude, the only person that can keep a ship face into the waves and storm at the same time, is a good skipper. Stu stayed at the controls while the rest of us, held on for dear life. Lachie went to sleep, on his bunk. Abdalla spent considerable time in the sea toilet or clutching a bucket. No one laughed at him, even my sea legs were in danger of collapsing.

After about the first six hours I knew we had made it to the headland of Scotland. I could feel the wind move to the side and even though we were charging forward, most of the time, I knew the waves were hitting us side on. Stu continued his diagonal tack across the north of Scotland. We were just about six hours from home. But we had to cross the Pentland Firth. *An Caol Arcach*, meaning the Orcadian Strait This was an area of sea that every seafarer gave the utmost respect. It separates the Orkney's from Caithness. Not to mention the men from the boys, as far as skippers are concerned. Despite its name, it is not really a firth as that would imply that it is the opening to a river. The Pentland Firth lies between the northern Scottish mainland and the Islands of Orkney and has a well-deserved reputation among the world's mariners as a channel to be navigated with great care. Twice every day the tide surges through the Firth from the Atlantic to the North Sea and back again. The Firth is well known for the strength of its tides, which are among the fastest in the world, a speed of thirty kilometres per hour, that being sixteen nautical miles an hour, being reported close to the West of Pentland Skerries. The force of the tides gives rise to overfalls and tidal races which can occur at different stages of the tide. Some of the principal tidal races are as romantic in name as they are deadly in real life. Like the Swallower or Swelkie. This is a race at the north end of Stroma. Off Swelkie Point is known simply as 'The Swelkie'. It extends from the point in an easterly or westerly direction depending on the tide and can be particularly violent. The whirlpool of the same name was, according to a Viking legend, caused by a sea-witch turning the mill wheels which grinds the salt to keep the seas salty. The name derives from an old Norse term, Svalga meaning "The Swallower". In the past many captains and ship owners, preferred to make long detours north of Orkney, or South by the English Channel to avoid the roosts and eddies in the Firth. Many a fisherman has gone to Davey Jones's locker by way of this tumultuous stretch of water. I took a mug of coffee up to Stu. I could see the strain on his face. He had all the boats spotlights on and the lights inside the wheelhouse switched off. When the rain allowed, I could see the massive waves that Stu was navigating, with a combination of throttle in his right hand and steering with the small wheel held in his left hand. Waves were crashing over the bow and always threatening to drag the Catherine May down. I knew that almost six years ago Rosemary and Stu had spent a large portion of their 'Compensation' from SIS, on upgrading this boats engines and her props as well as realigning her shafts so that they were lower and deeper in the water, to accommodate the custom five bladed bronze props, that were around twice the size of the originals. This gave Stu the ability to give the power where and when he wanted it, without the delay of waiting for enough water to go under her keel. Even so, there were times, I could feel that as we crested a wave, the Catherine's arse was hanging loose so to speak. I could feel and hear her props, were biting into nothing more than the rain and sea spray. All this was driven by the howling gale that drove this bitch of a storm. It was the blackest of black that I had seen a night get. There were no edges to the clouds, nor was there moonlight. This was probably because it was one huge cloud. Day had come and gone without daylight. There was lightning but it did nothing to brighten the sky.

"Hows it going Stu?"

"We are lucky I think."

"Huh? How the hell can this be lucky?"

"If it were winter, we would be icing up and this is not a good stretch of water to be carrying an extra forty tons of upper decking"

"OK yes in that case we are lucky."

ACT 13

Karl had gone to the rig just before the weather had turned, he had given Stu our position. Stu had immediately set a rescue mission in place. Hence we were now safely on our way back home. As soon as the weather permitted we would mount an attack on RAF Dawes Hill and hopefully rescue 'The Suit' and his family. Then we would go after the head of the snake so to speak. Sir Philip's number two. However for now, the first thing I wanted was a hot meal. I could smell the food from the galley, I guess Rosemary must have put some food in the oven before setting out to rescue all of us. I entered the galley Petrá was there having previously relinquished the controls back over to Stu.

"Hello babe" she said with a big smile and then slung her arms around my neck and placed a big wet kiss on my lips.

I put one arm around her waist and pulled her even closer to me.

"I know you are pleased to see me Andy but can we dispense with the weapons" She said, pointing to me to my guns. Then she continued.

"You might want to have a shower too, you stink." and laughingly she pinched her nose. I kissed her back and went off to clean up. My cabin was pretty much the same as any of the others. Basic bed with storage space under and a cubical shower in the corner. After placing my weapons in the storage locker, I stripped off and entered the shower. It was a battle to stay upright in the small cubical but I persevered. The water was hot and with the help of the soap I managed to clean off the waxy camouflage paint and accumulated dirt and grime, from the past couple of days. I rolled around inside the shower cubical, so when I felt clean, rather than turning shower all the way to cold, and stand under the pounding stream of icy water, as I would normally. I got out and towelled dried and then shaved as best I could, dressed in a pair of denims and open neck polo shirt. I went back to the galley where the rest of the team were already tucking into some hot food.

"Coffee Andy?" Rosemary asked.

"Please."

"With or without?"

"I think its a with sort of day." I replied and she poured a good measure of Irish Whisky into the steaming black liquid. Abdalla was looking a bit better, being on a larger boat. That said we must have cleared the Pentland firth as the Catherine May, seemed to be climbing smooth rollers and going steadily back into troughs rather than being thrown about like a leaf in the rapids.

"Mr Andy, do you have a plan for when the weather is better?"

"Abdalla, I never have a real plan, you know they just tend to evolve, mostly with the help of the rest of the team. For now though, I think we should get back to the rig and take things from there. We will see what info, Oran has for us."

Hans entered the galley and sat down, Rosemary put a similar plate of food down to the one I was eating, which basically resembled an all day breakfast. Full of carbs to replace the energy we had spent over the last few days.

"Do you want to take over now Hans? You are the senior officer." I asked him.

He looked up from the table and finished what he had in his mouth, washing it down with his coffee.

"No Andy, I really do think it is best if you run this mission. I know that technically, I as the NATO commander should take the reigns, but once again, I would like you to command. I know that the rest of the team would prefer it as well."

Stu, who had been standing next to the stove, with Rosemary, came and sat down at the table.

"Good job Petrá, well done."

"Thanks Stu, but I think even a monkey could have done it."

"So how long before we get back to the Rig?" I asked him

"Well all things being equal, which they rarely are around here. I think if I push her as hard as I can in this weather, about another 3 to 4 hours. So early morning."

"Thanks Stu."

I finished my meal and went back to my cabin with Petrá. The last couple of days had been hectic and my adrenalin levels were returning to normal. The effect of the adrenal gland dumping loads of adrenalin into the blood stream, when we were in the firefight and even when we were on the Island, had now left me knackered. I really needed to sleep. I lay down on top of my bunk with Petrá by my side, and fell to sleep. The next I knew we were at the rig and Petrá was shaking me awake.

"Wake up sleepy head, we are home Andy."

Home, strange to think that we once owned homes on the dry land of the Highlands of Scotland, now what we really called home was far our from land and in the middle of the North Atlantic. They say (Those people that are 'They', and that nobody knows, who the hell 'They' are, anyway 'They') when building a house you should build it on solid ground, in order that its be safe. Well my original home had been built on the side of a solid mountain. Then it got demolished, so we rebuilt it in the same place, and it got demolished again. Both times because of the people that wanted us dead 'THEY' wanted us dead. Our home now was solid as a rock and fixed to the sea bead. It would be the safest place to be in a storm like this. I sat up and swung my legs over the edge of the bed, stood up and stretched. I felt human again. After a quick wash we went and joined the others on the foredeck of the Catherine May. Stu had already docked with our floating harbour under the gigantic, concrete legs, of the ex-Brent Bravo Oil platform. This was now our permanent home, out here in the middle of the North Atlantic. I jumped over the side of the Catherine May and gave Petrá my hand to help her over. I would collect my gear from my cabin later, for now I needed to get as much help as I could from our technical expert, Oran.

We took the lift up to the bottom deck area. The others went off to their apartments and I went to see Oran in his grotto. I knocked and waited, Oran greeted me with Cyber by his side.

"Welcome back Andy."

"Thanks Oran, what news do you have for me?"

"That would depend on what it is you wish to know."

"Lets start with any satellite imagery of RAF Dawes Hill. I guess after that, we will move on from there."

I followed him over to his computer setup, which really was three super large screens all controlled from his custom built computer. There were different things on each 70 inch plasma screen. Oran clicked a few keys on his computer keyboard and satellite images appeared on the central screen.

"Has there been any movement over the last couple of days? By that I mean since we left there."

"There was a Land Rover, left there this morning and then it returned about an hour later. Apart from that nothing. The bunker shows a small heat signature, which I would guess to be the exhaust pipe for the underground bunker there. That would indicate that they are running a generator, for power."

"OK Oran, good work. Now what can you tell me about the hard drives that you have been looking at?"

"The only thing that I could really get from them that seem to have anything at all to do with the ongoing situation, is that 'The Suit' was investigating rumours that there was a double agent working in one of the military intelligence services, although so far I have not been able to tell which one."

"What about the number two at SIS?"

"What do you want to know?"

"Is he the double agent?"

"If he is, then he is not being named in any of 'The Suits' files. What 'The Suit' was able to discover, is that enormous sums of money seem to be making their way out of the crowns coffers. That in itself is not that unusual. The security services pay vast sums of money out, for information. They pay it to informants from the Arab nations and the like. The only thing is once the money goes from SIS, there is no record of where it goes. There is a mention of the BOYS 50ATR, that is linked to a file on the SAS. I dug into the background of John Stevens. He went to Cambridge University and while he was there, not only was he in the same class as 'The Suits' wife, but he had a short term love affair with her. This was all before she met Sir Philip and became Mrs Reeves-Johnson."

"Thanks Oran. Now, I wonder why John did not tell us about that?"

"Cant say Andy. I hacked into John's computer and there is an email between him and Black-Tree, the American black ops company. They do a lot of work for the CIA, mainly in area's of the world where America has no official involvement."

"So what's it say?"

"Well most of it I have not been able to unscramble yet, but it is between John and some guy from Black-Tree who just goes by the name of Colonel. I would presume that he was previously in the American forces and is technically a retired officer. They are talking about a Taliban terrorist, that they have given the codename of Zorro. It would that seem he was recently captured. It does not say where he was captured, just that he is due for stage two interrogation. Apparently he is a non Arab but he holds the key to where the Taliban and ISIS are getting their funding and weapons from. Reviewing the political situation I would say the most likely country for him to have come from would be one of the ex soviet nations. Whilst they got their arses kicked in Afghanistan and they should have no love for the Arabs. They have less love for the West, who they now blame for all the ills that beset new nations. Things like poverty and crap governments. So the enemy of my enemy, becomes my friend sort of thing. It is strange though, that the number two of SIS has this information. Yet I can find no reference to it on any of 'The Suits' hard drives."

"That would not necessarily be that unusual for SIS, they have a nasty habit of keeping things compartmentalised, even between themselves. Perhaps 'The Suit' had given John, this to run with on his own. I am more interested in anything that we can find out about John and Sir Philip's wife. See if you can dig a bit deeper into the social life of John and also look into Mrs Reeves-Johnson."

I left Oran to do his work and headed of for our sick bay, to check on the young police officers condition. His condition had improved greatly over the last couple of days. Both of his legs were now encased in plaster and it would appear the reconstructive surgery had been done to his knees. All the other reconstructive surgery would be done privately. For his own personal safety it was agreed that he would stay on the Rig for the duration of this mission.

As soon as the weather improved Carl would take us back to somewhere near Daws Hill. We had talked it over and over and it was Hans who had come up with a plan to help us get inside the bunker there.

"The thing about blast doors is, they are intended to keep explosions out, as such all the strength is designed that way. The flaw with all of these older and cold war, types of complexes, is you can actually force them open with relatively small amounts of explosives." He said.

"How much in the way of explosives, are we talking about?" I asked.

"Mr Andy we should only require a couple of kilos of plastic explosives" Abdalla added

"Just where do you suppose we are going to be able put our hands on two kilos of C4?"

"We already have it Mr Andy, we still have a few Claymore Mines in the Armoury. They were leftover from our last mission. I can deconstruct them and remove the plastic, so that we just have the C4 and the firing mechanism."

"Oran can you sort out the optimal placing of explosives to open the blast doors?"

"Sure thing boss, I can do that in my sleep" He said and stuffed a lollipop back into his mouth.

"What about transport, once we are on the ground. After all, we cant ask the SAS to help us now." I asked Hans.

"I have some ideas and I will get in touch with some of my other sources in the British Army. Whatever happens we will have something suitable. And I am sure Lachlan will be able to drive whatever it turns out to be." Hans replied and Lachie just nodded his head.

We threw all sorts of ideas around in our brainstorming session. By the time we had finished it was almost night and we still had no firm plan, apart from we get there, get the transport, somehow get in and set the explosives, blow the doors off, go in and try and rescue whoever is in there. Then we make our escape and hopefully go back to our wonderful mundane and simple lives on board our Châteaux La Brent Bravo. We all went to our respective apartments. Petrá was waiting for me, with both the kids, who ran to me. I scooped them both up in my arms at the same time. Being a parent for me had been scary to start with. Not because of my own fear of death, but for my fear of not being there for them. The first 5 years had been magical, as we had no longer been involved in anything more dangerous, than going out for pleasure trips on the Catherine May. Now things were starting to get hairy. Like all the others I had made out my last Will and Testament. Everything I had went to Petrá and the children. I thought there was a very real chance of me being killed in our efforts to rescue 'The Suit'. I had not discussed this side of things with Petrá, I knew she was aware of the danger of what we were doing. She had watched me put on body armour and load up with firearms. Petrá was also aware of some of the things we had done on previous missions. I never lied to Petrá, I just never expanded too much on things. We were now planning to go up against some more rogue SAS soldiers, who were hiding out in a great defensive position. We had no idea just how many were inside the bunker. The more I thought about things, the tighter I held Finn and Aíná. I had been doing this subconsciously and it was only when Ainá said.

"Too tight Daddy"

I relaxed my arms a little so that I still had a firm hold of the children.

"Sorry Baby just that Daddy is so happy to see you" I said as I bounced them up and down. Petrá crossed the room and planted a kiss on my lips. I could see in her eyes that she had noticed that there was something different about me. Even if I had not noticed it myself, but she said nothing. I kissed them both and gently lowered them back to the floor. I wrapped both my arms around Petrá and pulled her close to me. We kissed passionately. The kids looked first at each other and then up at us. In unison the said

"Ewwe" I laughed and let Petrá go and chased the children around the room with my hands raised like claws.

"If I catch you I will tickle you"

They squealed and giggled. I caught them and tickled them we rolled on the floor and played as a normal father would with his kids, though there was nothing normal about their adopted father.

We fooled around some more and then Petrá sent them off to the bathroom to get ready for bed. I knew from the looks she was giving me, that we were going to talk after the kids were in bed. Petrá, tended to go quiet just before she would explode, not that we rowed, it was not so much how she would say things, it was the content. Nine times out of ten she would be right about a situation. I was the sort of man who tended to bury his head in the sand, at least when it came to domestic situations. After I said goodnight to the children, I sat down next to the balcony doors, the rain was still coming more or less horizontal in the gusts of wind that were blowing down from the north. I knew this kind of weather never lasted more than a few days out here. With any kind of good luck we might be able to carry on with the mission as soon as tomorrow night. My thoughts were interrupted by Petrá's voice.

"When are you going?"

"What?"

"Jesus Andy, you know what. You take off for two days armed to the teeth and then have to be rescued by Stu, and you waltz back, in like nothing has happened. I know you don't want me to know the details of what you do and I have never asked, but I also know from the way things are that you are all worried, about what is happening."

"Petrá I told you what my life was and why we live off the grid."

"You did Andy but you told me that was behind you."

"And it was darling. If it were me that had been taken what would you expect the others to do?"

"But its not, Andy. You have other responsibilities now you have to think about Finnbar and Ainá, not to mention me."

"They have saved my life so many times, these are my friends and yours. Without them we would not have any kind of life, without Sir Philip we would not have the children. So I owe that man everything. I know sometimes I curse him for getting me mixed up with SIS. In a way he gave me you Petrá." I held her close and whispered in her ear.

"I love you and the kids more than any other thing,"

Then I continued. As we stood facing each other.

"This is something I have to do. I promise I will be careful and come back to you. I need you to be strong and keep things running here. As soon as the weather clears up we are going back to the mainland to follow up on some leads. Morag and our parents will stay on too. The two scientists along with the medical people and their patient, will need your help while we are gone. Oran will be coming with us along with his teddy bear, but the other dogs are staying here. Now, you know we never put Oran in harms way, so you know I will be safe. Stu and Rosemary have said they will keep the boat here so you will have lots of company."

"Andy you fool. You are the only company I need. But I know no amount of talking will change your mind. Just know I am not happy about it."

She turned and walked out of the lounge and went to our bedroom. I knew how this would end and I hated myself for it. I would enter the bedroom she would be laid on the bed crying and curled up into the fetal position. I would then cuddle up to her and hold her till the sobbing ceased and then would would make love tenderly and fall asleep in each others arms. It was like I was using sex as a tool, to appease the argument for my failings. But I did it nonetheless. Morning came all to soon and I could see the sun starting to show itself on the horizon to the left of my bedroom window. It would set on the extreme right tonight. We never closed the blinds on the windows or balcony doors, who the hell was there to look in our windows out here. I would have taken the opportunity to make love to Petrá again, had it not been for the sound of a Helicopter approaching. I got out of bed and quickly showered. I knew we were going active again today, so dressed appropriately in my Nomex complete with full body armour. I would arm up after I had said goodbye to Petrá and the children. I know Lachie would be doing the same, as in he would not arm up until he too had said his goodbyes to Morag. It was not so much as a tearful farewell, but it was more uncomfortable than it had been up until now. I went to the armoury and took my two Sig's along with my AS50 complete with the new BAE advanced scope attached. I took suppressors but only fitted them to my Sig Sauer's. Abdalla had the VAL Silent Snipers Rifle, should we need to be quite from a distance. Abdalla had also deconstructed some Claymores and had them in a backpack ready to go. Hans had once again opted for his Desert Eagle 50 calibre hand canon along with a HK Machine Pistol. Lachie had chosen pretty much the same gear as me. All of us added to our kit with flash bangs as well as some real fragmentation grenades. We had been in firefights before and I always worried about the safety of my friends, as well as my own. This time however I was more than just worried. We would be going up against SAS troops that had complete cover. We were taking Oran because he could call up satellites and give us working plans, at a moments notice, he could also block any outgoing messages from the Bunker. I tried not to let my worry show, even though I was sure the others would be feeling the same. The strange thing about men is we are not keen on showing our feelings to others. When we were fully kitted we all traipsed back to the central kitchen for a last coffee and fill up on as many carbohydrates as we could in a short time. Like the others I had put handfuls of energy bars into my backpack, there was no telling how long we were going to be down at Dawes Hill. I did hope that we could take them by surprise, and it would all be done and dusted in a matter of minutes, but it could just as easily go tits up and we could be dug in for a couple of days. The longer we were there the greater the propensity of things going wrong and us all being either captured or killed. Carl had joined us for breakfast so there was now six men clad in Nomex sat drinking their coffee. The only person who looked strange in our unofficial battle dress, was Oran. Some time ago Rosemary had altered a Nomex suit to fit Oran, due to his small and skinny frame, it made him look even more like a stick insect, except that now fitted with full body and limb armour, he actually looked like some kind of super hero. As if on a predetermined cue, all the other civilian members and families joined us in the large kitchen to say their farewells and to wish us good luck. I hated these moments, I would rather have just gone without the fuss of a public goodbye. I had already said my farewell to Petrá last night and early this morning, but I went through the motions again. It was not that I did not care, it was because I feared I might not have the strength to leave my family. I quickly kissed the Kids and Petrá and walked out of the kitchen then up the stairs to the next deck and collected my Backpack and medical pouch, along with my firearms and extra ammunition from outside the armoury. I knew that the others would have followed my lead and would be close behind. I climbed the next two flights and up to the helipad. There was a British Airways Sea King parked there. I waited for the others to join me on the helipad. Carl came up and walked over to the chopper we all followed him and clambered in. Unlike the normal webbing seats, that we had been used to. There were comfortable leather recliner seats.

"I leased it from British Airways and I have filed a flight plan to RAF High Wycombe. They will not be looking for us to come in on a scheduled flight. So the transponder will click in when fly in over Dyce airport by Aberdeen and show us as a civilian aircraft on a set flight path. There will be transport waiting for us at High Wycombe. Hans joined his nephew in the front and the rest of us in the main cabin, even Cyber seemed happy enough to be here. I strapped in as the motors started up, I noticed Lachie had already assumed his position, which was with the seat relined and him laid back with his eyes closed. He would be asleep within minutes of take off. I would close my own eyes and try to power nap, but I doubted if I would sleep much. Oran had a set of headphones on and was listening to some Heavy Metal band or other. Abdalla was reading his Quran. This was something he did at the start of every flight, in about fifteen minutes he would close it and then like Lachie he would lie back and sleep.

ACT 14

I had not expected to sleep but it happened anyway, because the next thing I knew was that we were on the ground at the side of RAF High Wycombe. Lachie had woken me, by gently shaking my shoulder. I brought the seat into the upright position and climbed out of the chopper. There was a large Armoured Personnel Carrier Parked at the side of the Runway. It was painted in plain matt green and looked to be new.

"Its a Type 96APC and is on loan from the Japanese. They want the British Army to evaluate it." Hans said

It was an enormous beast with eight large wheels, a chisel style front. There was a machine gun turret on the top which looked to be a 50 cal. After getting our backpacks and weapons out of the Sea King we transferred everything into the Japanese Monster Truck.

"Lachie would you care to be our chauffeur for today?" Hans said.

A huge smile crossed Lachie's face, showing his perfect white teeth. As soon as we were all in, Hans shut the door and sat down opposite me in the basic bucket style seating. Oran had plugged his laptop into the APC's, dish aerial, and was busy typing away. I held My AS50 between my knees and felt the butterflies in my stomach start. Lachie pressed a large button on the expansive dashboard and the big Mitsubishi engine roared into life, from inside it sounded powerful, from outside it would be a petrol heads dream, even though it was a diesel engine.

"Nice" I heard Lachie say over the top of the engine noise.

"Please be careful with it Lachie, the army would like it back in one piece. The original engine, now has a supercharger, which means it goes faster and has more horsepower. It used to give about three hundred and sixty, horses, now it delivers four hundred and twenty. It now has a top speed of almost a hundred miles an hour. So take good care of this baby, or you will start a war with Japan again." Hans said

Lachie put this thirty foot monster, into gear and spun the steering wheel and the APC quickly responded to his control. Lachie's vision was through a set of four large monitors set in front of him, rather than traditional windows. These gave him full panoramic views from around this tank on wheels. There were cameras mounted all over the outside of this armoured transport and they fed the images direct to the monitors in front of Lachie. I could see he was enjoying himself.

"Do you have a plan?" Hans asked me

"Not so much of a plan. but a collection of ideas Hans. We go in to Daws Hill at night, blow the doors off, go in kill all the bad guys and rescue 'The Suit' and his family"

"Do we take prisoners for interrogation?"

"Only if they surrender. As far as I am concerned we are just here for 'The Suit'."

There was no more conversation as we drove along the roads towards Dawes Hill. I, like the others, took this time to check my weapons and kit. I checked that the BAE digital scope was fully charged and that the magazines for my guns were full and free working. Oran had a satellite image on his screen of the surrounding area.

"Andy, there is a wooded area to the rear of the bunker site. It looks to be a lightly wooded area. You should be able to come around the back of the bunker without them seeing us." Oran said

Lachie spun the wheel and I felt the big armoured carrier leap off the road and onto rough ground. Lachie slipped it into a lower gear ratio and dropped the speed down. The roar of the engine now went down to a warm burble. Being inside this vehicle was like being in a boat going over rough seas. The APC went over humps and ditches with ease, as all of its eight wheels were now in full automatic mode. I looked at the monitors in front of Lachie and watched, as the slim trees were just cut down by the chisel shaped front, of this Japanese ATV on steroids. Lachie stopped in the middle of a small copse of birch trees. We were about forty yards outside the wire fence, that was effectively the demarcation line of the secret bunker. We painted our faces and exposed skin in dark woodland camouflage. Then attached our PDA's to our forearms. These were linked to Oran's computer, which in turn was linked to some satellite.

At the moment it showed our APC with dots of warmth showing. Those dots were us. Because our PDA's were fitted with transponders, we would show as blue or green dots and anyone else would show as red dots. Hopefully this would mean that no one could creep up on us. Last time we had been here we had attacked from the front. This time we were going to initially make our insertion from the south of the bunker. Abdalla would be placing the charges, where Oran had indicated would create the most damage. Then when the doors were off, we would be able to attack within the safety of the APC. That was the plan, at least for now it was. We left Carl in the APC with Oran and Cyber. Keeping ourselves hidden as much as we could, we carefully made our way to the fence, that surrounded the bunker complex. Last time we had been here we had just cut through the fence, even though it claimed to be electrified. This time though, you could hear a gentle hum coming from the wire. The sign said Danger 2,000 volts, more than enough to cause severe damage or even death. The UK uses alternating current which in theory would mean that if you touched it you would be thrown backwards, unlike the American system, theirs operated on DC or direct current, touch that and you stick to it. Either way it was not so good. Hans pulled a reel of plastic covered copper cable from his backpack and a polythene bag that contained about 20 or so crocodile clips. He cut several lengths of cable about six feet in length, to each he fitted a pair of crocodile clips too. Then he started to clip them to the fence, before cutting a large hole in the fence. Then he taped the six wires to the top of the opening he had created. We crawled through the gap in single file. Then carefully made our way toward the bunker. The sun had set and it was a still and quiet night. Not the best sort of weather for an attack. When we were about three hundred yards from the bunker we huddled down in a hollow for a quick rerun of our plans and then Abdalla crawled out of our natural fox hole. The rest of us spread out in a defensive line about twenty yards apart. I followed Abdalla in my scope, I knew the others were doing the same. Just like we had been taught by Hans and Abdalla every couple of seconds, checking our own surrounding area. I saw Abdalla on my PDA he was on top of the entrance to the bunker. The plan was to place four charges on the hinges of the Blast Proof doors. They were made of steel but they were set into the concrete frame. It was this concrete, that would shatter from our IED's. Then with the force of the blast the doors should fall open. I followed him as he carefully made his way across the grassy mound to the side of the door. I knew he was also attaching an electronic fuse wire to each of the pieces of C4 explosive. Abdalla made his way back to my position.

"Mr Andy. Would you like the honour of setting the charges off?" He said as he passed me a small box with four wires coming out of it. I lifted the safety cover on the detonation switch and paused.

"Fire in the hole" I whispered into my Storno throat mike, I had waited years to use that term. I had seen so many war films where the hero says that as he either dumps a plunger or throws a handful of grenades. Then I pressed the button. The explosions sounded more like thunder and I felt the vibration of the shock wave rolling through the earth below my body. We quickly spread out, forming an arc behind and above the blast doors. The doors were still covering the front of the bunker.

"Fuck! Now what do we do?" I said.

"We try again" Hans said

"How?"

"We still have a couple of claymore's, we use them"

"How do you intend for us to detonate them?"

"Simple Andy, we attach a long trip wire and pull it?"

"How far away will we be when we do that?

"Not far." he replied

"Mr Andy I will do it. It is my job."

I knew there was no point in arguing with Abdalla, he was already slithering across the grass towards the entrance.

"Andy." Oran's voice came through my earpiece and continued

"There is some activity at the front gate. It looks like someone has a planned visit, because there is no way they could have mustered held so quickly."

I looked at my PDA and it showed three red dots close together, towards the front of the bunker. We would have to deal with them before we dealt with the blast doors. I raced out from my position and Lachie went from his side so that we could form a cross fire with our rifles. I lay down at the front left edge of the bunker and Lachie was on the right. I rapidly set my AS50 up on its Bi Pod legs and zoomed in on the military Land Rover that was just entering the gates of the campsite. There was a driver in the front and two men in the back. It was too dark now to make accurate identities, so I did not know if these were regular soldiers or airmen, who had a legitimate right to be here, or if they were part of the rogue SAS unit. It is impossible to shoot someone with a 50 cal and just wound them, due to the size and velocity of the round. The AS50 is a snipers rifle but it is a kill weapon.

"Andy how do you want to do this?" Lachie said in my ear.

"We need to be closer and we need to identify them"

"Roger that Andy going down the side now"

Quickly we both slithered down the side of the hillock that made up the entrance. At the bottom I held my body to the damaged blast door and covered the three men who were sat in the land rover. They had not moved from there since they entered the compound of the bunker area.

"Cover me Andy, I am going in for a closer look" Lachie's voice whispered in my earpiece. I watched him as he crept around the wooded area to the front of the bunker.

"Andy they are just sat there and they are not moving at all."

"Get back here Lachie I have a real bad feeling about this."

A few moments later Lachie was beside me.

"Something is way off about them. Its like they are waiting for us to go down and attack them."

"Oran can you backtrack that Land Rover and see where it came from? I need you to do it as fast as you can please"

I sat and waited with Lachie in silence.

"Andy. They were here almost an hour ago. But there were six of them at that time. Two men returned on foot and one man got out as soon as they got here he is somewhere near the front gate. He must have an aluminium blanket over himself or there must be another entrance by the gate, because there is nothing showing now on the Sat image now."

"Thanks Oran."

I called Hans and Abdalla over and waited with Lachie for them to get to my position. I wanted to brainstorm with the others. The three guys in the Land Rover just sat there doing nothing. Abdalla was the first to arrive quickly followed by Hans I explained the situation as we saw it.

"Mr Andy it is a trap"

"I guessed that much Abdalla, How did they know we would be here at this exact time?"

"Mr Andy perhaps it is just bad luck on our part. I have seen Boko Haram do something like this. They take innocent people prisoners and make them sit on mines in a car. They tell the prisoners if they move they will blow themselves up. Then they wait until someone comes to rescue them or just to ask what they are doing. Then the terrorists explode the car, usually by radio or Mobile Phone, killing the rescuers or the police and army around it."

I picked up my AS50 and I unclipped the sights off of it, so I could use it like a monocular. I zoomed in on the Land Rover until I could scan each part of it. The people inside still were not moving. They showed warm on the scope so they were alive. I switched to High Resolution night vision and the thermal colour picture was instantly replaced by a sharp black and white image of the scene in front of us. Then I saw it. Behind the men in the back were two barrels, both of which seemed to have some form of electronic detonator on top of them. So this was definitely a trap, meant to kill anyone who would attempt to rescue the men in the Land Rover.

"Oran?"

"Yes Andy?"

"Can you set up a jamming signal to stop any telephone or radio signals?"

"I can but it will interfere with our transmissions."

"OK can you tell me a couple of seconds before you do it. I want you to block all signals for exactly three minutes. And by exactly I mean 180 seconds not a second longer or shorter OK?"

"Roger Andy stand by."

We talked it over amongst ourselves and formulated a plan, albeit a rushed one. I clipped the sights back onto the AS50 and covered the Land Rover. Lachie moved back up to his original position on the far side above the blast doors. Hans and Abdalla prepared to carry out the plan. We would be unable to communicate for three minutes. Each of us would be on our own. I waited and silently prayed that Oran would get things right. I knew that if anyone could then it would be him.

"Radio's down in ten seconds" Oran's voice sounded and he counted down.

As soon as he reached zero both Abdalla and Hans set of running at a low crouch to the Land Rover. I could only cover the front of the Bunker. I knew Lachie from his position would now also be covering the area as well. I saw the small personal door to the right hand side of the blast door open, they had failed to turn the lights off inside and the light spilled out, silhouetting their sniper who would have shot at either the bomb in the Land Rover, or at our men. I knew the moment that I caught sight of him, that I would be taking another life or maiming someone forever. My reactions had been trained into me by both Abdalla and by Hans, they were the real experts in Hostage Rescue scenarios and Offensive warfare. There was already a full metal jacketed round in the breach of my rifle which was cocked and because, we had planned things, the safety, was already set to the off position. The man standing at the door, had made his own fatal mistake, by not having a round chambered in his own rifle. It was that one and a half second delay, that would cost him his life. I set my red dot just below his neck and centrally between his shoulders. I did not pause to recheck the target. I just increased the pressure on the trigger, I felt it pull back on its sprung loaded tension. I saw him cock his rifle and chamber his own round, by the time his thumb had reached the safety of his firearm, the firing pin of mine had reached its target on the rear of the 50cal shell casing. The firing cap did its job and provided a small spark for the main charge in the shell. The bigger explosive charge instantly impacted upon the base of the murderous projectile, sending it down the barrel at over 2000 miles an hour. His finger was just rising towards the trigger guard. By now the flame had shot from the end of my barrel. It was pushing the bullet at supersonic speed towards its target. He may or may not have seen the flash in his peripheral vision. His other eye was now moving towards the sights of his long barrel rifle. It was at this point his life ended. The bullet actually struck the bottom edge of his rifle where his hand had been holding his rifle. His hand vanished in a cloud of blood, flesh and bone, before he felt the pain. The bullet now carried on forward and struck the rifle this was forced backwards and upwards in two broken pieces. Slowed to subsonic speed but no less deadly, in fact it was more destructive now. Previously the projectile had been sent spinning forward by the rifling of the barrel, now it was sent tumbling end over end and at a slightly lower target than I had intended. The force of the impact on the rifle he was holding had now dislocated his right shoulder and started him on a reverse spin, back towards the light spilling out from the bunker. My now deformed bullet hit more soft flesh and bone as it hit the base of the sternum. It tumbled around inside his chest cavity and ripped through that with ease, before striking the spinal column taking a four inch section of it out though his back ripping the skin and clothing apart as it did so. The blood and bones mixed with bits of his rifle and clothing now poured freely like a balloon has been filled with water and is then pierced. His body had now completed its turn so that he was facing inside towards the bunker. His broken rifle was still up in the air. it would reach the ground almost a half second later than the man. The bullet hit the front of one of the main blast doors and ricocheted off into the trees on the other side, where it fell silently into the deep undergrowth. All this took just a second to happen. Had he been more prepared and a half second faster the outcome could have been horribly different for us. I kept my sights fixed to the door. In my own peripheral vision I saw Abdalla reach the side of the Land rover. My semi-automatic AS50, chambered another round and fixed my dot at chest height of the now open door. Again I could see out the corner of my left eye that people were coming out of the Land Rover. Not via the doors, but instead they were using the windows to exit the vehicle. I moved my vision completely to the door again. I did not like the silence in my earpiece. The block that Oran had put on had also wiped out our PDA's. I saw movement just inside the door of the bunker someone else was trying to shoot the bombs in the back of the Land Rover. I could only see the rifle and his arm. The arm was the easier of the two targets. I would have to snap of a series of rounds, in order to at least buy our guys some time to get the three men from the Land Rover to safety. My first shot missed his arm by inches, which was as good as missing by a fucking mile mile. The second shot whined of into the night as it hit the steel door frame. I steadied my breathing and gave myself a second. The first two rounds I had fired, made the guy a bit wary and slowed him down a bit. He would be careful with his next shot in the same way as I was going to be careful with this shot. Look, target, breathe, calm, and fire all in the space of one second. My bullet left the barrel followed by the dragons breath of flame and a vortex smoke ring. Even before it left the barrel, I knew that it was true in its flight to the target. So much so that I actually let my rifle barrel drop down. In the blink of an eye I watched as the firearm, that had been pointing out of the door, was now flying upwards in an arc, while the arm that had been holding it was already bouncing off the body of the man who had fallen previously. The sheer power and velocity of a 50cal supersonic bullet had ripped the lower arm off at the elbow. The person who owned the arm was now out of the conflict. Again from my peripheral vision I saw Hans and Abdalla dive into the undergrowth to my left. The next thing that happened was my body was blown backwards to land about twelve feet from where I had been crouched. I felt the heat to the side of my face and I smelled my hair being singed. Fortunately my mouth had been open when the explosion happened which meant I was still able to breathe. I no longer had my rifle and I had no clue as to what just happened. I had been almost thirty five yards away from where the Land Rover used to be and I had been sheltered by the side wall of the bunker. Somehow they had detonated the bombs. I doubted that they had used radio and it seemed to me that less than a minute of the three minutes I had asked Oran to provide us with. Then pieces of metal and other detritus of what used to be a Land Rover started to rain down from above. A wheel attached to part of the back axel just missed me as it came back to earth. It was like deja Vu of the previous mission. I had ended up in hospital after that one. Only then, the rear axel of Lachie's Range Rover, had landed on me, after it had been blown up. I was still on the ground when Abdalla and Hans got to me Abdalla set up to cover Hans and me. The radios came back on.

"You guys OK?" Oran asked

"I think so I replied" although I was not entirely sure I was. I felt like I had sunburn to the left side of my forehead. Hans helped me to sit up.

"Did we get all the guys out OK?"

"Yes Andy looks like they managed to get a shot off from inside the bunker and that detonated it. From what I saw I would say that it was diesel and fertiliser in a couple of big barrels. You are damn lucky Andy. Had you not been partially screened by the bunker wall you would have been dead."

"What about Lachie?"

"I am OK mate" He said from behind me. And continued

"We Rock Apes know when to keep our heads down, I guess they don't bother to teach that sort of thing to you medics."

"Ha ha" I replied and then stuck out my hand

"Give me a hand up then"

Lachie grabbed my hand and helped me to my feet. I could now see my rifle which had landed about five feet from where I did. I gave it a quick check. It seemed to be OK. I replaced the magazine with a new full one.

"We need to keep the front covered and we should also get the APC down here. They have left the gates open, so I am guessing they either have reinforcements coming, or they were getting ready to leave. I think it was the latter. So let's hold them here in their bunker and take it from there. Does that work for the rest of you?" I asked

I got lots of nods

"So who were the guys in the Land Rover?"

"They claim to be the real SAS and claim that these guys are fakes. They were kidnapped and held inside here before being used as bomb bait for us."

"You believe them Hans?"

"Yes I think I do."

"OK they should be able to tell us something about who they have in there, along with the number of men they have. Let's get some quick answers."

My ears were still ringing and I think I may have a slight burn to my forehead and a bald patch, where there used to be hair before it was burned off. Still by the sounds of things I had got lucky. I followed Hans and Abdalla into the wooded area, while Lachie covered the front of the bunker. The three men that were squatted down were still trying to remove bits of duct tape from their wrists and ankles.

"My men tell me you are the real SAS guys, so how come you ended up as bomb bait?"

A stocky man with short crew cut hair and a nose that said he had been in many fights and perhaps not won them all. Stood up and answered me.

"Yes we are the real guys, we were all kidnapped along with Sir Philip and his wife. This lot came down pretending to be another Unit of the SAS and they had the right paperwork for Sir Philips office at SIS, so we let them in. The next thing was they caught us with our pants down and they later executed some of our guys and captured the rest of us along with Mrs Reeves-Johnson and her son. Then they split us up. They took Sir Philip in a black van, his wife was taken off in one of the Jaguars and we, along with the boy were brought here."

"Any ideas where Sir Philip and his wife, were taken?" I asked

"When they had us tied up in the bunker, I overheard a conversation something to do with Black-Tree and a terrorist. They kept telling the boy to do as he was told, then he and his mother, would get to live."

"I don't suppose you know who was on the other end of the telephone, do you?"

"No not really only that it was an international call."

"How would you know that?"

"I could hear it ring, like he had it in speaker phone at least until it was answered. So you know that here in the UK it rings twice and then a short pause before ringing twice and so on?"

"Yes so?"

"Well my wife went on holiday with our daughter just a few weeks ago. I would ring them every day to make sure they were OK. So when I rang them. It rings once and then pauses and then once and so on. That is the way that this call sounded before it was picked up."

"Don't suppose you caught who it was on the other end when they answered?"

"Yes. I just told you Black-Tree Enterprises, after that it was taken off speaker-phone."

"Thanks you guys sit tight for now, we might want your help, once we check you out to make sure you are who you say you are. No offence intended but of late, I have found its best not to take anyone, at their word. I live longer that way, at least until tonight that is" I said passing my hand over my singed forehead, where a blister was starting to form.

"Non taken and we will sit and wait, while you do whatever it is you have got to do. You know we appreciate the rescue and all that, but you never told us who you are yet."

"That's right we never did, lets just say we are friends of Sir Philip and leave it at that shall we."

"Fair enough, for now." he said and went and squatted down with his two colleagues.

The radio came back to life, I relayed as much information to Oran who was now on his way here with Carl in the APC. We did not have to wait too long. I heard its big powerful motor roaring like an amplified American muscle car and it was magnified, in every way, not just in the sound of the engine but in its muscular size. This is the sort of car you need when you are in a hurry to get somewhere. It roared in through the open gates of the compound and skidded to a halt to the right hand side, giving us cover from the open door of the bunker. Carl opened the back door so we could enter. Lachie, was still providing over-watch on us. Abdalla watched the three men he had helped to rescue. I joined Hans and Carl in the APC, with Oran and his ever faithful Cyber. I had taken the names of those we had rescued along with their units, I passed all this to Oran and he typed away for a few moments and then he took a small portable printer out of his backpack and attached it to his Laptop before printing off, copies if the front page inside their passports.

Before we could do anything else we had to first clear the bunker and see if any of the others that had been kidnapped were still in there. I pressed the transmit on my throat microphone.

"Lachie can you move so that you are directly over the open door, and drop a fragmentation grenade down there?"

"On it boss" he replied

"Carl can you work the 50cal machine gun on top of this, if required?"

"Yes Andy I think I can manage that"

"Fire in the hole" Lachie's voice said about 2 seconds before the fragmentation grenade went off. It forced the partially open personal door fully open. Which was good because we could now see inside, but it was also bad as they could see whatever we were doing.

"Lachie we set two more Claymores against the main hinges of the blast doors they are on long trip wires. The bunker should give you all the protection you need. If you lay flat when you trigger them. But wait until I get all the other folks, inside this tin can."

"Roger that"

I called Abdalla and asked him to bring the three men with him, to join us. As soon as they were inside I closed the door.

"Anytime you like Lachie"

Two simultaneous explosions to the two top hinges of the blast doors. We had not the time to deconstruct these two Claymores, consequently around 150 steel ball bearings were flying through the air. Most were contained within the concrete of the blast door and the frame, quite a few though had made it out and they were pinging harmlessly, off the outside of our APC. Their effective range was only about 100 meters, so there was no harm to anyone living near by. The doors were free from the top hinges and slopped slightly forward held for now by the bottom hinges. We were clean out of explosives. As if he were reading my mind.

"We need to attach a chain or cable to the top of one of those big doors and drag it down with this truck" Carl said.

"And just how do you propose we get a chain up there" I asked

"With this" he replied and pulled a heavy grappling hook from its bracket on the back door of the APC. Then he continued.

"We attach the rope on this, to the cable on the front of this truck. Then we fire the hook up using the grappling gun" he said taking it from a bracket that was below the one where the hook had been.

"Lets get to it then"

I pressed my throat mike and relayed what we were about to do, up to Lachie. Carl took the grappling hook which was attached to the rope after loading the hook into the grapple gun. Carl then tied the other end off to the cable that was attached to a winch under the front of the APC. Using the vehicle for cover, Carl fired the grapple over the bunker doors, to where Lachie was waiting to pull the excess rope up and then the heavy winch cable that carl was letting out steadily.

"Lachie can you find a place to attach the cable too? Somewhere near the top?"

"There is a big D ring on the back of the door, probably where they attached it to a crane, when installing it back in the 1960's, will that do?"

"Perfect Lachie, let us know when it is secured then go back to watching over us if you could please?"

Through the monitors that acted as windows on the APC, I watched Lachie pull the cable up and then give the thumbs up.

"OK Carl your turn, can you move us back away from the doors and then line us up centrally, before you start winding the cable back in?"

Carl moved us into position and wound the cable in until it was tight. He changed the gearing on the winch and it slowed but with double the torque. The APC started to lift its front wheels from the ground. Carl eased the cable back and then put the APC into reverse. This time with a combination of all eight wheels in reverse and the sheer weight of our armoured vehicle, in conjunction with our high tensile winch cable. The big blast door started to sway towards us, then it stalled for just a moment and it looked to me, that it was going to hang up. Then just like the slab of concrete and steel that it was. Gravity came into play and it came crashing to the ground in a cloud of dust. The light from inside the main hallway of this bunker now spilled out into the dark of the night. Carl changed gear and drove the APC over the cable and then drove forward and up onto the fallen blast door. Hans jumped out of the back door and unhooked the cable, then he returned to the safety of the Japanese tank. Carl wound the winch all the way back in and then drove forward into the bunker, being careful to avoid the body of the man, I had shot through the chest. Now he had driven over the demolished door, he parked us in the hanger like area of the bunker. This appeared to first glance to be empty. I knew Lachie was still keeping a watch from above, I also knew that we were limited in time, because someone local, was bound to have called the police to say there had been explosions at the old RAF Base, as well as gunfire. I finally got around to checking the printed of documents that Oran had given me and they matched exactly the three men we had rescued. Time to use them. They were all dressed in boiler suits. But still had their original dog tags. We could use them as gate guards. I gave them my Sig Sauer's, complete with holsters and Abdalla handed the other one the VAL that he had been carrying. We sent them off with instructions to close the gate and stand guard. They were to tell the police that there had been a series of explosions caused by old ordinance that had been stored in the bunker. But it was now being made safe by a BDU team. And that if the police wished to help they could do so by closing roads into this area until further notice. Lachie now came down from his position at the top of the mound and joined us inside. With the exception of Oran we had exited the APC and were starting to search the bunker and its various tunnels and rooms. We did it methodically. I found the man whose arm I had shot off, he was dead of course from shock and loss of blood. I shouted down the corridors not really expecting any reply. When suddenly a voice shouted out

"Down here, I am down here, Help!!"

ACT 15

I followed the sound down a side corridor, constantly covering all the angles as I went. Abdalla was walking behind me facing the other direction. Even though, he was covering my six. I still felt exposed and vulnerable in this enclosed corridor. All those years ago when we had been in training at the shooting range and the, hostage training site. Abdalla had told us that a tunnel or corridor is the worst place to be in any form of a firefight. Those shooting at you did not have to be all that accurate, as the corridor would funnel fire directly onto you. Yet here we were doing just that, going down a corridor that could have been a trap. Was the guy screaming for help just another trick like the Land Rover. I could not take the chance that it was not a real person in distress. I knew that there were three people who had been taken from the farmhouse, and that this sounded like a teenagers voice, that was screaming for help. I kicked open doors on the right and I knew that behind me Abdalla was doing the same thing to the left. Every time a door opened, I expected to be greeted by a hail of lead, every time it did not come, I worried more on the next.

The person was still shouting so I knew at least he was alive for now. Finally there were no more doors on my side of the long corridor. I turned to face Abdalla as he kicked open the last door on his side. The boy was in there he was alone in a room that was empty with the exception of a bed that was bolted to the floor. That much I could see from where I stood. I walked backwards and joined Abdalla in the room. The boy was chained to the bed with hand cuffs. There were several Pizza boxes on the floor and empty coke bottles. A slop bucket was next to the bed that from the smell of it, had not been emptied for a few days. I recognised the boy from one of the photos that we had lifted from 'The Suits' home. Abdalla shouldered his Sig and took a thin piece of metal out from the side of his boot, then slipped in down inside the handcuff that held the boy to the bed and in 2 seconds the boy was free.

"Kevin Reeves-Johnson?" I asked

"Yes, I thought they were going to kill me. Today is the first day the lights have been on. Then I heard all the explosions and shooting. They told me if anyone attempted to rescue me, they would kill me first. One guy went out then the second guy said, 'he was going to come back and kill me', but he never came back that was about thirty minutes ago."

"OK Kevin we are friends of your father. You are safe now and no one will hurt you. Do you know where your parents are?"

"No they took my mother somewhere else and my father was taken away for questioning and he never came back."

"OK Kevin come with us, we will talk when we get you out of here. I need you to put your hand on Abdalla's shoulder and follow him out to the front. We have three more men waiting there and they will protect you. There are some bodies out there, they are the bad guys. Don't look at them OK?"

"OK?"

"OK What?"

"I wont look at the bodies"

"Good Lad. Ready Abdalla?"

Abdalla nodded and we went out to the front, like a little caterpillar. Kevin was holding onto Abdalla and I was holding onto Kevin. There were no incidents. We got to the APC and loaded him in. I asked the real SAS boys to see if they could search the scene for anything that would give any useful leads. I was sure that Kevin would be an absolute mine of information, on not just the people that took him, but also what had happened to his parents. For now though we had to be gone from here. Not only would the police be headed this way, but I was bloody sure that these guys had contacted their cohorts and told them that we were here. The real SAS guys said they would make their own way back to their base. After recovering our firearms, I took a personal contact number from one of the SAS guys and told them we would be in touch. Then I too jumped into the big APC with the others. I would make the introductions when we were safe. Carl shifted the big tin can into reverse and we moved back over the debris of what used to be the big blast doors of the Dawes Hill bunker. Once out, he picked Lachie up, then he turned us around and headed back down the road, using as many back-roads as he could he took us back to the British Airways Sea King chopper. When we got there, we did a quick decamp and loaded everything into the chopper along with Kevin, who to be fair, was holding up pretty damn well, for a young civilian. I guess he was made of the same stuff as his father. Once we were airborne, Carl called in a fictitious flight plan to Wick Civilian Airfield via Dyce Airport near Aberdeen. Now we were on our way home I made the introductions and passed him a couple of energy bars along with a bottle of water. Lachie had assumed his usual mode for flights, which was to switch off and go to sleep, his jacket was balled up and pressed against the window next to the seat he was reclined in. All in all it was a successful day. Chalk up a bunch of bad guys down and none of us even wounded, with the exception of my new hair style and light sunburn. It would seem our luck was still holding.

We did actually Fly to Dyce and then refuelled and went on up to Wick. Then Carl logged another flight Plan out to another Oil rig in the North Sea, not ours of course and then from the other rig, to our home. Later he would fly over to Dyce and then back to Wick, with the leased BA Helicopter. So he had a long night in front of him. I knew Hans would go with him to help and then they would get back to us, probably on the Catherine May. Kevin did not seem at all phased by Cyber and Cyber loved the fuss that Kevin was making of him. I was having a drop out from my adrenaline rush. So closed my eyes and made the best of the down time flying home. We landed in the small hours of the morning. After we got all our gear out of the helicopter, Hans took the control of the chopper, then Carl and he vanished into the still night air. I led Kevin to the lift and we went down to the main deck area. I knew that Rosemary would have cooked some food for us, as Carl had radioed in from Dyce. All the girls were up and they were sat in the bar area waiting for us. Kisses and hugs were exchanged before we started talking. I could smell the food from the kitchen and led Kevin through and sat him down at the slab of teak that served as the communal dining table. The girls followed us into the kitchen, Rosemary took a large casserole dish out from the oven and put it on a trivet in the middle of the table. Then she brought over some plates and cutlery.

"Lamb Hotpot, I hope you are all hungry as I made a lot of it." Rosemary said. I looked at Kevin.

"I am starving." He said and then sat and waited

"No one stands on ceremony here young man. Help yourself before these hooligans, dive in and eat it all." She said as she passed him a large serving spoon.

Petrá was coming around, with a large jug of coffee and filling up our mugs.

"With or without?" She asked generally

All of us with the exception of Kevin said "With" He looked around the table a little bewildered. So I helped him out.

"With, means with a shot of Irish Whisky in it, and if you wish, I would say you have earned it. After all you have been through, but make sure you eat plenty of the casserole the our Rosemary has made"

"Can I have it with, please" He said. I guess his parents had taught him good manners as well. It was nice to see, in these times of goby youngsters, that did not respect their elders. We would have to get into debriefing, as soon as he had eaten. I told Petrá this, so that she would be able to go and get some sleep. We would do a team style debriefing and would bring Hans up to speed as soon as he was back. So after the meal was finished we went from the kitchen and into the bar area. Petra insisted on applying some burn cream, to my forehead and cheek. Rosary would cut my hair in the morning so that at least it was all the same length. Rosemary and Petrá went off to prepare a guest room for Kevin. Morag said she would clean up after we had eaten. I got Kevin another coffee, this time it was without, at least until he told us all he knew.

"Kevin, I want you to tell us every thing, that happened, from the time you got home, to when we rescued you."

"Don't really know much, I came home from boarding school, for the half term. We were supposed to be having a family dinner, when John turned up. He said something about due to an internal leak, of security details. That we would be having a new security detail. Half an hour later they turned up and they changed over. Then John said he had to talk to my Mum and Dad, so I went to my room there was a lot of shouting. I went downstairs to see what was going on. I went to the library, dad was sat in a chair and John had a gun pointed at him my mother crying and sat in another chair. Then three men came in and they took my father away. Another two took my mother and myself.

"Do you know why any of this happened?"

"Not really, just John kept saying, something about he loved Mum first and if we behaved ourself, then no one need to die. Then someone put a cloth over my mouth and nose and I ended up where you found me."

"And you cant think of any thing else? Nothing at all?"

"Just something about a terrorist"

"OK Kevin, My wife Petrá will sort you out with some clean clothes and a room. We will talk more in the morning when you are refreshed."

He left us alone. Not a lot wiser than we had been before.

"What do you think Lachie?"

"Well mate apart from the bit about his mum loved John first, nothing more than we already knew."

"Mr Andy there is also a link between SIS and Zorro not to forget the Black-Tree link."

"Yes you are right Abdalla, Oran see if you can get some more information on those links, I think we need to pay Mr Stevens. another visit. This time an unannounced one. But lets make sure we are totally prepared and have a full team when we do it. I am sure that he is the key to everything that is going on. I never liked the weasel. There was always something sycophantic about him. So for now I say we get some rest and wait until Hans gets back here." I said as I finished my coffee and then went to my apartment. I undressed and showered, then dried myself of and climbed into bed with Petrá. She was already asleep so I just snuggled up next to her. The morning came I showered and dressed and went to the main kitchen. Petrá was already up and had the kids fed, she was getting them ready for their home schooling. They probably did more school work than those at regular schools. Whilst we did not have set school times, or for that matter set lessons, the children not only did the basics but they were schooled in world politics. Petrá had correctly said that in our line of work it would be important for the kids to be well prepared for the outside world, or they would be otherwise closeted and protected from all the evils of the world. So they were encouraged to watch the news, from multiple channels, and then there would be a question and answer session to follow. We were all apolitical, they saw what was good and bad in the world. I guess if we had any political leaning it would be towards socialism but with a good measure of enterprise thrown in. I saw nothing wrong with wealth so long as it was not used for evil, or to be flouted in the face of the poor. In the same way as some well off folks, go on holiday to third world countries, flaunting their wealth by wearing diamonds and watches that cost more than the average person from that country, could earn in ten lifetimes. I like wearing a good watch as much as any man, but not for show. I wore a good timepiece because of reliability. So I would wear a stainless steel Omega as my daily watch. It was not flash looking and unless you knew watches, it would look just like a run of the mill watch. When diving I wore a stainless steel Audemars Piguet Royal Oak Offshore. It was an expensive watch but it could stand the pressure of going down five hundred meters under water. No gold or diamonds on it Just a neon face with luminous hands and a yellow rubber strap. It was a watch for a man who did deep sea diving or as I did parachuting. Unlike a gold and diamond encrusted Rolex which was the, sort of watch could get you killed in a poor country. For me though my watch, It was just another tool of my new trade. I would have been just as happy wearing a Timex, if I thought it would work in my new environment. When the children were old enough then they would be given the tools to see them through life, for now though it was an education. They would learn the basics that most kids learn, then they would learn how to survive.

I had learned that over the last seven years. I had good teachers in Abdalla and Hans. The things they had taught us, were the things that had keep us all alive during the last few years, when we had been semi retired from life. The children had spent time learning more life skills. They could swim and dive. They knew how to quickly evacuate from the rig. They could fish and shoot obviously not the big guns that we would use. They would use 22's and shoot at target that we set up, either overlooking the ocean or targets that we put on the ocean in order that they could hit a moving target. They were never allowed to have firearms on their own, least ways not for now. That day was yet to come. They were skilled in the use of computers and Rosemary gave them cooking lessons. I taught them first aid. Stu taught them sea navigation and also how to know, where they were by the stars. Oran taught them basic computer programming. Then there were all the languages they were learning from all of the team. I had just poured myself a coffee when Hans walked in with Stu and rosemary behind them.

"Morning Andy"

"Hi Hans. Coffee folks?"

"Please" They said in unison.

We carried them out to the lounge area where Lachie, Oran and Abdalla were sat. Oran had a pile of printed papers spread out on front of him.

"You should see this Andy" Oran said as he passed me a sheet of paper. I read it and then read it a second time.

"So Stephens, is the man who discovered this double agent come terrorist, that goes by the name of Zorro?"

"Yep and there is more too Andy." Oran said as he handed me another sheet of paper. And continued

"As you can see, not only did he discover who this terrorist was, but he was also able to deliver him into the clutches of the Americans. I have looked through all the CIA databases and I cant find anything other than his codename. Until just about ten weeks ago no one in the entire world knew who he was. Yet this John Stevens, who is a desk jokey for the SIS. Suddenly he can do, what no field agent working for SIS, CIA, MOSAD or any other intelligence agency, has been able to do for the last 10 years. Does that not strike you as just a little strange. Surely if anyone from SIS would have discovered it, then that would have been Sir Philip?"

"Agreed, so what are you saying?"

"I am not really saying anything, I am just thinking out loud."

"OK Oran, think louder and share those thoughts with us."

"Lets suppose that Stevens, for whatever reason, wanted to get Sir Philip out of the way. Say he planted evidence on Sir Philip, to make it look like he was Zorro. After all, we know that Zorro, is supposed to be a high up figure in the intelligence community, come double agent. Lets say Stevens, then gives Sir Philip to the yanks. So that Stevens, can become number one at SIS and then climb the monkey puzzle tree, of the political mountain to become the next MOD or even deputy PM. Then make that final jump, to Prime Minister. We all know that Stevens is a sycophantic bastard, with an ego the size of Donald Trump's"

"Its a bit of a stretch, but I kind of get where your are going with it. Good work Oran. Anyone else got any ideas?"

"So why take the wife and the kid?" Lachie asked

"Don't ask me Lachie. Its not me that is thinking out loud." I said.

"Oran?" Lachie asked

"Sorry I don't know any more they were just thoughts."

We brainstormed for about another two hours and the best we could come up with was, that we would have to go down and ask John Stevens directly. We would have to do it at his home, rather than at his office. Thankfully Oran had managed to get that location and some really good satellite images. He lived on a much bigger place than 'The Suit' did, well he had more land than Sir Philip owned. Stevens was part of the horsey hunting fraternity. So had stables and horses, along with lots of fields for them to run in. Plus he had the land to run them at a gallop. He had two roads in and out of his property, one led right to the stables and fields, the other led to a modern expansive detached house with large ornamental gardens and an outdoor swimming pool, next to which were tennis courts. He seemed to have a much more lavish lifestyle than even a high ranking civil servant, should have. It was of course possible that he came from a family with money, just he seemed to lack the subtlety that old wealth has. He had that New Wealth rudeness to him, that alone, should have rung alarm bells of his employers.

"Oran can you look into the financial records of Stevens and see where he gets all his money from" I said and Oran went off to his computers.

"Mr Andy, Kevin said something, about Stevens said that 'He loved Mrs Reeves-Johnson first' do you not think we should try and follow that up as well?"

"You are right Abdalla can you go to Oran's Grotto and see what you two can dig up between you."

I asked Hans to keep Carl on standby so that we could get down to the Stevens home. Lachie and I went for a walk with the dogs up on to the helicopter deck.

"What's up Andy, that you wanted to be all the way up here, rather than in the lounge area."

"Lachie, I worry that Hans could be caught up in the shitstorm that will go down if even a fraction of what Oran has said is true. He is our friend and his career is at stake, especially if we fuck things up."

"Then we had better not fuck things up"

"Seriously Lachie, I want to ask Hans to drop out of Team Seven, at least temporarily. I want him to have that plausible deniability that 'The Suit' always talked about. He is the only one of us, that is still officially employed by anyone. Even the slightest bit of a scandal could ruin his career. I know him and Sir Philip go back a long way but this is getting beyond personal for him."

"Have you spoken to Hans about your feelings?"

"No Lachie I have not"

"Personally I think it is his choice to make, not ours. Even though, I understand your reasons."

Just at that point Hans appeared behind us.

"Andy I caught the tail end of your conversation, I understand your concerns and I was going to point out that because of my links to NATO, I could be of more use to you there. BUT all of it would be unofficial. NOT because I am worried about what would happen to my career, but because inside the top of NATO, is worse than being in an old fish market. There are no secrets there, in fact it is the least secure place for secrets that I know. So that is why I will now take no official part. If you need anything ask Carl he is at your total disposal. I will ensure that you have whatever resources that you need. I understand that you are planning to gain entrance to John Stevens home? I can tell you that he requested extra security, so much so, that he has a ring of armed guards for two hundred metres around his home. In fact not even his guards are allowed to come closer than that. So either there is something there that he does not want anyone to see, or he is scared."

"Thanks for that Hans be careful. If they can get to Sir Philip, they might want to get to you, whoever they are."

"I will Andy, In a minute I have to go. Carl will take me to the mainland and then he will come back here. I just wanted to come and tell you in person that I have to go back to NATO. I don't give a shit about my position. It is just I am in the middle of doing some good things and I would hate for them to be thrown away by some new broom sweeps clean sort of thing. Also I can keep my ear to the ground. As you know the CIA have a large field office inside Iceland. I get to hear things about their civilian contractors like Black-Tree."

"Thanks for everything you have done for us Hans, you will be missed."

"Carl is every bit as good as me and he is younger and fitter."

"Yes" Lachie said

"What?"

"He is."

"What?"

"Younger, fitter and faster" Lachie said with a smile and reached out to shake the hand of Hans. Hans in turn put his hand out and then changed his mind and they exchanged man hugs, as did I. Just then Carl came up with Hans's backpack, which he threw into the open door of the Sea King and climbed in after it. The rotors started and Hans climbed in and slid the door closed. From the Co-Pilots seat he waved us farewell. The dogs all laid down flat on the deck as the helicopter lifted off and turned towards land. Then just like that Hans was gone.

ACT 16

After Carl returned from the mainland, we sat back down in the communal lounge area and brainstormed ideas as to how we were going to get into John Stevens home or office. It was actually Oran that hit on the idea first.

"We know his home is like a fortress and that we would probably be shot on sight, if we even went anywhere near there or Whitehall. So why don't we grab him between home and work. You said before that the mobile protection detail is normally a two man team who follow and that there will be a driver plus one other in his Jaguar. So that is just four men to take out. I have seen you guys in action and that should be easy enough for you?"

"Oran on paper it sounds easy enough, but you have to remember that these guards are highly trained and they are going to be on high alert."

"I know that Andy but I have taken a look at the route that he takes to work. In order for him to get to the M25 he has to use a small B-Class road. The road that he has to take, has current ongoing work being completed on it. Can we not form some sort of a plan, in order to take him at the roadworks?"

"Mr Oran. That is not such a bad idea, especially if he has been encountering this work on a daily basis." Abdalla said

We talked and drew plans and drank lots of coffee. Then went to bed as the sun was coming up. The following day with Carl at the controls of the Sea King. All of us including Oran and his faithful guardian, Cyber beside him, said goodbye to our families and friends. Then we set off for Buckinghamshire. Hans landed at a small civilian airfield and there were three private hire, Ford Transit Vans along with a low loader which was complete with a bulldozer on its trailer, also on that trailer, was a sheet of inch thick steel about 12 feet long and 6 feet wide. There were Steel barriers and steel cables along with all sorts of road work tools. Oran and Cyber went in one of the vans, with his computer equipment. Lachie would drive the HGV Low Loader. We would split up out arms and ammunition between the other two Transits along with some of the other road work tools. We all wore our Storno radios along with full Kevlar Body armour under our boiler suits and Hi Vis Jackets and Trousers.

Oran had fabricated some magnetic signs that we attached to the sides of the vans and HGV. He had researched and found out, that the road works were being carried out by a third party for Buckinghamshire County Council. Oran had gone to this companies website and downloaded their logo and incorporated that onto the signs, that we had now attached to the transport. We would have to get to the area of the roadworks long before the start of the normal working day. Carl would stay with the helicopter but would be on standby. We drove without any incident and found the roadworks easy enough. Then we set the trap and waited. The contractors arrived at 6am on the dot. They were of course surprised to see, three more transit vans like the one they had come in. We were easily able to bring them into our custody and after relieving them of the keys to a large shipping container that was being used to store their JCB Digger, Generator and Compressor, all of which we emptied out before locking the bound and gagged workmen inside. We set up the traffic lights for manual operation. Then dragged the sheet of steel off the low loader by using the JCB. The sheet of steel was dragged along the road until it was exactly next to the steel shipping container. After which we offloaded the Bulldozer and parked it facing back down the road in the direction that we knew John Stevens would be coming from. We parked the two transit vans, on the opposite side of the road from the Shipping Container, then the JCB slightly further down from that. The result being that in order to go past the shipping container you would have to drive over the sheet of steel. Because we had parked the other vans parallel to the container. This would only allow single file traffic, to pass between the container and the vans, with almost no

room to spare. Then we set up the usual things that workmen do and
let the traffic come and go. We knew that Stevens would be coming in
a Black Jaguar, with another following behind with his security detail.
Oran was sat in the other Transit van about half a mile further down
the road, he had set up a sign showing roadworks ahead, in order that
his parked transit, would not look suspicious. We waited. If this went
off as Oran's plan then we should be able to pull this off without a
single shot being fired.

"OK Satellite shows that the two car convoy, has left his home they
should be here, in less than 30 minutes"

"Thanks Oran" I replied and called Carl to be ready for his part.

There was very little transport using this small side road and that
would work in our favour. We waited I was nervous, I was sure the
others were, though they showed no signs of it.

"They have just passed me, and it is just the two cars. Stevens
in the front car with a driver and two more men in the support car"
Oran's voice said in my headset.

I switched the traffic lights to red at both ends of the roadworks.
Right on cue. Abdalla was in one transit, and Lachie in another. I was
the spare man on the ground, so to speak. The bulldozers blade was
down and facing towards the traffic. The two jaguars moved perfectly
into place. The second vehicle had deliberately kept close to the first
in order that they would not be separated, by any traffic event. That
was one of the things we were hoping for. Because we had parked the
Vans on the other side of the road the cars then had to pull very close
to the Container. Again this was another part of the plan. Oran had
now arrived behind the convoy and pulled off the road and out of their
direct line of sight. He then reappeared in the JCB digger, with the
bucket down and dove it force-ably into the back of the rear Jaguar,
forcing it to the rear of the lead jaguar and up against the blade of the
Bulldozer. While Oran was doing this Abdalla and Lachie pulled up
on the drivers side of the cars with the Vans. They were now effectively
blocked in. The steel container stopping them from opening the doors
and also from shooting out of the windows of the passenger side of
the cars and the vans doing the same for the drivers side. I knew Carl
was on his way and told Oran, to block all radio and satellite signals
from this area. This would ensure they would not have reinforcements.

Oran had set a red light half a mile down the road, where he had originally been parked and I had done the same down the opposite end of the road. So there were no civilians, apart from the men locked up in the shipping container. Abdalla and Lachie were now out of their vans and were attaching cables to the steel plate that the lead Jaguar with John Stevens in, was sat upon. I was standing with an RPG to my shoulder pointing it at the two cars and I looked at the worried faces within them. John Stevens had put down the paper, he had been reading prior to his car being stopped. He had picked up a mobile phone, in a vain attempt at calling on help. The cars may well have been bullet proof, but at this range, they would not be Rocket Proof. The Crash barriers, we tied around the lead car on the steel plate. The barriers were attached to steel cables, that Abdalla and Lachie were rapidly fixing to the large steel plate with the lead Jaguar on. So far we had only used a minute of the estimated three minutes that we would require. Carl brought the large chopper into a low hover over the lead, car with Stevens, in. Lachie and Abdalla were now both on the roof of the Jaguar attaching the cables to a heavy winch under the belly of the Sea King. As soon as it was attached Carl took up the slack and slowly moved away. I kept the other car coved while Lachie moved the big Bulldozer forward and blocked the support Jaguar between it and the large yellow JCB digger's bucket. As soon as that part of the plan was completed, Oran went and got Cyber and drove off in the real contractors van. All the guns we had taken and not really needed we transferred to this van. The Jaguars were fitted with bullet proof glass, whilst those inside would be protected from gunfire it also meant that they could not fire out. There was no space at the sides so escape that way for them was not an option. We knew that the Jaguar with Stevens in would have a digital tracker fitted to it. But Oran had created a little gadget which we slapped onto the roofs of his both Stevens's car and to their support vehicle. As for his detail, they would have to stay in their Jaguar until they were rescued. I kept it covered with the RPG, until we were ready to leave. Then I walked backwards towards the rear doors of the waiting transit crew bus. So far everything had worked like clockwork. Oran's plan had been simple and genius. I closed the doors behind me and we raced off down the road to a prearranged spot, where we would meet up with Carl. Which was approximately five miles down the road at a disused cement works. We had a large box-Luton panel truck waiting in a storage hanger. All the transport had been arranged and paid for including an extra large bonus so that the small company that we hired the transport from would not ask questions. The truck, like the transport that we had already used, would be reported stolen by them in about four hours. For now though, we had to get John Stevens, out of his Jaguar. Carl lowered it to the ground and we surrounded it with not just one but two rocket launchers pointed at it. The Magnetic radio blocker was still attached to the roof so they would not be able to trace the Jaguar until the batteries died or the driver escaped. That was not going to happen anytime soon.

"Throw your guns out of the car window, and then get yourself out the same way. You have thirty seconds to do so, or I will give the order to blow it up. Don't even think about trying to make a run for it. Make your choice and do it now." I shouted

I could see the driver talking with Stevens. The driver was shaking his head and then he wound his window down about three inches and slid out his Glock 17 stock first and then he lowered the window a little more as if to put another one through, the stock of an MP5 appeared and then it spun around I dived for cover as did the others the engine of the Jaguar roared into life, but the tires just spun on the smooth steel below. The barriers that had been attached to the steel lifting cable held the car firmly in place.

"Last chance throw out your weapons or die in the car." I shouted.

This time the MP5 was thrown out of the drivers window and was promptly followed by both of his hands, palm outwards.

"You too Stevens, put your hands out the window." I called to them. The rear window came down and his hands appeared. With my Sig Sauer pointed directly at the drivers head I walked towards the car.

"With your left hand wind the window all the way down and then slide your hands out of the car but keep your seat belt on" I said as I moved closer. This time he did as he was told. I quickly cable tied his hands to the metal guard rail that was around the car.

"Stevens wind your window all the way down and slide your body out. Be quick about it."

He too did as he was asked. Apart from a lame attempt of the driver, at escaping, everything had gone exactly to plan. We had not even had to kill anyone. Oran with Cyber at his side walked over to where Stevens was standing, Stevens looked more worried than he had previously. I walked over to the driver and injected him with enough Morphine to make him drift off into a happy drug induced sleep, for several hours. After Lachie had secured John Stevens hands behind his back, he then put a set of ear defenders over John's ears and a Blackout bag over John's head. We clambered into the big van, with the rest of our equipment. I knew John could not hear or see anything but I still whispered to Carl.

"What about this Chopper? Is there any way of tracing it back to you or us?"

"No Andy, it was hired through a shell corporation, then subleased to another shell corporation and then on private lease to a Russian Oligarch. He is actually wanted for crimes against Georgian businesses. There is no way that Russia will approve an extradition order, as he owns half the high up folks, in their government. He will naturally deny any involvement and the British government will naturally disbelieve him. They know who we are, but they don't know where to find us. As such they will now assume that we are getting help from Russian criminals. Hopefully they will start looking for us in Mother Russia and her friends. Meanwhile we will be in our base in the North Sea. We are not going back by air. We are going to drive back up to Wick, which is where Stu will collect us in about twelve hours from now. First though, we need some answers from Stevens. We should at least find out from him, where Sir Philip and his wife are"

"Agreed but let's relocate somewhere far away from here" I said.

We drove for about an hour going deeper into the countryside until we found an out of the way wooded area. After throwing Stevens out of the van none too gently Lachie pulled the hood and ear defenders from Stevens and then Lachie set about the softening up process. In the case of John Stevens, this did not talk long before he was begging to tell us everything.

"Where is Sir Philip?" Lachie Asked

"I don't know" he whimpered back

"Where is Sir Philip's wife?"

"She is safe."

That answer was rewarded with closed fist blow to his face that knocked Stevens to the ground. As his hands were still zip-tied behind his back he had trouble getting back from the floor.

"Lets try that again where is Mrs Reeves-Johnson?" Lachie demanded.

Stevens started to say "Safe" but all that came out was "Sa" before another stinging blow to his solar plexus, sent him choking and crumpling to the floor. Lachie did not give him time to recover.

"Where is she?"

Even if Stevens had been going to answer, the reply never made it out of his mouth before Lachie kicked him in the gut. This time however Lachie, let Stevens collect his breath and was just getting ready to launch another blow from his right boot when Stevens shouted.

"Alright! Alright! I will tell you. She is unharmed and is at the Shoulder of Mutton in Wendover."

"I know that place." I said and continued

"But it seems a stupid place to hold someone prisoner. A bit too public."

"She is not being held prisoner, well not exactly" he said

Even I did not see the slap coming, but I heard it a full blown open hand slap from Lachie. It spun Stevens around. He had previously been on his knees, but the slap sent him spinning across the forest floor. Lachie walked over and picked him up by the scruff of the neck.

"We don't have time for puzzles. Say it exactly as it is, or you will be of no further use to us. I am sure you know what that means?" Lachie said.

"I told her, I would kill her son and her husband. So I paid for her to stay at the little pub. Her son, I believe you have already rescued."

This time it was Abdalla who went over and picked Stevens up by the throat, so that his legs were dangling a foot off the floor. For most men this would have been a difficult achievement with two hands. Abdalla managed it easily with just his left hand.

"I despise those, who use women and children, to hide behind, or to use as a bartering chip. You will now tell me, where Sir Philip is, right now, or I will choke the very life out of your worthless little body." Abdalla said.

Rarely did Abdalla raise his voice, this was no exception to that rule, but Stevens could not have doubted the seriousness of the words. The words that Abdalla used were deliberate and slowly spoken in his deep bass voice. I could see that Abdalla's left thumb was in danger of crushing the larynx against his own forefinger. So I touched Abdalla on the shoulder. Rather than just let Stevens down Abdalla threw him bodily up against the closest tree. Stevens bounced off it and was left gasping for breath on the carpet of pine needles that served for the forest floor. I walked over to him and offered him a drink from my water canteen. But he just shook his head. So I sat him up against the tree trunk and gave him time to catch his breath. After thirty seconds I asked him'

"Where is Sir Philip"

"I told you I really don't know" he almost screamed at me.

"Oran can I borrow you and Cyber for a moment please?"

"Sure thing boss" Oran said and walked over to the tree where Stevens was sat and I was standing over.

Abdalla can you hold his arms back to the tree? And Lachie can you sit on his thighs.?" I asked them

Abdalla cut the cable ties that bound Johns hands. They both did as I had asked but Lachie gave me a 'What the Fuck' look. Then I pulled out my Bussé knife and after pulling off his right shoe I cut his trouser leg up as far as the knee. Stevens could not see his lower legs because Lachie was sat on his thighs, nor could he look around him, because Abdalla, had Stevens back, pulled tight against the tree, using his own arms.

"Cyber come here boy, OK what you will feel in a minute John is a Caucasian Shepard dog, having a light snack on your leg. So if I were you I would answer my questions without delay and do it honestly without games. Understand?"

"Yes but please you don't have to do this."

Out of his sight I had poured a handful of water from my canteen into one hand and held my knife in the other. Then I pushed the blade of the knife, into his shin and at the same time trickled some water over the cut. I then offered the rest of the water to Cyber so it would look and sound like Cyber was licking up his blood.

"So where is Sir Philip?"

"Honestly I really don't know" and then before I could say anything he continued.

"Black-Tree have him."

"What?"

"Black-Tree, they have him."

"Why the fuck would Black-Tree have him?"

"Because I arranged for it to happen"

"Why? Why take him, his son and his wife?"

"Because we, were meant to be together, but she chose him instead of me. She would not leave him. Yet I know she would have loved me like she used to."

"Are you saying, that all this is because you wanted another man's wife?"

"It is not like that. She loved me once and she would again."

"Do you realise the number of men that have died because of your childish behaviour. And what has the Boys Rifle got to do with all this?"

"I had arranged, for a specialist SAS Unit to be equipped with the rifle. Then there were to be big kickback payments, to the SAS commander and some of his men. I was also going to arrange for some wealthy Arab nations to have this weapon."

"What nations?"

"The Saudi's, they were offering to provide information in return as well as cash. They were going to finger some of the worlds worst terrorists. It would have been a win win situation. The world would have been a safer place. She would have been proud of me because of that."

"Are you completely fucking nuts?" Lachie screamed in his face

"So you say Black-Tree have Sir Philip. How do we get him back?"

"You cant. They know who he is. They believed that a high up member of the security forces, is in fact a double agent working with some extremest Islamic terrorists. There is a paper trail that shows it was Sir Philip, that was the person behind selling the BOYS to the

Saudis. I told them he was the terrorist, that they and us have been chasing for years and they just took it on good face."

"Let me guess you sold him out as Zorro?"

"How did you know that?"

I could almost hear his shoulders become dislocated as Abdalla increased the pressure. Stevens screamed in agony. We were not a lot further on, than we had previously been apart from we knew the American Private Security company Black-Tree Enterprises, had 'The Suit'. We would be able to get Mrs Reeves-Johnson and keep her safe. But we had to find, where Sir Philip was being held. Abdalla would contact the Kenyan arms company and give them the heads up, that we knew about the scam, and that if they followed through, then we would let it be know to all the security services of the world. This would effectively bankrupt the company. So that end of the mystery could be put to bed. It was just about the greed and of one man. The other part though, was about one man's desire for another man's wife and that part was pure madness.

I knew that Cyber would growl like he was going to attack if you grabbed him by the back of the neck. Even though it was just playful growling. Stevens however did not know this. I pushed the knife in with my left hand and pulled Cyber's head down towards the bleeding leg of Stevens. Cyber duly growled and shook his head back and forth, while I moved Johns leg about with the point of the knife pressed up against the bone of his lower leg. He screamed and screamed. So much so that I thought an entire county would hear him.

"Where are they holding him?"

"Please I don't know"

"Last fucking chance before this dog eats your leg clean off."

I moved the knife around and at the same time played roughly with Cyber, who growled even more fiercely. John suddenly went white and his eyes rolled back in their sockets, his entire body stiffened and then went limp.

"Shit, he is having a heart attack. Lay him on his back" I said as I stood up.

Lachie and Abdalla laid him flat on his back. I felt his carotid artery. Just a very weak pulse almost nothing at all. I listened to his chest, he was in full blown cardiac arrest. He was no use to us dead.

We needed him to let everyone know that he had told them a pack of lies, or we would stand no chance at getting Sir Philip back. I started compressions. After he had wiped most of the blood and broken teeth away, Lachie started on filling his lungs with air via mouth to mouth. I stopped compressions and felt for a pulse. Nothing. Without a hospital or even an ambulance, filled with all the cardiac equipment they carry, there was only one other way I knew, of starting a heart after a massive heart attack like this one. If I did not get it started soon, his brain would be starved of Oxygen and we would get no more information from Stevens.

"Oran get my bag from the van please"

Oran ran to the van and returned seconds later with my canvas medical bag. I went in and found the longest needle I had, that was one that I would use in the field for a collapsed lung. I did not even know if what I was about to do, would work, but I had to try. I attached the large needle to the end of a disposable syringe and then drew up 2cc of Adrenaline, after making sure there was no air in the syringe I ripped open John's shirt and felt for the fourth intercostal space between the ribs then pushed the needle in. I was aiming for the ventricular space of his heart. When I thought I was there, I depressed the plunger of the syringe. I don't really know what I was expecting but whatever it was, it failed. Nothing no change. I looked at his eyes. No reaction to light and dark. I smashed my fist down onto his chest three times, nothing. I knew I must have broken the sternum. That would not kill him though but there was a fucking good chance the heart attack would. This heart attack would be his swan song.

"Fuck! Fuck! Shit and double Fuck." I screamed to no one. Then I kicked his lifeless body in the nuts.

"How in the name of fucking hell are we to supposed find 'The Suit' now?" I asked again to no one in particular.

"We need to get home boss. As soon as his driver wakes up, it will only take him a short time to escape his binding and then go for help" Oran said.

He was right and I knew it. I had fucked things up, by frightening Stevens too much, or by allowing the others to batter him. I should have realised that Stevens was nothing like the rest of us. He was a desk jockey. We were fit and battle hardened. There was not much left in life, that we had to be afraid of. We had faced our fears way back in the early days of Team Seven. We had been hunted down by everyone including SIS. We had been beaten, shot, stabbed and threatened with the worst evils of the world. We had literally held the life of billions in our hands. So it was really difficult, to stress us to the point of a heart attack. I was sure John Stevens was a regular at his local gymnasium and squash courts and he had stress from achieving targets and making deals. He had never though been a field agent, so he had never had to face the possibility, that someone would ever take his life. We left his body there on the forest floor. Limp and lifeless, his eyes looked like those of every dead person I had seen. The glassy surface turned to dull and they would soon be covered with a grey layer that death bestows upon all of us. Shit happens. We had just lost our only lead to where the suit was. We were in deep shit too, we had just killed the head of SIS. That was what had happened to us. Shit Happened to him, that was just it, Shit Happens.

ACT 17

After swinging by Wendover and The Shoulder of Mutton pub, we collected Mrs Reeves-Johnson. I was amazed that there was no extra security on her. I guess the very thought, that harm would come to her husband and son, was enough, to hold her in place. After introducing myself. She came with us willingly, when we told her that we had rescued her son and that John Stevens was now dead. I paid her bill at the Pub and left a serious and overly generous tip, asking the owner to forget ever having seen us or 'The Suits' wife.

We took turns in driving and were always careful to wear baseball caps and to keep our heads down when passing through any of the towns and cities on the way back up to the highlands. We refuelled once just outside Inverness and then followed the A9 all the way up to Wick. The Catherine May, was docked against the great granite blocks, that made up the wall of the harbour. I made a quick radio call to Stu and asked him to bring our large backpacks with some of our clothing in. We always kept spare sets of clothes on the Catherine May. We could not really go unnoticed wearing our full battle gear, even in the Highland harbour of Wick. As we waited we loaded all our firearms into one big sports bag along with the body armour.

Stu arrived about 20 minutes later and we all changed and carrying our kit-bags walked back down to the Catherine May, looking like any other fisherman getting ready to go out to sea for several days. Jeans and jumpers with boots and wool hats. It was a uniform of the Highland Fishermen. With the exception of Mrs Reeves-Johnson, who even in jeans and jumper still managed to look like a genuine lady. Once we were onboard, Stu took us out to sea and towards our home. After getting showered and freshened up I went down to the galley and a decent cup of coffee. I would have to contact Hans but I would do that from our base, via dead drop email. This was a method that we used, to be secure. We would use a web based mail system and write a message but not actually send it to anyone, it would be saved to the drafts folder. Any one, who was away from our team, would check on a daily basis to see if there was a new message there, if there was, they would amend the message with a reply and again save it to the drafts folder. This way, no message was sent so it could not show anywhere, or under any search engine. The only way to read the message was to have the password to the webmail. Nothing sent, nothing received. As we had an encrypted password that actually required a piece of hardware to access. It was double safe. It would be a few hours before we got home. Stu and Rosemary had used their trip to Wick as a restocking mission, not only for their boat but for the rig as well. Now one of the holds was almost full of frozen and chilled goods. Along with a large variety of dry goods. I guess it must have been one of the Bi-Annual stock up trips. I lost track of things like that and had left it up to the non-coms to arrange. To be quite honest I was beginning to lose track, of the people that had been affected by all of this. We were becoming the protectors in-facto for more and more people.

I would arrange for Mrs Reeves-Johnson to join her son on the rig, in one of the guest apartments. We were looking after the young policeman. We had two scientists and two extra medical people on the rig. Our own families were growing. It was not that we were drastically short of space. Before we had purchased the Rig, it had been the home and workplace to over 100 men. That said we had made it far more luxurious, complete with all the accessories that we wanted like spacious accommodation along with our swimming pool and gymnasium. Not forgetting the shared area like the communal kitchen, bar and lounge area. The more people that came, the less secure we would be in the future. That part of things worried me, although I had not shared my thoughts on this, with anyone else. I went to my bunk and lay down on the cot and let the movement of the sea rock me to sleep and wash away my worries. I must have been in a deep sleep as Rosemary was shaking me awake.

"Andy we are home, or at least we will be in a minute" she said as she handed me a fresh cup of steaming coffee.

"Thanks Rosemary" I said and she left pulling my door closed.

I sat up and looked at my face in the mirror opposite. The man looking back at me, was not the man I wanted to be. Today another man had died because of me. I was becoming something worse than just a Sniper for SIS. I was becoming the very thing I hated, a bully. When this mission was over, I wanted out for real. I would take Petrá and the kids and make a new life far from here. Perhaps by a smallholding and pretend to be a farmer. God knows I did not need the money. I felt the Catherine May touch our floating dock, far below the platform. A knock at the door called me away from my day dream. Lachie opened the door and entered the cabin.

"How the hell are we going to find the suit now? The only man that actually knew where he might be, is dead and we have no clue other than, those cowboys at Black-Tree might have him. If they do, they have wrong intel that shows him to be this international terrorist, come double agent. If we contact them, they will say they have it right, as all the proof came from the head of our own security services. We cant get any denial on that. The new head of SIS, will again, have false details left by Stevens, showing 'The Suit' to be guilty and probably shows him to be involved in this Boys Rifle scam."

I wiped the shaving foam from my face, then balled the towel up and threw it at my bunk.

"How the fuck should I know Lachie? You all ask me these questions and expect me, to have all the fucking answers at hand. Well hear this, news flash mate. I don't Fucking Know!!"

Lachie stood facing me and look right into my eyes. I could tell that my outburst had hurt him deeply. But I continued unabated.

"I am tired, of being the one, who has to make the fucking decisions. I am tired of all the death and fucking destruction that seems to surround us, wherever we go. I am sick to fucking death of it all, Lachie. I only ever wanted to be a medic. I helped kill Stevens, no scrub that, I fucking tortured him to death myself. I murdered Chang. I have murdered all in the name of keeping others safe. Our parents have been attacked, our families have to hide. The kids can never have any kind of normal life. Lachie you know we are more than just friends. We have been like siblings since we were young kids. So I love you like my brother. Every fucking day, I ask you to be at the front of things, while I stay for the greater part safe at the rear. I am tired of it all. I am really fucking tired."

Lachie just stood there, he never said anything to begin with. Then, he just smiled.

"So does that mean you want a coffee with Irish then?" he asked

"What? Have you not been listening to a word I have fucking said Lachie?"

"That will be with then. See Andy, I feel more alive when we do this shit, than I ever did as a Rock Ape in the RAF. Yes I know you are a Medic and all that shit. I will always have your back mate, not that you really need it. You have become a real soldier and not just that Andy, you our our spirit level. You are the one that stops us from going all primal, when things go to shit. Would you really have preferred to be 'Just a Medic' or being part of our giant and extended family. Yes we live in the middle of the North Sea. But look at it this way. You met Petrá and the twins because of this, and you have a good life ninety five percent of the time. A life where you can do what you want. We have more space than a mansion. Andy, people look to you to lead, because you can. Hans used to say you would have made a great policeman. He was right, you see things that others don't. I remember Hans once made the comment 'you dot the joins' and we told him that you join the dots. We are the dots Andy and you are the line that brings us all together."

"Fuck!"

"Fuck what Andy?"

"Like Fuck, where and when did you get all philosophical and deep?"

"About two minutes ago, when you started to feel fucking sorry for yourself. Stevens was a twat of the first order. Who cares if he died. Hell, he caused the deaths of at least 20 men. We might not have him to answer questions but we have everything from his computer, well Oran Has. We have access to NATO info, via Hans. We will find where they have 'The Suit' and I know you will come up with some ridiculously dangerous plan to get him back. So once again I ask you, is that a with or without?"

"With a large Irish." I said and all the tension was gone.

We helped tie up the Catherine May and with the help of everyone else. We first offloaded any supplies for the rig and then we took the lift to the platform. After going to my apartment and seeing the kids and Petrá. I went to the communal kitchen where the others were and snagged a cup from the rack on the side. I sat down at my usual seat and poured my coffee from the pot on the trivet in the centre of the table. Lachie passed me a bottle of Jameson's Irish and I topped the coffee off, with a large slug. It is quite amazing just how much better yo feel after a shower, a good talking too, followed by a great coffee, topped up with whisky. Carl had joined us at the table. Lachie to my left Abdalla to my right and next to him was Oran. Stu and Rosemary were also with us. Petrá was in the class with the kids. Mrs Reeves-Johnson was now with her son and they both looked the better for it. Our parents were on the floating dock with fishing rods. I had asked them why they bothered, when we had the use of a bloody big trawler? We could have as much fish as we could ever want. They said it was not the act of catching the fish that they enjoyed, it was the act of relaxing with a rod and having a good chin wag. The two medics and William, were playing some card game in the communal lounge area. While the two scientists read books in the garden area. Morag was helping Petrá. I knew that the girls would help The Reeves-Johnson's settle in and see that they had everything they required.

"What next?" Carl asked.

"We find where 'The Suit' is and we get him back"

"I can help, with looking deep into John Stevens files and also his background and contacts. I will try and come up with some kind of a map of what happened to 'The Suit'. The with a bit of luck, we will get an Idea of where he is being held. I am also going to try and hack, into Black-Tree Enterprises. At least if I can get a list of names of their head people, then perhaps I can get some links between them and Stevens."

I thanked Oran and he along with Cyber took of for his grotto.

"Lachie?"

"What?"

"Got any ideas?"

"On what?"

"Anything?"

"The egg"

"What?"

"The egg came first."

Abdalla almost choked on his coffee, which unlike ours, would have a good shot of Havana Club in it. The others started to smile, but almost dared each other to be the first one to laugh. That was Lachie all over, he could relieve tension with a childish quip. But normally he would do it like a shaggy dog story, and wind up to it. This time though it was just a quip.

I knew I would have to contact Hans. There was no use in contacting any of the UK Security services or even the Americans. This was something that we would have to do on our own, with very little help from anyone else. I was sure that 'The Suit' would have been vilified amongst the security services of the world.

Some like the Russians would be glad to see Sir Philip out of the picture. I knew we would try, I was not sure if we could succeed. Hopefully Hans could find something out at NATO. I would have to talk to 'The Suits' wife and son, just to see if there was anything at all that Stevens, or any of his men had let slip. Even the smallest piece of information could be the thing that solved the puzzle.

ACT 18

After several attempts we managed to get Hans on video conference and gave him an update. He said he would contact the Americans and see if he could get any information from them. Although he already had papers on his desk showing him that Sir Philip, was the double agent in the security services, as well as supposedly being the terrorist that some fool had named Zorro. Yet according to Hans he could find nothing about Zorro anywhere, no acts that he had been involved in, but he had managed to make it all the way to the top, of the most wanted terrorist in the western world. According to Hans, Black-Tree had small units all around the world, whilst they got paid by the American's it was all done indirectly, in the form of contracts, that had little or nothing to do with the American Military. The payments were always made in a way the USA, could deny any official association, with any of the nefarious actions of the well known company.

Black-Tree's own website, claimed that they provided Logistical support, in areas of the world, where it would be difficult for the military to operate. They claimed also on another site, that Oran had found. To be a Private Security Company, offering solutions for the Mining and Oil Industry's. They recruited exclusively from Elite Military Units of the USA and from Nations friendly to the USA. They were listed as having an annual turnover in the Billions of dollars. Yet when Oran checked on the number of employees, he could only get figures on the Administrative staff that they employed. There seemed to be no control over the weapons, that they could acquire. If they needed it, they got it, via one contract or another.

Hans said he had composed an email that would need editing, which was his way of saying that he had used the dead drop email.

"What's in the dead drop Oran?" I asked

Oran clicked away on his keyboard and brought the page up on the big screen.

'Andy

I pushed a friend in the C.I.A. They tell me that the Black-Tree Unit you are looking for, is headed up by a Colonel Jay Demontford Rtd.

He was previously a Captain in Delta Force but has promoted himself over the last few years. His men are all hand picked from the units, he used to command, whilst in the employ of the US Forces. He has worked in the Oil Pipeline Security and has a bit of a name for getting results.

A few years back he was accused of wiping out an entire village of North Western Peru. There was a small indigenous tribe that did not want a pipeline going across their lands. The Official story is that there was a Large explosion caused by the native people, who were trying to steal oil directly out of the pipe. This supposedly caused a massive explosion that killed the entire village. No one could prove otherwise and the Peruvian government made a lot of money out of the deal so they did not care.

What did raise a few heads, is that they are suspected of having dropped a Daisy Cutter directly on the Village. Where they obtained such a weapon, is not known. But the only country the could have got that particular item from is the USA.

Back to This Colonel Demontford. I can't find out where he is, perhaps Oran would be better placed. He should work forward from the Peru incident and see if he can find any other serious incidents, involving Black-Tree.

I have a possible line that I will look into and should have answers for you tomorrow.

Hans

"Wow they sound like they are crazy bastards" Oran said when he had finished reading it.

"Oran can you get on this Demontford bloke, I want to know EVERYTHING about him, right down to what he eats for breakfast. I am sorry to put pressure on you so soon after we just got out of the shit, but the sooner we have the information, then the better chance we have of getting 'The Suit' back to his family."

"On it boss" he said and instantly went back to his computer. After printing the Email off, he wiped the mail and closed the account down. Oran was well aware of computer security and Dead Drops.

"This Colonel sounds like one crazy bastard, and worse he sounds like a dangerous crazy bastard. I mean anyone who, when retired, then goes and promotes themselves, has to have some kind of mental issue"

"I agree Lachie. But he would not be the first to do that, remember Idi Amin back in the 1970's? He even awarded himself the Victoria Cross not to mention a Knighthood as well as crowning himself King! He was also responsible for Murder and Genocide."

"Aye a right fucking nutter. And you are planning to go up against someone like that?"

"Lachie I don't know what I am planning yet. For now I just want to follow down the leads we have and see if we can find 'The Suit'. Besides how tough can it be, say compared to being chased by ALL the worlds Security Forces, or rescuing the twins families, out of a North Korean death camp, going in via China."

"When you put it like that Andy, it does not sound quite so bad."

There was an audible bing from the computer.

"Hans had just logged back into the email server." Oran said.

I looked up at the large screen and watched the text form in front of me, sometimes it was backspaced and corrected as Hans typed his new message to us.

'Andy

Can you ask Carl to stay on location with you. His big brother is on his way as we speak. He will assist Carl. I have an unconfirmed report of Colonel Demontford, being in Syria last month. Black-Tree were used to reclaim an oil refinery for one of your nations Oil Companies. Again there were a large number of civilian casualties. There are claims that he (Black-Tree) machine gunned a group of locals who were apparently making things difficult for the Syrian Government.

Everyone here at NATO, seem to know about this Colonel, but no one can tell me what he looks like or even give me a Photo ID. He must have someone really good covering his financial and social tracks. Perhaps he has

an alter ego in the real world that is diametrically different to his military
one. Have Oran look into that aspect.

When I worked as a policeman. I followed a few rules. Number one,
most murders were committed by spouses. Number two, who benefits? And
most importantly of all "Follow the money" This should save Oran some
time.

Hans'

"On it boss" Oran said even before I could ask him.

"I will leave you to it Oran, I have to go and check in with Petrá
and the children. Not to mention my dog who will probably now
thinks of me as a stranger and rip me to pieces the moment I walk
through the door." I said as I turned as left Oran's grotto.

Lachie and Carl followed but Abdalla remained.

"So who is your brother?" Lachie asked

"I don't know" Carl answered blankly.

"What do you mean you don't know, do you have more than
one?" Lachie asked

"Nope."

"So you only have one?"

"Nope"

"No what?"

"No I don't have more than one....................And no I don't
have even one."

"I am confused" Said Lachie.

"I know" Carl replied and continued

"You are a man and yet you wear a skirt and ...."

That was as far as he got. I had to stop the playful Icelandic Pilot,
before it got out of hand and some one got hurt.

"STOP I said louder than I had intended, but it got their attention.
Carl what do you think Hans means by the message about your
brother?"

"He has either managed to get me another helicopter or something
else of use to us. But right now I am going to have some of Rosemary's
wonderful food. Field rations are for field mice. Are you coming
Lachie" he said with a wink and his hand shot out to shake Lachie's
own extended hand.

They went off in the direction of the communal kitchen and I went to see the young police officer. He was in his temporary medical bay. Before today, the last time I had seen him he was in a pretty bad way. Today he was sat in a wheelchair in a pair of sports shorts and a sweatshirt. Presumably Stu had collected some clothes from the mainland. Both of of the legs bore full length casts. And his facial wounds seem to be well healed. I just wanted to check on his health and to explain that for now he could not leave the confines of the Rig, not just for his safety but also for the safety of every one else here. I would want his assurance, when and if, this matter was concluded, that he would never reveal where we lived. He promised, that because of all we had done for he he would stay quiet. I would arrange for him to have a new identity either through Oran or if we got 'The Suit' back, through him. The medical and scientific people were the responsibility of Hans. But again I would prefer they stayed here for the duration. Given the line of our work, extra medics would always be useful.

Finally I made my way up to my apartment and went in. Immediately the children ran to me and I cuddled and kissed them both before putting them down and embracing my beautiful wife. I looked at her and she was indeed beautiful. Her eyes were almost like glowing Emeralds, It did not really matter how much sun, Petrá sat in, her body would go bright red and then return to its milky white colour, covered in brown freckles. Her hair in some lights looked like fire spilling out from her head. It was the most natural red hair you could imagine. She was slim, but not that bony skinny look, that those super models go for. Petrá was just built slim and fit. I would pinch myself just to make sure I had not dreamed her up. She never wore make up, not even on our wedding day. Once she had been shopping with Morag and Rosemary and had come back with various face creams and mascaras. She had put some on and then washed it off. After I had said playfully.

"Are you trying to improve upon perfection?"

That was my Petrá she was perfection. She was smart too, a lot smarter than me, she completed several degrees, since moving to the rig. These she did through the Open University. All the mail was sent to her home and then my father sent it on to the Hotel in Keiss where

Stu would collect it once a week. I was lost in my thoughts as I held and kissed her.

"What Andy?" she asked in a furtive way

"Nothing, just thinking how lucky I am"

"Yes you are. Mr Andy McPhee and don't you forget it my Andy Andy Andy" she sang it out.

Just the same way as she had all those years ago in the back room of her shop in the Faeroe Islands.

"Petrá, as you know some bad people have taken 'The Suit' and the man who was his second in command was involved in it."

There were no secrets between us. Petrá had joined us about a year after we rescued the kids. But we had initially met after we had tracked some Neo-Nazis, down to a whaling station on the small Island next to her Island. I had used her fathers Ship to Shore radio to get help. Then All I could do was think about Petrá. Her, face her silly words and accent, they filled my days and nights until I had given in and gone and collected her and shown her our home. Next day she came to live here with us as my partner and then as my wife. So she knew what we had done in the past and she knew what we were involved in now.

"You said was? When you talked about his number two"

"Yes, He is dead."

"Because of something he caused to happen?"

"Yes Petrá, he sold 'The Suit' out to some really bad men."

"Andy, did you Kill him?"

"Yes Petrá I guess I did, but not as directly as shooting him, or something like that. We were asking him questions and he had a heart attack. I tried everything I knew, to save him but it was a massive coronary. He was afraid we would hurt him and he just died. You know the business we are in Petrá. I should say, we were in. But now as you know we are trying to save our friend. So I will not lie to you. I don't think it would be nice, to go into too many details. After we get 'The Suit' back I was thinking about moving to a nice warm country and have a little farm. I am sick of all this cloak and dagger stuff."

"OK Andy I will not ask details. Just be safe. I will not pretend that I like what you do. Do you really think that you can ever be free of SIS?"

"Yes I think so Petrá. We have enough money to afford to live anywhere you like and I am sure Oran can build us new identities complete with a past."

"Do you not like living here on the Rig with your friends?"

I had not thought for a moment until now that Petrá might actually enjoy her life here in the middle of the north sea. Yes we had made it glamorous and comfortable. But only because we need to hide from the rest of the world.

"You like living here Petrá?"

"Andy look at where I lived and grew up, it was not as nice as our home here. You saw my house it was small and cold. I had a small shop with three customers. My father and brother were fishermen from our Island and they both died at sea. I see more people and have more friends here on this Oil Platform, than I had ever previously had. So yes Mr Andy McPhee, I am very happy to live on this Island on Legs. Unless you think that there is some immediate danger to the children or us. Then I do not need a fancy farm in the sunshine."

"Ohh I see" was all I could muster. Fortunately for me the telephone in our apartment rang. Both the children raced to answer it. Aíná got there first.

"Hello this is Aíná. ......Who is it?" she said in her sweet voice. While Finn sulked because his sister had beaten him to the phone.

"Yes Uncle Oran....... I will get daddy. .....Daddy, Uncle Oran wants you" She said as she held the phone out to me.

I listened to what Oran had to say, and then put the phone back on the receiver.

"You are supposed to say Goodbye, when you finish on the phone daddy" Aíná scolded me.

"Yes you are right Darling, that was rude of me. I have to go and talk with Uncle Oran in his apartment. I will be back in time to kiss you good night"

"OK Daddy don't be long then"

Petrá looked at me, not angry but not happy either. I kissed he on the cheek and went out and down to Oran's.

I knocked and waited to be invited in.

"Yo! Its never locked and you are always welcome."

How Oran managed to actually survive in here was beyond me and I am sure that if a Pizza delivery company would deliver out here, then his place would be cluttered up with empty or worse partially empty boxes. It was not exactly a mess but it was not tidy either. Each apartment had a washing machine, but Rosemary had once offered to do the washing for everyone and Oran had been the only one that had accepted. Consequently there were stacks of clean clothing that Rosemary had done for him, but that Oran, had not found the time to put away. There were Hard Drives, stacked up on the floor, along with various connector cables. In the middle of his floor was his gaming chair, which unless he was working, he would be sat in for a minimum of twelve hours a day, fighting a global war in some game or other. Lachie was already there as was Abdalla, Carl and Stu came in behind me.

"What you got for us Oran" I asked when everyone had cleared a small space to park themselves.

"This Colonel Demontford bloke, he gets about a bit. He was in the UK at the time 'The Suit' got taken but according to the records he never made it past the security at London's Heathrow Airport. He came in on a US Military Flight, which is not that uncommon. They land there all the time and they have a special area, for the military to go through customs. Initially they assumed because he was carrying military document with his name and rank on as well as an American Passport, that he and the five men with him, were all bound for a base in the UK. As you know when going through a civil airport, all firearms have to be in a lock-box. They arrived with that, but they were also wearing concealed under arm holsters with firearms in. They created a bit of a Fuss and SIS were contacted. It being a diplomatic matter it was directed to John Stevens. He sorted it by sending transport and the correct documentation, for them to carry firearms, on British soil. They returned to Heathrow later that day but this time there were seven men that boarded the American Military aircraft. We know this because even military plane are required to process document for every person on board. Guess what name was used?" Oran said, nobody answered

"Go on Oran you tell us"

"Sir Philip Reeves-Johnson. They used his real name and real Passport."

"Where did the plane go?"

"You are going to love this. It took a non stop flight to Cuba"

"Cuba? I thought the Cubans, fucking hated the Americans since the Bay of Pigs debacle and the Cuban Missile crisis. Don't they still have some kind of blockade or trade embargo on the Cubans. I am sure I remember Castro saying something about the Americans should stop their illegal grip on the Cuban Economy."

"Yes that is true Andy, but what most folks don't know is that the USA still has a lease on a plot of land on the southern tip of Cuba. You will probably have heard the name but not really associated it with Cuba. Guantanamo Bay, or GitMo to the initiated."

"I thought that the American Army ran that place."

"They do and they don't, they run the jail end of it and the civilian contractors run the black ops side of things. They are a law unto themselves. They do not have any oversight from Congress, or an other official body. As Cuba is not a signatory to the Geneva Convention and the black ops folks, don't actually exist there. They can pretty much do as they please with impunity."

"Oran how sure are you that it was 'The Suit' that they took out on the plane."

"Well we all know that Stevens was a desk jockey and not a field agent. If he had been a real SIS agent, then he would know that Heathrow, has more cameras per square metre than any other place on earth. Wiping the images from one or two camera's is a relatively easy, if time consuming task. Trying to do it from the thousand plus cameras, in Heathrow and the thousands of cameras, outside on the roads, would be impossible. So I have hacked into the mainframe security server, via the G4S server there. And now I can pull up all the footage over the last month. All I have to do is locate the ones that will have captured him."

"Jesus Oran, that sounds like an impossible task and one that could take time, that we just don't have"

"For mere mortals such as you Andy, you would be correct. But you forget I am Oran, a God of the internet. That, and I stole a program from Hans, and one that he borrowed from the CIA."

"Hans borrowed a program from the CIA?"

"Well not exactly Andy, he borrowed from Homeland Security through the CIA."

"OK Oran why do I get the feeling that I really don't want to know this part, but go on"

"Well yes just knowing that we got this from Homeland Security, would probably put us on a wanted list, pretty close to the top. Anyway they have a new facial recognition program, that they actually got from their NSA. The algorithms that it runs, are truly amazing and I would not mind deconstructing the program, to take a look at it in more detail"

I rotated my finger in a 'Lets a get a move on and to the point' sort of thing."

"Ohh right, yes. OK so like I say, they have this program that can run 10,000 faces a minute. Which is like fast man, so I also have a program that Hans gave us before. You remember that PRISM program? well I have used that to mine the cameras at Heathrow and linked it to the FRS, that's the facial recognition software. So with my own algorithm, embedded in the prism software, I have been able to get it to scan the entire camera database, of Heathrow as well as the Roads and Motorways around the Air Port. That way we will be able to back track."

"So?" Lachie asked?

"What?" Oran replied.

"Now is not the time Lachie. What he means Oran, is where are we with it at this moment"

Lachie gave me the Bird.

"Its running and now we have a day and a rough time, I should have the images in moment or two."

Oran hit some keys on the keyboard in front of him and the main screen was filled with lots of small windows each was comparing faces to those of peoples passports or driving licenses and even social media accounts. Anything that had a photograph on and was in any form of database was being scanned against faces picked up by security cameras. They were comparing the distance between eyes, size and shape of nose placement of ears, mouth, chin and all the bits that don't change. It ignored hair including facial hair. Even if you tried to disguise by wearing dark glasses the program would then discount that part and then look closer at other parts and then extrapolate the rest. Then one of the small windows, suddenly increased in size and took up half of the main screen, while the other side continued to scan thousands of faces every minute. The image was captured on a dashboard camera, of one of the airport utility vehicles. It showed a man walking between two other men. With four more men walking behind. The man in the middle at the front was Sir Philip.

"That's him Oran. Can you back track from there?"

"Can you shoot?" He asked me and continued

"Already doing it."

Images flashed across the screen three Range Rovers going backwards. All the way to RAF Dawes Hill.

"OK Oran we already know what happened there, just needed to check it was 'The Suit' they had."

"Andy what I don't get, is why did he go so quietly? From what I can gather he is a bit of a hard man in his own right."

"Oran what would you do to save the ones you loved and the people you were responsible for? They had his Wife and Son and then at some point, they would probably want to know where we live. So he went to save the ones he loved. And he would know, we would come looking for him"

"What about us?" Oran asked a little worriedly

"Mr Oran, Sir Philip will die before he gives up our names and or location. This much I am sure of."

"Abdalla is right, which is all the more reason that we have to go and save him."

"Andy, there is no more secure location on this planet than Guantanamo Bay Cuba. It is like a triangle. Two of the sides are open to the sea and the other shares a no man's land, with the Cuban forces. They don't even know how many mines, are around the outside of the camp. They have radar, they have patrol boats. Guantanamo Bay is just 100 miles from the USA. They can have jet fighters over Guantanamo in a matter of minutes. It is constantly scanned by satellites and these satellites are monitored 24/7. Where you went in North Korea is like walking into an empty field by comparison to this place. They shoot people who even get close."

ACT 19

Carls 'Big Brother' arrived at 2am. It was a Bell 505 Jet Ranger with Hans at the controls. Unlike the previous helicopters which had been plain white this was painted in a red livery. When the blades had wound down Hans opened the door and jumped down on to the Helipad then walked over and greeted us.

"I thought you were sending Carls big brother, rather than yourself."

"Andy even at NATO Headquarters, the walls have ears. In fact they probably have more ears in the walls there, than at any other place in the world. With the exception of the Kremlin, that is. So what information, has young Oran been able to get you so far?"

"Quite a lot actually, we tracked 'The suit from the bunker at Dawes Hill, all the way to the military section of Heathrow Airport and then we tracked the plane to Cuba."

"Gitmo?"

"One and the same Hans, lets go down to the bar and we can talk some more." I said.

I had been woken an hour previously when our own Radar has picked up a small blip on the radar heading our way. That in turn had set our alarms going. Which brought our own defence systems online. Hans had radioed five minutes out, which was just as well because if he had left it another two minutes then we would have targeted the chopper with a one of the SLSAM's that we had confiscated from the Neo-Nazis in the last operation. The shoulder launched surface to air missiles were not much cop for taking down high flying fighter jets but were a really good defence against a helicopter, or a high speed boat. I left the dogs up on the heli-deck, as we went down to the bar area.

Abdalla had already got a map showing the coast of Cuba. Oran had printed it off from google. There were some aerial shots of the Guantanamo area but they were no where near, as detailed as we would require. We already knew that the CIA, would not give Sir Philip back as they believed him to be a terrorist, going on the information that they had falsely been given, by John Stevens. The same applied to Black-Tree once they had a top target, that target invariably vanished to some black op site, that is not even listed. Black-Tree had a reputation of getting information from the terrorists, who they had been given to interrogate. By using this independent contractor, the USA could claim, that they never knowingly harmed any prisoner. Nor did they, as signatories to the Geneva Convention, harm or abuse any captured combatant. Even when the worlds press and the International Red Cross were given access to the prisoners at Guantanamo Bay. They were never able to see any atrocities committed. Because, the prisoners that Black-Tree and the other independent contractors had in their sheds, were not on the prisoner list that the Commander of Guantanamo Bay Prison Camp had.

There were some prisoners who had been there for many years just on the word of someone within the intelligence community. They were held without a shred of evidence. This is how it would be with the suit. Many of those, who were holding him, would doubt that he was Zorro, but 'The Suit' still had secrets, they would love to know. So, he was a high value target, for everyone. They themselves, would all deny that Sir Philip was there, or ever had been there. If we did not rescue him soon, he would be lost forever. After stowing Hans's bag in one of the guest rooms we went down to Oran's Grotto. This time instead of scanning faces, Oran, had hacked in the USN SEA BEE's mainframe.

"Andy all recent construction, even of the temporary buildings at Guantanamo Bay, were completed by SEA BEE's Battalion One. Now, like all good military units, they keep impeccable records. They are accountable to not just the USN but to US Congress as well. They account for every brick, plank of wood, nail and sewer pipe. They like all good construction companies, work to a plan and have blueprints that they can refer too. I have just copied those blue prints. So we have that Part covered for now.

The USA have the NSA satellite scan Gitmo every time one of their satellites pass over Cuba. I have found a 30 minute window when American satellites are blind. During that time they use one of the Euro Sats. That said the satellite is controlled by the Germans and they like to review it first, before they pass the feed to the yanks. It is in that 30 minutes we can actually redirect the Euro Sat to cover something in Europe that has some high security event going on. Then the Germans can say that they were using their own satellite and as such, could not have it cover two places at the same time. That is where Hans comes in, as he can authorise it. All we have to do is find an event and then request the satellite. When I say we, I do of course mean the IDF, or perhaps something to do with NATO. I can also force a re-boot, of the USA satellite that is due to take over from the Euro Sat. This will buy us another 25-30 minutes. That gives us half an hour to get into Gitmo get 'Sir Philip' and about the same to get out."

"Wonderful Oran, when you say it like that, it sounds easy."

"I never said it was a plan I just said I could buy you some satellite blindness. You still, have to work out how to shut down their electronic stuff, as well as half a battalion of prison guards. Not to mention several units, of crazy contractors. There are land mines and there is also a heavy Naval presence, in the form of high speed gun boats, that patrol the waters around Gitmo. Unlike North Korea, They expect an attack from the air and have Anti Aircraft guns, surrounding the place. We cant risk using any commercial flights, nor can we take a military flight to Cuba. The Cubans are very touchy about bringing weapons, into their country. We need to plan how we get there, where to be, when we get there and how to get out. when we have 'The Suit'. Assuming that we do actually manage to find him." I said

We all went back to the lounge area next to the bar and kitchen and brainstormed for the next four hours. We were still arguing about things as the sun came up. Rosemary, without any of us asking, had started to cook breakfast. It was not long, before every one of our team and families, were tucking into a full cooked breakfast. This was eaten, over the now well used slab of teak, that served as the communal dining table in our kitchen. We did not stop talking about our plans or hide maps, the wife's were part of the team every bit as much as any of us. The had defended the Catherine May in the past. They all knew the business that we were in, and they all knew Sir Philip as a friend. A further two hours of talking, got us half way there. We would first, load up the Catherine May, with all the equipment that we thought we would require. Then the majority of us, would head of to St Johns Point in Newfoundland. We would take on extra supplies, that will have been transported from the IDF Stores in Iceland, by mutual agreement between Iceland and Canada. From there we would down to the Bahamas and then across to the Cayo Coco's of Cuba, where we would lay off and work on our plans. Petrá would stay and look after the children and the Reeves-Johnson's. They would keep things functioning on Château Brent Bravo. The Icelandic nurse would stay to take care of William. The IDF Doctor though, would be coming on board the Catherine May with us. Our Parents would stay and look after two of the dogs. Oran would not go anywhere without his protector Cyber. The two scientists would be staying on the rig. It was good to have another medical person along with us. I would imagine that 'The Suit' would require medical help, when we finally got him back.

Stu would skipper his boat and Rosemary refused to stay at home. She correctly pointed out that she had been in the thick of it on the last two missions so she had earned her wings, so to speak. Morag flat out refused to stay aboard the Rig and said that if Rosemary went then she was going too. They were like twins these days and completely inseparable. Lachie, Abdalla, Hans and myself were there because we were the official team seven. Carl, was an extra as was Oran. I had no worries about Carl, he had shown his grit and determination, during the firefights in Iceland and in the Faeroe Islands. We needed Oran, for his techie skills. There was enough room on board. Hans had not told us what it was we were collecting at St Johns, just that it would be required. The only person among us that looked like he belonged anywhere near Cuba was Abdalla. None of us had even the slightest tan, as such we would stand out like a spare prick at a whores wedding. I knew this was not going to be a quick trip. All I could hope and pray for, was that Sir Philip could hold on until we got to him. Assuming that we could actually get to him. One thing for sure, the Americans would not take kindly to our actions. The next morning after Hans and Carl had returned, we said all of our goodbyes and promised that we would be careful. The basics were, get there, get in, get out and get home without getting caught.

The first part of the trip was simple enough as we would head around the north coast of Scotland and headed west towards Newfoundland.

Hans had said that we should not make definite plans as things would be fluid when we got there. So all we did was familiarise ourselves with the layout of Gitmo and with special attention to the Delta sections.

From the Satellite shots, we had we could see the section of the camp, that was set aside for the civilian contractors. What we had no way of knowing from here was just which civilian contractor section, was the one belonging to Black-Tree.

The Sea Bees plans, were good and showed us the entire site. From Canteens to prisoners blocks. Even the sewage outlet that was at the extreme south point of the shoreline. The Sea Bees map, also showed us where they had removed mines, in order to complete some more construction. Some work had just been completed, on the East side of the camp, which was the area closest to the contractors compounds. I looked at the map and the blown up pictures of the Black Ops end.

"What is that building by the fence?"

"Its the water treatment facility, they don't trust the Cuban water supply so they have their own facility, it feeds the camp and the living quarters, well actually it is the water supply for anything American in Gitmo"

"Oran how far is it from the beach to the left of the harbour to the camp wire?"

"About a kilometre. That said as soon as you leave the beach there is a minefield"

"So how do they get down there?" I asked pointing to a group of sunbathers that showed clearly on the satellite image.

"I am not sure Andy, but I will find out for you."

"Mr Oran, I see from the welcome brochure that they hand out to new families and servicemen at Guantanamo. The have fresh fish caught by local fishermen. Where do those fishermen come from? Do they land elsewhere and then bring their catch by road or do they bring it ashore at or near the base?"

"Again Abdalla I don't know, but I will see what I can get from social media sources."

"What are you thinking?" Lachie asked me

"I am not really thinking anything yet. We have a lot of time for that ahead of us. I just want to get as much information as I can, between then and now. The more we know about Gitmo, the less fuck-ups, we will have to face. The thing about jails, is mostly they are built to keep people in. Gitmo is a bit of an exception to the general rule. When they built it in the early 1900's it was just a naval base and as such they made it to keep people out. Since then and more so now, with the high value targets that they keep there, they have beefed up not just the internal security but the external stuff. They have high speed RIB gunboats that patrol the coastal area. So a direct approach is out of the question."

"Andy why does it have to be a single approach?" Oran asked

"Mostly because we are only a small unit." I replied

"But cant you like, stagger your approach?" Oran said

"I'm not sure I follow you Oran, care to be a bit more specific?"

"We know that they use a central water supply, so that is a weakness there."

"Oran all the pictures I have seen show the army personnel drinking bottled water."

"They might drink bottled water, but I guarantee that they cook with the water from, this treatment plant. They probably fill their coffee pots from the taps as well."

"Go on?"

"Well we can spike the water with some thing that could incapacitate them in some way."

"Oran you are talking about attacking a US base with chemical weapons, at least that is the way they will see it. It would not be the first time that a friendly country has done this sort of thing to another. I will think about it. Anything else?"

"Lots actually Andy. They allow scientists on to the beach, to do research on the wildlife and also archaeologists go there to study the Sea Glass."

"Sea glass?" I asked to no one.

Oran continued. As if I had asked him personally.

"Yes it is a beach that has lots of sea washed glass on it. There are all sorts of rumours and folklore about why this beach seams to have more glass on it the most beaches in the world. Some would say it came from the 1700's and 1800's from trade ships that foundered on the coral reefs, to pirate ships that would smuggle rum. True some bottles and pieces of glass on the shore do come from that period in time. But now there is a much more specific reason for the glass. Since the late 1800's and early 1900's there has been a naval presence in Guantanamo Bay. And since that time the navy has been throwing its waste into the sea around Guantanamo. From the mid 1900's though they became a little more conscious of waste and there is a large landfill next to the sea. The way the weather is there, it has caused coastal erosion and lots of the trash was washed out to sea and then due to the tides around here washed back in again. So Historians sometimes get permission to go around the beaches to look for bits of the past."

"How do you know all this Oran?"

"I just read it on the Guantanamo Bay social website. Its quite amazing just how much info they stupidly put out there for the public to see. Why cant we enlist local help?"

"Go on Oran."

"Well much as most Cubans hate the Americans, and Fidel would be happy to see the Americans go. The local situation is quite different. Most of the locals rely on the Base to support the local economy, in the forms of jobs in the service industry, as well as the Pseudo Tourist industry around Gitmo. So if you are looking for help from the locals you need to look more to the places that don't benefit. Havana is OK but you start asking too many questions there and you might incur the wrath of Policía Nacional Revolucionaria. If I were to look for help, I would go to the poorer areas in the countryside and around the Cayo Coco's. From what I have read so far, there is no love for the Americans there. In fact they blame the Americans for everything that is wrong with the country. Contrary to the popular believe held by most folks in the west. The vast majority of Cubans have a love for Castro and don't so much as see themselves living under Communism.

But see it as a Socialist country. They have education for all, medicine for all. The poverty though is Americas fault for banning trade."

"Wow you are a fountain of knowledge"

"Not really Andy. The internet is the biggest library in the world, with instant access to billions of books. It gets bigger by the day. The truth be told Andy, there are very few secrets any more, especially if you know where to look. If it is written, then it is on the internet somewhere or on some form of storage system. There are acres of storage and most have backups. The more people that use computers, then more storage is required."

"Sounds a bit 'Big Brother-ish'."

"You have no Idea just how close, you are to the truth there Andy. There may be another possible way in. I told you that Gitmo, have a welcome site for their personnel, Well one of the things they encourage the men staying there to do, is to take up scuba diving. There are lots of coral beds and some Spanish wrecks to dive on. The picture of the beaches shows lots of Americans dressed in Scuba gear both in and out of the water. Sounds like an easy way to mix?"

"Good work Oran. OK lets take a break, Oran can you make sure everyone has copies of the maps that we have here. As well as any relevant info on the water facility. See if you can get some hi-res images of the ground between the Cubans and the Americans. Remember this though, we don't only have to get in, but we also have to get out and then get away from American soil and waters." With that I ended the meeting and went to my cabin.

ACT 20

Mrs Reeves-Johnson and her son, had given us quite a bit of information with regards to things that they had overheard from Stevens. The whole thing, had been about insane jealousy, as well as John Stevens desire to be the head of SIS. This he perceived as a position, that would not only launch him into the political world, but would also allow him to remove any competition, in his efforts to become the political leader of the UK.

I had come across many megalomaniacs in my time with SIS, but none who had been as slimy or as envious, of other people as this. To deliberately frame a man, in order to steal his wife and his life, was a completely new low on the scale of reasons for power. Then he had used the Royal and Political protection units, to do his dirty work and after that he then turned them lose on each other. I doubted if the Officer from the SAS would have been allowed to live, had we not intervened in Stevens plans. Now that officer would die, because once his own men, had learned of how members of his unit had been sold out, for the promise of backhanders. Like Stevens, those within the SAS, who were responsible, would quietly vanish to an unmarked grave, on a remote welsh mountain side. In the military, as in the rest of life, there are unwritten rules. We would be forgiven our trespass against the men, we had killed. In order for the information against those, that we had not yet caught up with. As of yet. I did not know who we could trust in the intelligence community of the UK. For now we would do it all on our own. If and when we could find others, that we could trust to assist with the rescue of Sir Philip. Then and only then would we ask of help.

Now we had Hans and Carl back in the fold, we had two extra men, that I had previously not counted on. I was concerned that we would be carrying civilians on the Catherine May. Rosemary could not be dissuaded from coming, as the boat belonged to her and her husband I could not demand that she stay on the rig. The insertion team was to be Hans, Lachie, Abdalla, Carl and myself. With us also and because we really needed his technical expertise. Stu would be skippering his baby. The IDF Doctor was also along, as I had a feeling we would at some point require more medical help that I was capable of providing. I had been unable to stop Morag from joining Rosemary. She had correctly pointed out that whilst we were going to be launching a rescue mission. In order to do that we had to have some kind of cover story for the Catherine May to be in the area of Cuba.

The Catherine May was registered as a Luxury Fishing boat for hire, to those who could afford it. And by having two wife's on board legitimised it as a fishing holiday. There was no way Oran would come without Cyber, so this was to be our team, complete with Cyber.

After saying our farewells to those on the rig, we set off on the first part of the journey and headed west towards the Newfoundland coast. The time was spent brainstorming and checking our firearms, looking at maps, as well as sea charts of the area around Guantanamo Bay. On board we had all the dive equipment that we had kept from our first enterprise with SIS. Full face anti-mist dive masks complete with wet and also dry suits. The maximum depth of the waters within 3 miles of the US Guantanamo Bay base, varies between 10 and 450 metres.

Commercial fishing around Gitmo, was banned for all but a few small boats from the village of Cainmanera. It used to be a thriving small town but nowadays there are just a few families who scratch a living from the sea. Whatever they caught, was supposed to be sent to the canneries or other larger towns. They do sell some illegally, to Americans, or they trade their catch, for other goods such as Goat Meat or Fruit. Even for cigarettes or tobacco. It was this black market that could be our way in. The Cuban people come from a varied background of ethnicity and culture. The majority being Spaniards and Afro Caribbean. As such Abdalla, would be easy to blend in, especially with his ability to speak fluent Spanish. Of course Abdalla had grown up in Northern Kenya and in the faith of Islam, although

Cuba was a communist and socialist state. The vast majority of the people followed the Roman Catholic faith. Abdalla though could not see any problems with this as he said he would be able to blend without any conflicts in his heart. So Abdalla would be our man on the Island, unless we could find a better option. Hans, had said that he was working on some other plans, but would not say what they were, at least until he was sure they would work. Oran was keeping us updated on troop movements as well as where the Americans went, when they crossed over into real Cuba. When they did this they had to pass through a Cuban checkpoint and then return the same way and then go through an American checkpoint. This could be the way out, but there was no way we could get in that way. Strangely it would be a lot easier entering into this small Communist state, than it would be to get into this little portion that the USA had on lease. It would also be a lot easier to get out of Cuba, providing we could first get into and then out of Guantanamo Bay. During one of Stu's many upgrades, he had installed a false floor into the two forward holds of the Catherine May. It had not been intended for us to use for smuggling, more of a just in case, sort of scenario. Previously we had stored all of our weapons in a water closet, which we called the armoury. Now though sailing into international waters and without the backing of any of the security services, it was better that we be seen purely as a pleasure boat. Even the hold where Oran would normally have set up a huge NSA like communications centre. Now it just looked like it was used as a lounge area with a single computer and a large screen where TV could be watched. There was even a small drinks bar in the corner. This was all done quickly to legitimise our trip as a bunch of super 'well off' individuals, on a Caribbean holiday. When we got to St Johns, Rosemary and Morag went ashore and purchased clothing that would suit a sun soaked holiday. Stu refuelled and then took on extra fuel in barrels, which he stored in the second forward hold, which neatly hid the access panel to our cash of arms. The dive gear, was all held in wire cages at the rear of the Catherine May. Rosemary also took on board some fresh produce as well as a good supply of dry, tinned and frozen goods. We were unsure how long we would be at sea other than it would be more than ten days and hopefully less than a month. There were some small crates waiting for us at the Harbour masters office.

They all had customs stamps on them stating that they were engine parts, from Iceland. I knew without even looking that they would contain more arms, ammunition and the sort of equipment that only a few people in the world would ever require. By using Saint Johns Point in Newfoundland as a resupply, we attracted almost no attention from the authorities. Not so much due to any influence, that Hans may or may not have in these parts, but more because the people here made their living from the sea. We were just another fishing boat, albeit a somewhat fancier boat. These crates we would only open once we were on or way South towards Cuba. Like flying, there is no such thing as a straight line between two points of the ocean. Tides and the curvature of the earth along with winds, means that the route is a curve. So from the North Atlantic Ocean to the South Atlantic Ocean, or the Labrador sea down to the Sargasso Sea. The weather and the seas in these areas, are as changeable as the seasons. I have heard tales of large fishing vessels foundering in the waters off St Johns, and of great liners going down in the Sargasso during hurricane season. We were headed towards a tropical storm that was building to the east of Cuba. At the moment it was sitting of the coast of Cape Verde. Whilst that was on the other side of the Ocean from where we were headed. It would only take a slight shift in the jet-stream and that tropical storm, would move to the west and pick up power, from the seas moisture. Then it would either head North or East. It would take a few days for us to get anywhere near the North coast of Cuba.

The plan being that we would try and pass ourselves off as a tourist boat and dive on coral reefs. We would look the part. I and the others, spent as much time as I could on deck in an attempt to get a suntan. We would spend about 10 days going around the coastal waters of Cuba, but still outside their territorial waters. As with all tourists, we would work on getting a tan. When the time was right, we would deliberately bring ourselves to the attention of the Cuban authorities. We did nothing to hide the registration of the Catherine May nor its occupants. Part of the Plan would be for the Cubans to help protect, us even they did not know it yet. Our passports all stated that we were British. We also had a passport for Philip Reeves-Johnson, again we would require this providing we managed to get 'The Suit' back. We still had no cast-iron plan, just a series of partial plans. I was sat on the foredeck catching some sun with paper and pencil in my hand, trying to break down the sections of the rescue mission. I started writing.

1: *Make contact with Cubans Legitimise our presence*
2: *Scope out the waters around Gitmo*
3: *See if Oran could get 3 of us inside Gitmo on one ruse or another*
4: *Attempt to locate 'The Suit'*
5: *Rescue Him*
6: *Get some form of Political asylum in Cuba Proper*
7: *Get Him and the rest of us back home safely*

I had no clue as to how we were going to accomplish, any of the stuff I had written down. I knew if we were discovered, before we had actually managed to get to step 5, then we would either be held prisoners by the Cubans for spying. Failing that if we were caught by the Americans, we could kiss our life goodbye and the best that we could hope for would be life in a supermax, that no one had ever heard of. Being shot would seem like bliss compared to being tortured for the rest of our lives. The reality of our situation was really starting to weigh heavy on my shoulders. I made a real promise to myself. If we actually managed to pull this off, then there would be no more SIS, no more Team Seven. I had a wife and two kids that needed me. I had friends who should never be put in harms way again. We were still a couple of hundred miles from the Bahamas. The weather had been getting not just warmer but sunnier all the time. Between the sea breeze and the sun we were all looking like tourists who had spent 10 days on some sun soaked beach. Stu had stopped the boat and cast out a sea anchor. Hans and Lachie going through the items, that we had unpackaged from the crates, which we had taken aboard at St Johns. Most of it was extra Dive gear but there were also other bits that were more military than civilian. All items they were fixing to the bottom of the hull using heavy duty, waterproof electro magnets. When attached the looked like power bulges. These were similar to the ones you see at the fronts of sports cars. What they were in reality were large storage pods. Hans had told us we were to pick up an extra passenger off the coast of the Bahamas. He had not given any more details than that. This was fine by me and the others as we trusted

Hans, not only with our lives, but with those of our families and friends.

Stu had decided that we should travel at half of our normal speed, so from this point on until we required the extra power, we would stick to a maximum of 20 knots. That would be about right, for a modern steel hulled fishing boat. There were up and down sides to this down side was it would now take us longer to reach our destination. The up sides were that, should we be tracked by anyone, we would not look any different from any of the 100,000 pleasure craft, that cruised around the Caribbean Sea, at this time of year. The other up side, was of course we had more time to tan our bodies. Consequently having a real tan, could literally be the difference between life and death. So, we would have around another week, to build our already tanned bodies to a golden mahogany. I was happy in a way that Petra was not with us, as in this climate she would have burned and then pealed and burned some more. I had worried a bit about Hans and Carl but like most military folks, they travelled the world on a regular basis and went in and out of tan with the seasons. We spent as much time as we could on the deck either Rod fishing for Barracuda or just laying there soaking up the Caribbean sun.

I was on front deck in a pair of well worn shorts, looking more like a member of Jaques Cousteu's crew, than a member of SIS. Most of SIS members, wore suits and ties and were more likely to resemble James Bond, than James Pond. Even in the time it had taken us to get here from our home on the Rig, my beard had grown so I really did look like a fisherman on a protracted fishing holiday. The radio sprung into life and in the still and quiet of the ocean it sounded like a fog horn.

"Ahoy Catherine May, This is the Ocean Voyager. We are about thirty minutes out with your final passenger" The radio squawked.

"Ocean Voyager. Roger that, look forward to seeing you" Stu replied

Try as we did we could not get any more information on our new team mate, from Hans. All he would say was, that he had skills and knowledge, that we needed. Being wary of any boat that would approach us we stuck a few baited rods in holders at the side and stern of the Catherine May. The sea was calm enough that we had no problem in seeing far into the distance such as we could, which was of course about 3 miles to the horizon. Although if we climbed the mast we would see for perhaps another mile, on a clement day like today. The radar however can see much further than that. Officially we had a standard marine radar, which had a range of approximately 50 miles. Ours though was a military spec radar, which gave double that, although it could be electronically dumbed down if required. So we already had a picture of all the boats that were in the ocean around us. Now we had one boat, that was around 20 miles away and heading in our direction. Lachie and Hans came back aboard and stripped down to their swimming trunks. We had attached two dry-bags to a pair of the fishing rods. The contents of the dry bags were automatic machine pistols that were already loaded and cocked. I hoped we would not require to reel them in but stood ready to do so. Soon we saw the shape of a small fishing boat appear. It was a 20 foot wooden hulled traditional fishing vessel. Painted in sea blue and white with a small wheelhouse in the middle of her deck. Black diesel exhaust poured from her stern. But it moved through the still waters with grace and ease. As she grew closer I could see a large man standing on her deck and another person of indeterminate size in the wheelhouse. There were, what looked at first glance, windows to the wheelhouse but this turned out not to be so. It was just an open framework to support the roof which had a Ship to shore aerial and a couple of life preservers. I could hear the engine as it spluttered on, not racing and not missing a beat, just a regular clunk, clunk, clunk. It might be a main contributor to global warming, but it would probably continue to do so for many a year. She was now less than one hundred yards away and the rate of the clunk clunk clunk reduced. The black smoke that had been coming from her stern was now more blue-grey in colour. I could see it had been a long time since she had been painted. The varnish over the craved wooden nameplate, attached to her front, had long since come adrift. The wood was now sun-bleached grey. Although now she was near us, I could read 'Ocean Voyager'. It had been carved into the wood by some skilled artisan and then filled, in gold coloured paint, before being varnished. Now all that remained were small streaks of gold on grey. The man who had been standing on her foredeck was now dropping old tires over the side to act as a cushion as she came alongside. From six feet away he threw two lines over to us. I grabbed one and Abdalla the other, we tied the small fishing boat to the side of the Catherine May. Hans reached forward for the man's outstretched arm.

"Good to see you Alé"

"Likewise my friend Hans"

"Folks I would like you to meet Alejandro Fernánadez, although his friends call him Alé. He knows more about the land and sea, around Guantanamo Bay, than any living individual. He is also a senior member of MININT which is Ministerio del Interior de la República de Cuba. I first met him when he was a member of the Cuban Elite Special Naval Force. I worked with him on bringing some drug cartels down, strangely enough those very drug cartels were funded by the CIA. Alé was the underwater team leader. Better than that though, he is related to José Abrantes Fernandez, who until recently was Minister for Internal Affairs. So in the unlikely event that you get captured by Cuban forces, you will not be sent to Combinado del Este, you will perhaps only be shot!" Hans said

"And that would be a good deal? How?" Lachie asked

"Why, because you would not have to live on a diet of maggot and flies, with the other 5,000 prisoners, who have committed crimes against my Cuba" Alé said with a friendly smile.

I could not tell if he or Hans were joking about us going to a Cuban jail.

Once all the introductions had been done and Alé had brought his large backpack, on board the Catherine May. We untied the small fishing boat, which went on its clunk, clunk, clunk, way. I asked Alé what was a Cuban fishing boat doing so far from Cuba. He then told me it was not a Cuban boat, just another boat from the Bahamas, but that it was owned by a family friend. We went down below to the air conditioned galley where Rosemary was cooking some of the fresh tuna, that we had managed to catch. The vast majority of the tuna we caught had been thrown back into the sea, however we had kept one to eat and to act as further bait for the barracuda that swam in these warm waters. Once we had eaten the galley table was cleared and charts and maps, took up the space that had previously been filled with plates and cutlery. Much discussion was had about how we would be getting ashore. Then assuming we had managed to rescue 'The

Suit' would we be coming directly back to our boat or would we travel overland to a friendly part of Cuba and then make contact with the Catherine May.

Alé's knowledge would be paramount in our incursion. His family had a small farm near Gitmo, so he knew the land, around the camp. He had fished in the waters and more importantly he had dived in and around the coast of Guantanamo Bay. He knew where the under water mines and traps were, and he knew the blind spots on the beaches. Although Hans had filled us in on the basic exploits of Alé, Ale himself had said very little, with the exception of saying he was part of a skilled elite anti dug unit.

Alé was a slim but muscular man, of just about six feet tall. His head was shaved and smooth. To most people he was fairly innocuous looking. He was wearing a traditional Caribbean style shirt which was unbuttoned to the middle of his chest. It revealed two small round scars to the right side of his chest. These I recognised and small calibre bullet wounds, presumably from his life fighting the drug cartels. He never mentioned them so I did not ask. What it did tell me was he got those injuries facing his enemy, not running from them.

All of Team Seven were accomplished divers but Ale suggested that we learn more about reef diving especially as many of the species of sea life around Cuba was either poisonous or aggressively dangerous. So we pulled in the sea anchor and once again headed off around the Bahamas and towards Cuba. All the time the weather was getting hotter and more humid. The sea was still calm and there was little or no wind. When we approached Cuba, Alé said we should call ahead, to the Cuban Authorities and apply for a visa. This we would require, if we wished to take our boat, into Cuban territorial waters. It would also mean allowing Cuban sailors, to come on board the Catherine May, to do a drugs and illegal contraband search. He explained this would be a cursory search and they would ask a few simple questions, look at our passports and have us fill in a green visa card. This we would have to pay for with either Cuban Exchangeable Pesos, or they would accept Sterling but it would not be at the exchange rate but at a one to one rate. After this, we would be allowed to do two things. We could fish in her waters, providing that any excess fish that we caught, we would give to the local harbour, so they could send it to the government canneries. The second thing that we would be allowed to do would be to step on to Cuban soil as regular tourists. This was of course providing they found nothing untoward, on the Catherine May. Because Alé's uncle, was a well known figure in the MININT things should go quick and easy.

ACT 21

"You know what they say about the best laid plans?" Lachie said

"Aye, They can oft times go astray" replied Stu

The Cuban territorial waters, like most countries extended twelve miles out into the sea. That being the case when we were fifteen miles out, from the Cayo Coco's, we radioed our boats Name and call sign, to the Cuban Navy. We were told to enter Cuban waters and await a Cuban Naval Boat to come to us. This we did.

All or our firearms were now in a secure box attached to the hull. The only firearm we had on board, officially that is, was our Distress flare pistol. We took the time when we were waiting the arrival of the cutter to check and double check all our belongings to make sure we had nothing illegal on board. Nothing found, all things should have been equal. The Cuban high speed patrol boat radioed us first and asked that we make ready, for them to board us. I must admit I was expecting to see an old boat from the 1960's Cuba conflict. But what came darting towards us at an alarming speed was a brand new Chinese made high speed armoured torpedo gun boat. The bow of this armoured boat was riding high in the water and her wake spread out an an ever increasing trail behind her. There was a roar coming from her exhausts, that told of a large and powerful turbine engine below her deck. This was a modern piece of military hardware. Fifty yards out, her bow dropped back down into the water, forcing the wake to catch up and her nose to break the water in front of her with a large splash wave. Her skipper skilfully pulled alongside us and reversed the motors, before engaging the clutch and the engines sound reduced to a burble. Four AK47's were pointed directly at us and an officer in green fatigues, proffered a smart salute. Then in impeccable English

"Permission to come aboard your boat"

I assumed this was more out of politeness, rather than a real request. I was equally sure that had we refused his pseudo request, that he and his men would have boarded us anyway. Stu who was on deck stepped forward under the careful gaze of the soldiers. He offered his hand to assist the office on board.

"Please do and welcome aboard my boat, the Catherine May"

The officer accepted the hand and he came aboard rapidly followed by the four men who still pointed their rifles in our direction.

"Why do you come to Cuba?"

"I am here with these guests on my boat, for leisure and to enjoy the fine weather that Cuba has to offer. We called ahead because I know that my passengers and myself require visas although, we do have a Cuban passenger on board." Stu said indicating with his hand to Alé

"Passports" The officer said and held out his hand. I noticed that he now had his right hand on the butt of his side arm. Stu obliged and handed over our passports. The officer took them and then handed them to one of his soldiers who went back to their cutter.

"Cómo te llamas" he said indicating to Alé

"Mi nombre es Alejandro Fernánadez estoy con la fuerza de respuesta naval cubana. Estas personas son mis amigas que he invitado a disfrutar de nuestro país" Alé replied and I looked at Abdalla. Who whispered back to me

"Alé just told him his name and that he works for the Cuban Navy"

The officer said nothing to begin with. There then, followed a heated exchange between Alé and the Officer. Abdalla just shrugged his shoulders.

"Kneel down on the deck all of you, and put your hands behind your head." the officer shouted.

Alé started to protest and the officer drew his pistol. Alé indicated we should comply.

"No talking" he shouted as we all knelt down. The Soldier that had taken our passports came back and handed them to the officer and then he saluted him and stepped back.

"You" he said as he tapped me on the shoulder

"Stand up"

I stood up and turned to face the officer, still with my fingers clasped behind my head. I suddenly noticed he had our British Passports in his hand, rather than the fake Irish ones we had previously been using. I looked quickly at Stu and then at Oran, who gave a tiny nod.

"What is your name?"

"I am Andrew McPhee."

He leafed through the passports until he found mine. Then he opened it and looked at the photograph inside.

"This is you?" he said as he turned it to face me

"Yes that is me."

"Why do you have no beard in your passport and now have a beard on your face? Are you trying to disguise yourself?"

"No Sir. We left Scotland some time ago, on this long holiday and I have not shaved since we left home. That is all"

"It says on your passport that you are a medical person? How would a medical person be able to afford to pay for a trip like this. This is a Private Charter? No?"

"We all are friends and we have saved for many years to pay for this trip, so we decided to make it a really good one. We all like Scuba and Snorkelling. We also like sunshine as we do not get a lot of that in Scotland"

"How is it that you know Señor Alejandro Fernánadez"

"Sir if you look back through my passport you will see that I visited Cuba some years ago and that is when I met with him. In fact he taught me to dive."

I had been to Cuba before, but it had been entirely, for a 10 day slice of relaxation. It was not long since I left the Military and ended up in the clutches of SIS. He thumbed back through the pages. Then he looked at Alé.

"¿qué hacías fuera de Cuba? ¿Dónde están tus papeles?" He said

I had no clue as to what he had just said. I knew that it would antagonise the officer if I asked Abdalla. Fortunately Alé answered in English

"I was working with the police in the Bahamas to stop drugs coming into our country. I contacted my friends as I knew they were coming to Cuba and they kindly offered to pick me up and give me a ride home on their nice boat. You can check with the Policía Nacional Revolucionaria. They will confirm that I am currently attached to the anti terror and drugs unit."

The officer said nothing. Then he tapped Rosemary on the shoulder.

"You. Stand Up."

Stu made to move and I stopped him with a glare.

"You are Rosemary Anne McCormack?"

"Yes"

"You are a Chef?"

"Yes"

"Where is it you are a Chef?"

"Here on this boat, we have bookings for most of the year, I can show you our logs they will tell you where we have taken the rich people"

"Why would a boat so small like this for less than 12 persons need a chef? And not just a cook?"

"It is my husbands boat and I was a chef before I met him"

"Where?"

"What?"

"Where were you before?"

I thought for a moment that Rosemary was going to pull a Lachie on him

"Oh sorry, I did not understand what you meant at first. I was a Chef to Queen Elizabeth the Queen Mother."

The officer seemed duly impressed and then asked

"Where?"

"In Scotland"

"Young lady are you trying to lie to me?"

I had to step in

"Sir what she is saying is true. The Queen does live for most of the time in England but her mother, the Queen Mother, had a Castle in Scotland where she used to spend her summers. It is called Mey Castle. That is where Rosemary was a Chef."

"And you do not do this now? For your Royal Family?"

I knew Rosemary to be a bit of a Scottish Rebel at heart. I was worried she would say that the Royal Family was not her Royal Family, and that she only cooked for them because she needed a job with a good wage. Fortunately all she answered was No.

The officer indicated that Alé, Rosemary and myself should kneel back down.

"You stand up"

Abdalla did and looked down on the officer. The officer pulled out the light blue passport belonging to Abdalla. He thumbed through the pages.

"You were recently in Kenya?"

"It is my home."

"But then you were in the United Kingdom."

"Yes I went to see my good friends here at their home."

"It says you trade is a Machine Engineer?"

"That is correct I make parts for machinery"

"You are a Muslim" It was more of a statement than a question.

Abdalla did the right thing and just stayed quiet. The officer went around the others looking at their faces and comparing them to the passport pictures. Amazingly he never asked a single question of Lachie.

"My men will now search your boat" He said to Stu

If we find anything is not as it should be, then you could be in a lot of, what is it you say in England? Boiled Water?

"Sir I request that one of us be with you when the search is made, just in case you need access or wish to ask about any thing." Stu said

"You Andrew McPhee come with us."

Two of the guards remained on deck with their AK47's pointed at the others. I went with the officer and his two men. I had a sudden chilling thought. Oran was on the deck but Cyber was in the Boats hold, come coms centre.

"Excuse me officer, before we can enter one of the rooms. we much first have the little man that looks like a Hippie, to come with us. He is the small man. But he has a very large dog that protects him."

"I too, have a large dog at home, an Alsatian, I have no fear of big dogs, It will not be necessary. Why was the dog not on the deck?"

"Because of the heat, the room he is in, is air conditioned."

"Then we shall go their first."

I tried and I tried, to get the officer to agree to allowing Oran to come with us, but he stubbornly refused. We arrived at Oran's door.

"Can you at least ask your men to shoulder their arms so that the dog does not see it as a threat."

He just nodded and they shouldered their firearms. Slowly I opened the door. Cyber was sat in the middle of the room. I had been worried that he might charge at the door and tear them to pieces. I entered first and the two soldiers behind me followed by the Officer. I swear the soldiers went almost white as they looked upon this canine monster that was Cyber. I stepped aside in order to let the officer get a good look at the room and more importantly at Cyber.

"Now are you sure you would not rather I get Oran to control his dog before you search his room."

"Mr McPhee that will not be necessary" he said as he backed out of the room.

Cyber still sat motionless in the middle of the floor. The two soldiers squeezed past me in order to exit the room.

"Let us go back to the deck he said after a cursory look around the internals of the boat."

I went on deck followed by the two armed guards and then the officer.

"I am sorry I can not give you Visa's"

"Why not? We are just tourists, who will spend money in Cuba and provide fish for the Cuban Canneries."

"You do not understand me. You can not have visa's because we no longer issue them at sea, they have to be issued by the local port or harbour. So you must first follow my boat into the Cayo Coco's where we will get your visas stamped and issued."

"Oh...... OK so everything of OK?"

"Yes but because of Rabies and other animal problems the Dog will not be allowed to come ashore. It must stay on board your boat."

The officer and his men left and went back to their boat after they untied they moved off towards the main Island of Cuba.

"Why the hell did you give them our real passports?" I shouted at Stu.

"Don't blame him Andy I told him to do that, your false passports were compromised. There was a leak of some form, Oran had just told me about it before the Cuban gun boat arrived. I dropped the fake ones over the side in a bag with a weight in it. They are gone mate. We can still use our real ones inside Cuba. They don't share information with the Americans and they are slow to share with the Brits. So in a way, we are slightly better off. The Yanks will be searching for us under the false names. With the exception of Abdalla, its been years since we used our real ones. We are only going to be in Cuba for a week at most. Then lets see what happens. Remember apart from us NO ONE knows where Sir Philip is. Stevens is dead, the guys that snatched Sir Philip and his family are dead. There is no record of where they took him. Sir Philip will not even have given his name, let alone ours. The only reason that they will not have killed him yet, is they believe that he is a high value target, with lots of information on terror cells throughout the world. He is worth nothing to them dead. They will work on him for weeks. So the fact we used our real passports, will not lead us back to SIS. They always gave us false papers and remember Oran, has been inside their system, and removed all our names from any of their documents. He did the same thing through all the other agencies. So our names and passports are clean. Lets try to keep it that way." Hans said

Stu went to the wheelhouse and started up the engines. We followed the gun boat towards Cuba. The first glimpse I got of Cuba's Cayo's, was of a long bank of coral Islands the water was crystal clear and even with the naked eye I could see all sorts of fish swimming in the water below our boat. We were taken to the Marina Jardines del Rey. Because of the size of our boat we had to leave it anchored with Cyber in charge while we transferred to the gun boat which took us in to the small Marina come harbour.

We landed and followed the officer to an office which was just a glorified shed. We filled in our visas and paid the charge in sterling then our passports were stamped along with our visas.

"Before you leave Cuba you must come back here and have your exit visa stamped. You must not go anywhere near any of our naval or military installations, they are clearly marked on this chart." He said as he handed us a rolled up chart which cost us a further £25

"If you wish to change some currency then you can do so at the bank, which is just up from this office. You will need to take your passports with you to the bank. We have a closed currency here in Cuba, so it is illegal to take any Cuban money out of our country. You are now free to go. My men will ensure you get back to your boat. Welcome to Cuba"

Between us changed we £5,000 at the bank and got our receipts along with a large wad of Cuban pesos. Then after Rosemary had purchased sack loads of groceries, we headed back to the Naval boat and then to the Catherine May. We were now officially in Cuba for up to 30 days, which was a lot longer than we expected to stay there. We had brought with us, all the usual touristy things with us which included a Canon SLR Camera with a variety of lenses. This was fine to use in the areas where the tourists were. For all the other places we would use our BAE scopes, or to give it its full title, Advanced British Aerospace Electrical Systems Digital Scope, which fitted on any firearm with an attachment rail. It would give us natural, night, thermal and infrared all in High Definition. Normally it would be mounted on one of our AS50 sniper rifles. Most true snipers would use a smaller calibre, we were trained snipers, just we preferred to make sure our targets went down, even if we were slightly off with our aim. We could sit almost two miles from shore, if the sea was flat calm we would stand a good chance of hitting our target. On land it would be a given, if it was in our sights, then what ever it was, would be hit. That could be man or machine. We had found the BAE Sights to be a complete game changer. With these attached to any rifle, wherever you put your dot was where your bullet would strike. Lachie had been the first to remove the sight from the rail of his AS50 and put it on the rail of his Sig Sauer. Something of an overkill to put it on a pistol, but Lachie had been injured at the time and could not hold his AS50, so he had used it as a night sight on his automatic hand gun, to great effect. Now we had been checked out by the Cuban Navy, we were unlikely to be searched again. So when we were far enough from shore and on the horizon. Hans and Lachie went under the hull and brought up some of the items we would require. These were our skin tight dry suits along with the full face Ocean Reef dive masks, they looked like something out of Star wars but allowed us to use our Storno encrypted radios under water. Our dry suits even came with dry pouches so we store our radio packs. We would be going around both sides of Guantanamo Bay. There was an exclusion zone around Gitmo but the demarcation line to the Cuban side. We were able to use to our advantage, we were allowed to sports fish within 500metres of the shoreline. This would happen tomorrow. The first part of the plan we would make things ready. After checking that half of our compressed air tanks were full they were tied together. Firearms were bagged up and explosive charges made ready. Tools were checked and double checked. The AS50's would remain on the boat, with Stu, Rosemary, Morag and Oran, to cover us. The Doctor would also stay on board the rest of us would be going ashore. The insertion point was to be on this side of Gitmo, which was in fact the closest point from the actual camp. The reason we chose this was, that Alé had family and friends, he said would help us once we were ashore. Assuming we got that far, we would then wait until the next night, to scope out the prison camp. Then on the third night we would, hopefully make our rescue of Sir Philip. Finally we would make our escape on the opposite side of the Island we had come in on. We would need to swim the 500m in and then get all our gear to the safe house, that we would be staying in, on the first night. It would mean, that we would be throwing away half of our compressed air bottles. We had some mini air bottles that you just bit down on unlike the tanks we wore on our backs. These mini ones, were about the half the size of a coke bottle and came from an American company called Spare Air. Hans had managed to get these some time back when he had good relations with the CIA and they had obtained them from the US Seals. These would be our only Air supply for about 15 minutes. After that and all things being equal there should then be full sized dive bottles laying on the ocean floor at a pre-arranged point. Oran would then send that info to the PDA units that we would be wearing on our arms. So, one day to get there, one day to scope things out and another day, to make good on our plan and then to escape to the Catherine May and get 'The Suit' Home. It did not matter how many times we went over the plans, I could not find a perfect solution, let alone one that I thought we had any chance of pulling off.

Oran had attached digital markers to the back of all our dry suits which he claimed would allow him to locate us from 30 miles away and track us down to an inch. So much of our plans, we had laid in the hands of a man, we had never met before today.

Alé seemed to be the linchpin to our mission. He was coming with us and would face the same dangers as any one of us, perhaps more as he was also placing his family in danger. Whilst Fidel, had no love for the Americans, he would have less love for foreign agents conducting a covert operation, on his soil. Technically though the actual operation would be conducted on American Soil. That would be the way the Americans would see things. Their soldiers had a shoot to kill policy, in and surrounding Gitmo. Personally I had a feeling they would prefer to first catch us, then interrogate and then shoot us.

ACT 22

Stu sailed us to the point where Alé had indicated, on the Charts. The lagoon to the South East of Gitmo was on Cuban territory. The place we had to get to was a small farm to the East of the there. We would sail to a point out at sea, that was closest route, then we would swim ashore and bury most of our equipment in the sand. The Problem that we faced here was, this close to Gitmo and on the Cuban side was constantly patrolled by the Cuban Army as well as Cuban gun boats. We were taking a change of clothing, in order that we would at least look like Cubans, given a cursory. glance The daytime temperature in this region of the world was 30c and with an almost 100% humidity. On the upside, whilst we wore our dry suits the mosquitoes would have less flesh to feast on. Alé had promised his families home had good air conditioning.

On the blind side of the boat we dropped into the water. This would be the last we would see of our support vessel for three days. Carefully so as not to make too much noise. We had a lot of equipment to take with us on this part of the mission. The strange thing about Cuba even the water is hot, and I wished we had opted for normal swim clothing, but I knew we needed the dry suits, they were essential for the protection they offered our sensitive equipment, that we wore under, not to mention the pouches that we carried the ammunition, scopes and detonators in. Each man would be carrying about 75lbs of hardware, that alone would be sufficient to allow them to drop to the ocean floor, with out the aid of extra weights. Under water this weight would not be much of a problem, overland and in this heat and humidity, it would be torturous. Stu and Oran had been talking about the tropical storm that was currently sitting to the east of Cuba. Oran assured Stu that the American Weather stations had been plotting its expected to run north and miss Cuba by almost a thousand miles. That did not stop the humidity that seemed to be building by the hour. It was like drinking air.

I, like the others, had my dive mask on and I slipped beneath the ripples. You would think at night the sea would be dark. Not tonight the moonlight was almost like sunlight. The floor of the ocean at this point was almost 30 feet down. Soft sand and a few fishes, though fairly quickly there were schools of small and medium sized silver and blue fish. I looked to the others and then started to half walk, half swim towards the shore. Wearing our air tanks and dragging another 75 pounds, was hard work even for folks who were a fit as ourselves. We had taken our passports just in case we were captured by either side. Whilst we had not taken much other than equipment of war, we had each taken 500CP, to use for food and buying the things we could not carry with us. It would also be useful for bribe money, especially in this poor third world economy. The Cuban people were generally quite happy with their lot in life and almost all of them, looked to Castro to guide them into the future. Wages being 40CP a month on average meant that an extra 100CP, would get you a very loyal friend and could open a lot of doors as well as close them, to hide you if required.

All these thoughts were going through my mind as we followed in a serpent like line, behind Alé. Nobody spoke and we never used a light but just trusted Alé to be a true guide. I looked at my PDA through its clear plastic window on my wrist. Each of us showed as a worm of red dots. Hans had been the one to stay behind on the boat as the protector and co-ordinator. So the team was Alé, Abdalla, Carl, Lachie, and me. A small enough team so we would not create a ruckus in the neighbourhood, but big enough to get the job done. The green dot of our boat was now reaching the extremity of my PDA and I had to zoom out to bring the green dot back into view. Oran had said we could zoom out to a radius of 30 miles and zoom in to a radius of just 12 feet. Theoretically that would mean we should never be out of contact with anyone. I hated theories. We had used these PDA's before to great effect, when we were on a container ship during our last mission. That did not mean I trusted them. My father had told me once, don't trust anything you cant see with your own eyes, hold with your own hands, hear with your own ears or taste with your own tongue. Everything else is speculative.

I was sure I was sweating as I dragged the large dry bag behind me. It was causing the sand on the sea bed to become disturbed and the sand flowed up in small clouds. Small fish darted in, out and around the clouds. Bigger fish came to eat the smaller fish as they to ate even smaller things, that we could not see with our naked eyes. Suddenly a small barracuda raced across my vision and all the other fish disappeared from sight. That is the law of the jungle, so to speak. Its all about being the big fish in the pond. Yet here we were the little fish heading right towards a bloody big American barracuda. Alé motioned for us to stop. I looked down at my watch and it showed we had been under water for 20 minutes, the gauge on my tank told me it had about 10 more minutes of air. From the feel of the water pressure on top of me I would say we were no more than 10 feet under water now. The gentle slope of the sea bed made it difficult to tell if you were much closer to the shore or not. Normally when going to the shore there is a distinct uphill slope, not so tonight. Alé moved ahead on his own and then returned to us 5 minutes later. He gave a thumbs up signal, which was the normal for everything is as it should be. He turned and started to walk forwards and we followed. Now though I could feel the lack of pressure on my suit and soon my head popped out of the water. I stood still and shut my eyes tight for a few seconds to improve my night vision. I kept my mask on, just in case I needed to dive back down for any reason.

There was a small light being flashed from the shore. It was flashing in groups of three. Alé flashed his penlight back and the one on the shore flashed once more then went out. Picking up our dry bags we followed Alé up to the top edge of the beach there was lots of foliage covering the ground and large palms overhead. We grouped ourselves together and Alé went and spoke to the person who had been flashing the torch from the shore. While he did that, we buried our dry bags and face masks, the nearly empty air tanks we buried next to the full ones that we had taken with us. After quickly changing into street clothes, which for Cuba was chino shorts and short sleeved loose fitting shirts and deck shoes on our feet. Wearing the loose shirts allowed us to carry our firearms in the back of our trousers with the shirt over. So now the only things we had on us were personal side arms our Storno Radios and some money. We carried the spare stuff in our backpacks. After making sure our equipment stash, was covered with fallen palm leaves. I used one more, to sweep out our footprints from the waters edge, all the way up the beach. Suddenly from about three hundred yards away I could hear an engine. Alé indicated we should go towards that sound. Keeping as much as possible, under cover of the trees, we stayed in the shadows. The engine belonged to an old soviet era flat bed truck. There was a man and a boy standing next to it. Like the conspirators we were, we crouched down next to it in the dark. Alé spoke with the man and told us to get in the back, then the driver and boy threw a Tarpaulin over us, this was followed by lots of dead palm leaves that had been piled up next to where the truck was parked. Until now I had not really noticed the mosquitoes, now though it seemed that they were everywhere. It was almost impossible not to slap and scratch.

The Truck started up and moved off, over the uneven ground, we were jostled and bumped around. Then obviously, we had hit a proper road, as the ride became a little smoother. Five minutes later the truck stopped abruptly. And there was a voice from outside speaking in Spanish, our driver replied and then the discussion became a little heated. I had my Sig our and in my hand, like most people, who's lives depend on a firearm, mine was already cocked and loaded with a round up the spout, even before I had my magazine inserted. This actually allowed an extra round. The safety though was switched to on. As quietly as I thought I could, I slid the lever forward. I heard the tiny click as the firearm became useable. The sound to me though, in my mind, was amplified 100 fold. I was even able to pick up the sound from my team, as they too made ready for a firefight. The argument continued in muffled Spanish, and then there was a grind of gears as the driver struggled to get the old truck going, the clutch probably should have been replaced 30 years ago. The truck moved forward and continued on for another 3 minutes then it pulled off the road and back onto a dirt track, before jolting to a stop. The engine though refused to die quietly and gurgled a few times, before a backfire and then silence. We waited for what seemed like and eternity and then the tarpaulin was pulled back by two men who were greeted by our combined arsenal pointing back at them.

"Hola mis amigos y Bienvenidos a Cuba" he said as he raised his hands above his head.

"Hola" Alé said and indicated things were OK, by putting his Pistol in the back of his trousers.

I like the others climbed off the truck and dusted myself down, then slapped away a few mosquitoes. Our hosts though did not seem to notice them. Alé went into the house, which was really a bit of a euphemism. It was a building, made from bits of wood and plastic. which seemed to be held together by the rusty corrugated tin roof. Chicken scurried out of the way to let us pass. Inside it was dimly lit, a small portable television was tuned into a baseball game and three children sat as if glued to the screen. A rotund lady was cooking on a two burner gas stove. Neither she nor the kids paid any attention to our being there, or so it seemed. The air conditioning that Ale had promised, turned out to be an open window that allowed a small draft of air to flow through the house.

Alé spoke some more Spanish to the driver of the truck and then told us, we should sit down at the table. The table itself had seen better days and none of the chairs matched. This seemingly in the West, was now a cool thing to do. Although here, it was because that is all there was. As soon as we sat at the table the woman, who had been stirring a large pot on the stove, suddenly sprung into life. Like something out of Disney's 'The Sorcerers Apprentice' with Mickey Mouse. Plates of random shapes sizes and colours appeared in front of each of us and the large pot from the stove, was placed into the middle of the table.

"Eat please" she said in perfect English, as a large ladle was inserted into the steaming pan.

Having been to Cuba before I knew that Rice and Beans were a big part of the food, they were the bulkers to which small amounts of meat or fish would be added. It was not really one style of food it was more an amalgamation of cultures that made the diet. Afro Caribbean, Portuguese, Spanish and African all mixed into one. The food was tasty and spicy and even though we were not really hungry we ate heartedly. The generosity of those who have little or nothing, seems to be a world wide thing. Whilst the majority of those who had lots, seemed that they would die, if they gave some away, for no other reason than a kind deed.

We introduced ourselves and the conversation was light and friendly. The family that was hosting us was the uncle and aunt of Alé and they had a small holding, on which they grew some Sugar Cane and Yams. They were also fishermen and fished the big lagoon that we had come into. They would fish for any fish and anything else unlucky enough to swim into their nets.

Alé's uncle Carlos, would be our guide, as he knew the area. Although he was over seventy years old, was still fit and lithe. He had been a labourer to the Americans, when they had built the perimeter fence that not only went around Gitmo but was previously on his fathers property. There was an area of about one hundred yards, that was the mine field which also surrounded the camp. Carlos explained that there was a Cuban army checkpoint on the edge of his property, which he actually objected to, and every time he went through it he insulted the guards for protecting the Americans from good Cubans like him, who fed the Cuban Army with his crops and fish. Getting back to his home was easy, because he could put fallen leaves on the back of his truck or crops from the fields. Coming the other way though, would be difficult, as he could not hide us under anything. It would look suspicious if he took crops back to the fields. I explained that we would not need him to take us back through the checkpoint but we might need him to collect some of our equipment from the beach. I wanted the one bag with the VAL and our scopes in, plus it also had a small but very powerful thermal lance. We needed this to cut a hole in the fence.

That would be tomorrow night. What I needed him to show us tonight, was where the Civilian Contractors were, in relation to the rest of the camp. Then help us find a way to the fence, without us being seen and without being blown to pieces, by some old land mine. The children were dispatched to bed and the table cleared. I laid our map of the camp on the table. Carlos produced a bottle of Havana Club and like the plates, a variety of glasses appeared. Then we got down to the real business. We drew small plans copied from parts of the big plan and then annotated them. It turned out that the Private Contractors who had extended their section on the extreme eastern side of the camp, had laid a new sewage pipe which went down the middle of the minefield about ten yards out from the camp. This pipeline went all the way down to the sea. It was an eighteen inch wide pipe, but there was no way that we would be able to enter the pipe, as the Sea Bee's who installed it had put a series of one way valves so that nothing, and, or no-one could come back up the pipe. The one saving grace was, that no one on either side of this fence, had relaid the mines. All we would have to do is go down to the sea, and then come back up from the shore. Then we follow the newly turned earth, all the way back up to the area, where the pipe came back through the fence line. Carlos said in such a matter of fact way that made it sound simple.

I knew that at the time, we were supposed to be entering the camp, the Catherine May, should be about 500 metres out, with Hans behind the sights of an AS50 kitted out with his BAE sights. I asked Carlos if there was any way he could get us close to the point, where the pipe entered the camp. We needed to see things for ourself before we made any more plans. He said he could lend his motorcycle to Alé, as there was a footpath that completely missed out the check point, but that sometimes there were random foot patrols, of Cuban Army walking around the outer perimeter. The Americans, did not bother, because they had electrified the fence with a lethal voltage. Then you had to cross another mine field to their internal fence. It was agreed that Alé would take me and we would try to get as close as we could to the sewer outlet from the fence. Alé found the track with ease and the old Honda 50cc motorcycle that like the truck had seen better days, but still managed to carry us forward. Alé was driving with me as pillion. If we were stopped and caught with guns, we would be in the infamous political prisoners jail in Havana and never see the light of day again. So we left our automatics back at the farm. Soon the path came out of the trees and bushes and I could clearly see the fence. There were spotlights shining down on both sides of the divide, which was the minefield. I got off the back of the Honda and Alé laid the bike down at the side of the path. I could really have used one of the BAE sights at this point, but like the guns would have landed us in jail if caught. Reeking of Rum which we had deliberately spilled down the front of our shirts we started walking along the path, that seemed to follow the minefield. This pathway looked well worn, so I felt safe walking it. An hour later we came to the point where the private contractors part of the camp was and even at night, I could see where the sewage pipe had been laid. Because the ground where it was had first been cleared of mines and then filled back in afterwards, it was more fertile that the ground around it. Consequently it was lush with short plants which stood out next to the dry barren ground that was filled with mines and death. I could see some of the private huts and containers near the fence. The Humvee's that were parked at this side of the camp were gloss black, the military ones on the other side of the camp were in desert camouflage. Inside the camp there was another wire fence that separated the contractors from the US Army/Navy. This meant we would have to enter and leave by the same route. Having seen what we needed to, we started to walk back to where the motor bike was. Halfway there I saw two lights swaying back and forth.

"Be so drunk that you cant stand properly and if you could be sick on cue that would help! But whatever you do don't talk or answer any question, even the ones I ask, which will be in Spanish." Alé said

I started staggering and dribbling out the side of my mouth. I could see that there were two armed soldiers walking towards us. Their lights had not picked us out yet but Alé started to sing. Whilst it was in Spanish I knew it was song exalting the praises of Che Guvara

"*La primera cancion esta escrita*
cuando nuestro Comandante en Jefe
leyo la carta de despedida del Che

Aprendimos a quererte,
Desde la historica altura,
Donde el sol de tu bravura
Le puso cerco a la muerte.

Aqui se queda la clara,
La entranable transparen.............."

His singing was interrupted as the lights were shone in our direction. The Cuban soldiers shouted a command at us

"Usted allí para"

Even though I did not know the language the inference was almost clinical in its simplicity as the shouldered firearm of one of the soldiers came to the ready position and pointed at Alé.

We stopped and I deliberately leaned on Alé then when the soldiers were almost on us I turned my back to them and pushed two of my fingers, deep into the back of my mouth and throat. The result was almost instantaneous. The large plate of food, that I had eaten and followed with a large glass of rum, forceably ejected itself in a most spectacular fashion down the side of Alé's trousers and over his sandals. The soldiers said something more in Spanish as I dropped to my knees and on all fours I puked up the remnants of the meal and then dry puked some more, before falling face down in my own puke. Hopefully my actions were almost Oscar award material. There was a further exchange in Spanish and then one of the soldiers started to laugh and they moved off into the night. Alé, helped me to my feet and I staggered forward for a bit until we rounded a bend in the path and the soldiers were out of sight.

"Sorry about that Alé, but it was all I could think of doing that would stop them wanting to talk to me."

"That's OK Andy but I would prefer you had missed my feet."

We found the Honda and made our way back to Carlos's home. I showered in cold water around the back of the house, without taking off my clothes, they would have to dry on me. Alé did the same. Though I was sure there was enough moisture in the air that I could walk and wash at the same time. After I had washed I went back into the house. Abdalla, Carl and Lachie had already had their laugh pointing out, that I could not hold decent rum inside me. I was offered more food by Alé's aunty, which I accepted. Not normally a smoker, though an occasional cigar smoker I accepted a 'Romeo y Julieta number 2' from our host, which I smoked in the warm air outside the home. The added enjoyment of the rum and cigar, was the fact that the mosquitoes did not appear to like the blue smoke, that hung lazily in the heavy air. So for a short time I was free of the incessant high pitched buzzing and biting of any exposed flesh. We worked the plan and with the equipment that Carlos and his eldest son had retrieved from the beach, we were now good to go.

During the next night Carl set up a hide in the wood opposite the point where the sewer pipe entered the camp. He messaged us to let us know and to curse us for choosing him to be the one, to be drained of blood. by these 'Fucking Insects'. I knew this was partly true and partly banter. We were all sniper trained, so were aware of the importance of setting up your nest a long time before you were due to be in action. He would lie there and allow the insects to feed without even moving. Nothing would give away his position to any vigilant eye. Abdalla had taught all of us and trained us to be in an almost dormant mode yet to be fully awake when required. If he was caught short. He would go in a bottle. If he was unable to move then he would just piss in his pants. He could not stand up or move around even after the sun had gone down. He would be there for the next 18 to 20 hours. Carl's only friend for that time would be his VAL Silent Sniper Rifle, Its sights although covered now so that nothing could reflect from it, would already be set for that point in the fence that we would be entering. The equipment that we carried now from the bag, Carlos had retrieved Blackout suits, complete with balaclavas the mini thermal lance, our Sig Sauer's with suppressors, our Bussé knifes and some cable ties. We waited until the sun had gone down, and made our way back to the beach, by a circuitous route. Now all we had to do was make our way back up following the fresh soil until we got to the entry point, all the time remembering we would be crawling almost five hundred metres, through a live minefield, whilst at the same time avoiding the lights from both sides of the wire and any other booby traps that may have been laid over the past thirty or so years.

Earlier the television in the house, had the news and weather on, when we were eating our final meal there. The topical storm looked to have changed course and had now been upgraded to a Hurricane, someone had given it some name or other. I was more interested in the direction that it was headed, which was directly for the Southern tip of Cuba. They said it would hit Cuba in 6 to 10 hours and that Cuban people should tie any loose items down. Cuba has seen many Hurricanes over the years and the Cuban people mange all but the worst of them. As a category 2 hurricane they were not at all worried.

"Ready?" I asked and they all nodded.

ACT 23

We played rock paper scissors to decide on the order we would follow the sewer pipe up to area, which was officially designated Delta Holding Cells. This though was government speak, for we know nothing about this and we don't want to know anything, about it. We lease it out as storage space to private contractors.

The thing about rock, paper, scissors, is that sometimes it can be a thirty second game and other times it can be endless. So after five minutes, I gave up and started on up the fresh dirt, leaving them arguing the toss behind me. Eventually though Lachie tapped my heel and Alé was behind him with Abdalla taking up the rear guard. We had our Storno encrypted radios, but we had agreed to only use them as a last resort. We knew the position of our fellow team mates from the small PDA units, attached to our forearms. We did not have the luxury of wearing our usual body armour, there is only so much hardware you can lug around, besides being shot would be the least of our problems if things went tits up. With every part of our body covered in black and even a black mesh material covering our eyes, so not even our eyes could be seen by others. I knew from the documents that Oran had managed to steal from the Sea Bee's servers, that the main part of the camp had thermal sensors around the wire. The Delta portion though was an addition to the main part and what they had actually done, was to cut a large hole in the fence and then put a big set of gates on it, before creating an annex and then wrapping that in a razor wire fence. Hopefully so long as we were not physically seen, we would trip no alarms. The first part of our crawl went easy enough, the next part was the real test. We were now just outside the edge of the prison boundary. Raising my head from the ground a little, I could see the cages of the main camp, as well as the row upon rows of wooden prison huts. There were some cages in the middle that had prisoners kneeling with their hands zip tied behind their backs. There was one cage, that had four prisoners in orange jumpsuits they wore chains and a black hood over their heads. I guessed these were important prisoners or new prisoners in for 'induction'.

I put my head back down and continued to crawl forward. There was a flash of lightning but without the roll of thunder. The sudden flash startled me for a moment then after a few moments another flash of sheet lightning. Thunder storms in this part of the world were not uncommon especially at this time of year. I turned and looked back towards the sea, There was a swell but I would not describe the sea as rough, just it was not as calm as it had been when we came ashore. I continued forward following the fresh ground and keeping my eye open for booby traps and trip wires. So far I had seen no sign of the mines that should have been to the left and right of me and I was feeling pretty lucky right up to that point.

I felt a tug on my boot and stopped. I turned to face Lachie and then looked to where he was pointing just over my head. Well about a foot over my head there was a thin shiny piece of stainless steel wire that was travelling down at an angle from the top of the razor wire to a point about 6 feet to my right, where it connected to an anti personnel mine. I could see the fins sticking out of the hard packed earth. Carefully we all removed the back packs that we had been wearing and shoved them in front of us as we moved along, just in case there were more of these. By pushing our packs it slowed our progress and we had to stop many times to regain our energy. We encountered six more of these booby traps along the way. More lightning out as sea, there seemed to be several storms forming and circulating but so far there was no thunder or rain. After almost an hour of hard work we arrived at the point, where the pipe turned in towards the fence and then into the contractors compound. The first thing we had to do was to poke, a blackout cloth through the electric fence. In order to do that I had to first put on a pair of heavy duty rubber gloves. The blackout cloth was actually a fire retardant sheet. Our insertion point was behind one of the buildings, so we would not be seen unless someone came close. As soon as the cloth was in place, Lachie passed me the mini thermal lance. I had to cut a hole through the mesh part of the fence but without cutting the wire that went along the top middle and bottom. So I cut a six foot wide hole in the bottom section. Carefully so as not to allow the section I had cut out, from touching any part of me while it was still in contact with the rest of the fence. I moved it to the side and laid it gently down next to me. Then I unrolled a rubber mat and laid that over the bottom wire. I fixed a bungee cord to the middle wire and connected it to the top wire of the fence, effectively giving us a bigger crawl space to get inside the Delta Camp. So long as we were careful when we went through, we would be OK. Now would come the real challenge.

There were perhaps a dozen wooden huts that looked like offices and sleeping quarters for the contractors. There was also a block of four shipping containers. Then next to them, was another small locked compound. That was all behind a corrugated iron fence. The gate into that compound and it was padlocked. This is probably where their hardware was stored.

My bet was that one of the large shipping containers, is where we would find the suit. We could not risk going and looking without first, putting all the guys in this part of the compound out of the playing field first. The main gate into the compound was locked from the inside which meant that they were all at home. I reasoned this because they did not have a gate guard waiting to let others in. We would try to do this without killing anyone, but we were prepared to do anything to get our friend back.

We split into two teams of two, Abdalla with Alé, and Lachie with me. I knew that Carl was just 300 yards on the outside of the fence and I knew he would be following our movements not just on his PDA but also through the BAE sight fitted to his VAL Silent Sniper Rifle.

The VAL had been a present, from Hans some time back and it had seen action on the last mission. These were originally invented by the Russians and given to their special forces in Afghanistan. So much was said about this rifle, that fired heavy subsonic 9x39 parabellum rounds, the rifle became legendary and the Afghans set out to capture one, which they eventually did, but not before giving the poor Russian soldier, to the Afghan women to literally skin him alive. They had then slowly roasted him over an open fire. After the Afghans captured it, they used it to great effect and even managed to get a few more. When the Russians pulled out of Afghanistan the Americans moved in to fight the Taliban. The Russians then gave a few more of these VAL rifles to the Afghans. Then it was the US forces that wanted this original rifle, they knew where it was and the man that now owned it. But he was a major player, in the Afghan conflict. Whilst the USA backed the Afghani's against the Russians, later it would be the Russians that backed the Afghan Rebels against the Americans. A trade was done, that provided a lot of arms and hardware for just this single rifle. The Americans then replicated it and finally the Brits got their hands on them. The SAS had three at Credenhill, before one went missing and came our way. Abdalla said that it was OK for shots under 500 metres and providing the person you were shooting at was not wearing body armour. Which is why Team Seven as a rule went for the AS50. The VAL was a relatively close quarters sniper rifle. From 25 metres you would not hear it and providing you could cover the muzzle flash you would never know where the shot came from.

I went right, towards the first hut with Lachie behind me. I knew without being told that Abdalla and Alé had gone left. We had our Sig's out ready. About six months ago Abdalla had suggested that we cover them in a thin layer of matt black paint in order to stop light reflecting off them in covert situation. We were completely black and in the shadows we would never be seen, but in the light we would stand out like a sore thumb. I knew also we would have to switch to our Storno radios in order to update each other.

The door handle turned easily in my hand and I felt the door give. I just hoped to fuck, that they oiled their hinges in this salty humid place. I pushed the door open a fraction and it opened silently. The hut was set out so that there were two bunk rooms one on either side and then an open space with the wash-room down the far end. I stepped inside and felt Lachie behind me. He closed the door as silently as I had opened it.

"What do you want to do Lachie? One room at a time or both together?" I asked

"Both together on three" he whispered back at me

We both grabbed hold of the door handles and carefully turned them in unison. The room I opened had a single bunk, I looked back towards Lachie and could see that his room was similarly accommodated. In two strides I was across the room and had delivered a heavy blow from the base of my Sig Sauer, to the mans right temple. Had he been awake, it would have put him to sleep for several hours. I zip tied him in a Hog-tied configuration so that if he did wake up then he would go nowhere fast. I did not like duct-taping an unconscious persons mouth, but if it came down to him croaking and me escaping, then that is the way it would be. Lachie had likewise managed to surprise the man in the other room. After a quick check of the rest of the building, we declared it safe. I keyed my throat mike.

"One clear"

"Two clear" Abdalla's voice said in my earpiece

We exited the building as carefully and as quietly as we had entered them. Then we moved on to the middle building on our side, as Abdalla did the same on his. It would seem that no one locked their doors here, but then again, who would be dumb enough to try and steal something, from a bunch of ex delta guys. They were now, not much more than mercenaries for hire. These were as it said on this door 'Bad Ass Only'. Well they might be 'Bad Ass' but we were desperate, and to me that 'Desperate' would would trump 'Bad Ass' any time. We entered the same way as we did before and went to enter their rooms, on the silent three count, played out on my fingers. I opened the door to mine and the bunk was empty. I quickly turned and raced towards the door. Lachie was coming out of the room he was in.

"He moved" he whispered

"What?"

"He moved so I had to shoot him"

"Oh...Right"

As we were whispering a man dressed only in a pair of boxer shorts came strolling up the hut from the wash room.

"Hey what are you guys doing in here, this is Blac........"

It was as far as his last speech in this life, was going to be, as both Lachie and I turned to face him at the same time. We both fired two shots to the chest and one to the head in unison. The result of so much lead hitting an unprotected body, completely destroyed his head and left him with a large whole in the front of his chest, not that he would be worried about that one now. I was glad that it was almost dark in the room, but could only imagine the mess that lay behind with the crumpled corpse.

"Too Much?" Lachie asked and I just shrugged my shoulders.

I was a long way, from where it all began. When SIS decided, they needed us out of the military and into their ranks. I had seen dead bodies in the military but I had never before SIS, been the cause of them. Now it would seem I would leave a trail of mangled destruction wherever I was. It had followed me like a dark shadow of violence that it was. It was now almost automatic for me to kill, these were becoming my muscle memories. Turn, point, shoot and kill. It sounded easy, when you said it like that, but they would always haunt me, in slow motion.

"Lachie we need one of these guys alive and by alive I mean with the ability to talk to us like right away."

"Don't blame me you shot him as well" he replied.

"Clear here" I said into my mike

"Clear" Abdalla's voice said

"Keep one for interrogation" I said

"Roger"

I really wanted two alive and scared enough to talk and I wanted ideally them both, to tell me the same answers to our questions. We left the second hut and prepared to enter the third. A man dressed in battle fatigues was walking across the compound towards us. We were out in the open and although he had not seen us yet, the moment we moved he would sound the alarm. He stopped and shielded his eyes from the bright white floodlights atop the fence, and behind the huts that we had just entered. His other hand went to the side arm strapped to his leg in cowboy fashion. His hand had reached the Velcro clip that was holding the large automatic in place. He stopped where he was and looked down to his chest and then followed the red dot that had appeared. The dot then rapidly moved to a spot between his eyes. Before he died he would have seen the flash of red laser and then nothing. The heavy subsonic round from just 300 yards out, entered at the top of his nasal cavities and the sinus's, between his eyes then it ripped through the base of his brain, turning it into boiled mush. Already flattened by its initial impact, the much slowed round, hit the back of the skull and tried to force its way through. The result of this forced his head back in a whiplash movement. The inertia caused a whiplash ripple to move down his entire body, reaching his boots, his legs kicked forward, as his head and shoulders flew backwards. His body crashed to the ground landing hard on his back throwing up a small dust cloud. Time for him had stopped a full second ago, but for us it still seemed to stand still as well.

Abdalla who was closest to the man raced, over and grabbed the man by the shoulder and dragged him behind one of the Humvee's then he picked up two handfuls of sand from the ground and covered as much of the blood that lay on the floor.

"Thanks Carl"

"No problem" he said in my earpiece

We continued to the third hut and like all the others it was unlocked and had two rooms. Two men were sat at a table playing cards, we shot them, as soon as we saw them. There would have been no chance to capture them, and if we tried to wound them, they would have been a threat. Like a wounded animal they scream out, or if there is enough life in them they fight wildly. I hoped Abdalla was doing better.

"We are clear" I said

"We are empty" he replied

The other hut was empty of everything no furniture of belongings. So that left us with the large shipping containers. I asked Abdalla and Alé to meet us, in the first hut that we had entered. The two men were still unconscious and they would both be for several hours, they might have brain damage. Its not like the movies, where they wake up after a minute, with a slight bump and a dribble of blood. When you hit someone on the temple, with a big lump of metal, which is weighted down by a full magazine of bullets, made of lead and brass. The thinnest piece of the skull, is at the temple so it breaks. Swelling will cause pressure on the brain. This can lead to permanent brain damage and in some cases death. There will be a big swelling to the outside of the head and a one to three inch gash, caused by the edges of the gun's stock. All head wounds bleed profusely and tend to look worse than they really are. So the sight of the guy I had hit, with so much blood on his sheets, did not surprise me.

"What now boss?" Lachie asked

"Well I would have preferred a live one, that could have talked to us. I am as much at fault" I said pointing at the unconscious guy I had hit

"Mr Andy I have an Idea" Abdalla said

"Please share"

"Why don't we use the thermal sight on Carls AS50 and get him to turn up the sensitivity and scan this area, perhaps it will find Sir Philip."

"Will it work through those shipping containers?"

"It might not be very clear, but it will show a heat source."

"OK Carl, Abdalla will give you some instructions on how to adjust the thermal settings, on your scope. When you have done it, can you scan this portion of the camp? See if you can pick up any thermal sources apart from us and the prone bodies, in these wooden huts"

"Roger" he replied

Abdalla then proceeded to take him through the settings menu on the BAE Sights. For those who use them normally, they are simple to work with. However when you are new to them, its like trying to set up an old VHS Video recorder. It took him a couple of minutes as Abdalla had to also tell him how to reset it back to normal afterwards.

"There are heat signatures in the two end containers. The ones nearest the main compound. One has four who appear to be doing nothing and the other one closest to you has at least three, with two moving around." Carl said in my earpiece.

"Plans anyone"

"Why don't we put on the uniforms of the guys we have taken out. And just walk into the steel containers." Lachie said.

That's what we did, well three of us did. We could not find anything to fit Abdalla. If he started to walk around then he would be seen very quickly. It was the simple plan that Alé suggested we do. Abdalla stripped down to his shorts and I used some of our duct tape to secure his Sig Sauer to his back. Providing one of us was behind him, then no one would see the gun. We put more tape over Abdalla's mouth. We smeared some of the unconscious man's blood down the side Abdalla's head to make it look like he had been beaten. We cable tied his hands, but we put the cable ties, on back to front. I did this, so that they would slip open at the slightest pressure. We set off with Alé behind Abdalla, Lachie to the left and me to his right. We walked across to the closest container and opened the door, then walked in like we owned the place. Two of the contractors, were busy with an interrogation of a naked man, who was cable tied to a chair. The man in the chair had his head down on his chest.

"Who the fuck are you?" one of the interrogators shouted at us

"Well if you would have read your fucking email, or even answered your fucking telephones, then you would have known we were bringing this big bastard, in to you for debriefing" I replied

I could almost see the cogs, working in his brain. Trying to visualise his recent coded emails and messages. I had to pile on the pressure and give him an overload of information.

"C'mon fuckwit, the Colonel, personally told me he had messaged you, to expect us tonight. He wants as much info as you can pull from him. He is Zorro's number two. The Colonel, also wanted to know, how far you have gotten with Zorro?"

All the time we were walking forwards, toward the two men from Black-Tree. There was a look of total disbelief on their faces, as first Abdalla pulled his hands free, and then reached behind his head and came out with his Sig Sauer, complete with its suppressor.

"What the fuck?" The taller of the two contractors said.

They were so surprised by Abdalla, that they never even noticed the rest of us pull our firearms. Like all good interrogators, they were trained to leave their own guns, out of reach of the prisoner. They looked towards the table, where their guns lay. One of the men, made to reach for the table and Abdalla shot him in the knee. He went down squealing like a stuck pig. The sound of a man screaming from this container, would be normal and not attract any attention at all.

"What the fuck did you do that for? We are all Black-Tree operatives?" he whimpered from the floor, where he now lay holding onto his shattered patella. The blood was oozing out from between his fingers and running in rivulets across his hands.

"See now, that is where you have got things a bit sideways. We are how should I say it? Independent Contractors. As in independent from you. Now you have a man want and we have something that you want and something that some of you will never get?" I said

"Who is it you want?" he asked

"Wrong question first" I replied?

"What?"

"You should have asked. What we have the YOU want?"

"What's that?"

"Your life's in our hands, you get to chose today, if you wish to die? Or if you wish to see your families again?"

The man on the floor, suddenly became brave again and tried to reach up to the table. Abdalla shot him in the hand. Three fingers and the bottom part of his right hand disappeared in an instant. The man howled in agony. Alé walked over to the table and picked up the firearms and knives, that were there.

The interrogator who was still standing and looking totally confused. He could not work out, why members of the same company would be doing this to him? Then finally it struck him, that we were there to rescue 'Zorro'

"Who really sent you?"

"Zorro did." I replied

Lachie zip tied the man's hands behind his back. Then kicked him heavily at the back of the knees forcing the man to kneel on the ground. We ignored the man they had been interrogating, as he was probably a real terrorist anyway.

"Where's Zorro?" I asked again.

"I don't know who you mean" He said defiantly.

That got him a swift and solid kick to his kidneys, from Lachie. He would probably be pissing blood for weeks, providing he lived that long. I gave him a minute to stop writhing in agony on the floor and nodded at Lachie. Lachie reached down and grabbed the man by his shirt collar and brought him back up to the kneeling position.

"Remember the two questions. I told you work with? So once again where is Zorro." I asked.

The man who Abdalla had shot, suddenly gained a voice over his sobbing.

"For fucks sake Rick, give him up, the fucker never talked anyway."

"OK now see Rick, if you don't tell me where Zorro is, then I am going to put a bullet, right trough his head" I said pointing to the sobbing man.

"He's in the next container" the sobbing man said quickly and then followed it up with.

"I ain't taking another bullet, for that piece of worthless shit. I don't even think, he is who they say he is. Probably just some low down moron"

"Watch them" I said to the still nearly naked Abdalla who must have looked pretty fucking fearsome to them, standing there in his underpants, with his body covered in tribal scarification, and on a body that was so muscularly toned, glistening in the sweat, that now covered his entire body. He looked like a Mr Universe or a superhero of some form. I guess that was not far from the truth. Just without the cape,

"Carl cover us"

"Roger"

Lachie and I went to the next container and pulled open the door, the first thing we noticed was the stench. It was a smell, I had often smelled in the mortuary. It was the smell of dead and rotting flesh. It was the smell of muscle that had been turned to liquid by maggots. There was a buzzing noise and a cloud of small black flies covered the top part of the container. It was dark as night and there was no electricity in this unit. I pulled my penlight out and flashed it around the container. There were at least four dead and rotting corpses. That smell had mixed with the smell of urine and faeces. Interrogation is one thing this was a completely different level. This was depraved. I looked at the living faces and I could not recognise 'The Suit'

"Sir Philip" I called out. I got no reply.

I ventured into the dark and hot cavern. The dead bodies had literally been slow cooked and those that were chained to the walls no doubt during the day were forced to endure incredible heat. As is if on cue a huge clap of thunder and a flash of lightning. That told me the storm was directly overhead. It could not be the hurricane, as that was over a hundred miles away. I walked down the line of men on the right. They were chained, so that they had to stand on their tip toes. I poured some water from my canteen, onto the face of each man as I passed along. I did not see 'The Suits' face in any of them I looked at the human carcases of the men, stacked up at the far end of the steel box. I accidentally stood on a corpses leg and all the flesh slid away from the bone as if it were a piece of slow cooked pork, I almost threw up what little I had in my stomach. I walked back down the other side and repeated the same process, as I had on the first pouring water from my canteen on the faces, of the mostly dead men hanging there.

It took me a while to recognise him. Even then, I still could not believe the change, in his facial features.

"Sir Philip?" I asked in incredulity

He lifted his head and I looked into his eyes, they were both bloodshot, but the grey blue of his eyes showed. He was hanging by his wrists which were shackled to the side of the container. He was totally naked and covered in filth and grime. He had been beaten and his face was distorted. Both of his cheekbones, had been broken and his lip split. Some of his lower front teeth were broken and one of his upper front teeth was missing. There were burn marks all over his chest and he was bruised all over.

"Help me get him down" I called out to Lachie. Between the two of us. We first unshackled him, then we put his arms over our shoulders and carried him back to the air conditioned container. He struggled against us as we opened the door and half dragged and half carried him inside.

"No....no more please......no more I don't know anything..........." he called out in a weak voice.

"Mr Andy, he thinks you are his torturers."

Abdalla was right they had broken Sir Philip as a man but they had not managed to get any information out of him. Lachie and I laid him down on the floor as gently as possible. I looked down to his feet. The soles of his feet had been beaten so often and so viciously that there were parts where you could see bones protruding. Without strong antibiotics a serious infection would set in and then that could rapidly lead to septicaemia. If his injuries didn't kill him the infection would.

I would have gladly murdered both of his torturers on the spot had Abdalla not done so first at least to the already wounded man. He walked over and put his big muscular arm around the man's neck. Then lifted him clear of the floor before turning rapidly around so that the back of the man's neck was now against Abdalla's own shoulder. Another rapid movement by Abdalla, and there was an audible snap, followed by a death gargle of air, as he broke the wounded man's neck. He then dropped the limp lifeless body to the floor.

I was fully aware, that he wanted to do the same to the other torturer, but I needed information on the Colonel, that ran this operation. So for now I needed at least one of them alive.

I held my hand up to stop him. Alé went back to the first hut and retrieved our clothing and we quickly changed. After carefully washing and dressing as many of 'The Suits' wounds as I could, we then dressed him in the clothes of the man who was still alive. He now was dressed only in his boxer shorts.

The interrogator did not know the location of his boss, that became obvious quite quickly. I zip tied him to his dead comrade. The man in the chair who have been the one they were interrogating when we entered the room. Had said nothing the entire time we were there. My beef was not with him, but I could not allow him to be treated in the same way as they had with the suit. Like an injured dog, I gave him a way out without pain. A single shot to the base of his skull. I would do the same to the other men in the containers before leaving. As the murderer I had now become.

"Carl we are coming out"

"Roger"

ACT 24

Abdalla looked at me just before we left. I knew what he was asking. It nevertheless seemed wrong, like two wrongs don't make a right. This was vengeance, in its purest form. For all the pain of everyone, who had been killed or hurt in some way, since this began. I gave the slightest of nod's and Abdalla's Sig Sauer fired twice in rapid succession. The shots placed so close together that it looked like a single wound to the chest. He dropped to the floor and Abdalla fired another round into the man's brain. Now the only ones who were alive, were those who were unconscious and unlikely be able to give much information on who we were. I knew we had almost no time to play with. There were big drops of rain starting to fall. Before leaving I took all their mobile phones and Laptops not forgetting their satellite phone and one of their portable radios. The ground was becoming wet and in some places the water was pooling.

We had to Gag 'The Suit' and tie his hands and feet together. This we did to first keep him quiet and secondly to make him more manageable, for our ex-filtration. He still was unsure who we were, such had been the brutality used against him. Carefully we carried Sir Philip over the live wire at the bottom of the fence and onto the earth beyond.

"How are we going to get him down to the beach?" I asked to no one in particular.

"Mr Andy if you could tie him to my back I will carry him. We can leave most of the equipment behind, we don't need it now."

Abdalla was right we had brought a lot of tools expecting things to be much more difficult than they were. With Abdalla being the biggest and the strongest of us. We used our last two rolls of duct Tape to bind 'The Suit' to the back of Abdalla. The rain was becoming quite heavy now and the wind had picked up. It was too rapid a change, to be the Hurricane. It was most likely, one of the many almost instantaneous, thunder storms, that sprout up on a nearly daily level over the ocean, due to the high humidity. The heavy rain, would hide our presence but with the ground all around becoming muddy and worse, it was becoming increasingly difficult to see where the Sea Bee's had buried the sewage pipe, in the minefield.

Alé led the way back to the beach. It took longer because we were crawling through ever deepening mud. We cut the six trip wires so that Abdalla and 'The Suit' could pass them. Eventually though we reached the shore and Carlos was waiting there for us. Abdalla refused to let any of us take turns in carrying 'The Suit' back to the old truck. We got to the truck and repeated the process we had the previous night.

At the checkpoint, once again Carlos argued with the guards. Only this time it was a shorter conflict, due entirely to the rain, that was threatening to strip all the leaves from the trees and the palms. When we reached the dirt track to Carlos's home, I could feel the wheels dig into the mud and spin uselessly, until they found grip to propel us forward to the next mud hole. Eventually we reached his home.

We carried the suit in, Carlos had his wife, take the children out of the room and then he cleared the dining table for us to lay 'The Suit' down on. Carlos's wife returned and put a large pan filled with clean water, on top of the stove.

I cut the bindings and removed the gag. When the water was hot she helped us remove the boiler suit from Sir Philip and then we washed him down properly. He never even flinched when I cleaned his feet, then dusted them down with antibiotic powder. After I had done that, I then bound them in bandages. There were burns to his chest back and even to his testicles. We were way beyond embarrassment. He looked so weak and broken. I knew inside though, there was a man fighting against torture, both mental and physical. For now though he was hidden so deep. It would be days before he was even aware of his surroundings. I inserted a dextrose drip in one arm and a saline in the other. Alé held the saline while I forced the Dextrose into Sir Philip. There was no point in even attempting to ask him any questions, at this time, because all he knew was pain and torture.

Now we had cleaned him we redressed him, in some of Carlos's clothes. They were loose fitting, but the covered the majority of the injuries, the lay below the dressings. His face was cleaned of filth and dried blood. Alé's aunty carefully washed 'The Suit's' hair in water, until she was finally able to rinse it, and the water remained clear and clean. Then she dried it off and combed it back. The man on the table now looked a bit like Sir Philip, although his face was puffed up and covered in blue green bruises. The cuts to his face were at least clean and I had placed Steri-Strip bandages over them. Carlos and his wife went and re-appeared with a single mattress, which they laid on the floor and covered with a blanket. Between the five of us, we gently lifted this brave man, from the table to the floor. I hung the refilled drips on two picture hooks in the wall and then covered him with a mosquito net from my medical kit, which now looked depleted.

I took an ampoule of Morphine and injected it into the catheter on his right hand. This would reduce the pain, from all his injuries as well as sedate him. I could do very little else for him at the moment. It would help him, to have a peaceful sleep. We were now inside Cuba, so there was no way Americans would come after us. That did not mean that the Cubans would not. They would be aware in the morning that there were escapees from Gitmo. They would be able to see the hole in the fence from their side of the wire. I needed to get 'The Suit' some proper medical treatment. He would require emergency surgery, on his feet and he would require more treatment from a maxilla facial specialist. The rain was thunderous in its sound on the tin roof, the wind was definitely gusting at 40 to 50 miles an hour. I asked Alé to find out from his uncle, if the hurricane had hit the Island, or was this just a tropical storm? After a few minutes of fast Spanish Alé said

"This is not the hurricane, it is to the East of the Island and is still three hundred miles away. This is a new one that is forming and it is less than a hundred miles from us. My uncle says that soon the military will come, to evacuate this area. It will be a mandatory evacuation they think that this new hurricane will be a bad one. Perhaps category four or maybe even a strong category five."

We tried to contact the Catherine May, but got no reply. The effects of so much static electricity in the air, made any long distance communication nigh on impossible. Between the gusts of wind, I could now hear a klaxon wailing.

"I guess they know, that we have broken someone out of Gitmo"

"No Lachlan. That is the mandatory evacuation. The Government will be sending buses, to take people to safety. We have to go to the school in Yateritas. If you dress in normal clothes, we might be able to get treatment for your friend. They have a hospital there. You must not look like military, I can put you in my uncles truck and take you with my family. If we get stopped. I will say you are my extended family from Moron, which is in the Cayo Cocos. My uncle says this hurricane, will destroy much of the land around here. The stadium at the school, in Yateritas is built to withstand the worst storms. It is also on higher ground, than we are here. The storm surge if it happens will put my uncles land under water and the house will also be destroyed by the storm." Alé said.

"Will the Doctors, not ask about Sir Philips injuries?" I asked him.

"Yes, but if you pay some extra money, they might forget ever seeing him."

"OK Folks that works for me, and we don't really have much of a choice at the moment. We cant contact the Catherine May. We cant stay where we are, and I cant give Sir Philip the treatment, that he is in need of immediately. He is so weak his body is liable to go into shock. We bury anything that we don't need and anything that would show us to be anything other than poor Cubans."

That is just what we did. Then Carlos and his family along with Team Seven, and 'The Suit'. Who we carefully laid into the back, The we put him on the mattress, then under a small tarpaulin. The rest of us would just have to get soaked. We kept with us, in a small and battered suitcase, that Carlos had provided. One of our Storno radios, as well as the radio and telephones from the Black-Tree, men. Each of us kept our Bussé knifes and we had our Cuban Peso's.

It worried me not having our firearms, or any of the high tech equipment like the VAL and the BAE sights. All the armaments we buried deep, in the mud outside the perimeter, of the land that was the farm, allocated to Carlos by the Government. Lachie, Carl and I, had no more understanding of Spanish, other than ordering a couple of beers. It would be up to Alé, and Abdalla to do all the talking for us. There were many tourists on the Island, they would be carrying their Passports and Visa's. We carried them, just not openly, at least not until we were in a tourist area. Carlos and his family only took a few personal items with them.

The sky was in continual lightning mode and it was impossible to tell if it was one, two or three storms, raging around us. The rain now, was like nothing I had ever seen in my life. The actual raindrops seemed to be four times the size of a normal drop of rain. It was like being covered in a power shower on full pulsating mode. The water was flowing out the back of the truck. We bounced from puddle to puddle, eventually we reached what passed for a main road. There was no traffic on it I guess most of the people had headed out earlier, for the shelter of the concrete stadium at the school in the town. I looked over the top of the cab and down at the two headlights of the truck. They only cut a few yards through the curtain of rain, which seemed for the greater part to be horizontal. At points the road seemed to be completely flooded, with the water up to the axels of the old truck.

We came to a road junction, the sign pointed left to the town of Yateritas and right to the Hospital. We turned to the right and came across some traffic going in the other direction to us. Presumably they were seeking the shelter, of the stadium. We followed the road, for about another mile, and then saw a large green sign for the hospital. Half of the sign had already been ripped away, by the winds, that were now accompanying the relentless rain. A streak of lightning hit a tall palm tree, that had been defying the wind, by remaining upright on its own. While all around it, its peers had given up and their roots had let go, to send them crashing to the ground. This one remaining tree, exploded as if there was a charge of C4, buried deep inside its trunk. The flames were rapidly extinguished by the torrential rain. The wind was now roaring, well more like screaming. Bits of wood and tin roofs were flying through the air, like the deadly missiles they were. I had no doubt that if anyone, were unlucky enough to be caught by a sheet of corrugated roofing, that they would be decapitated.

We pulled up at the doors of the Hospital and we got 'The Suit' out along with our suitcase. Then said farewell to Carlos and his family.

ACT 25

We carefully carried the suit into the hospital and gently laid him down, on one of the bench seats. I had most of the money that we still had, in my pockets. Abdalla went to the reception desk and hit the brass bell several times. Nobody came and then the lights went out. I guessed that the main power station had tripped out or the lines had gone down.

"Fucking great, an empty hospital and no power" I said more to myself than to anyone else. And then continued.

"What's that down there" I said as I saw a gentle glow from down the corridor.

I went with Abdalla to investigate, while Alé, Carl and Lachie stayed with 'The Suit' We walked closer and the light remained steady. It was coming from inside an office, with a half glass door. The inscription on the door said 'Doctor Juan Pablo Fernandez'. I knocked and waited. No answer. So I knocked again only this time louder. This time, I saw a shadow pass across the light, from inside the room the shadow moved towards the door which was then opened.

"Hola, ¿qué haces aquí? El hospital está cerrado"

"Necesitamos su ayuda por favor" Abdalla replied and motioned his arm towards the reception area. The Doctor who was wearing a white coat over green scrubs followed us, down the corridor to the reception area, where 'The Suit' was laid, dripping wet on the bench seat. The Doctor became agitated and gesticulating that we should leave.

"No soy un doctor de la gente. Este es un hospital de animales"

I understood the word 'animales' and 'doctor'

"Doctor do you speak English"

"Si a little. You must go to the Hospital, in the City"

"Doctor, my friend is hurt really badly, and he will die, if you do not help us. I can not go to another hospital, where they will ask a lot of questions. If I am honest with you, will you help us?"

Just in case he did not understand the inflection of what I was saying to him, I had Alé translate everything I was saying. I told him most of what we had done and how we had rescued our friend from the bad Americans. The doctor took a penlight torch from his pocket and started to examine 'The Suit'

"Your friend is indeed very sick, but I tell you again I treat only Animals."

I took the large wad of Cuban money, from my pocket, then split it into three, two thirds I put back into my pocket and I offered him another third.

"This now and the rest when you have treated our friend"

"I am not licensed to treat humans"

"I do not care if it is legal or not. Can you treat my friend, Doctor?" I almost shouted at him.

"Si I can, but I can not promise you anything good."

"OK Doctor, please do it"

The doctor left and returned with a large trolley. We carefully lifted 'The Suit' on to the trolley which the doctor took to an operating theatre and again we transferred Sir Philip to a large table in the middle of the room with pull down light over.

"There is an emergency generator in the next room that will need to be switched on before I can work."

Lachie went through the door and moments later the lights came on in the theatre.

"The power only works for this room and the X-Ray. Nothing else will work. My staff have gone home apart from the one nurse, who is back in the office where you found me." he said

Alé raced back to the office and came back with a plump nurse who it turned out spoke almost no English, which made us even, I guessed. The Doctor told us all to get out of the operating theatre, but I insisted that one of us stay and that it would be Abdalla. The rest of us made our way back out to the waiting area. A large tree had fallen against the sign for the hospital. The wind was definitely stronger when the lightning flashed I could see all sorts of debris flying through the night sky. Mostly it was foliage but some sheets of wood or light gauge metal. The rainwater was flooding the surrounding area. The drains had no hope of clearing such a downpour. The thunder no longer rolled, it boomed with a frightening ferocity. A flamingo caught by the wind and its feathers soaked in water and black mud, was thrown against the main doors of the hospital and slid down to the step where it remained motionless and dead. I had seen big storms before in the seas around Scotland, but this was the fiercest storm over land that I had ever seen. We were forced to go back down the corridor towards the Operating room, as the glass front doors of the Veterinary Hospital, gave in to the wind and debris. Within seconds the front foyer was flooded with water and whatever else the wind carried. This was not the Hurricane, the American weather station on CNN, had been talking about. This was a new storm, that had been born in the warm seas to the South of Cuba. Possibly two thunder storms colliding and then the up-draft, of warm air filled with the moisture, of water evaporating from the ocean, who's temperature, was approaching the high 20'c. It would mix, with the really cold air, almost at the edge of space. The friction caused as that moisture is rapidly cooled, then formed into ice partials. This resulted in the fantastic light show, of lightning. This cold moisture filled air, now falls as hail and rain and with the up and down drafts the wind is fuelled. This would be a self generating storm and it would not loose its destructive power, until it hit the USA mainland. This is where there would be enough solid ground and dry land, to starve the storm of moisture, which was the storms fuel.

For now though, comparatively speaking, Cuba did not possess enough land mass to quell this natures beast. I prayed that the Catherine May, had found safe shelter. They had the power to outrun this storm, and I hope they had used it to do so.

In a storm like this, even the steel hulled 170ft Catherine May, would be tossed around like a dingy. The waves would be forming into great swells I did not have to see them, to know it was happening right now. The ultra low pressure of the storm over the sea, would allow the actual sea level around the Island of Cuba, to rise by anything up to twenty feet. The waves coming in would be nothing short of disastrous to the small homes around Cuba's coastal regions. The storm surge would only add to the flooding, caused by the torrential downpours.

Even some of the modern glitzy hotels, that were starting to surround the sand covered coastline, would be in danger from this rapidly growing storm. Two windows to my left shattered, as some piece of debris, carried on the wind hit the glass. The rain poured in the hole, like it it had been opened especially for it. Soon the floor was covered in water. With nothing to board over the hole from the inside the rain and wind would cause more damage.

"Lachie how do you feel about coming with me outside and see if we can block that hole up?"

"Beats doing nothing" he said and we forced our way out into the storm. We found a sheet of wood that presumably had been on someone's roof earlier tonight, It was a struggle but we managed to wedge it into place and then quickly returned to the relative dryness of the interior in the Veterinary Hospital. When we were back in, we brushed away as much of the water as we could and then mopped up the rest. It was so dark that without looking at our watches, it was difficult to tell what time of day it was. When I did finally look, I was surprised. It was 10am and still it was still almost as black as night outside. The thunderstorms rumbled and roared on and the rain had not abated in the slightest.

The wind though did seem to be less fierce. 'The Suit' must have been in surgery for almost five hours, when the Doctor and his nurse, came out of the operating theatre. They walked down the corridor to us. We had taken their paraffin lantern from the Doctors office.

"How is he Doctor?"

"Your friend was badly beaten?"

"Yes by the American forces"

"The injuries to his feet will require some skin grafts, I can not do that here. So long as you keep the wounds to his feet clean and change the dressings twice a day, then get him to a hospital within a week to start on grafts. I had to wire both his cheek bones into place and his jaw was broken I have also wired that and removed the broken teeth. Almost all his fingers were broken, so I have straightened them out and strapped them with aluminium splints. I treated all the burns to his body, including the burns to his genitals. The men that did this must be sons of the devil himself. I sutured some of the big wounds but some of his other wounds, I left with the butterfly stitches I believe you put on?"

"Yes Doctor, they were evil men and they will not be hurting any more people. Thank you Doctor. I was only able to give emergency treatment at the time we got to him."

"Your friend can sleep in the theatre for now, I have put another drip into him with saline to reduce the strain on his heart. We do not have human blood here. I have also added an antibiotic drip with penicillin. The anaesthetic will keep him asleep for another couple of hours. As soon as the storm is over I will take you to somewhere safe."

"I am 'O' Negative, Doctor can you use that on him. I know it can be used universally"

"Yes I can but I can only take a little from you"

"Then do it. How much do you need?"

"I can not take more than 1 litre, any more than that and it will be dangerous for you, I will give you a glucose and drip after to replace volume and bring your blood sugar level back up."

I went to the operating theatre where the nurse was watching over 'The Suit'. He was not yet conscious and had two drips in his arms. I knew one was antibiotics and the other would be either glucose or saline. I sat down on a chair and the doctor put a cannula in my right arm and then connected that to an empty glass container, with a rubber sealed top. Presumably even animals would need to give blood to save other animals, of the same species. I watched as my dark blood slowly filled the glass bottle. Then the doctor removed the tube from, the cannula in my arm and the connected it to a dextrose drip. The bottle of blood was now connected to the left arm of the suit.

"As soon as our friend, has got all the blood in him. We will take our leave" I said

"You would not make it past the army patrols. They will see you. They will think you are looters. I have a Veterinary Ambulance in the garage behind the Hospital. I can take you anywhere in Cuba. With the lights flashing and they will not stop me. You and your men can hide in the back."

"That is very kind of you Doctor" I put my hand into my pocket and took out another third of cash that we had, to give to him.

"This is what I owe you"

The Doctor put his hand up and refused it.

"No you have paid me more than 2 years wages already. I would ask one thing? Your watch? I have not seen one of those? Would you give me your watch as payment?"

I undid the strap of my A.P. Royal Oak Offshore. I knew the watch was worth more than the entire wad of money we had started off with, but for saving our friend it was cheap at twice the price. I passed the watch to him and he immediately undid his Casio and gave that to me as a trade. I put it on and we shook hands.

"We cant thank you enough and if I can ever do anything for you I will"

I dare not tell him what the watch cost, for fear that he would not accept it. We took turns in watching over 'The Suit' for the next twelve hours as the storm raged. The doctor and his nurse shared the little food that they had with us. It was the wind that decreased first then the thunder and lightning and finally the rain stopped.

ACT 26

True to his word the Doctor brought the old van converted to an ambulance with the name of the Veterinary Hospital painted on the side. A light bar was attached to the roof along with a chromed two tone air horn. After removing the large and small animal cages from the back of the ambulance we made a bed with some blankets and carefully carried Sir Philip and laid him down on the makeshift bed in the back. For just a moment Sir Philip looked at me and beckoned me to come close. Then he whispered to me. What he said to me, was something that would change me forever.

I raised the Catherine May on the Satellite Phone that we had stolen from the Black-Tree men. The Catherine May, was anchored in Havana Harbour. I knew this was at the other end of Cuba and it would be a very long drive for the Doctor even with his nurse sharing the driving. But he insisted he would take us anywhere. For the first time in days I was able to close my eyes and dream that we might get home safely.

The Cuban roads were not the best in the world. Where there were police checkpoints, the Doctor or Nurse would put the emergency lights on and if required the two tone klaxon style horn. Several times along the way we had to stop to refuel. At a small town outside Havana, we stopped for some hot food at a roadside café. We topped up on coffee and burritos. It was in the early hours of the morning when we got to Havana. It turned out that the Hurricane which had been a category five, with wind speeds gusting at over two hundred miles an hour.

The Southern tip of Cuba, had bourn the brunt of it. The Americans had practically shut down Guantanamo Bay Prison, just leaving a skeleton staff. The families and majority of staff had been evacuated to the USA. Without doubt the Americans, would be unhappy about us breaking out Sir Philip, from the Delta section. That is assuming they did not cover it up, out of sheer embarrassment. After all they could not say 'oops we lost a super high value target from our delta section of Gitmo'. If they did they would never get any more work from the CIA.

'Zorro' would be marked up as 'died during interrogation'. We pulled up next to the Catherine May, which was tied off, at the international section of the Harbour. There was no one around when we loaded The suit and ourself back on to her. I thanked the Doctor and gave the Nurse the rest of the money that I would have given to the Doctor. She was crying with delight, perhaps she had never seen 500CP before It would certainly change her life for the better.

We had already made sure we had a passport for the Suit and Oran had printed some forged stamps, for his passport and visa. We were all back safe and sound and we had rescued 'The Suit'. Stu contacted the Harbour master who sent a young female customs officer down to stamp our Passports and Visas. She never even looked at them just used her red rubber stamp and handed them all back to Stu. She then informed us that we had six hours to leave Cuban waters. We thanked her and waved her goodbye as Stu started the Twin diesel Turbine engines. Lachie cast of the forward rope and I did the same at the stern. Alé stayed on the dock and waved us off. I for one would not feel happy until we were in international waters.

Now we had the IDF Doctor, to treat Sir Philip, not that I was not grateful to the Cuban Vet. According to the IDF Doctor, the vet had done an amazing job, especially on the feet and the suturing was the best he had ever seen but it would be a long time before Sir Philip would be up and about. It would be a couple of days before we could carefully debrief him. For now though we were heading home. As soon as we were outside the Cuban territorial waters, I was going for a long hot shower. I went down to my cabin and striped off and entered the small shower cubical and let the water pound on my back, I was not sure how long I stood there, before I turned the water to cold. Then I towelled dry and after cutting my beard off, I shaved and then shaved again. I dressed in shorts and a loose fitting shirt. It would be some time before we would need warmer clothing.

I joined the others in the galley. Rosemary and Morag had cooked up a storm, boiled ham, potatoes and cauliflower cheese. Served up with copious mugs of strong Arabic coffee. Stu produced a bottle of Jameson's and all of us even Abdalla had a good slug added to their coffee. A single round of drinks, killed the entire bottle.

"Thanks Stu for keeping them all safe." I said and we all raised a glass to him.

The Auto pilot on the Catherine May took us on a heading to Saint Johns Point we would be there in a couple of days, if he powered things up, and if the weather was fair to us. It turned out that the weather was fair. We could not trust taking 'The Suit' to any hospital, until we had cleared him of all the charges that had been levelled against him. So we would treat him on the Rig and would get the best specialist to come there and treat Sir Philip. We already had our medical bay and a lot of equipment. Hans had said he would get specialists from his country, in the same way as we had done for the young policeman. We should all have been happy. We had gone out on a mission to rescue the suit, from Black-Tree and to bring him back home. We had been 100% successful and we had lost no one, not even had any of us been injured. Yet there was something dragging us all down. I had a feeling what it was, but I would not share it with anyone until we were all safe and sound back home in our castle above the waves. I spent a lot of the time in my bunk.

We had left some stuff buried outside the farm in Cuba, we had even left some stuff on the ocean floor. Hans had said he would take care of it. I had promised to myself and to Petrá that this was the last mission, even though I knew it was a lie at the time, well not really a lie but it was not entirely honest either. There would be another mission. Oran was busy on his computers, cleaning things up as he called it, which normally meant he was inside someone's server deleting any file that connected to us. Normally a gregarious person, I kept myself to myself on the way home. I looked in on 'The Suit' and checked continually with the Doctor as to the state of his patient. He gave me the same answer every time. Sir Philip was resting he had been brutalised and traumatised. I knew 'The Suit' was not the sort of man who just gave up, yet to see him laid in his cot with his eyes blank and staring worried me. On one of my walks up on deck Oran came up behind me with Cyber.

"How is he?"

"Same, its like he has left his body, I have known him for over six years and in all that time, I have never seen the fire leave his eyes, until now. Those bastards did a real job on him." I answered.

Cyber pushed between us and put his snout to the wind at the front of the boat. It was like he was smelling for his home back on the rig.

"Oran If I asked you to do something and not let Hans or anyone else know, would you do it and just trust me?"

He like Cyber, seemed to to be pushing his face into the wind. Almost like he too was searching from something that could not be seen, but that he knew was out there.

"Would it hurt anyone in Team Seven and family of those on the Rig?"

"No, I can promise you Oran, it would not"

"Then I will try to do whatever it is you wish me to do."

"Thanks Oran, I will let you know more when we get back to the rig."

Stu opened up the big turbines and the front of the Catherine May lifted clear of the ocean, on her hydrofoil blades that were pushed out, on their hydraulic rams at either side of the boat. The twin screws with their custom made props, dug deep into the salty water below and the Catherine May, rode the surface of the water, like the queen of trawlers she was.

I looked around at my team members as I walked down into the galley come lounge area. With the boat on auto pilot and the anti collision switched on. Stu could spend some time with his wife. Lachie was sat with his arm draped over the shoulder of his wife Morag. She and Rosemary were sharing some girlie time and were smiling.

Hans was playing chess with Carl. This Uncle and Nephew team had pulled us out of many a sticky problem. Abdalla the biggest and strongest of us, yet he was also the kindest and most gentle man you could ever hope to meet. He would be getting married and I was sure would raise the big family he had always wanted.

'The Suit' had formed us all into a single team, right from the time when he had taken Lachie and me from the RAF. He had created us in the image, almost of himself perhaps 30 years earlier.

Abdalla, he had taken our basic shooting ability and refined that to a skill that put us in the top half dozen snipers in the world.

Hans and Sir Philip they had taught us hostage rescue, which by a cruel twist of fate, we had used to rescue the very teacher. We had been taught interrogation and anti-interrogation techniques. We had been able to hone our own skills in parachuting, diving and combat. But the greatest skill that 'The Suit' gave us was to work as a real team, always having each other's backs and being there for one and other. There was nothing that one would not do to help another. God help the person that picked a fight with Team Seven. Because they would be picking a fight with the most elite single unit in the world.

I looked back at the things we had done. We had complained about the tasks, that we had been given but we never shied away from doing, what needed to be done. They say there is a time for everything and they, whoever 'They' were, were right. I knew that time was fast approaching. Oran was back to his computers. I walked back to my cabin and lay down on my bunk. I closed my eyes and fell into an uneasy sleep.

ACT 27

We arrived at Saint Johns Point, without any drama, took on more fuel and headed for our home in the north sea. Oran had dead dropped an E-mail, letting those on the rig, know that we were all safe, and that we had rescued 'The Suit.' We also let his wife know, that Sir Philip was injured but not fatally so. In order that the sight of him would not be such a shock. We took on more supplies and immediately headed back out to sea. Hans had arranged for the specialist medical team to be ready to transfer to the rig shortly after we would be arriving. The weather was clement so it would be a simple trip home.

I found myself feeling distant from the others even from Lachie. I could not explain the why or the how, just that I now felt different. There was a coldness in me. Something had changed me back at Gitmo. I went to the galley and grabbed a beer and headed up on deck. The scene in front of the Catherine May was like a picture split into two but with just a single colour BLUE. That was the feeling, I felt blue and down, there was a light blue sky and a dark blue ocean. I was struggling to maintain myself in the mid line between them. I asked myself if I was going mad? I don't know how long I had been standing there but it must have been some time. The bottle of beer I had taken from the fridge was now warm, but I had drunk none of it. I drank it anyway and then went back down to the galley. I sat and talked with the others, even though all the conversations seemed to be hollow. I knew this would not be finished, at least not until I had done one more thing. Yet the impossibility of that task frightened me. I was not frightened of death or even of pain. I was scared shitless I would fail. I went to my bunk and showered scrubbing the imagined filth from my body. Towelled and then dressed in clean clothes. Then went to see Lachie. We had been friends since childhood, he had always been more like a brother to me than just a mate. The first time I got drunk it was with Lachie, I was 13 and we had gone to a house warming party near Golspie. I puked all the way back home. Lachie was a big lad, even back then. He had thrown me over his shoulder and carried me back to the school digs, where we were staying. We had caught our first fish together, even shot our first stag together. We joined the military together. He had been my best man, at my wedding and I at his. I knocked on his cabin.

"Come in"

His voice sounded as warm and friendly, as it always did. The soft West Coast accent mixed with the Highlands, a reminder of where we came from. The strange thing is we don't hear our own accents, just that of others. I guess my own accent was not that far removed from his. I opened the door and went in to his cabin. I told him what I had going around in my mind. We sat and talked for most of the day and well into the night. We went to the galley and had a meal and then I made my excuses and went back to my cabin. There I lay down and tried to sleep but without avail. I got up and grabbed a pen and some paper. I would try and sort into an order of some kind, just what it was that I had to do. I knew it clear as day now.

We arrived back home and the first thing we did was to arrange with Hans, for a specialist team to be sent to the rig in order to look after 'The Suit'. Then we reunited with our families both close and extended.

We let Mrs Reeves-Johnson, have as much private time with her husband as we possibly could.

Oran went straight to his grotto and started work on the task that I had set him. For most of the time he kept his door locked. Normally there was never a locked door on the rig. The Children knew, not to go in other peoples apartments without being invited. But it was not for the children's sake that Oran now kept his door locked. Fortunately no one else had noticed.

Lachlan and I spent a lot of time in working out the how and where of what we had to do. This was something that we would do together, without the help of the others, not that they would not be willing and able to do so. It was just that it had to be us. I don't think I could have explained it, if I even tried. There was a darkness in me that never existed before and I had shared this darkness, with only two people, Lachie and Oran. I would not tell my own wife, who I previously had no secrets with. I knew that Lachie would not tell Morag. Oran strangely enough, was the man that kept the best secrets. That had been his way of life, before joining Team Seven. He was the man who stole secrets and raided banks and electronic vaults. He did all this from his own computer. Then Hans had come into his life and Oran had then stolen secrets, from nations and terrorists. Hans said there was no system, that Oran could not hack. I had murdered the only other man who could hack as well if not better than Oran.

Oran was not helping me, because I had killed his enemy. Oran was helping me, because he was a full member of Team Seven. Lachie was helping me, because he was my brother. I would need one other person to help us that would be Abdalla.

I knew the who, I needed to know the where and most of all, I needed to know the why, the real why that is. This time it would be for keeps. What I was planning, was nothing short of a reign of retribution. Then Team Seven would cease to exist, on paper and micro chip. Oran would be the man to fix that. For now though, I would spend my time with my family and wait until 'The Suit' had recovered, however long that might be.

I had not mentioned him, in the micro team, for what we were planning, just that it was a given. That would mean, we had at least six months to work on things and probably a lot more. Given that we normally worked on the fly and still managed to survive, then within ninety days of that, we should not just survive, but we would conquer.

Our parents went back to their shop on Fugloy. The young police officer had a new life in the village of Keiss. Hans and Carl, had gone back to the IDF taking the scientists with them and in a few weeks time The Icelandic Medical team. Would leave us.

So for now 'The Suit' remained a wanted terrorist, all his possessions and property had been confiscated. Oran had offered to clear his name on paper by proving his innocence. Sir Philip had refused and would stay a wanted man, until we had fixed things his way. That was the reason that we could not involve Hans and Carl. To do so would not only place them in grave danger, but would destroy their careers.

Petrá kept asking me, what was wrong? And I just kept replying there was nothing wrong. I know she had asked Morag about Lachie. It had created a tension not just between me and Petrá but between all of us on the rig. The conspirators and those who were not involved. This was to be a secret so tight, that our wives, would hate us, for even thinking it. Time passed slowly for us. Sir Philip was now able to walk with the use of sticks. It had so far taken almost seven months. He was still not able to look at his wife without crying. This once proud man, had been reduced in a matter of days, to an introverted sickly old man.

I remember the very first time I met him. He had told me 'The is no out for you' What he was telling me at the time was, once you were in SIS you were a life time member. Some of its members had died, strangely enough in the first mission we had been involved in, we had actually dispatched several of them. Now we would be looking to see who facilitated things this time. We would do nothing until Sir Philip, was able to join us in what had to be done. This was his mission and we were nothing more than the tools for the job. I would not question a single command nor would the others. Another three months later saw us in summer again. Sir Philip's feet had completely healed all bar the scarring being tight. He was now able to wear his leather brogues. He worked out in the gym for almost 6 hours a day. He would run around the deck with Kyla at his side. Then the day came, as I knew it would.

"Andy? Are you sure you are up for this?"

"Yes Sir and I think I can speak for the others when I say we are all with you." I replied

We were all down in Oran's grotto at the time, and they all nodded. There was a strong chance, that we might not all, survive this mission. Even though officially it would never be sanctioned and no record of it would ever exist on computer or on paper. This was not an SIS Mission. This was to be purely personal.

Oran had done his research and had then wiped any digital trail he may have left behind. He had put together a digital package that would be sent to every authority in the world. To prove beyond doubt that Sir Philip was completely innocent, of any and all charges. Also all his property and finances would be replaced.

The time had come to tell our families, that we would be going away for some time and that we would be out of communication, until what we had to do was done. This could be for weeks, or even months, before it was completed. That night after our communal dinner we told them. We would be going to the mainland with Stu, after that we would go dark. They all knew what it meant. There were arguments and threats from spouses and friends. But to no avail. I went to the armoury and collected my stuff, then went to my apartment. I told the kids how much I loved them and that I had to go away for a while. Hell I did not know how long. I stood up and told Petrá how much I loved her. She slapped me and for the first time ever she screamed at me. She said if I really loved her and the kids, then I would tell her what the hell was going on. I didn't and she slapped me again. I told her I loved here, but this was something I had to do, in order to put a complete end to things. When Abdalla, Lachie, Oran Cyber and 'The Suit' were onboard the Catherine May. I passed a large sealed letter to Stu and told him if we were not back in three months then he was to give that to Petrá. Lachie and Oran did the same, as did Sir Philip.

"So where to then"

"Aberdeen"

It was a simple enough trip from Château Brent Bravo down to Aberdeen. During that time we went over our plans until we could execute them in our sleep. We assembled and dismantled or firearms blindfolded. We worked on a silent code of hand signals because we would not be using radios, nor would we be using telephones except to identify the guilty. We would use our skills, built up over the last seven years. Perhaps this was to be our destiny. I don't know if I believed in Karma, Destiny, Gods will, or just sheer fucking bad luck. Years of seeing death and destruction, of the human body. Along with taking part in said destruction, had made me who I was now.

They say, again, just who the fuck are they? But they say life is a journey. If that was the case, then the roads end, was just up. Ahead. It would be a dead end. We had taken large sums of money with us, because the last thing we wanted was for us to be linked to an area, by going to the bank, or hole in the wall. I had taught Oran how to use the VAL and the digital scope. He was proficient with the Sig Sauer's. His skills were so important to us now. It would be all very well us going in guns blazing, and it turns out the person we are seeking is not there.

Oran would find those that we needed to find. He would destroy any trail. We would be ghosts. Normally there would be all sorts of banter, black humour. This time it was all business. Cold as ice and as direct as a laser beam. I have always been a great believer in the punishment should fit the crime. But what about when the crime was so heinous and barbaric? ....

The forever internal struggle between right and wrong.

Stu brought the Catherine May into Aberdeen's big port, come marina.

"Over there" Sir Philip pointed to a huge luxury yacht. Carefully Stu brought us alongside this yacht that was bigger even than our super fishing vessel. There was a set of steps that led down the side of her hull. We tied off and I followed 'The Suit' up to this classy boat. It actually made the Catherine May look like some old tug boat from the Clyde.

"A gift from a true friend" he said as he walked up to the Wheelhouse.

Underneath a lifebuoy, there was a small key safe, with a combination lock. Sir Philip punched in a code and then entered the wheelhouse. Again it made our own boat look complex. Just two throttles and a tiny almost redundant wheel to guide the boat with. This though was only for when you wished to use manual control. This luxury boat might as well have been a luxury apartment, or the penthouse suite at that top of fine building. Everything was beautiful and shiny.

"Where's the crew?"

"We are it. Oran will control it in the same way as the Catherine May. This has full automatic control, with collision awareness. Only this baby if far more accurate. You put the destination in, it finds the best way. I am afraid though unless you want to cook, then there is a freezer full of ready meals. She is fully fuelled and at our disposal for as long as we want it."

"When you say its a 'Gift' Don't they want it back?"

"Well yes, they would prefer it back, but for them its not a big deal. Lets get our gear on board and then we will see what else my friends have left for us?"

That is what we did and then we said farewell to Stu, Rosemary and the Catherine May.

"Just to be safe, Oran can you take us out sea and then we will work things out for there."

"Aye aye Skipper" Oran said with a cheeky wink.

He plugged his laptop into the USB slot in the control panel and set the course for a point 30 miles from the coast of Aberdeen. As if by magic huge turbines sprung into life and the boats external lights came on. As did the lights in any room that you went in. If you did not want the lights on all you had to do was say lights off. Such was the level of high tech ingenuity of this automated vessel. Finally out to sea, Oran let his faithful hound have the run of the deck areas.

"I don't think the decks will wash themselves Oran" Lachie said with a smile

Whilst Oran was busy controlling the boat and sluicing down the deck area, where Cyber had decided to leave his mark, the rest of us went on an exploratory mission around the boat. Lachie said we should start at the bottom and see what she was loaded with. The engine room would have been impressive had there been anything to really see. The engines were covered is a metal shroud and there did not appear to be any way to control the boat from here apart from plugging in a laptop to one of the many ports that appeared almost everywhere we went. To the rear of the engine bay there was what could only be described as a hanger.

On a winch in the middle of the room was a small four man submarine. There was pretty much all sorts of dive equipment and it was all top end stuff. Then there were two sixteen foot RIB crafts with twin Honda engines. The RIB's were mounted on rails and faced towards the rear of the boat, in a similar way to Stu's twin life boats. There was a pair of four wheel ATV's and even a pair of off road cross bikes. On racks at the side there were mountain bikes. In short everything apart from a plane. There was a choice of taking an elevator up to the next level of taking the stairs. We took the stairs we found ourself in another smaller area about the size of a large garage and that as it turned out when the lights came on was just what it was. Pulling back a dust-sheet, there was a brand new Jeep Grand Cherokee. The doors of this garage opened out to the side of the boat and a ramp could be deployed either manually or automatically via the boats control system. The next level seemed to be all accommodation and luxurious bathrooms. The next deck up from this had the Galley and bar with a large seating area that doubled as the dining room. Above this appeared to be set for crew quarters or auxiliary accommodation. Above this deck, was what could euphemistically called, the wheelhouse or control deck. The top deck was semi open and was another relaxation area with leather seating and another bar. To the rear of the boat there was a large wooden deck area probably big enough for a dance floor. To the front there were decks and walkways. Then there was the most interesting room and I knew Oran would spend most of his time in here. It was some form of control or security room there were monitors showing all the areas of this boat. Calling it a boat seemed to somehow be demeaning of such a big and beautiful vessel. I had always imagined a yacht to be something with a sail stuck in the middle. So it did not really fit there, it was more like a small luxury ship than a big boat.

I looked all over but could see no name, nor could I see an identifying number that would say where it was registered to and who owned it. I guess I really did not need to know that. I knew that without looking, that above the top deck its roof would double as a helicopter pad. So we had everything here to go on sea, under sea and over land.

Target number one and there were several, would soon be making our acquaintance. We were going to ensure that there was a bit of a house cleaning. We all went and joined up with Oran.

"Target One Brigadier General Sutterton the SAS Commander"

ACT 28

Brigadier General Sutterton, was currently the commander of the SAS at the Credenhill Barracks. Some people occasionally referred incorrectly to it as simply 'The Boathouse' Usually they were the ones who claimed that they were Ex-SAS. The truth is most Ex-SAS don't go around advertising the fact that they were in the SAS. Because people knew that the SAS did the things that other people would not do. This time though it was not so much about a military action, that had been conducted by the SAS. It was about money and power. As with most of these money and power things, the money goes to the military but the real power ends up going to a civilian. We were not going to be so bold as to attack the SAS Barracks, whilst we might just about get to our target, there was a much bigger chance, that we would either be shot or captured and then locked up as the terrorists, that they claimed we were. Oran, by his research had found out that the Brigadier General, was a bit of a sailing buff and had shares in a classic yacht. The Suffolk Regatta would be on in two days time. There would be many boats like ours anchored off the coast, to watch their spoiled sons and daughters, take part in one of these annual events. Where the incredibly rich of Britain and the rest of the world, would come out to play, as if they were on the French Riviera. I was sure that the Brigadier General, knew of Sir Philips escape, from the Delta wing at Guantanamo Bay. He would have assumed then, that Sir Philip, who was close to death when rescued and would probably not survived. Especially now, we were more than nine months or so on from our daring escape and still we had not surfaced. He would be feeling pretty confident, that he had gotten away with murder. He would be in a relaxed and happy mood, at the Regatta. There was always a party of one form or another going on especially the night before any race were to start. Most of the yacht races did not start until the afternoon. I was not sure if that was just tradition, or if it was so that the sailors and watchers, could have time to recover, from the previous nights over indulgence and exuberance.

Oran set course and we chose to sleep, until the boat told us we had arrived. We would anchor near, many of the other large vessels, belonging to the worlds billionaires. They would be the only type, to own a vessel like this, as such no one would even notice us. We arrived and we would anchor, as if we were a lost sheep going back to a flock. Our flash boat came to a stop and dropped her anchor about half a mile from the shore, to be in amongst a fleet of boats, of her own kind. I was sure I even spotted an identical craft to ours.

There was to be a dinner party for the most powerful and rich on the beach. The Brigadier General had been invited, whilst I say invited. It was the kind of invite that you paid for. Seats at this dinner would set you back a cool £50,000. This in itself should have been a pointer to the security services, that even on a brigadiers wage, that was above his pay-grade. At this dinner, deals would be struck and billions would be made. That worked fine for an industrialist but not really where a military man, should be. We knew who he was meeting and I knew why. The BOYS AT-S Silent, was going to be launched to the worlds military and the manufacturing rights were up for grabs. If the Brigadier General said, that his men had been using this in tests, or even in actual combat, lets face it, who would be able to check and see if the SAS, had taken out a target, or if it had been another unit. So the Brigadier General would claim it was as silent as the Kenyans claimed. We knew it was not. The kick back that the Brigadier would get would be far beyond his fifty thousand pound, ticket to sit down with the Saudi Princes. This deal alone would no doubt net him somewhere between five and ten million pounds. Quite a nice retirement plan. We were going to ensure that retirement plan was retired, even before it came into play. We were going to bring him back to our boat and then leave. Oran stayed on board our boat, yacht, or ship. I actually doubted if anyone other than Oran could make it work the way it was supposed to do.

Lachie gave himself a haircut with a number two, all over. I did likewise and both of us shaved. Then we dressed in black tux with a white dinner jacket, crisp white linen shirts and black bow ties complete with patent leather shoes. We would look the same as any of the other three hundred or so guests. Oran had managed to print off some very realistic invitations to the dinner. The only thing that we would be carrying that other guests would not, would be some ceramic knives.

'The Suit' would be driving the RIB and he would be staying with the small boat, until we returned with our quarry. For his part he had dumbed down his usual garb, so that now he wore a pair of oilskin trousers, a dirty sweatshirt and a woollen beanie cap on his head. Instead of his fine Oxford brogues he would be wearing turned down Wellington boots. Now he just looked like the poor hired help. There were many similar men in all forms of small craft, that had taken their rich occupants ashore, for their banquet.

We made it past the first line of security as we went up from the harbour, leaving 'The Suit' behind in the RIB. The second level of security, comprised of a G4S minimum wage security guard, in a smart pressed uniform and even a peak cap. It did not make him any more vigilant than the other guy down at the harbour. He looked at our invitations, but in the half light on the edge, of the 'rich' area he nodded and passed them back to us, which we put in our inside pockets.

The tables were laid our in long rows. There were areas set aside for visiting dignitaries. I could see some of the rich had brought their own security with them. They were the ones dressed like us in black Tux's. Their necks seemed far too big, for the shirt collars, that threatened to choke them to death. A lot of testosterone on show here tonight.

Abdalla with Oran's help had identified the Kenyan delegation. Not that they need had bothered. We saw them almost immediately. I had expected them, for some reason, to be dressed like most of the others. They however were in their traditional robes with the Kenyan colours. Perhaps he was a prince or a king. Who cared, he was going to help me find our target. Obviously, no one wore name tags. I guess at £50K a ticket it would have been a tad crass. Lachie and I wandered around the many guests that were milling around. This was the time for polite conversation. The real money talk, would come over and after dinner, over fine Cuban Cigars and equally fine French Brandy. We would be long gone by then. What had to be done, had to be done openly, just not here.

The Kenyan delegation moved on from the woman they were talking to and to a military man. There is this thing, about a military man whilst still in the military, they stand out like a Jewish penis in a catholic boys choir. He was military. He was not anything other than a pen pusher. All those years behind a desk had made him soft and had killed his keen sense of spacial awareness. Twenty years ago he would have noted any possible threat. He would have looked for the best exits and escape routes. The quality paid personal security had their back to the outside and their heads on a swivel stick. They would be able to see where their charges were. The optimal route to get to them and get them out in the case of an emergency.

Lachie and I split up and he went left, I went right. Like Lachie, I had a flute of fine champagne in my hand which had been presented to me as soon as I had entered the big covered area. The Brigadier General, was here on his own. Because he could not afford a second ticket even with a possible big payday looming. That played right into our hands. No one to miss him, when he was gone. No one would report him missing for at least 48 hours. Because of the secretive nature of high finance and business, there were no security cameras. A lot of the people here, like the Brigadier General, did not want their presence advertised. The time now to see if Oran's magic, was as good as he said it was. I sidled up to one side of the Brigadier General and Lachie did the same on the other side. We did so in a way, so that when we were at his side our, faces were facing out into the night air, of the sea beyond. I took out what looked like a mobile phone. In fact it was just a digital photograph display unit, as used by professional photographers to check their shots. The picture showing was the daughter and grand daughter of the Brigadier General. The picture, through the powers of Adobe Photoshop, showed the woman and child being held by a man with a large machete, at their throats, below was today's newspaper being held by the child. The picture looked pretty convincing to me and I was seeing it with calm eyes. Through the eyes of a father and grandfather the picture would conjure up all kinds of horror, especially given the line of work he was in.

"We have your daughter, if you make a noise or a fuss they die right now." I said as I drew his attention to the picture in my hand. He said nothing to begin with but then as we expected the next thing would be bravado albeit quietly

"Do you have any clue, as to who I am, If you have done anything to them, I swear................." he said

Lachie cut him off by saying

"Yes. We know who you are and blah blah blah blah Here is the thing now, we have your child and granddaughter. We will kill them without so much as a thought. So come with us now and they will be released."

He looked flustered as well he should. To anyone looking at us it would look like we were discussing things or looking at a mobile phone.

"Call her" I said

He took his own mobile phone out and pressed a speed dial button. Due to a telephone hijack device in Lachie's pocket, his call rang twice and then connected to Oran on our boat.

"What... Who the fuck are you. I will kill you." he hissed, into the phone.

I reached over and took his phone from him and switched it off. I turned to face him and used his body to cover my actions. I took his phone apart and removed the Sim Card and the battery. Then I broke the phone in two and put it in my pocket. I would put it in the first waste bin I came to. Lachie now had his ceramic knife in his hand he showed it to the Brigadier General.

"We are leaving now" Lachie told him

"But I cant. I have important people to meet. You must understand that I have a powerful job." he said in a low voice. I took out the picture.

"If we are not in the harbour in 5 minutes they die. Do you value your meeting, over their lives?"

"Lets go" Lachie said again and took hold of the Brigadiers elbow.

"As we go, you best look happy to be with us, because if we don't get out of here clean. You die where your standing. Then all your family will die, five minutes later. So fucking move it" Lachie said with a smile on his face, as if he was having a jovial conversation, with an old friend. I led the way and he followed with Lachie all the time at his side whenever there were security guards, we would turn our faces the other way.

Soon we were away from the throng of the wealthy and corrupt and heading back to the harbour. 'The Suit' had seen us coming and had brought the RIB to the slipway so we could get in quickly. I forced the brigadier general to sit while we made our way out of the harbour. Then we were away from the small vessels and out to where the real money, was floating. We were anchored the furthest out. Oran had the RIB ramp ready and with a twist of the throttle, 'The Suit' ran the RIB up the ramp and into the belly of our beast. The Ramps came up behind us and a door slid down, to close off the boat hanger. His phone I had ended up dumping, on the walk down to the harbour.

"Who the hell are you?" he almost shouted at us?

"Imagine that Lachie. He had people try to kill us and he does not even know who the hell we are"

"I will take a bet he knows our boss?" Lachie replied as he dragged him out of the RIB and onto the internal deck of our big boat.

"Who is your boss then? And what do you want with my child and grandchild."

"Our boss would be that gentleman, over there and unlike you we don't harm innocents." I said

"But I saw the picture"

"Jesus for a member of the SAS, you are really fucking stupid. It was a mock up. We got their pictures from their social media and then photo-shopped them. C'mon the SAS have been doing it for years. And as for our boss let me introduce to you. The Right Honourable, Sir Philip Reeves-Johnson." I said as I made a sweeping arm movement towards 'The Suit'.

"But I was told you were dead." he whimpered back at us.

The Suit removed his beanie hat and walk over to where his first revenge victim stood.

"You Bastard, you are not fit to lick the shit, from the boots of the men, who I have had the greatest honour to serve with. Before I was in SIS and even before I was recruited into MI6. I was an officer with the SAS. Never did I use my men, to forward my career, or to make personal gain from them. But you have stooped even lower than that. You deliberately murdered, men in your own regiment. It is for that, more than any other crime, that you are to be taken to task for. We know all about the backhand bribes and fake reports, that you signed off on. The BOYS ATR50, is still as useless as it was, in the second world war. The only difference in it now is, it shoots further and has a bigger bullet also the rifle makes a bigger bang. But it does not even compare to the AS50 or the VAL-SS. Yet you would have sold it with a false bill of goods. Do you know, how many men died because of you and John Stevens? Do you know how many innocent people you killed through this? You attacked my family, in my home, using your men to murder my detail. Then you set it up, to look like it was an attempted hit. You sent your men, to not only to get me and try to extort our countries secrets, which quite frankly are way above your pay-grade but you tried to murder my friends, on numerous occasions. You had me kidnapped and branded a traitor of the worst kind. You had me handed over to those animals, at Guantanamo Bay. Were it not for these brave men, who risked their lives. Not because they were ordered to, and not for money, they did it for friendship and a loyalty. That quite frankly you could never comprehend. Loyalty and Friendship along with a sense of duty."

"I have money" The Brigadier General pleaded.

I kind of expected the reaction that would get. I had seen 'The Suit' pissed off before and it went exactly the same way, as it had done the first time I saw it happen. This 60+ year old man. We were never really sure just how old he was. He struck out with a single hand, the first two knuckles, of the now healed fingers, on his right hand were tucked in under the rest of the fingers, so that they formed a perfect wedge shape. He sent his forearm flying forward from where it had been resting in line with the side of his body. It was sent forward with such speed, that even I was caught unaware of what was happening, until it was all over The Brigadier General was on his knees, on the deck and puking and choking on the very expensive floor. He was struggling to breathe. By the time he had hit the floor 'The Suit' was already walking away. The general would not die yet. That was still to come. No one was going to walk away with just a slap this time.

I zip tied is legs while Lachie did the same to his hands and then we hog tied him and threw him back inside one of the RIB's. We would sort something more secure, when we were underway from here and on our way to the next target. It would have been John Stevens had he managed to live until now.

He though could not have done what he did without help from above. Someone, who would gain, by the loss of Sir Philip. The one man who could control the money in SIS. The Chairman of the Executive Defence Spending Board. Such a secretive position, that they are only appointed out of one of the security services themselves. It is incredible easy, to make money disappear, in MI5/MI6/SIS. You just say spent on ensuring security of undercover operatives. Operatives often bribe people, in foreign nations, in order to gain secret information, that is useful to our nation. Alternatively, sometimes we want to make a country conform, to our mindset, that costs even more. So money can be taken from a slush fund, without any real control.

The Suit had before being kidnapped, been looking into where large sums of money were going. So when John Stevens was presented the opportunity to protect that income. He combined that with a jealousy, that was burning deep inside him. He was never quite as good at anything as Sir Philip was. He even failed to get the bride that 'The Suit' got. Never the less here was a chance, to close an enquiry.

Mr Robert Halliwell chairman of the committee and long time friend of John Stevens. Halliwell had nothing to do with the BOYS rifle scam, nothing so complex. He was just outright stealing money from the slush fund, in order to supplement his extravagant lifestyle. Parliament like Schools, has set dates for its holidays. That is how we would get him. He was at his holiday home, on the tiny Island of Alderney. This was a place where the wealthy went to relax and some to spend their ill gotten gains. Halliwell even owned several expensive properties in his property portfolio.

ACT 29

We found the perfect place on or luxurious boat to place our prisoner. The Anchor, Chain Room. This was located at the wonderful pointy end of the boat, which was good because, we were at the nice flash back of the boat and did not have to listen to his perpetual whining. We removed his ties and gave him a bucket. He was given basic food and water. Any time anyone went to check on him we would take Cyber to the door, just in case he was stupid enough to try something.

So we were now sailing to get number two on the list. There would definitely be payback, but for now we had to round up the hens, as the Americans would say. One of the busiest shipping lanes in the world, is the English Channel. It is also one of the most dangerous, not so much because of tide races, though there are some of them. More so because of shipwrecks that lay close to the surface and even worse, gigantic tankers and freight ships. Unlike a small boat a tanker can take up to 5.5 miles to stop and have a turning circle of around 2 miles. So you have to have your wits about you on this stretch of water. The one thing we did not want, was to show on the radar as we crossed. Oran had it figured though.

"We piggy back"

"And how are we going to do that Oran?" I asked in my stupidity.

"Its simple man." He said sucking on his lollipop and continued.

"We come within 50 yards of one of these gigantic oil tankers and maintain a parallel course. I then capture their responder signal and relay it on. What happens then is it becomes a ghost signal and their big boat cancels out our small boat sort of thing. Trust me Andy It will work."

"I trust you Oran, I just don't understand you." I replied and that just got me the bird.

It would seem that since Oran had become a seasoned member of Team Seven, he had become quite brave in his responses.

"So Boss. Now we know where he is, what is the plan on grabbing him?" I asked Sir Philip

"This is where Mr Mohamed comes in"

"Sir Philip, I am not sure what it is you wish me to do?"

"Mr Mohamed, as with all men like him. He is driven by greed. A lot of very rich people in the UK, live on Alderney. He will have tried to get money, at some point, from all of them over the years, and will be looking for someone new to con money from. That will be you, Prince Karim Mohamed of Sudan. You Andy will be his translator and money man. You will find there are some royal robes in the walk in wardrobe in your room Mr Mohamed. Or should I say Prince Karim. Andy there is a business suit which should be the correct size. There is also a large aluminium briefcase which is filled with £50 notes." I put my hand up to stop him.

"Just who is the friend, you got this boat from and how come all the bits we require, wherever we go, just happen to be here?"

"Mr McPhee you should know by now, when it comes to things that I do, they are generally well thought out and planned. I know who my team are and therefore I had a pretty good idea, the items, that we would require and when we would need them."

"OK Just asking" I replied

Sir Philip continued

"Mr Henderson you will be the driver and will be driving that nice black American car that is in the hold. Mr Abdalla will, as the Americans say 'Flash The Cash'. You will let it be known, that you are there on the Island, looking for something to spend your money on. Property, Boats, Cars even Artworks. Mr Henderson is to be the driver come body guard, you Mr McPhee as I said, you will be the translator come money man, for the Prince. I will stay on the yacht with?????? Oran ......what is your last name?"

"I have not had a last name since I was thirteen and that's the way its gonna stay. Just plain Oran no middle and no last name" Oran said after he a sucked some more of his cherry lollipop and then promptly, popped it back into his mouth and continued to suck upon it.

"Very well Mr Oran and I, will stay on board this boat. Remember unlike previous missions, no radios, phones or other devices that can be tracked or listened in on." 'The Suit said.

"So where do we find this Halliwell person?" I asked

"Do not worry about that Mr McPhee, he will find you. Oran will find you the most expensive hotel and get you booked in there for a week. Use the Casino, if they have one, and tip well."

We shadowed a large American oil tanker and then we shadowed a large ferry boat into the main harbour. Oran brought us dockside and extended the landing ramp from the garage, at that point

Abdalla, Lachie and I, left our luxury yacht for land, using the Jeep Grand Cherokee. The windows were black privacy glass, The wheels were 20" with chrome rims. The interior had been pimped out so that the boot space had been removed and the seats moved backwards. The bench seat had been replaced with something that resembled a luxury U shaped couch. There was now also a privacy screen between the passengers and the driver. The doors were thicker than normal, which showed that they had been armoured. The suspension must have been toughened up to support the extra weight. The roar of the engine when it started up also told a tale. This was meant for speed, comfort and security before anything else. Lachie took us down the ramp and onto the concrete peer. Oran as quickly as he had docked us, withdrew the ramp and the unnamed boat, headed out for the open sea and the English channel. When we were ready for collection I was to go to the side of the harbour and to a shale covered beach, then shine a green laser exactly due east on the compass. I must say, I was not a big fan of no lines of communication. The only Hotel that we had been able to get booked in was the Old Government House & Spa complex.

Lachie pulled up to the front doors and a Porter came and went to open the back door, to allow 'The Prince' and myself to exit. Lachie beat him to it and stood looking like he was the hired muscle. I let the be-robed Abdalla, exit before me and then followed, carrying the aluminium case filled with cash. After going to the front desk, to check us in while 'The Prince' sat in a large chesterfield in the waiting area. Lachie brought in some crocodile skin suitcases, which had been loaded up with clothing and any items we might require. By coming into this Island but not using the ferry, we bypassed any form of customs. The harbour-master never even had time to notice our boat that had come and gone in under 5 minutes. A porter quickly collected our bags and took them away, presumably to our suites. We had the entire top floor, as was befitting of a Prince. Our suites were next to each other, a connecting door between my room and that of the Prince. After our car had been valet parked. We all took the elevator to the upper floor. We were shown to our rooms, I deliberately opened the case in full sight of the bellhop and took out a £50, which I gave him as a tip. His eyes nearly fell out of his head.

"If you need any thing at all, just call down for me. My name is Jimmy and I can get anything you desire, I do mean anything,"

"OK Thank you Jimmy that will be all. On second thoughts. His Highness has a specific dietary requirements, please can you have the chef, sent up as soon as possible." I said as I held the door open for him intending that he should now leave.

When he had gone, I opened one of the Crocodile skin suitcases that were laid on the bed. These were superb quality as were all the clothes that were inside. Strangely all in our sizes. I knew that the best stuff was for Abdalla and then next would be mine and poor old Lachie ended up with the lowest quality. That was not to say his were rubbish they were fine quality just not Prince quality. In one of the suitcases there was a watch case with a choice of what seemed to be real, Rolex, Omega, AP, Philippe Patek and some others that I did not recognise. Rings and men's bracelets along with other expensive accoutrements with which a prince might adorn himself, especially if he were flashing the cash. I replaced the A.P. Royal Oak Offshore, that I had lost in Cuba, with one from this case. I hung my clothes and Abdalla did the same. I was sure Lachie was doing pretty much as we were. There was a knock at the door I answered and Lachie was standing there.

"Where do you want the hired muscle?" He said

"We have muscle?"

"Yes"

"Where?"

"Here! You twat"

"I guess you should be on the outside of the door, patting down everyone."

"What about the maid?"

"You can try, but I bet you get a slap"

The elevator bell dinged, Lachie gave me the bird and turned to face outwards as I closed the door. A minute or so later there was a polite knock at the door.

"Enter" I said

The door was opened by Lachie in a very professional manner.

"The Chef to see his Highness Sir"

Lachie said as he opened the door wider, to show a portly man dressed in crisp chef's whites and carrying a large notepad in one hand. The other hand was folded neatly behind his back. I looked at Abdalla, the Prince. He gave a barely perceptible nod and I indicated that the Chef was free to enter. He stood in the middle of the floor and started to introduce himself. I held my hand up to stop him and then walked over to where Abdalla was standing in his green white and gold robes. Abdalla made like he was whispering to me and I nodded occasionally and then went over to the Chef.

"His Highness would like Tamil Stew, followed by Halal Roast Lamb, with rice. His Highness would then like English Earl Grey with Lemon and clear honey. Do you think you can manage to do that?"

"I do not know if we have Halal Lamb, would ordinary lamb not do?"

"No it most definitely will not do. We, that is His Highness is Muslim and it has to be Halal. The Prince quite happy to pay for Halal meat, to be Helicoptered in. Money is no object. However please ensure that there is a Halal certificate with the lamb"

I went to the case and took out several hundred pounds which I put in the chefs hands.

"If that is not enough please come back and see me and I will arrange for more funds."

"Thank you, I will have Halal meat, sent over from France, by helicopter. It will be here in time for dinner at 8pm?" The chef said.

I walked back over to The Prince and pretended to be in whispered conference again.

"That will be fine"

The Chef backed out of the doorway like he had just had an audience with God himself. But it would be money well spent. Managers of hotels can keep secrets, about who they have staying at their establishments. However when the kitchen staff know, or worse the low paid bellhop. Then word will get out, about this foreign prince, that was just giving away £50 notes, like they were confetti. And what's more he does not even speak English. What a patsy!!!

I changed into a light charcoal, original Armani suit. After we had all changed we made our way to the elevator. Lachie walking ahead of us, by eight feet or so. The elevator arrived. As we were the only ones occupying this floor, there was no one but the Bellhop in the lift. Lachie motioned for him to get out which he did. The prince and I entered followed by Lachie. The bellhop went to follow Lachie in. Lachie placed his palm on the boys chest and gently pushed him out of the lift.

"Take the Stairs" Lachie said and gave the boy another £50.

When we reached the ground floor. Lachie led us out into the beer garden. He found a table sat on its own with a high wall behind it. Almost every head in the Room turned to watch the Prince and his small entourage. Then Lachie motioned us over. Abdalla and I took our seats and Lachie stood with his back to the wall, until a young waitress came over, to take our order. She first spoke to Lachie who then spoke to me and I indicated that she could approach the table.

"May I take your order please" she said politely

I made, like myself and the Prince, were once again having a hushed conversation.

"May we have a bottle of Gordon's Extra Dry Gin and make sure its unopened. Also Schepps Indian Tonic water, again ensure the bottles are not opened. Please can bring a bucket of Ice. Can we have two glasses and some sliced lemon?"

"I don't think we serve it by the bottle sir"

"My dear you don't understand. The Prince has, because of his immense wealth, many enemies. They would perhaps, try to poison him. So he would prefer his bottles unopened thank you." I replied and carefully slid two £50 notes onto the tray she was carrying.

She Hurried back to the bar, where she had an even more hurried and animated conversation, with the Bar Man. Within a minute she was coming back with a Silver tray complete with a Bucket of Ice, a Large bottle of Gordon's Extra Dry gin, a bottle of Schepps Indian Tonic and two lead crystal glasses there was a fresh lemon and a knife as well on a small plate. She carefully laid all the items on the table and then backed away. I poured two drinks for Abdalla and me. Then under my breath and just loud enough for Lachie to hear.

"Sorry nothing for the hired help"

Equally mumbled, Lachie replied

"Fuck You"

We drank our very nice G and T and then motioned the waitress over.

"Thank you we are done now you can clear the table" and I left another £50 under the bottle of Gordon's.

"Excuse me Sir, What do you wish me to do with your Bottle of Gin?" She asked

I was feeling generous as it was not even my money

"Because of your good service, the Prince has asked me to give you this small tip and to tell you that you are to have what is left, not the Hotel, and not the Barman. Just you. Thank you" I said

"Thank you your Highness" she said

Abdalla made a flowing gesture with his arm, to show he was happy with her service. Then we stood up and left the bar. We wandered through to the main foyer and to the dining room. Again Lachie went ahead and first spoke to the Maître-d, who then motioned, for us to follow him to a table that sat on its own. The Maître-d pulled the chair out for the prince, and Abdalla sat down. I followed and Lachie stood behind Abdalla. The meal had been pre-ordered, as such there was no delay. The lamb was beautifully cooked and tender. After 'The Prince' had his Earl Grey Tea, we ordered another bottle of Gordon's Gin and again Tonic, Ice and Lemon. Once again after just one drink each from the bottle we left it on the table with a £100 tip. As we had the best table in the house, there were plenty of witnesses to this flamboyant Prince who was literally giving away money. Lachie asked the Maître-d to ensure that our car was brought around to the front of the hotel. We all left and started to look at anything that had a for sale sign on, which was actually quite a lot. On a small Island like this you cant do something like we were doing, and not get noticed.

We returned to the hotel Abdalla in his flowing Robes and me in a fine Italian suit. Headed up by Lachie in his Brooks Brothers 'Secret Service' style suit. He politely moved waiters out of the way in order for his Royal Highness Prince Karim of Sudan to pass. We went back to the bar. When we were seated and Lachie once again ever watchful standing ready. Abdalla sat down and had a pot of Earl Grey Tea, I gave it a miss and opted for an Arabic coffee, this they served in cup that bore a closer relationship to a thimble! Lachie almost lost the plot when he saw me trying to drink my coffee out of something smaller than an egg cup. I watched a fat balding man talking to the Matrádee. He crossed the head waiters hand with a few £10 notes.

The man started to walk, directly towards our table. Like a real security man, Lachie had seen the threat and was already putting his body in front of our table and between the prince and the threat. As the fat man reached to where Lachie stood. He started to reach into his jacket. Lachie grabbed the man's arm and held it firmly where it was.

"Please remove your hand from your jacket sir" Lachie said quietly into the ear of the fat balding man.

The man slowly took his hand out empty from the jacket.

"But you don't understand I am Mr Halliwell. I am with one of our Governments Select Committees I just wanted to Welcome your Sheik to our little Island."

"Prince" Lachie said firmly correcting the fat man, still holding the man's arm

"What?"

"Not a Sheik"

"He's not?"

"No"

"Sorry"

"Are you?"

"What?"

"Sorry"

"Why?

"Why? What? Sorry I don't follow"

"I Know?"

Lachie could be like that any time he felt that he could wind someone up until their brain melted. I stood up

"That's all right our security can be a bit.............well you got the picture. Peter Smythe-Holland. How is it His most exulted Highness Prince Karim of Sudan, can be of assistance to you?" I said as I introduced myself and held out my hand for him to shake.

"I just understood that the Sheik was looking to buy property or possibly invest, in our small but exclusive Island.

"That would be a NO and then a Yes" Hell, Lachie was infectious I then continued

"That is to say his Highness, is not a Sheik. He is a Prince and yes, he is looking to increase his portfolio. He also likes a bit of a flutter, every now and then."

"Well then, this is a fortuitous meeting, because I can help on both of those fronts you Highness."

Once again I made the well practised mumbles and whispered conversation. With the Prince nodding occasionally and a flick of his fingers to show that the conversation between staff and him was over. I told Mr Halliwell that the Prince, would like to hear more of his Ideas and would be happy, if he would meet with the prince at the side of the harbour, at 10:30pm as the Prince like to walk, when talking business. With the meeting arranged, we finished our drinks and went back to the rooms. Anything we had touched, was wiped down. We would be leaving most of the stuff here, with the exception on the heavy briefcase, filled with dosh. The car too would have to stay. We drove it to the beach at 10pm and wiped it clean. Then sat on a bench seat and waited.

Halliwell arrived five minutes early, which was fine by me. I got up and greeted him. This was going to be a lot easier than the last one. While I was talking, Lachie was walking down the length of the beach with Abdalla, using a pocket compass He flashed his laser pen into the dark of night and received a single green flash back. The good thing about lasers apart from being used to light things up, or to act as a targetting aid. They can also be used to measure great distances within a millimetre even from several kilometres out. 'The Suit' had the exact spot where Abdalla and Lachie were standing. Sir Philip, was already on his way to us, in one of the RIB craft. I led Mr Robert Halliwell down towards 'The Prince'. First I reached out to take 'The Princes' hand and bent in deference to his Royal position. I then introduced Mr Halliwell to the Prince. He too took hold of the princes outstretched hand, then bowed. That was as far as Halliwell got. I hit him across the back of the head with money case. Abdalla caught him as he fell forward. I pulled some Zip ties out of my pocket and secured his hands behind his back. Then from my other pocket I took out a black bag, which I put over Halliwell's head. I heard, rather than saw the RIB racing towards our position. Obviously I had not hit Halliwell hard enough because he started to come too and even started to shout "Hel....." That was as far as he got, before I hit him again. Just like before, he folded and went quiet.

Almost to the inch 'The Suit' drove the boat up onto the shingled beach. We loaded our prisoner in and were about to go.

"What about the Jeep? Wont the guy that owns it be pissed if we leave it here?" I asked

"Not really he has lots of shares in the company. They will just send him a new one." he replied.

We pushed the small boat back down and into the sea, then set back off for the fancy yacht. As previously, we went back into the boats hanger. This time we put Mr Halliwell in the starboard Anchor room. We had two of the men responsible and that left two more to get. The third man was located Belgium. Of the four he might be the hardest target to acquire. Sir Philip explained.

"This is, or I should say was my opposite number in the CIA. Unlike us Brits, they take security of their top guys very very seriously. Especially those officers stationed at NATO Headquarters. But I do have a plan to take him down. So lets go Belgium. So Oran if you could plot a course for Ostende."

"I thought you said your man was stationed at the NATO Headquarters in Brussels?"

"Yes I did Oran, but like all greedy men, they always want more, even if they have millions they still want more. Mr Conrad Levitz likes to gamble, especially with other peoples money. There is a big open poker tournament on at the Ostende Casino Kursaal. Normally he would have a protection detail with him but the casinos don't like that sort of thing. The only people around their casino with radios and earpieces are their own casino security. Mr Levitz's security team will drop him off at the Casino and then they will pick him up when he calls using the Casinos own land line. There are no mobile devices of any kind allowed in the Poker Tournaments in the Casino. So we will be waiting for him when he arrives. His detail will drop him off at the front and then they will drive away. We will be inside and take him as soon as they leave." 'The Suit' replied.

We followed the same pattern as before by shadowing larger craft. When we came close to Ostende Harbour I joined Abdalla with Lachie and 'The Suit' in one of the RIB craft as soon as it was dark. This time though Sir Philip would be joining Abdalla and me. Lachie would stay with the small RIB Boat. I was once again dressed in my fine Italian suit, Abdalla had also opted for his Princes outfit. The suit was dressed like he always had, from when I first met him all those years ago in the Commanding Officers office at CDE Porton Down. Harris tweed 3 piece suit, with a pair of brown Oxford brogues on his feet. A light check shirt from some Saville row tailor or other. Finally he wore a his SAS regimental tie. He looked sharp, especially for a man. who just almost a year ago, had the living shit kicked out of him. Abdalla was unarmed as was Sir Philip. I though had a pair of evil looking ceramic knives. We walked up from the beach and around the rear of the Casino. During the daytime the beach would have been full of tourists and locals alike. At night though the sand was dark and deserted, except for the odd dog walker. The area around the Casino, was filling up with people looking to have a good night, out on the town and many of them like us would, be heading for the casino doors. As we entered, we walked through the security barriers and as I knew it would, our watches set the alarms going. Then we were wanded by security and allowed to enter. Abdalla made his way into the casino proper. All the time making his way as far back, into the main area where the tables were.

I cashed some Sterling, keeping my back to the cameras as much as I could, although I knew that once we were out Oran, would in his geeky wizardly way, manage to wipe any digital recording. He would not be able to do the same to any old analogue system, but the quality on those were so bad, that we would not be recognised if they ran them later. The suit played a one armed bandit that faced the doors and I played on one that faced into the main casino. We played and waited. At 10pm on the dot, 'The Suit' scratched his head. This was the sign, that our target had just entered the casino. I waited and watched Sir Philip for the next signal, which would tell me if Levitz, had passed me to my left or right. He passed on my left and I followed him deeper into the casino. I could see Abdalla easily by his shiny flowing green and gold robe. He was sat at the High stakes table playing poker with a small pile of chips in front of him. Abdalla threw a chip at the croupier then stood up and walked quickly towards Mr Levitz.

"Conrad! My Dear Friend Conrad. It is so good to see you again. It has been some time, since we last met." Abdalla said as he stretched out his arms to Conrad. Then continued.

"Please let me buy you a drink, for all the good fortune that you brought me."

"I am so sorry, my memory lets me down. You are?"

"Conrad I am with the Kenyan Arms Company, you can not have forgotten so soon. How is your friend, the wonderful Brigadier General. We were working on a deal for the BOYS ATR" Abdalla said

"For Christ sake keep you voice down man, you never know who is listening. Are you here for the big game?" Levitz replied.

"No I am here to introduce you, to my friends. The man with the very sharp blade pressed against your spine is Mr Andy McPhee and you of course know my other friend Sir Philip Reeves-Johnson. Now if you don't wish that blade to sever your spine, then you need to follow me. If you make a sound you will die. shake my hand if you understand?" Abdalla said in hushed tones that left no doubt as to the seriousness of the situation.

Levitz shook Abdalla's hand. Abdalla turned and led the way Levitz followed with 'The Suit' and myself close behind ensuring that the point of my blade, remained pressed against his spine. I knew that the point had pierced his skin and that under his black dinner jacket his white linen shirt would be getting stained with his life's blood. Abdalla made for the corridor that led to the gentleman's rest rooms. It also had a fire door at the rear. The low ceiling was just what we required and it was an area that did not have a camera. Abdalla quickly took out a Zippo lighter and held it under one of the automatic fire suppressors until the wax melted and all the alarms and fire suppressors let loose, water rained down all over the Casino. We used the fire exit at the rear and moved through the crowd of onlookers. Then kept walking, until we got to the beach. Everybody's eyes, were on the casino who's patrons were now spilling out, in wet clothing. Amazingly police and fire services arrived in minutes. We though, were now down on the beach and loading Mr Levitz, into the RIB. After zip tying his hand and feet I pushed him into the rubber sided boat. Then we pushed the RIB back into the sea, after getting on board we made our way back in to the dark of the night and the sea. As before, we went back up the ramp to the luxury boat. We put our new guest in the bilge pump room. Then went up to the lounge area.

"So we have three of them Sir, who and where is the fourth man?"

"Mr McPhee I am sure you remember who he is?"

"The Colonel?"

"Yes indeed, the where though, I don't know exactly, where he is. I only have an approximation. And we have to go and let ourself become bait." Sir Philip said.

"So where to this time boss?" Oran asked.

"We are going down to the Horn of Africa, via the Suez Canal"

"So long as we keep shadowing other boats, it will take us about a week, If you want us to get there quicker then we will have to more visible."

"A week is perfect Oran it gives us time to plan and organise. Andy can you ensure that the prisoners are quiet whenever we are close to any other boats, they will only need water and energy bars. If they bitch turn their lights off."

I followed the orders and the prisoners behaved. They were let out for 15 minutes to empty their slop buckets and then to rinse it out, then back into their individual cells. They had no contact with each other at all. People often talk about going after the head of the snake. Well we knew who he was in name alone, we did not know the man. Oran found everything and anything on this 'Colonel' as he could. His company seemed to make a lot of money and it also appeared that he was a very hands on man. Sure he let his men work on their own, but when it came to getting new contracts, no matter how big or small they were. That was entirely done by him. He negotiated the terms the price and he told the customer, just how many of his men would be required for the job. The Colonel, trusted no one but himself to get the best possible deal, for himself that was.

ACT 30

We arrived at the Northern end of the Suez Canal. I remembered the first time I travelled this maritime passage. Nothing seemed to have changed on this stretch water that connected the Mediterranean and the Red Sea. Just over one hundred miles of canal. This was the water motorway, for the world container and oil ships. Although small boats like ours, if you could call ours small, also used this aquatic shortcut. We were head down to meet with a man 'The Suit' had trained with at the end of the Gulf War. Other than that we knew nothing of this contact. Although Sir Philip made no secret of the fact, that his friend was somehow or other, still involved with security, in some way. Not so much by telling us, but by not telling us.

After the Suez, we made for the Egyptian port of Al Adabiya. Then we followed it on down to the southern end of the port. To one of the many private marinas. Oran had created the correct paperwork for an Irish registered, pleasure craft, which was the flag of connivance that we were currently sailing under today. Our three prisoners had been given a good dose of barbiturates and were sleeping. Lachie would stay on board and keep watch over them, as we set off to meet up with 'The Suits' nameless friend.

The Egyptian children, that would normally beg from foreign tourists, they gave Cyber and us a wide berth. Even the hawkers thought, that the better part of valour, would be to walk away, from us as we walked down the dirty side walks. We arrived at a cafe located in a very narrow side street. Canvas shades went almost from wall to wall cutting out the burning sun. So much so that just stepping into this street felt like a 10c drop in temperature. At first, the man would not allow us in with Cyber, but the suit said something to him and handed him one of the £50 notes we had. It would seem that even in Egypt the British pound or the US dollar, is still good even if they don't like our countries. We went through the small cafe and out into an enclosed courtyard at the back. There were some tables with Egyptian men playing dominoes. A man dressed like a Berber came from one of the doorways that entered this courtyard. He waved his hand and the men finished playing dominoes and just left by the doorway, we had come in by. The man pulled back the hood on his cloak and smiled. He looked a bit like Omar Sharif, only taller.

"Marhaba Philib ، ahla" his voice was soft and cultured as he greeted 'The Suit'

"Shakira lc ya sadiki, now let me introduce you to my friends here. Mr Andy McPhee, Mr Abdalla Mohamed and Mr Oran along with his faithful companion Cyber" Sir Philip replied.

"I am most pleased to meet you. My name is Radwan." He said

We all shook hands and then he indicated that we should be seated. He waved his hand in the air and a young man came with a tray which had six glasses on it and a large pot of sweet green tea. When the tea was served the man went back the way he had come.

"How is it I may be of help to you Philip?"

"We are looking for the man who is in charge of Black-Tree Enterprises, he calls himself the Colonel. Do you know of this man? Or where we could find him?"

"Most of those, who are involved in our line of work, know of this man. He is a privateer and gets results. He does not care how he gets results. Most of his work is in the form legal protection rackets. But he also contracts for the CIA, though I hear you know of this? What sort of trouble are you in my friend?"

"Radwan, I do not know of this man personally. He though was responsible for framing me as the terrorist named as Zorro, even though he knew I was innocent. It is because of him that I am now here. I need to find him and then get him to come to me. How shall I say this? He owes me for pain, he has caused me and my family"

"By, come to you. You mean under a fictitious name?"

"Yes Radwan. What have you heard about my predicament?"

"They say you are a terrorist, and you have a big price on your head. Some people say that you escaped from Guantanamo Bay?"

"Well yes and no Radwan. I am not a terrorist. I was set up. I did not so much escape from Guantanamo, more like, my friends here, came to find me and they helped me. How big is the reward?"

"$10 million" Oran interjected and then continued

"I did not want to upset you with the details"

"Why would I be upset Oran?" Sir Philip asked

"Because its ONLY $10 million" Oran said and that lightened the mood instantly. We drank our tea and talked amicably, then got down to the nitty gritty of things.

"So I am guessing you already know that the man you are looking for is working out of Mogadishu. He sells protection to ships and boats sailing anywhere in the Arabian Sea."

"Yes Radwan. What I need from you, is some more firearms for me and my men I also need a way to get the Colonel to come to me." Sir Philip said.

"Then you are in luck, because I am bored and I really would like to have a sea trip. You know that I work with the Egyptian government, on a freelance basis. So with my documents I can get you whatever you require. I know you speak Arabic and Abdalla I am sure you as well. But the Somali language is not the same as either Arabic or really any other African language. Once again Philip you are in Luck because it is one of the languages I speak. So when do we leave?"

"Just as soon as you can load us up with the equipment we need." Sir Philip said and passed a small slip of paper to Radwan.

We said our goodbyes and made our way back down to our flash boat. We refuelled and awaited the delivery and our extra passenger.

The man that came aboard was no longer a Berber it was a sophisticated Egyptian wearing a fine suit and lots of gold. Shortly after, a beat up Iveco truck arrived, and several large wooden cases, were brought on board and put in the hanger, that was the bay, where the Jeep had previously been stored in. Oran laid in the course and we set of for the Port of Mogadishu.

Radwan as it turned out, was not only our contact, but he was also a great Chef in consequence the next few days, we are as if Rosemary was on board. Our trip down to Mogadishu was uneventful, with the exception of the crates that we had unpacked. Small firearms as well as several long range rifles. We did not have the luxury of our BAE digital scopes but the 16x scopes would do the job. There was however, a heavy Ma Deuce 50 BMG- M2HB machine gun on a quadrapod stand. This we set up on the front deck of our Yacht and we threw a tarpaulin over the top. The small arms and one big military style machine gun. This would be more than adequate for what 'The Suit' had in mind.

The plan was first to head for the port of Mogadishu and then directly South in a route that would take us to the east of the Sechelles. We knew this to be an area of high activity, for the Somali Pirates and we were ripe for the picking, at every little port down the Red Sea. We had flashed the cash and shown off expensive jewellery. Word will no doubt have gotten out about these stupid British people in a big expensive yacht. We wanted to be attacked, in order that we would have to make a run, back to Mogadishu. We were reliably informed, the Colonel was offering his firms services, to any boat or ship that could afford him. Some people even thought that his men, might actually be the ones who were attacking boats, that were not protected by him. In order to make them, take up on his offer. This was a protection scam, of the most basic order. Again before leaving Mogadishu we splashed the cash and talked loudly about the millions we had made from our last business deal. Then the following morning on a crystal clear day we set sail. The waters were perfect for fair-weather sailors that we pretended to be. We stuck two rods over the end of the boat and sat in our luxurious chairs, awaiting the fish to bite. We did not have to wait long, about five miles out to sea, we picked up one large and three small boats, on our radar.

"Oran take us 30 degrees to starboard and keep the same speed, see of our shadows match us." 'The Suit' said

"Aye Aye Capt'n" Oran replied in a fake pirate accent.

The boat moved course and I watched the wake curve out behind us in white froth over the deep and bright blue of the ocean below. I could not see over the horizon to where the boats that had popped up on our radar were, but I instinctively looked for them anyway.

"They have come about Capt'n, do you want me to heave too" Oran was milking the power that he had over the yachts direction.

I was not sure what made a boat. a boat or a yacht. a yacht or even a bloody ship, a ship. I just knew it was big and luxurious.

"Oran just bring us back onto the original course and see what they do." Sir Philip said

Oran was just about to make his pirate reply when a look from Abdalla silenced him. And he went about his computer work controlling our direction.

"Boss the three small blips have moved away from the bigger one, but they are all heading our way.

"Well we best get ready to greet some guests then" Radwan said.

He then went to the Heavy Machine Gun, after removing the cover he fed the belt of bullets in and cocked the gun before replacing the tarpaulin over. Sir Philip handed out or personal firearms which were ex British military Browning automatic pistols. These he handed out with two spare fully loaded magazines each. Then he laid down the long range guns on the deck chairs that were around the rear deck area.

"Let them Come, remember we don't shoot unless they do, just be ready. Oran do you want to put Cyber below decks"

"OK boss where do you want me?"

"Can you control this boat from the lounge area?"

"Sure can Boss"

"Then take yourself off down there." 'The Suit' said.

That left the five of us on deck, Lachie and I with rods in our hands, Abdalla pretending to be steering the boat but actually looking at the radar. Radwan and 'The Suit' sat at the side pretending to be playing Backgammon.

"Sir Philip, the small boats are picking up speed and heading our way. The big boat is still heading our way, but much slower. I think that would be the mother vessel and these three, are their Attack Fleet, so to speak. They are definitely using the normal style, of Somali Pirates. When they get within sight they will have one boat move ahead of us and the other two boats will take up port and starboard. Then they will make their move. They will be on us in thirty minutes minutes or so." Abdalla said in his bass voice.

Twenty minutes later they started to make their move and a skiff shot past us about a hundred yards out, they even waved at us. five minutes later the first boat slowed in front and the other two boats appeared in our wake. Then they moved up and took up positions at our sides.

"Hey English. Stop your boat" A skinny dark skinned man, shouted over the forty yards that was, now all that lay between us and them. Then the same from the boat on our starboard side.

"English stop or we will shoot you" Then he fired what looked like an AK47 into the water at the front of us. Like good tourists we were we dived to the floor. While Radwan crouched on the floor Abdalla stopped the engines by using the deck controls. The bow instantly dipped into the water and then rose back up as her speed dropped. When the boats were less than twenty yards apart, Radwan tore the cover from the 50cal and turned it to face the boat on the starboard side, that had originally fired at us.

The noise was the first thing I noticed as Radwan strafed the open hulled boat. Then the hot shell casings, were rolling around the deck, clinking and clanking off whatever was in their way. He swivelled the big gun around on it stand. So he was now facing the other boat and gave it the same treatment, as he had done with the first. By the time I looked up, both the boats were sinking and one of them was actually burning as well. Abdalla started our boat up and turned us about. The boat that had stopped in front of us, was now desperately trying to run, only not fast enough. Another burst of the 50cal canon saw the rear end of the small pirate vessel shatter into fragments of wood, just before it too exploded in a ball of flame. Abdalla stopped our boat and we surveyed the damage done by our canon. Three boats down and 9 pirates in the water, either dead or dying. We would not help them, they had made their choice a long time ago. The mother ship of this little flotilla was now coming up on our stern. When she was about 300 yards out there, was a flash of flame from her bow end and immediately there was a smoke trail.

"RPG I shouted"

There was no chance of it being heard above the roar of the 50cal machine gun that Radwan was still holding onto. Then the missile was about 50 yards from us and I feared certain death, there was a loud explosion and parts of flying shrapnel pinged off the top and sides of our boat the flash of fire and smoke told me that the wall of lead had been enough to save our hides. By the time the mother boat behind us had realised that the explosion, had not been on our boat it was already far too late for them, they took too long to turn their boat, not that they could possibly have outrun us anyway. The big cannon roared into life again and the concentrated fire ripped apart her wheelhouse and then her hull. Black smoke told a tale. She was going nowhere. Anyone in her wheelhouse would have been instantly cut in half. Another long burst and their boat was listing and getting ready to go under. Any surviving crew would be lucky to make it until night. They were far from shore without any real contact with their base. Nor were any of them wearing life preservers. Their boats would soon be completely submerged, with nothing to show other than shark food. After we cleaned all of our brass away and before shooting a couple of 9mm rounds through the glass of our lounge area then hiding our guns, we headed back to Mogadishu.

Once in Mogadishu port we reported our near miss to Somali Pirates and how we just escaped with our lives, thanks to the fast thinking of or skipper. Before outrunning them as they were shooting at us. We went to as many bars as we could and recounted our hair raising tale, adding to it, that we were now worried, about our trip of a lifetime from Port Saíd across to the Sechelles and beyond. We went back to our boat and slept.

In the morning as we were having the 'Pirates' bullet holes to our yacht repaired, a tall American asked permission to come aboard. Apparently he represented his boss, according to his business card he was the Vice CEO for Black-Tree Enterprises. We invited him aboard and then listened to him tell us, how this area of the world, was rife with pirates and that anyone who was smart, employed one of the many security firms, that operated out of these coastal ports. He said that while they were not cheap, that they were the best. Their men were all hand picked from Delta and Seal forces. They only employed Americans.

Sir Philip was deliberate in his absence, from the meeting. Just in case his face was known. Without doubt it would be known to this man's boss. We asked the terms of a contract with them and were then told, that any contract would only be completed by The Colonel, who was the CEO of their company. They guaranteed that we would have safe passage, wherever we sailed, if we were signed to them and that we would probably need between two and four, of their operatives on board. This would be at a cost of between fifty thousand and one hundred thousand dollars a day, per man, all depending on the level of service we required. He said that once we had got to where we were going, their operatives would make their own way back. After letting him know, that money was not a problem for us, as we were investment bankers. We agreed that we would meet with their boss, the next morning. The trap was baited and set.

ACT 31

With the Suit and Cyber out of sight, we sat on the rear day-deck of our luxurious big boat, or little ship and we waited. We had made a box frame to go over our 50cal machine gun, and then covered that with a tarpaulin. As we were enjoying our coffee, a gloss black Humvee pulled into the dock area and the driver got out. He then opened the rear door, to allow a smartly dressed gentleman to exit. This gentleman wore a crisp white linen suit and cream loafers. His face was deeply tanned and the was colour of burnished mahogany. On his head he wore Panama hat and a pair of Rayban Aviator mirrored sunglasses. In his left hand he carried a polished aluminium briefcase. He spoke to his driver and then made his way to our boat.

"Permission to come aboard." He asked while looking to see if he could see her name. Then continued.

"I am with Black-Tree Enterprises, I believe you are expecting me?"

I could not really place his accent, just that he sounded like a well spoken American, who was trying hard to be British. I decided that I too, could be something other than what I was. And with my best Belfast accent as we were sailing under the Republic of Ireland's Tricolour.

"Aye catch yerself on boy and be comin' aboard." I shouted back down at him.

He strode up the gangplank with confidence and the air of a man who knew, what was what.

"My friends just call me The Colonel"

"No problem then boy. Have yerself a seat then" I said. Indicating to the empty seat at our table. He removed his hat to reveal a head of crew cut silver hair, and then sat down placing his briefcase next to his leg. Unbeknown to him Oran was already scanning for any Mobile phones or other devices.

"Now my associate tells me you, went out on a trip yesterday but had to turn back. I am led to believe this was because, some people tried to attack you. I must say you are remarkably lucky. Most foreigners who get attacked by these pirates, simply disappear and are never heard of again. Their boat and possessions, stolen and sold off."

"Yes General, we were told this, in the bars last night. But we have a very fast boat and were able to outrun the buggers" I replied

Lachie and Abdalla continued to play backgammon and listened in on the conversation. I continued the conversation.

"Your man tells us that it is up to one hundred thousand a day per man?"

"That is correct."

"That is a lot of money. So what is it exactly that we get for our money?"

He lifted his briefcase from the floor and opened it. There was a mobile phone, as well as a satellite phone. Alongside them was a wallet and an old fashioned large diary under which were a bunch of papers with the Black Tree logo on.

"What we are really providing Mr?.........."

"O'Donnell"

"As I said Mr O'Donnell. What we are really providing you with is complete peace of mind. We are well known around these waters and the Pirates avoid us, like the plague. So we put men aboard your boat and you fly one of our flags from your stern. As soon as the pirates see that, they take off. Those who do not know about us, soon do. I would recommend that you have four of my men so they can work shifts, giving you complete peace of mind."

"Sure now, its easy to say that the blaggards out there, would be after giving your flag a wide berth. It would be another thing, to prove such a statement my boy." I was attempting to bait him into showing us.

"Why Mr O'Donnell, I could show you right now but I don't do any freebies,"

"You know money is not a problem to us boys, do you accept Sterling?" I said sweeping my hand about the rear deck of our flash yacht.

"I do Mr O'Donnell, but it would be for two men not just myself. I could have my driver come onboard and we could sail out and have a nice and SAFE day out on the ocean fishing. We would be able to show you just what we can do for you. My driver is ex-Navy Seal and an expert shot. He is well known in Mogadishu and feared by the Somalians."

Lachie just had to do it and I knew he could not help himself it was just his way, instead of faking an accent like myself he had stuck with his own west coast of Scotland accent interspersed with a touch of Glaswegian.

"Why?" Lachie enquired

"Excuse me?" The Colonel asked

"Yes nae problem"

"What?"

"Yea're excused"

"I am? For?"

"I dinne ken, but yea asked for it. anyway why is yer man known?"

"I don't follow, I am sorry, it is your accent making things difficult for me could you slow it down a little please" The Colonel looked perplexed.

We needed a little fun so I let it run for now.

"OK How is yer man known."

"Well he is an expert shot and well respected."

"Aye so why is he fear'd by the Somalis"

"Oh I see you want know why he is so well known and so feared?"

"Aye man, am I no after tellin' you so?"

"He has shot more Somali pirates than any other person. So much so, that when we fly our flag on a boat. Only the new and inexperienced pirates, who are stupid, try something. You will see later today."

I put an end to Lachie's games, before he started to interrogate the Colonel any further.

"Very well Colonel, what are you waiting for bring your driver on board"

"There is one thing Mr O'Donnell, you will have to sign one of our forms, that allows us to come on board your vessel, as paid security consultants. This allows us to bring firearms on to your fine yacht." He said as he put a Black-Tree form on the table with his gold Cartier pen. I signed and Abdalla dug out one hundred thousand pounds and gave it to the General. If we had expected some change then we were sadly mistaken as there was none forthcoming. The driver who was a bigger and slightly more ugly version, of his boss. Went around the rear of the Humvee and brought two heavy flight cases up to the rear deck and then returned to his vehicle and then returned with two large steel ammunition boxes, one in each hand which he placed on the deck next to the large flight cases. After returning to his shiny black Humvee, he parked it and locked it up before returning to the boat. Then we hoisted the Black Tree Flag under the Irish flag, we cast off, and headed out into the sea once more.

Lachie and Abdalla were on deck with the two Black-Tree guys. I went down to see Sir Philip and Oran.

"As soon as you can Oran can you block their phones and any other devices that can give our location."

"All ready done it Andy."

"Sir Philip, when do you want to take them down?"

"Just as soon as we are out of sight of the mainland. Lets make it a party lots of cold beer and Whisky."

"OK Boss, best get tooled up then and that goes for young Oran too."

I went back up on deck and opened the cooler which was filled with Budweiser and Coors Lite beers. Actually the cooler was half full of ice with lots of beer stuck into it.

"Now we're out of port, anyone for a cold beer?" I asked as I passed one to Lachie and Abdalla, then I offered one to The Colonel and his Driver. The Colonel refused but the driver accepted.

"I don't suppose you have just plain Tonic Water on board do you?" The General asked

"I think I have some in the galley, hang on I will be right back"

I quickly went down to the galley.

"Oran go to my cabin and grab my medical bag can you please, as fast as you can."

I looked in the fridge and found a bottle of Tonic. Oran returned and I grabbed an ampoule of morphine from it snapped the top of and then after opening the tonic water I poured the morphine into it. Then I got a tall glass and half filled it with Ice and carried that and the tonic up to the deck. I unscrewed the cap of the tonic and poured it over the ice in the glass, after which I cut a lemon in half and made a big show of squeezing it into the glass. Then gave it to the general. I Knew that Lachie and Abdalla, would be poring their beers over the side of the boat any time they could not be seen. The morning went on and eight beers later a slur was appearing on the edge of the drivers words. Several Tonics later and The General seemed to be losing concentration and becoming a little sleepy. Time to act. First we made sure we were all armed and able to cover the two men. Then Oran and his beast waited inside with Sir Philip.

With their physical and mental reactions slowed it actually took them a while to digest what was going on in front of them. The driver actually attempted to reach for a weapon, he was far too slow and Abdalla just pushed him over the side of the boat and into the sea.

"Allah will take care of him. If he has a good soul, then Allah will give him the strength to swim back to land. If not, then Allah will see him in the afterlife, before sending him to hell." Abdalla said.

"What the fuck? Why in hell did you do that. Turn this God damn boat around, and pick him up." The Colonel shouted

While The Colonel was looking over the side of the boat Abdalla stepped behind him and held his arms while Lachie Zip tied them. Then Abdalla threw him on the floor. The Colonel suddenly realised that there were several firearms pointed in his direction.

"Who in the name of fuck are you? and what do you want?" He shouted from the floor.

Lachie sat on his legs while Abdalla tied them. Then one by one we dragged the others from their makeshift prison cells and threw them down on the deck equally bound. The flag, that the Colonel had put up on our stern, as we left port, now flapped in the hot wind, that came off the deserts and over the sea. Sir Philip waited along with Cyber until the bound men were sat in a row with their backs against the side boards of the boat. Then he appeared on the rear deck with Oran and Cyber.

"Oran do you have a course set?" I asked

"Aye aye skipper"

"Good then lets get everyone on deck and see what is what"

The first to complain about things was of course, the Brigadier General.

"You boys, don't know what you are doing, or just who you are fucking with!"

"Is that so Brigadier? What do you suppose your own men would do to you? when they find out that you murdered their comrades? The punishment for treason is hanging! Andy what is the punishment for treason at sea? I seem to remember you invoking some old maritime code, for someone who murdered your fathers dog. The Rhodian Law?"

"Yes Sir Philip, they were the ones who invented keelhauling and later they actually were the first to turn it into waterboarding."

"I heard that sailors actually died of fright, at this punishment. Can you explain it some more to me, I seem to have forgotten so much these last few months."

"I would be happy to sir. As you may or may not know, Greece, was, even before the time of Christ, one of the worlds greatest trading nations. They had their own Laws and Greek laws are the basis of all our laws in the west now. On a ship the captain was omnipotent and all powerful. What he said was law. He dictated the punishment. Keelhauling involved the transgressor having his legs tied and a rope tied around their wrists, before being dropped under the front of the boat. The rope then being let out slowly, in order to keep the body close to the bottom of the boat, or keel. Their bare skin would be ripped by the barnacles. Later they would tie a canvas bag over the head of the unfortunate person making them feel like they were drowning. This was later refined into true waterboarding. That would be the short version Sir Philip. I do hope that's OK?

"Yes Andy that is perfect. So Brigadier what do you think about that. I experienced being water boarded for real recently and its true. You really think you are going to die. I know you SAS types practice this, and you even endure it for thirty seconds. Well today, you will experience it for real. I will ask you once once Who made the plan to attack my home?"

"I don't know what you are talking about."

That was the last proper sentence that the Brigadier General would ever speak in his life. Sir Philip went over and placed a canvas bag over the head of the Brigadier and tied it on with its cord, Then he lifted the Brigadier up on to the bench seat at the side of the boat and then tilted him so he fell overboard and into the water with his feet and hands tied and a canvas bag over his head. He was to experience, the same fear and horror, that Sir Philip had endured several times over and over. Before being revived to repeat it again and again, Horror after horror. That was the one blessing the Brigadier General had, he would only die the once.

"Mr Robert Halliwell. How many times have you been to my home and sat at the table and broke bread, with my family. Yet you were involved in this, for what? Something as little as money. Your base income is twice mine, yet you still want more, to feed your gambling addiction. I understand the Brigadier General, casting men and women into the field of battle. Where he knows they will die to protect one secret or another. You however did this for a much more selfish reason. For you it was all about financial gain. Whilst I was in the hands of your friend over there. The man known as The Colonel. He and his cohorts tried so many ways to hurt me, in the most unspeakable ways. You already know, I was water-boarded until I died and was then brought back to life, with electric shocks. My feet were beaten, until the broken bones showed through. All of my fingers and toes were methodically broken. I was burned with cigars. Even my testicles they burned using a lighter. They pushed things up my anus. They would put me in a small metal box, for days at a time in the baking heat of the Cuban sunshine. I was forced to eat maggots and sit in my own shit for weeks. Which punishment should you receive? Abdalla what does the Quran say about revenge for crimes against the innocent?"

"Sir Philip The Holy Quran, is much the same as your Holy Bible in this respect. Your bible talks about an eye for an eye and tooth for a tooth. The Quran teaches us that if we harm an innocent, then the same punishment, be metered out upon the transgressor." Abdalla replied

I knew what was happening was technically murder and it was revenge killing. There would be no records of this and the only people that would know of the incidents, taking place on the boat today, would be the members of Team Seven. Because there would be no other survivors. Personally I would have preferred, that we shot these men than let Sir Philip extract his biblical revenge, on these people. Then again, how would I be if it happened to me? Would I have been sane, after months of intense pain and torture. The light was going down and I switched on the floodlight that covered the deck space. No I would not be the one to stop him. I would watch, not because I wanted to, but because I had to know the pain, my team mate had endured. without giving any of us up to his captors. I doubted if I could have held out.

"Mr McPhee, did you do Shakespeare at school?"

"Yes Sir Philip, it was required reading in most Scottish High Schools"

"Mr Oran, can Cyber swim?"

"Yes Sir Philip he swims better than most dogs."

"Mr Henderson can you undo the bindings of Mr Halliwell please. And then lead him down to the swim platform."

"OK" Lachie replied.

"Oran can you command your dog to attack without faltering?"

"Yes sir Philip, what have you in mind?"

Sir Philip whispered something into Oran's ear, that I could not hear. Oran went white but nodded his head.

"Mr Henderson can you leave Mr Halliwell where he is and come to the back with the rest of us. Now Mr Halliwell, you have been judged by both the Holy Bible and the Holy Quran and have been found guilty of crimes against the innocent, for nothing more than greed. It is said that the hell exists and I suppose for those that believe in heaven then hell must be a given. Have you heard the term 'Let Loose the Dogs of Hell'"

Halliwell just mumbled he was sorry and please don't hurt me. I can make you all rich."

That was Halliwell's last statement addressed to the world, well to a small section of it, that was standing and seated on the lounge deck of a super yacht with no name.

"Now" Sir Philip said quietly to Oran

I could see that Oran was not comfortable and I nodded to him as did Abdalla and Lachie

"Kill him Cyber Kill him!!!! Oran screamed and pointed his skinny arm at Halliwell. Cyber was big even for his breed, of Caucasian Shepard Dog. Often refereed to as an Ovtcharka. It is probably one of the biggest and most powerful and fierce-some dogs in the world. Cyber weighed in at 220 pounds and not an ounce of fat. He loved nothing more than running up and down the stairs of our home on the Rig. The speed at which this breed can move is deceptive. Cyber struck Halliwell full on the chest and forced him back over the swim board and into the water beyond. The last thing I saw was Cyber's massive jaws wrapped around the Halliwell's throat and blood was staining, his white dress shirt. Then both Halliwell and Cyber were in the water. A few minutes later Cyber returned to the swim board and we helped him back on board. After allowing him to shake of most of the water from his coat, he went back to Oran's side and sat down. The other two prisoners who had remained quiet up until now, were starting to offer deals in exchange for letting them go. I knew even if they had been offering billions to each of us, they were not going to survive the day. Even though I knew this was the last mission for all of us. 'The Suit' would never work in espionage again. He would never pass the psyche evaluation, let alone the physical or the medical. So our team would be dissolved and we could live semi normal lives once again. I knew also that the days work, was not yet done and here I was, planning for tomorrow. Perhaps it was my way of coping or hiding things, just like the suit did

I was compartmentalising, locking the horrors away, in boxes and putting them way deep down, in my subconscious. Hopefully never to return, to the front of my mind. What would be the form of death, for the CIA Chief. Mr Levitz the chief of spies. This man made his living telling lies and then covering them up. Those lies always ended up with someone dying. Today would be no different, except it would be him.

"Mr Levitz because you and I, are for the want of a better description, spies. I will offer you the professional courtesy. In ancient times, when a soldier had failed, he would commit Hari Kari. This practice was carried out by the Japanese warrior class of Samurai. These men were honourable, literally to the end and would, as recent as WWII, they would disembowel themselves. When they felt that they had let down their Emperor. Or even the act of 'Falling on ones sword' which dates back to ancient Roman times, it is mentioned in the Plutarch records, in the Life of Brutus. Shakespeare also refers to it in Mark Anthony. Since the advent of firearms, Officers who have brought failure and shame upon their families, would feel the need to commit suicide. 'Death before Dishonour' is the motto of 41st Battalion, Royal New South Wales Regiment, of the Australian Army. It's also the motto of 90 Armoured Regiment, of the Indian Army. But was used by many of the aristocrats as an unwritten law. Again as recent as WWII, officers would shoot themselves with their own pistol if they felt, that they had failed their family name, or regiment. So Mr Levitz, you failed the CIA, you failed your family and you failed your Country. The motto of the CIA is 'Work of a Nation, Centre of Intelligence'. The unofficial motto is 'And You Shall Know The Truth, And the Truth Shall Set You Free'. You knew the truth about me. We have known each other for almost 30 years. I have saved your butt on more than one occasion. I could have thrown you under a bus, for your previous debacle, when you were involved with one of the branches of the CIA, which were funding the Neo Nazi Party of Serbia. Yet I kept your name, out of my report to NATO. How did you repay my kindness to you? You deliberately set me up for a crime I did not commit. You did this to me for what? Money? Power? Status? You are a disgrace to us all. But still, I will give you a final chance at honour" The suit said.

He ejected the magazine from his Browning, ensuring he cleared the chamber. Next he removed all the bullets from the clip, then lacing the bullets in his pocket. Then apparently as an afterthought, he took one of the bullets back out of his pocket and put it back into the magazine. then he reinserted it into the automatic.

"Mr Levitz can you stand up." Sir Philip said

Levitz stood and Sir Philip led him to the rear of the boat.

"Do the right thing and pay your dues" Sir Philip said. Then he handed the 9mm to Levitz. As Sir Philip walked away to Join us, Levitz lifted his pistol and put it to he right temple.

"Philip" Levitz shouted

Sir Philip turned around to face Levitz. The look on Levitz's face changed from resignation of his fate, to a defiant and rebellious anger. Levitz took the gun from his temple and turned it to point directly at Sir Philip.

"Honour is for you fucking stupid Brits. The USA could give a shit about all that 'Death Before Dishonour' shit. My personal motto is, 'Never Give An Inch And Always Survive'. So it kind of looks like the tables are turned. I have to admit I did not want it to end this way. Stevens was much slicker than you realised. Before he made the move on your wife, he managed to dig up some dirt on me. So when he made his move I was already in too deep to get out. Now tell your men to lay down their weapons, that I know they have behind their backs. NOW!" Levitz shouted

Sir Philip made a movement with his hands, indicating that we should lower our guns. I looked at Lachie and Abdalla and nodded. We laid our guns down on the deck. But well out of reach of either The Colonel or Levitz. I knew that Radwan had sneaked on board our boat that morning but so far had not shown himself.

"So what now Levitz? You shoot me, with that one bullet and my men kill you." Sir Philip said

"If you want to live and see your precious wife and son, you will do exactly as I say. Now turn around and put your hands in the air." Levitz commanded. Then he walked forward and put his free arm around 'The Suits' neck. I looked again at the suit and he made a movement with his palms downward. Once again the sign for us to do nothing at the moment. Then I saw why.

"Levitz I gave you a chance to take the honourable way out and you decided to take a cowardly route, once again showing yourself to be the most untrustworthy person that you are."

"Tell your men to throw their guns over the side of the boat."

Again I looked at Sir Philip. I now, knew his plan.

"OK Lads Do as he says" I said

"Be sure you pick them up by the barrels and then throw them into the sea. I might even let you all live." He commanded.

I doubt that he would have let any of us, apart from The Colonel live. But we did what he said.

"Well done man, now cut me free." The Colonel said

"You fucking incompetent moron. You had your chance to end this. When I gave you Sir Philip Reeves-Johnson. And you fucked that up. So do me a favour and shut the fuck up" Levitz said and smashed the butt of the Browning into the side of the Colonel's head.

I was not even sure if The Colonel was alive or dead at this point as I watched the blood drip from his head and pool onto the seating where he now lay motionless.

"You" he said pointing at Oran. And then continued

"Tie Those men up and if your dog moves I will shoot you first"

I nodded

"Its OK Oran do what he says" I said

As soon as we were tied up he made 'The Suit' tie up Oran after he had put his dog inside one of the cabins. Now we were all on deck with our backs to the wheelhouse and Levitz lording it over us.

We could see what Levitz could not. It was probably good for us that the Colonel was still unconscious or he would have given the game away.

"Its time to say goodbye Philip. If it is any consolation to you, I am sorry that it came to this."

"Levitz, I give you one more chance, to walk away from this with your life." Sir Philip replied to Levitz.

"And just how would you propose I do that?"

"You could put down the gun and release my men and me and then you get to live. But you could not continue in your post, you would have to pay for your crimes."

"Spend the rest of my life in some supermax? No Philip I don't think so."

"No Levitz, nothing quite so grand as a cushy super max in the USA. I was thinking more about spending the rest of your life in Guantanamo Bay as an international terrorist" Sir Philip replied.

"And on who's word would I be sent there? Yours? No. You see now all your men are tied up and I am the only one holding the gun.

I think I shall first kill you and then I shall do them, one by one. I am afraid that will also have to include, the incompetent Colonel. All he had to do, was to keep you locked up in Guantanamo, until he had managed to get all the secrets that you held and then he was supposed to have executed you. What did this incompetent do? He gave the job to another, of his equally inept staff. And then after you escaped and made them look like the fools that they are. He then accepts an invite from the members of the very team, that broke you out of Guantanamo. He could not even recognise, the infamous Team Seven. You see I have known all about Team Seven, from SIS, since the day you first came to international attention. Oh yes I know that you were all responsible, for the deaths of your former Secretary of Defence and the American Billionaire, Mr Douglas Crump in that 'Accident' on Gruinard Island. I also know that, you were the team responsible for the deaths of so many, of my own teams and the son of Douglas Crump. You managed to take the Korean Geneticist, that I had extracted from North Korea. Then you went and snatched his family from Gulag 22. I paid for them to be killed at Lossimouth. But what happened to the two little orphans? Yes I know about them as well Mr McPhee. What I don't know yet, but I am sure I will in the near future is 'Where' your base is and where you have been hiding them. You cost me a lot over the last few years. Even you Philip, you did not know what part I played in those missions. I used you, when you shared information with us, I used it against you. You Oran, my God! you have been a thorn in my side for years. I am surprised though, that you failed to figure out my part until it was too late. And the honourable Mr Abdalla Mohamed. The man who lives his life by a set of archaic rules. 'Never harm an innocent' Have you any idea just how stupid that idea is? The only way a person prospers in this modern world, is off the backs and pain of others. Power is not having money, power is not even being a president or anything close to that. Power is and always was about owning secrets. Not just the secrets owned by countries, like the world powers. It is about owning personal secrets. Those secrets I keep in my memory, so that no one else can benefit, except for me. How about this one. I know your friends own a fishing boat the Catherine May. I am sure if I have that followed, I will learn where your home is. And then I shall do to you, what you would have done to me. I shall destroy everything, that ever meant anything to any of you." He said

"I am pleading with you Levitz end this madness now."

"Really Sir Philip? All your men are tied up and I am the only one holding the gun. Tell me why I should not just shoot you now and be done with your perpetual British whining about fair play?"

"Because it really is your last chance to live" Sir Philip said

Levitz walked forward a few feet and pointed the gun to Sir Philips head and thumb went to the safety catch and clicked it to live. Then his forefinger put pressure on the trigger. I thought that Sir Philip, may have overplayed his hand, even taking Radwan into the equation. At the same moment the hammer clicked and nothing happened. Radwan was just one step behind Levitz. Levitz looked down at the gun in confusion.

"Dud round? Miss-fire. That's a dangerous thing, when you only have one round in a gun and the enemy has you covered." Sir Philip said

Just then Radwan slipped the steel wire noose over the head of Levitz and pulled it tight, He did it fast enough, so that Levitz could not get his fingers under the wire, not that would have helped his predicament. All that would have happened is that as well as him dying he would have lost some fingers to the razor sharp wire. This was not a garotte intended to choke. This was a garrotte intended to decapitate. Radwan pulled sharply on the wire and it cut deep into the flesh, blood gushed from his throat and carotid artery. Levitz eyes bulged as he struggled. The Browning clattered to the deck. As Levitz hands raced to protect his throat that was already so deeply severed that no amount of surgery would have been able to save him at this point. The wire bit through the skin, the cartilage and the muscle until it reached the back of the neck and with the spine now totally encapsulated by this sharp wire garrotte. The head was lolling uselessly to one side and the blood was rapidly draining from the brain. The flow of blood to it had also been interrupted and was pouring in jets onto the deck in front of us. Then with a sudden snap of his powerful arms, the garrotte became a single straight line again, dripping with blood. The head of Levitz hit the deck about the same time as his knees thudded into the highly polish wooden planking, that made up the deck on this boat. Then the body fell forward. With the now dead head facing back at it, with unseeing open eyes. Radwan stepped forward and took a knife from the leg of his dive suit and cut our bindings with the exception of the Colonel who was still unconscious since Levitz had struck him with the Browning.

"Thanks, why did you wait so long?" I asked

"Sir Philip told me to wait until Levitz tried to shoot him. He told me he would set him free and give him a chance. But that if he tried to shoot anyone, I was to wait until the gun was fired, and then act. Now I see he had it all planned out well in advance"

"Like Chess?" I said to 'The Suit'

"Very good Mr McPhee, you remembered one of my first lessons to you, always plan six moves ahead"

After we were all free and the body along with its now decapitated head, had been thrown over for fish food. Then the decking washed down with one of the fire hoses, until there was no trace of the man formally known as Mr Levitz the ex-head of the CIA. A man that served only himself. I went over to where the Colonel lay on the side bench seat and checked his pulse. It was good and strong, when he woke he would have a severe headache but I could see that would be the least of his problems. I knew that Sir Philip had been deeply affected, by what had happened to him in Guantanamo Bay. I also knew that in the interests of our safety, plus that of our families and friends The Colonel, could not be allowed to live. Especially after the things that Levitz had said. How his death would come about I could not imagine. I would stand by 'The Suit' whatever he did and I promised myself that I would not interfere. It looked like the executions, as that is what they were. Each, had been selected to fit the crimes that had been committed by the person against Sir Philip. The suit took the fire hose from me and turned it on The Colonel. This washed away the pool of blood but reopened the wound on his temple. The Colonel shook himself awake and sat up.

"No one, knows where you are Colonel. You ordered your men to hurt me, just for the fun of it. You know they beat me, even when I was unconscious. They burned me, they beat me, they invaded my body. Now you are going to feel the pain, as I ask you my own questions. You know I will have to ask you a set of test questions that

I already know the answers to. So I will hurt you first, then ask my questions. This is the way you like to do things yourself. I am going to ask my men NOT to interfere." 'The Suit' said and looked directly at each of us. We all nodded even though I personally did not want to. I really wanted it all to end right now, with a bullet.

Almost nine years ago, I had been a Medic in the Royal Air Force. I had been a lifer, having already served around the world. I was a Sargent. Then there had been that bloody incident, on the Breckon Beacons in the mountains of Wales. When I got there Lachie was already there having been on attachment to the SAS. Lachie had been a Corporal in the Royal Air Force Regiment. We had been placed at the scene by 'The Suit', because he needed two people in place. in the Highlands of Scotland. He had lost his previous team, that had been undercover there. Lachie and I just happened to have come from the exact theatre of operations. We were promoted and then posted to CDE Porton down to learn about Biological weapons. Then we were trained up as operatives for SIS. We were dismissed from the RAF, just so that we could move back to our homes. Unfortunately a member of MOSAD, who was supposed to be on our side and a member of Team Seven, was in fact, a double agent and working for the other side. We had been attacked and our homes destroyed. We had to go on the run, not just from the enemy, but because apart from Sir Philip, no one knew that we were the good guys. Consequently, every security force in the world including our own SIS, MI5, MI6 and some that don't even have names came after us. A kill order had been placed on not just Lachie and me, but anyone who had anything to do with us. We had escaped and saved the world, as in literally saved the world, from a biological weapon that had been stolen from CDE Porton Down. We got our lives back and our homes rebuilt and had only just got back on track, when our homes were attacked by the demented son of Douglas Crump, a man who I had personally killed at the end of the previous operation. This time my father was kidnapped and we learned of another biological threat the likes of which would have been the real doomsday scenario. We had effectively invaded a sovereign nation, by rescuing the Chang family from a prison in North Korea. The weapon as it turned out was not yet completely made, but was being made by Neo Nazi's. We had destroyed the basis of the weapon, we had destroyed all the data that was on computers. I had murdered the man behind the weapon. We had even destroyed the old whaling station on a remote Faeroe Island. My significant other Jane Miller and her father had both died on that mission. A lot of other people had died and once again, we, well most of us, managed to escape with our lives. We had chosen not to go back to our homes, but to buy and then renovate a disused oil platform in the North Sea. Living off grid was great and we even made a home for the twin orphans of the North Korean family, who had died because of our actions. I had met my wife and we were happy as were the others who lived on the rig. We had been safe even those extended members of Team Seven. Then we were dragged back out of our safe and wonderful lives, by men who were nothing other than power hungry and greedy. They had attacked Sir Philip all because his second in command was jealous and wanted Sir Philips wife and family. He wanted the power Sir Philip had. He then used that power, to help other people, who's greed was not emotional but was financial. The Brigadier General and his friend Mr Halliwell in the government financial bodies. Thought up a scheme to make money from the Kenyans. They then enlisted the help of the SAS and the CIA offering him power. Now we had killed dozens. I personally had killed with bullet, knife and even my bare hands. I had not done any of this for greed of for any kind of kudos. I had done this to protect my family, as well as other innocents, in the wider world. I had done this to ensure the safe return, of not just my boss, but my team mate and my friend. He would have done the same for any one of us. I knew that, I had not experienced the horrors of Gitmo, that he had been subject to. I had not had my wife and children stolen from me, as he had. Yet even with all this pain and emotional leverage, Sir Philip had not given us up. Sure the head of the CIA knew about the Catherine May, which none of us had tried to hide and was a matter of public record, that it belonged to the Late Sandy McCormack. This had then been passed to his down Stu. It was obvious from what Levitz had said that he still did not know the location of our home. Yet he surely would have done at some point in his future, if he had been allowed to have one. So it had all come down to this one last man. This man who had been responsible for the physical and mental torture of Sir Philip. By members of his organisation, in complete and utter breach of any morality. No I would not interfere. I would never be the same man I had been nine years previous. I would never have a psychologist share my secrets. Sir Philip broke my thoughts.

"Untie him" He said to no one in particular Abdalla sat the man up, none to gently then sliced through the cable ties that bound his hands and feet. The Colonel rubbed his ankles and then his wrists but said nothing. In fact since it had become known that we knew about him, he had become remarkably quiet. Previous to that he had been so full of himself and his abilities to protect us. He was so full of shit, now he could not even protect himself.

"Colonel or should I say Captain?" The suit paused to see if there was any reaction, but there was none not even a blink to show that he knew he had been found out.

"You were a Captain on the Delta Force. But there was an operation that went very wrong. It was based on flawed intelligence. You were supposed to capture a member of the Taliban and bring him back for interrogation, by a team not unlike the organisation, that you yourself head up. After assuring everyone, that you had the right man, you snatched him and he was transferred to the Delta section of Gitmo. You went about your life of being a soldier and even gained some notoriety. There was a problem though. The man you gave to the civilian contractors as the number three in the Taliban at the time. Was in fact an under cover member of Amnesty International. He was there documenting atrocities being committed by the military, on the local indigenous population. Of course when he was interrogated by the contractors they expected him to deny being the terrorist that you thought he was. It was only after he had been tortured for six weeks and by pure chance the International Red Cross and Amnesty International and they happened to recognise him in one of the cages at the edge of the delta site. He could not be identified by dental records because all of his teeth had been pulled out. His fingerprints had also been burned off to prevent external identification. However there was still DNA and it proved him to be a civilian with Amnesty International. It was all hushed up. The Americans paid a seven figure settlement which was agreed with both A.I. and their man. You were asked to leave the Military rather than being Court Marshalled. A Court Marshall would have shown the world, the crimes that were being committed by you and the CIA and all the others there at Gitmo. You were not sent to prison because you had already cultured friends within the CIA and their dirty tricks departments. It was they who set you up in business. That business was to do the things that the USA can deny doing. You and your men protected American interests around the world. That in itself was not a bad thing. It was the methods you used which included, murdering an entire village in Peru and Syria, you did the same on the edge of the Amazon. In fact anywhere there was an American business that was having problems with the local populous. You not only made the problems go away you made the people disappear. You employed the worst of the worst and you knew that they would not stay within the parameters of any civilized society. Just how many innocent civilians have you killed, no that is the wrong word. How many have you murdered or have been responsible for their murders. 100, 500, 1,000 more? In short, you are a man not unlike Hitler, or Idi Amin. For you, it is about the power that you can wield over another human life. None of my men have ever knowingly killed or caused harm to come to any innocent. Yes we are all soldiers and part of being a soldier is knowing, that at some point you are going to have to point a gun at your enemy and perhaps kill them."

The Magazine that had previously held the dud bullet, 'The Suit' swapped out for a full and completely working one was in the gun, held in his other hand. Then he continued

"So I do not see, that you hold any real rank and most certainly you are not the Colonel, that you promoted yourself to. Nor are you the Captain, that was rescinded, when you were asked to leave Delta Force. You are a civilian. That means you are not employed by the American military or its security forces. You hold no rank and you are no officer, or even a gentleman. The actions you took against all the other innocents, were in fact Mass Murder, of the worst sort. The action that you and you men, took against me, was unwarranted and done primarily for their own entertainment. Like you, they took joy in inflicting pain, on others. Though unlike most of the others the only thing that you were able to get from me, was the fact that I was not Zorro, because Zorro never existed. He was invented by John Stevens." 'The Suit' said

Before he then ripped open his shirt, to show off the scars, that whilst were fainter than they had been almost a year after his rescue, they were still clearly visible. He turned around to show the long lateral and vertical scars on his back. I knew there was a lot of scarring to the rear of his thighs, where skin grafts had been taken from, to cover the soles of his feet, which had been completely devoid of any skin, when we had rescued Sir Philip. I knew there were internal scars, both physical and emotional. I knew all the sins that had been conducted on his body. I had seen him cry like a baby, when we carried him away from Cuba. It was not because we had rescued him. It was because he knew. he could never again be the man to his wife, that he had been before. Not because of the jealous John Stevens, but because of the damage that had been inflicted to his genitals. I had seen him when he had considered suicide. Thanks though, to the love and strength of his wife and son, along with that of his true friends in Team Seven. He had returned from that precipice. Now we were at that cliff edge again, and I could not honestly say which way he would swing. I know what I would do in his situation. Oran had switched the all deck lights on as the sun hit the horizon in the distance.

"Men like you are the school ground bully. You fear nothing, except that your little gang, might leave you high and dry. I hate you for what you did to me. I hate all the things that you are. I know if I kill you, then someone in your organisation, will take your post at the top of the totem pole, in which you live. The USA would just change contractors and nothing will ever change. I hate most of all, what you made my friends see, when they rescued me.............." Sir Philip was stopped in mid sentence a volley of shots rang out from the port side of the boat.

"You English and American we want your boat." A voice said in broken English.

"Oran start the engine and full power" I said

"Do not attempt to run, we have many, many guns pointed at your boat. We just want the money and good things you have and then we will leave you alone. We will not shoot if you behave good" The Somali voice said in broken English."

"How Many Oran?" Sir Philip asked.

"Looks like 5, two on either side and one a little behind us, the only big one is the one behind the rest are small craft"

ACT 32

"OK Andy tie that piece of shit back up. Oran, pull us away from them and then turn us around and take us straight at them. As soon as we are free Abdalla can you set up that heavy Machine Gun. There were bursts of automatic fire that strafed the rear of our boat as we pulled away from the Pirates. I knew they would expect us to run and I knew also, they would not expect us to turn and attack. So much for the protection of flying the Black-Tree flag, I had guessed it was bullshit. The prow of our boat rose out of the water as we pulled rapidly away from their small but relatively fast skiffs. Soon their AK47's were nothing more than firecrackers in the night air. I retied the Colonels hands and feet. while Oran brought the boat around.

Abdalla pulled the cover of the big machine gun and ratcheted the machine guns mechanism. The two flight cases that had been brought aboard by The Colonel's driver contained smaller versions of the gun that Abdalla was ready to fire. They were, two GE styled Multi Barrel Mini Gatling Guns, that we took from their flight cases. They were lightweight and belt fed. I had seen pictures of these but never fired one. I fed the belt in and stood ready on the port side, Lachie was likewise armed on the starboard side. I hoped the this would be the last ever, fire fight that we would be in. Oran pushed the boat to her limit and then guided us into the area ahead where the four boats had been, giving chase from. When we were 100 yards out he switched on our forward facing floodlights and lit up the four skiffs which had three men in each. Two that had AK47's and one man steering their fragile craft. The AK47 is not a particularly accurate weapon unless it is in skilled hands. In the hands of a Somali Pirate and bouncing of the waves it is more of a distraction. With the guns that we were now firing at them, we did not have to be as accurate as we would normally wish to be. The sheer volume of lead that was coming at them, was not only terrifying for them, but it was as destructive as a tornado. Their small wooden boats were shredded into small pieces of of wood and splinters interspaced with a red mist of what had previously been a human, but would no longer be recognisable. Even I, who had seen men shot. I was not quite prepared for the power of this mini cannon in my hands. I knew the same was happening to the other side of our boat. We raced through the middle of them and the cannons spun down, with a whistling sound.

Now we headed to the mother boat. If true to form, for these new age pirates. Then there would just be one or perhaps two men on board. If they had any warning of what had just happened, then they would have turned and headed for home. Two miles from us the blip remained on a steady course to our position. Oran had now turned all the lights off and we were speeding down upon them. We would destroy their craft and finish our business. It was then and only then, I looked to where 'The Colonel' had been sat He was clearly dead. He must have been hit by one of the stray bullets. No big loss there.

"Get ready and light them up as soon as we are in range." I shouted above the noise of our engines that were probably being pushed up to and beyond their limits. Sir Philip, now with a loaded Browning in his hand was standing ready on the prow of our fast yacht. The lights came on and three cannons roared, Lachie was standing beside me as he had always been in my life. Abdalla was above us on the top deck Next to him was Radwan with an old WWII Sterling Sub Machine Gun gripped in his hand and held at the waist, ready for the impending battle. And the man who trained us and led us into many a battle was standing at the front of this boat, once again leading us into what would hopefully be our final battle. The only man missing from Team Seven was Hans. Even Oran was up on deck with my pair of Sig Sauer's He was standing beside Lachie and me. Cyber was safe down below decks. But times had changed. We though, had not changed in our loyalty to one and other. In my head, I had heard that classic line from a Shakespeare play and King Henry V says.

"Once more unto the breach, dear friends, once more
Or close the wall up with our English dead
In peace there's nothing so becomes a man
As modest stillness and humility
But when the blast of war blows in our ears
Then imitate the action of the tiger"

Those thoughts that cross your mind. in time of battle. It is not caused by fear, rather it is caused by a heightened awareness, of your own mortal existence and for those around you. The people that stand beside you through thick and thin. The ones that protect you. The ones you love. My thoughts were now, only to point and shoot. The scream of my mini gun and that of Lachie's beside me. I could feel the burning brass piling up around my feet occasionally one would bounce up singe some exposed part of flesh. There were more men on their boat, than I had expected and they did not run. It was not for bravery they stayed to fight it was the stupid belief, that apart from a warship they could attack any boat they chose and steal. Spent brass rolled down from above and hissed as it bounced and landed in the sea. I saw from my peripheral vision the suit in classic stance firing his Browning at much more carefully chosen targets. I watched as he drew a bead on one of the pirates, who then fell backwards over the edge of their boat. Oran copied 'The Suits' stance, first with his left hand pistole and then his right. We swung by their boat and repeated our run from the other side. We fired until there was no return gunfire and the boat they had used was already sinking. Oran waked back to the pseudo bridge and turned the power down and our luxury, although bullet ridden yacht, which sat back down in the water. The winding down of twin mini guns like a pair of train whistles. I looked at the floor around me and the ammo case at my feet, showed that I had almost emptied my allotted ammunition. Whilst all around me there were empty brass casings. Who ever owned this boat was not going to be a happy prince, when he saw the damage. The smell of gunfire lingered around me. I looked to Lachie and we touched knuckles as we had as children, in the Highlands of Scotland, when we had shot a Stag, or perhaps a Hare, with a long range shot. This time though it was to signify that we were safe and sound. I looked up to Abdalla and he gave a thumbs up from where he stood behind the monster 50cal machine gun that would have not looked out of place on a tank. Radwan gave a formal salute. Oran was busy making a fuss over Cyber, who was probably a bit worried by all the gun fire. Sir Philip raised his hand and started to walk back towards the middle of the forward deck. He took three paces and dropped to one knee and then the other. His other hand had been holding a wound on his right hand side. I dropped my gun and raced to his side, while shouting at Oran to grab my bag. Sir Philip had been stuck by a ricocheted AK47 round and it had done a lot of damage. Rather than being a clean projectile fired from a gun. It had been a bent and misshapen bullet by the time it struck him. It had entered his right front side, just above the waist line and exited near his right hand kidney. The dark red blood that was pouring from the wounds told its own tale. His liver had been shredded and probably his right hand kidney. The internal damage I could not fix. I knew it the moment I saw him. Long before Oran arrived with my bag. Sir Philip would not last more than 5 or 10 minutes. He knew it too.

We sat with him and talked about how he made us a team. There is a love that a man can have for his brother. Sure there were times that I had openly hated 'The Suit'. It seemed so wrong, now that we had rescued him after he had been captured and tortured in Guantanamo. He had pretty much recovered, only to die by a pirates stray shot. We all held him as he passed, even Cyber lay his big head on 'The Suits' feet. We had lost our leader and we would take our fallen home with us. After cleaning his body I wrapped him in cling-film and put his body in the freezer. It was the only way we could transport him back. Oran contacted Stu, and told him to meet us at a halfway point, and not to bring any of the girls, not even Rosemary. Without Sir Philip I had no idea who owned the boat we were on. Hell, I could not even find a name on it anywhere. Truth be told that was the least of the things on my mind. No doubt who ever owned it, would be in contact with SIS, and they would be able to re-unite them with it. The mood was solemn and dignified as we made our way to the mid way point. At at St Johns Point in Canada. I paid for a private mooring and set the term as indefinite. Oran set it up so that payments for the mooring were made from an offshore account. We had transferred 'The Suits' body the night before we arrived at St Johns. We cleaned up the boat and transferred all the guns the brass casings we had dumped at sea. The bullet holes that we could see were filled and painted over. We switched everything off and left the boat all locked up, although it was missing a Jeep and a few other smaller items. We left it tied up and boarded our own Catherine May.

ACT 33

Once on board the Catherine May and as soon as we got underway, I called everyone to the galley. There was a bottle of Jameson's in the bottle gantry. I took it out and placed some glasses in front of me. Team Seven had lost its leader, the real leader. He was a man who inspired Lachie and me. I had met him at CDE All those years ago, then the team had grown. Abdalla already knew the suit because he trained all the members of SIS, how to shoot and what gun was the right firearm for them. Hans met him around the same time as us when we were teamed up. Stu had met him on several occasions sometime as an adversary but mostly as a hidden friend. He had put us all together because he knew each of us had a talent that would fill in where another's talent left off. Sir Philip knew what it took to make a team and that included, those that were on the edge of things, our wife's and families as well as the lifelong friends.

You can build a specialist unit in the military, by taking men and or women and give them all the specialist training in the world. You can give them the best equipment there is in the world. That team would be good perhaps even great. BUT they would not be a family. Team Seven, were that family and because we for the greater part, lived together, we really knew how to read each other. It was probably why, we survived so long. We had been hunted down by the top military units in the world, we had fought against delta teams and won hands down. We had even fought for our lives, against SIS's, own wet work team and taken them out. We did that because, we made them bring the fight to us, on our own home turf, in the Highlands of Scotland and in the Islands surrounding her rocky shores. I can honestly say, this was one end I never thought I would see. When we went to rescue 'The Suit' I was not sure if we would be bringing him back home at all, or even if he would survive after we got him out. Then all those months of recouperation. We went out to extract revenge on those who had even the slightest involvement, in the kidnapping of Sir Philip and the murder of so many innocents, or in an attempted cover up. We had completely succeeded in that mission, 'The Suits' Last mission. The men behind it had been sent to their makers. Only for the suit to be killed by a skinny Somalian pirate. who could not shoot for shit. His shot had stuck something solid and spun off into the unlucky recipient of the ricochet. In this case had been Sir Philip. Somehow it did not seem right and in other ways it was a completion of a circle. I knew that 'The Suit' would have hated to have died from a heart attack at a desk. Or worse in some care home, He had died in a fire fight, as a soldier. The very vision of him on the prow of our boat, bold and upright. Firing at the enemy until his gun was empty. He did not falter nor did he drop until the battle was won. It would not say that on his headstone, but it would say, he had died a hero in the service of his Country. Sir Philip Reeves-Johnson DSO.

When all of the team that we had on board, were around the table, I cracked open the bottle and poured our drinks and left one extra for our fallen comrade.

"Sir Philip" I said as I raised my glass

"Sir Philip" a chorus of his friends said as one and raised their glass and then put their empty glasses back down.

"Oran send a message to Hans and Carl, let them know we are taking Sir Philip's body back to his wife and son on the rig. Ask them if they can meet us there with a big brother"

"OK Boss." was all he said.

Oran had met the man we nicknamed 'The Suit' when we had been invited to a dinner come meeting at the Springers Hotel on the Island Of Unst. All of us had been dressed for a formal dinner with the solitary exception of Oran, who when he was introduced to us looked like a petulant teenager. His long lanky hair down to his waist with a stringy student type beard. He wore a T-Shirt along with a pair of worn out denim jeans and a pair of baseball boots. This was to be our one full time official civilian member. It was Hans who had brought him into the team. I, was not his biggest fan to begin with, but like the others I soon saw the skill set, that he brought to the table. So much so that he was probably the man, we would protected most on any mission. It had been a long time before we even let him touch a gun. Yet it was with 'The Suit's' blessing that he joined team seven. There were times that I thought Sir Philip, had sold us down the river. Times when I had made him prove his loyalty to us. We were almost like his prodigies. What he did not know, he went and found someone to teach us. He was an old school spy. And if there is a secret to be kept, then two of the three people that know it, have to die. Well that is what he told us once. I was not even aware, of the conversation that was going on around me. I was lost in my own personal thoughts of Sir Philip. Now I would have to explain to his wife and son, that their husband and father gave his life to help save ours. He had needed to go out and complete this one last mission. It was his mission.

Mrs Reeves-Johnson seemed like a really nice lady and they had raised a polite and intelligent son. I knew they would be able to go back to their home in the green fields of Buckinghamshire. I would ask Hans to talk to the new head of SIS, and see if we could be left in peace, after our service to the Crown? I intended to be there for my children. I intended to be there for my wife and I intended to be there for my friends. Life was way too short for this kind of shit. Money we had even before this mission. I wandered off to my cabin and took probably one of the longest showers I have ever taken. I had not realised, that as I held Sir Philip, as he lay dying, most of his blood, had spilled over my clothes and now lay thickly crusted on my skin. I could not get the water to run clear and even then I scrubbed myself down twice more, before finally turning the shower to its ice cold setting and allowing it to pound the tension out of my tired and aching muscles. I slid down the wall of the shower cubicle and my tear ducts erupted in an instant moment of deep and pure grief. It is surprising just how being on edge makes a person tired. How draining the loss of a good friend can make you feel. I felt his loss physically and mentally. There would always be a void where his character had once lived. I doubted if any man or woman would be able to fill it.

"Andy" Stu was shouting from outside my cabin.

"Can you turn your shower off mate, you are emptying the fresh water tank."

"Yes, sorry mate I fell asleep in the shower" I lied and turned the water off. Then just sat there. I was not even sure how long that was. But it was Lachie's voice that stirred me from my thoughts, once again.

"Andy? You OK Mate?"

"I will be Lachie" I answered through the door. And continued as I stood up and wrapped a towel around my waist before going to the door and opening it for my friend.

"Come in Lachie"

"He was a hell of a man mate." Lachie said.

"Yes he was Lachie. Did you see him on that last run at the Pirates?"

"Aye he looked good, standing on the prow, a proper John Wayne moment like Rooster Cogburn in True Grit."

"I don't think there are many men like that, but I think he wanted to die. I think no matter how wrong he was about it, I think he felt that his manhood was taken from him in Gitmo. I doubt his wife saw it that way, but he did. I think just before he died he was more alive than he or any of us have ever been."

"Aye"

"OK Lachie I will be up in minute" I said and Lachie left me. I dried and dressed, then went to see Stu.

"You got the letter I gave you?"

"Sure do Andy" He replied and reached under his map drawer and pulled out my letter to Petrá. I folded it and put it in my pocket. Then walked on to the deck. I ripped it in two and threw it over the side of the Catherine May and then returned to the wheelhouse

"There is another one here for you, The Suit gave it to me." He said and handed that to me.

"Why me?"

"I guess to answer that Andy, you will probably have to read it. But he was adamant that you should read it if anything happened to him and you were to read it before you spoke to his wife"

"Thanks Stu" I said and went back to my cabin and sat back down on my bed. I was loathed to open it and even more loathed to read its contents, although I had a suspicion of what it would say. I peeled back the flap of the envelope.

Andy
Well if you are reading this letter, then you already know that I am dead. I hope I died well and with honour. I cant really complain about the first 68, of my 69 years of living. Before I go too far in this letter, there are some things, I want you to tell my wife and Son.

Tell my wife. I have loved her since the first time I laid eyes on her. Tell her I am sorry, for any pain she has had to bear because of my work. Can you tell her, she does not have to be a widow for the rest of her life and that she must look to find happiness again. Tell my Son, how proud I am of the man he has become.

Now to you Andy, and Team Seven.

Andy you and Lachlan, have been the core of one of the most successful teams, that I had had the delight to put together. I saw in you, a man who could lead by example. Unlike most people who work for our security services, you never chose to be in SIS. Yet you have worked tirelessly to protect our Country. I believe that you have earned your right to leave SIS.

As your direct Commanding Officer. I grant you your wish, and I do so with thanks for your impeccable service to SIS. I recommend that you and your team (listed attached to be given to the new Director of SIS) be justly awarded

Mr Andy McPhee
Mr Lachlan Henderson
Mr Abdalla Mohamed
Colonel In Chief Gunnerson
Captain Carl Gunnerson
Mr Oran(No middle or last)
Mr Craig McPhee
Mr Mark Henderson
Mrs Petrá McPhee
Mrs Morag Henderson
Mr Stuart McCormack
Mrs Rosemary McCormack

All the above listed are due payment agreed upon previously (with myself) as paid members of SIS. The Sum of £1,000,000 each. This sum to be paid for services rendered to UK security services. As before this is to be a cash settlement to be delivered at a point of their choosing. Also as a severance payment, they are to be granted full immunity for any and all actions, taken by them, whilst in the employ of SIS. All of the above will be granted new identities and complete anonymity as any member of our Secret Services is granted upon retirement.

In a letter I left for the PM, to be opened upon my death or to be given back to me on my return. I have made the request that you be fully honoured for all the actions that you and Team Seven have done in protection of not just the UK but your service to the World. It is my recommendation that all the military and ex-military members be awarded the D.S.O. and all the civilian members of Team Seven be awarded the George Medal.

Please tell all the team, I thank them so much for never giving up. Andy I once told you there is no out for you. I release you and all the above from any contractual obligation, actual or implied.

Thank you Team Seven you were my extended family, the brothers and sisters I never had and always wanted.

Sir Philip Reeves-Johnson D.S.O.
Director
Secret Intelligence Services UK.

I re-read the letter and folded it then put it in my pocket. I would action it, as soon as we returned to the rig. He was right about a lot of the things he had said. Especially when he called us a family.

A couple of days later we arrived back at our home. There were tears, all around and I sat down with his wife and son then passed on his short message to go with the other letters that he had left with Stu. Hans had arrived with Carl. All of us went down to Sir Philips home in Buckinghamshire for the private funeral. The only people there outside of his now extended family, were the Prime Minister and his new head of SIS. We were granted all the things, Sir Philip had requested in his letter. Hans and Carl went back to Iceland. Oran decided to stay with Lachie and me, and our wives on the Platform. My father and Mr Henderson went back to the Faeroe Islands. Abdalla eventually got married and settled back down in Northern Kenya. Stu and Rosemary, ran their luxury fishing boat and still visited the Rig, bringing supplies to us. We were finally civilians once again. Though we still had the abilities to become much much more. Oran's skill with the computer gave us a new direction. We did occasional work in finding missing persons. This was in our new roles as Brent Investigations.

The End

Will there be more for Andy McPhee...and Lachlan Henderson....

Other Books
By
Kenn Gordon

Altered Perceptions (c) 2018
Return Of Seven (c) 2019
Dead End (c) 2019
Chaplin, A Not So Short History of Chaplin Films (c) 2018
911 The Firefighters Remembered (Audiobook) (c) 2001

Coming Soon

So You Want To Be A Professional Musician
(The Biography of Kenn Gordon)

Brent Investigation Company.